Bright Moon

First published in the United Kingdom by Coppersun Books in 2014
Copyright © Srinivas Arka, 2014

The right of Srinivas Arka to be identified as the Author of the Work has been asserted by him in accordance with the Copyright, Designs and Patents Act 1988.
All rights reserved.

No part of this publication may be reproduced, stored in a retrieval system, or transmitted, in any form or by any means without the prior written permission of the publisher, nor be otherwise circulated in any form of binding or cover other than that in which it is published and without a similar condition being imposed on the subsequent purchaser.

This book represents the opinion of the author and is not proven to be factually correct. Any references made to organisations and businesses are mere representations of the authors' beliefs and opinions. The author and publisher do not make factual assertions of any kind with respect to this book or its contents. In addition, the author and publisher do not represent or warrant that the information accessible via this book is accurate, complete or current and that the use of the guidance in the book will lead to any particular outcome or result. The information provided in this book is not advice, and should not be treated as such. All characters in this publication are fictitious and any resemblance to real persons, living or dead is purely coincidental.

A CIP catalogue record for this title is available from the British Library.

Hardback ISBN 978-0-9929430-0-4

Typeset in Calluna by exljbris Font Foundry
Cover design by Flowing Graphics
Research Support by Alison Bann

Printed and bound by CPI Group (UK) Ltd, Croydon, CR0 4YY

www.coppersunbooks.com

Bright Moon

Srinivas Arka

*This novel is **dedicated** to the **memory** of **my beloved father***

April

Full Moon: 12.20 pm on April 6th

I

Chris McKenzie – Dreamer Extraordinaire

The boy gazed out over the sweeping expanse of San Francisco Bay, his eyes transfixed by the silvery glow reflecting off the rippling water from the Bright Moon. The waves lapped and swished with a hypnotic regularity, buffing up against the pillars of the Golden Gate Bridge, whose merry illuminations twinkled like festive lights on a Christmas tree.

Lulled by the gentle rocking of the waves and nestling into the comfortable window seat he had fashioned by his bedroom window, the boy's silvery eyes closed gently, like a baby's - soothed to sleep by the loving lullabies being sung by his mother.

In this relaxed state, the boy could sense the Moon's song drifting through his consciousness and it made him feel so happy. There was nothing to worry about; he was safe and warm in a protective cocoon of luminous deliciousness.

He could sense the Bright Moon calling, calling him – yet it was not calling his name. He strained his ears to hear the name, but it was elusive, like a wild animal hunted in its own territory.

He sighed and stirred, thoughts beginning to well up in his mind. His name, Chris McKenzie, rolled awkwardly over his tongue like stubble being brushed with cotton wool. He had never felt comfortable with this name. It just didn't fit, like a square peg in a round hole. His mother had changed his nickname at his request many times: China, Bolton, Johan and Austell – to name a few – all sitting awkwardly on his shoulders as if meant for someone else. He wanted to be called Zenith and had once plucked up the courage to ask his mum to call him this name, but she had only laughed and told him not to be so silly, he had a perfectly good name already which she had chosen with his father – now absent as his parents had divorced.

He stared sadly at the Easter card which had arrived from him the day before. He'd read the loving message and proudly placed it up on the shelf next to his 12th birthday card, also from his father – another beautiful picture of the stars and the Moon. He longed for his father– his absence made Chris feel like his right arm had been cut off. He treasured the cards, but they were no match for seeing his dad face to face. It had hurt him deeply not to be able to see his dad on his birthday, but he knew his parents would end up fighting after what had happened last year.

The memory of the terrible day his dad left had imprinted a scar on his heart. It had been the day of that stupid party for his 11th birthday that children from his class had been invited to. Most of them weren't even his friends, but his mum had insisted that he should have them over for his birthday like any normal boy would do. He could picture it now; all their jeering faces around the table, singing the happy birthday song to him with the most despicable insults substituted for the real words. He could feel his face burning as he relived the shame of it all – and then his dad had stepped in and told them all to get on their bikes and leave.

Much as he had loved his father for standing up for him,

he knew it certainly hadn't helped his popularity at school. And then there had been that terrible row between his mum and dad, the shouting had been worse than ever, sending him reeling to the safety of his room, hands clapped over his ears to shut out the noise. He had retreated then to the safety of the Moon – staring desperately at its face, seeking answers to the strange behaviour of people.

After his mum had thrown his dad out, Chris had withdrawn from everyone besides his grandma, who he rarely saw now. His dad had been the only one who listened to him and tried to answer all his questions, but now he'd gone, moved out and started a new life running a store that sold spiritual oddities – gems, stones, healing amulets, books and such. He hardly ever heard from his dad now, apart from the occasional phone-call if his mum allowed it. He liked to hear about the store, to imagine what it must look like, with all its exotic and bizarre contents buzzing with mystical stories ready to be discovered. When his dad did call, he would tell Chris of the exciting visitors who had come into his store – healers, astrologers, psychics and the like – not that Chris really knew what they all did.

He knew a lot about astrology though – his dad had made sure of that. When Chris was younger, they had spent many enjoyable times together discussing the cosmic bodies of the Universe, their positions and identities, focusing wide-eyed and awed at the celestial constellations, through the eye-piece of the telescope his dad had bought him for his seventh birthday. Or there had been the mythological stories, the mystical allegories, the spiritual quests and the philosophical quotes which his father regularly imparted, each one sowing a divine seed of inspiration in the boy's fertile and budding intelligent mind. Yet so often his mother had interrupted, made a scene, dragging them away from distant horizons to come back to Earth with a bump, expressing her frustration at their incessant daydreaming.

Unlike his mother, his dad and grandma had always been a willing sounding-board for the boy's incessant questions about the heavens, which invariably turned to the subject of the Moon. Why did she have to drive away the two people that he loved the most? In their absence, his mum kindly tried to answer her son's myriad of questions, but soon lost patience with him, losing interest as soon as he touched on any topic that didn't seem firmly rooted to the ground and reality. It was funny how she seemed so upset by his questions – it was almost as if she felt physical pain every time he posed another conundrum concerning philosophy, religion or spirituality. After all, he was only following in his father's footsteps with his line of enquiry, and who can deny one's heritage or identity?

Perhaps that was the problem; he wasn't sure of his real identity somehow. His thoughts often turned to such questions as Who am I? What should other people call me? What's in a name? Is it just a sound symbol, or should it refer to one's personality? Or is it just a collection of letters compiled into a word to make a name? Why must I even be given a name? And why should I only be called by that name? Does it have any influence on me?

Sometimes his thoughts strayed to wider issues of identity... Do I really belong to these people around me? What is the real name of the parent of the planets and the Universe? Where did this name come from – who gave him or her or it a name? Or did it name itself?

Other times he pondered the development of speech... What was the first human language? Why do we have so many languages? How is it that meanings can be common to each other, yet words and sounds are different?

Such thoughts ruled his head most days. His mother often threw up her hands in despair, exclaiming that he thought too much, that boys of his age should be out playing basketball or baseball, not holed up in their rooms daydreaming all the time or with their nose stuck in yet another book about the Moon. Chris had turned to the Moon as if it were a surrogate parent, asking its ever-changing face the surge of questions that arose daily from his heart. 'Mooning around' his mum called it, yet why couldn't she understand that he was just being himself and there was no point him trying to be like the other 12 year old boys. Why couldn't she just accept him the way he was?

He'd hated the baseball kit his mother had bought for him his 12th birthday. There was definitely more to life than just sport, which required degrees of coordination that his tiny muscles never seemed to want to comply with. He stared at his skinny arms and legs sticking out from his scruffy black T-shirt and shorts. He knew he would never make the school baseball team or impress the girls with his puny body, but he had to be good at something.

He stared into his rocket-shaped mirror propped up against the blue wall, gazing at his reflection. He eyed his tousled blond curls that had grown long and shaggy, but as he hated getting his hair cut he had to keep it that way.

Looking into his silvery eyes magnified behind his thin-rimmed glasses, he felt sad, almost tearful. People always seemed uncomfortable when they spotted his silver eyes. They thought he appeared weird and freakish; most would make a rude comment or just back away from him. Surely he was just an ordinary boy though? Why couldn't people understand that? He might seem a bit different from other people, but surely he still deserved to be treated with respect.

Perhaps people didn't understand him because his name

didn't fit. Perhaps he should be called by a more meaningful name that helped others to understand his nature and his uniqueness. He sighed audibly and turned sadly away from his reflection, back to his celestial friend in the night sky, hoping to find some answers about his identity.

Many a night passed this way. As he exchanged his thoughtful lines of enquiry with the Moon from one night to the next, it seemed to lead him to discover more and more about himself, such that he often changed his perceptions of who he was and consequently of what he should be called.

Sometimes he would ask his mum several times in one day to stop calling him Chris. She would answer in exasperation – 'Well, what do you want me to call you, son? Tell me what would make you happy?' Yet this question always stumped him, as if the answer was always just a little too far out of reach, tantalizingly close yet too far to grasp.

In this sea of change, uncertainty and confusion that life seemed to entail, the Moon was an ever-present friend – a companion, a confidante, a certainty in an uncertain world. Much of life just foxed the boy; the way people like his parents – that should just love each other – just stop talking and shut each other out, the way perfectly innocent children could become his nemesis in Nikes as they discovered how much fun they could have bullying him. If the world was like that, then he wondered if he really wanted to be a part of it at all.

As his grandmother used to say – 'Focus on the good in the world, Chris, and you won't go wrong.' Yet what do you do when you realize that there is very little good in the world? He found himself retreating inwardly, lost in the safety and goodness of his thoughts, seeking that inner heaven that his dad used to hint about. Many days he would block out the world to the point that he could no longer see what was happening around him. His focus would be drawn ever inward much to the frustration of his mother, who blamed his introspection on pre-adolescent hormonal mood swings.

Some days were so bad, he would speak to no-one at school and just stand as a lonely, awkward figure in a corner of the playground, lost in his own world of thoughts. The other children milled around him as if he were invisible. Sometimes they would suddenly notice he was there and shout insults at him to appease their lack of understanding. His teachers would step in and rescue him from the taunts, yet they also had a hard time comprehending his ways. Sometimes he was so intelligent; he amazed them with his lists of facts about matters of science and religion. Yet at other times he was like an island, lost in his own thoughts and unable to bridge the gap between his world and theirs.

Such days as these, he would come home from school and just lock himself away in his room. He would switch on his bedside lamp, which was in the shape of the Moon, observing its light projecting all around the bedroom, casting eerie shadows wherever it fell – on the telescope, on the model rockets hanging from the ceiling, on the model of the solar system, on the bookshelf rammed with books on astrology, philosophy, and endless stories about the Moon.

Then usually he would sit in his comfy window-seat, his silvery gaze transfixed out of the window on the silvery Moon in the evening sky. He would pose more questions to the paternal 'man in the moon', such as 'What is the world? What is it composed of? What is our destiny? Why are beings even born at all if they ultimately must die anyway? Why are there so many creatures? Are there any creatures out there in outer space? Why don't we have the mastery of interpreting their language so that we can expand our understanding of the world? Who has authority over this world? Why can't this authority come up to the genuine truth seekers and give them light, clarity and answers where everyone can be convinced without conflict and misunderstanding? Where are all these answers found?'

He would stare for hours at the crests and troughs, the mottling and the radiance of the Moon's mysterious face. Sometimes he saw the shape of a leaping giant rabbit. Other times he saw a white elephant with five trunks. On one occasion he even thought he could make out an outline of his mum and dad kissing, (although he had to admit he was particularly tired that day). One time, the boy was even convinced he saw the Moon wink at him. Such was the power of his imagination, ever fuelled by his insistent curiosity about the Moon.

Every birthday the other boys in his class would request the latest toy – perhaps a Power Ranger, or a Spiderman, or a bike, or soccer kit, or a baseball glove, yet he would always ask for something of an astronomical bent – something that would help him find out more about the Moon. Sometimes it was a book, then he would scurry the book away to his room and absorb its facts such that in a short time he could recite them all ad nauseam to anyone within earshot.

From a very early age, his conversations tended to be somewhat one-sided and to go along the lines of:

'Mum, did you know that the Moon has its own 'Grand Canyon' called 'Alpine Valley'. It's 130km long, 20km wide and 2000m deep. It's the Moon's biggest fault valley and it cuts through the Moon's Alps.'

'That's nice, dear.' Or;

'Mum, did you know that the Moon used to be much closer to the Earth than it is now. Can you imagine it looking even bigger than it does at Harvest Moon, Mum?'

'I see; what would you like for dinner, Chris?' Or to a school friend;

'Did you know that there are either 12 or 13 Full Moons every year? I have written all the dates of the Full Moon down in my diary here and this year there have been 13.'

'Come on, Chris! That's really boring! Haven't you got a Spiderman to play with?' Or when his grandfather was still alive;

'Did you know, Granddad, that during an eclipse of the Moon, the Moon turns orangey-red for about two hours, because sunlight is bending around the edge of the Earth onto the Moon'.

'Chris, that's nice. Can you please speak up; my hearing is not so good these days.' Or to his teacher;

'Sir, the mayfly only hatches on a Full Moon.'

'That's fascinating, Chris, but I asked you to find the square root of 256.' Or to a visitor at the door;

'Did you know that the Sun is 400 times bigger than the Moon and yet 400 times further away, so they appear to be the same size?'

'Kid, that's really awesome, but can you please ask your mother to come to the door; I have her groceries?' Or;

'Did you know, Pastor, that there is an Ancient Indian myth that the mineral Selenite was made by moonbeams playing on water and it was said to have remarkable healing powers.'

'Goodness me, Chris, whatever next; when are we going to see you and your family in church?' Or;

Bright Moon

'Mum, it says in my book that astronauts have taken samples of the Moon's rock surface and soil. What do you think it's made of?'

'Chris, will you please stop going on and on about the Moon? I'm trying to watch T.V. here!'

Yet things had changed since his mum and dad had divorced. Without his dad and his grandmother around, it had become more and more difficult for him to have a decent conversation about his interests, particularly as his mother reacted so badly to them. So he had become increasingly introverted, choosing not to ask his mother any more but to ask the Moon instead. He knew she was frustrated by him clamming up, but what else could he do?

Such was life for Chris McKenzie – Moon Gazer extraordinaire – or ordinary boy whom no-one seemed to understand…especially his mother.

Chris stirred and sighed. He knew his mother would come up soon to nag him to go to sleep, so he peeled himself away from the comfy window seat and the Bright Moon, to climb into bed, snuggling down under his orb-covered Moon-theme duvet. He stared up at the luminous planets and stars that stuck to the ceiling, letting his thoughts wander. He sang along to the sounds he heard in his head…

2

DONNA MCKENZIE – DOUBTFUL DIVORCÉE

Donna McKenzie – blonde, blue-eyed, age 35, mother of
one, divorcée, lawyer, realist.
Organized, outspoken, honest, direct and logical.
Prefers punctuality and commitment.
Enjoys domestic life – excellent cook.

She stared at her list, uninspired to think of any other words to describe herself in this submission for the lonely hearts column of the newspaper. Not that she was desperate to get back into dating; she was still nursing the wounds of the divorce. However, she had to admit she was pretty lonely. It wasn't much fun in the house with a daydreaming 'tweenie', however much she loved him. She knew he was upstairs in his room again, locked away in his ivory tower, in a state of reverie.

There once was a time when Chris was devoted to her and hung on her every word. As a little boy he had been such a sweetheart – a round-faced angel with silver-grey eyes that seemed to pierce through you, darting their inquisitiveness into every nook and cranny of life. She remembered his tousled curly blonde locks that fell around his rosy face, the way he would toddle up to her and try to give her such a big bear hug that she would squeal in pleasure.

He had been a very loving child – interested in everything; though, as he grew older he seemed to get easily overwhelmed. She remembered times at noisy parties when he had run to her with his hands clamped over his little ears, burrowing his head into her chest for safety. Or times at the mall when the crowds had got too much for him and he had lain down on the floor and screamed until she feared her ears would bleed, whilst she stood by him at a loss for how to help him, passers-by staring in disbelief and horror, her face burning in shame.

She had taken to protecting him as much as she could from crowds, noise, parties; perhaps from life itself. It was all for his own good; she was certain of that. She kept a strict routine, with plenty of structure (as long as Joe was not on the scene) which seemed to help him to adjust to the uncertainties of life. She had watched him grow into a very thoughtful young boy, with a real thirst for knowledge. He had his pet interests, which she had tried to keep up with at first, but now she found them somewhat tedious and bizarre as they had manifested into an obsession.

He had a way of questioning you persistently, as if nothing else mattered in the universe. In fact she often felt like he was lost in his own little world and she no longer knew the way in. He'd been this way ever since the break-up. Poor Chris, she knew he was still upset that his father had left. It was understandable. He was never going to understand what a waste of space that man was.

She worked all the hours she could as a lawyer at a reputable and friendly legal firm, to earn money for the family. When Joe was still around she felt he did nothing to help out. Joe had had no regular job, minimal income, no sense of routine or understanding of the practical needs of the family. All he did all day was daydream in his office, writing about crazy spiritual ideas and astrological hocus-pocus.

She never knew what he was talking about – it was so high-minded and whimsical. As for the mystical and metaphysical stuff Joe came out with, she felt he was clearly lost on a one-way train to Fantasyville. How could anyone bring up a family with such impractical attitudes towards life? Their irreconcilable differences had led to a severe breakdown in their relationship. No, she was glad she'd divorced him and life was going to be so much better for them without Joe dragging them all into his unrealistic idea of life.

Although she didn't regularly go to church anymore, Joe's New Age beliefs had never sat right with her Christian background. As far as she was concerned, God was in charge and we all had to obey him or else we would be in big trouble; God had our life mapped out for us and would take care of us when we shuffled off this mortal coil, provided we said our prayers every night.

Yet, her ex had all sorts of funny ideas about people creating their own destiny and attracting the life that they wanted. 'Vibration-this and energy-that.' Ah it was all rubbish. All that daydreaming never got anybody anywhere. Life – she believed – was about working hard and playing hard. Life was a struggle; if you got to the end of it without having broken one of the Ten Commandments, then you were going to get a golden handshake from the Big Man in the sky.

She used to get the shivers whenever she saw Joe sitting with closed eyes with Chris, certain he was trying to brainwash her son into some newfangled New Age spirituality rubbish. There was nothing that got her hackles up more than seeing them together 'contemplating'. She thought it made them appear other-worldly and far-off, yet a small part of her recognized that she was really only upset because she felt excluded and alone.

She hoped that Chris would shake off this way of thinking now that his father was safely out of the picture. She knew Joe had set up some sort of New-Age hippy store somewhere with money from his mother, so he was welcome to go and live his life with all his spiritual cronies, as long as she and Chris were left in peace to get on with a more normal life.

Her thoughts tended to hover around this word 'normal'. Much as she hankered after a normal life with a normal family, sometimes she really wondered whether she could actually describe her son as normal. It was not that he was abnormal as such, just that he acted a little strangely sometimes and she didn't quite know what to make of it.

She very well knew that he had an obsessive fascination with the Moon. At one point she had thought it was just a passing phase. She consoled herself with the idea that the next one might be far worse – it might be a crush on a girl. Yet somewhere inside she knew that it was far more than that. She had to admit, the Moon had been a constant presence in her son's thoughts.

Often, when tidying Chris' bedroom, she had found various scraps of paper littering the floor showing detailed facts about the Moon, such as;

"The Moon is on average 380,000 km away. Light travels at 299,792.458 km/sec, so light takes just over a second to arrive from the Moon."

Now, this sort of thing could just be put down to homework assignments, or perhaps a hankering to be an astronaut, which surely many young boys would dream about? Yet the facts would continue to arrive and litter the floor, until day in – day out, there were facts smothering not only the floor, but also written on post-it notes stuck to the walls, the rocket-shaped mirror, the desk, the wardrobe door and even the ceiling, dotted between the glowing luminous plastic stars and planets that he had loved since he was a young child.

She would chide her son for creating such a mess and would beg him to tidy his room. One day, when she had made the bed she found a piece of paper hidden under the boy's pillow. Upon it she had seen words scribbled in Chris' handwriting, that seemed to be in the form of some kind of poem – an ode to the Moon or something. She had read the words, somewhat guiltily, as if aware that she didn't really want to know what it said.

> *"Bright Moon Gazing*
> *Oh bright silvery Moon with your face so pale*
> *I know in my heart that you have a tale*
> *To tell to us all should we prevail*
> *To listen intently – please do regale*
> *Of your truths within so we cannot fail*
> *To learn of your wisdom as ours is so frail."*

Her heart skipped a beat, aware of the depth of his thoughts, but she quickly rationalized her emotional reaction as one of annoyance that he was hiding things from her. He was evidently still obsessed with the Moon. He was probably dabbling with romantic lunar poems in the hope of impressing a girl or something. She slipped the poem back under his pillow and gathered up his moon-covered pyjamas to throw in the wash-basket, trying to think no more of it.

She had put this event to the back of her mind, but there had been more strange incidents. She had heard him talking to himself on numerous occasions in his room and wondered what he was doing.

Every few weeks he seemed to go through a phase of being particularly vocal in the evenings after school, singing strange songs and chattering away as if there were someone else in the room. Yet these phases came and went; she thought perhaps he was just a little lonely without his dad or many friends to socialize with.

Sometimes she wondered if he might need some sort of counselling; perhaps he was experiencing separation issues to do with his father, yet for some reason she could never bring herself to address this. Maybe subconsciously she blamed herself for the break-up.

3

JOE LARKIN – DIVORCEE OF DONNA

Joe reached his large hands skywards in a long stretch above his head. That feels delicious, he thought to himself. He blew out a long breath that he imagined took away all his negative thoughts. Shifting position, he rearranged his long, flexible limbs into a new triangular pose with bare feet set wide apart on the squishy yoga mat.

Joe took a long deep breath in, stretching his diaphragm and then his muscular chest. His lithe muscles held him steady and still, a picture of lean fitness. He eyed his reflection in the mirror, checking his posture. Not bad for a middle-aged man, he thought to himself. Restructuring his bronzed limbs into a one-legged balance pose, he stared straight ahead into his reflection, into his self-assured silver-grey eyes. Wobbling a little, his chestnut brown hair flopped forwards into his shining eyes.

He suddenly inverted his pose in one deft movement; as he balanced precariously upside-down, the yin-yang symbol that hung on a black cord around his neck fell into his mouth. The veins in his strong arms bulged as they supported his weight easily. He breathed in and out deeply then flipped out of the pose to a seated position.

After rubbing each wrist around the bracelets that he

always wore, he pulled his hands into a prayer position and closed his eyes ready to meditate. He tried to clear his mind of thoughts, but as so often happened, his thoughts wandered to his ex-wife.

Joe felt no ill-will towards Donna. In his mind, she remained as wonderful and unique as she always was. Way back when they had first met, he had fallen in love with her pristine good-looks, her mane of glossy golden hair, her dazzling brightness and organized character. She had been a constant and reliable linchpin in his life, whose dedication to their son, Chris, was second to none. Harsh as the break-up had been, he had tried to understand her reasons. He felt certain that she was only doing what she knew best – reorganizing their lives for optimum efficiency!

He was well aware of his own words and actions – he seemed disorganized at times, uncommitted, yet he was organized and much committed to his work and vision, frequently lost in his own thoughts. He often wished he was more audacious, well aware that only a few would dare transform the rain of thoughts into crystals of actions. There was no doubt that Donna, however, was a doer; she completed things on time and for this quality, Joe was always in awe of her.

He was also aware that their parenting styles were radically different, which had always been a source of conflict for them. He felt inclined to allow Chris as much freedom as he wanted to explore his own ideas about life, to experience the 'space between the lines' – be it in his formal education or his spiritual development.

Joe felt that it was more important for his son to be a good human being, to understand life and its meaning at a deeper level, than to surf along the top with the shallow subjects usually offered at school. He didn't want to force his beliefs and interests on his son; the boy had naturally taken to ideas of astronomy and spirituality.

He had always told Chris to follow his own path, encouraging him in this from a very early age, but without forcing him to have any great ambitions. Nor did he believe in conditioning his son's mind. Joe taught an alternative approach to life; to have an objective but not to become possessed by it, to flow with things and to adapt to circumstances.

Joe fidgeted on his yoga mat, aware that he was having trouble settling into meditation today. He breathed in deeply trying to relax then blew out hard to expel his thoughts, but try as he might they wandered back to Donna and his son Chris.

Although Donna had often accused Joe in the past of neglecting his son due to his lack of structure and involvement in Chris' formal development, he vehemently denied this, declaring the depths of his responsibility towards his son and his concern for Chris' spiritual and emotional welfare.

As a result, Donna forbidding him from seeing Chris was like a thorn in Joe's side and an assault on his heart, but he could see how his spiritual and philosophical interests lead to recurrent fights and a difficult atmosphere for Chris. For now he just had to accept the pain of the separation for the sake of his boy's stability. He hoped for the best that by being absent, she would develop a better relationship with Chris, and hopefully be less critical and more accepting.

There had never been much empathy from Donna's side for Joe's interests in philosophy, religion and meta-physics, which he had tended to share with his son. It seemed like much of his belief system was currently beyond her, as if she was unable to relate to any of the ideas they upheld, nor could she resonate the passion they instilled in him to serve humanity.

Donna's idea of community service extended no further than an occasional coffee-morning held in aid of a local charity. It was hard for her to understand the drive he felt to better himself in order to better the world and, however much the break-up had hurt him, it had served as a blessing in disguise.

The positive effect of it was that he had been able to spend more time exploring his interests. Using money loaned from his mother, he travelled to faraway places and bought mystical treasures to set up a store. Then he became involved with many like-minded people who had a similar thirst for humanity's spiritual and conscious advancement. He had a special gift for encouraging anyone who wanted to do something positive and good for people.

Any healers, alternative t herapists, or even psychics that crossed his path, showing similar humanitarian concern, were subject to his intuitive gaze. He had a knack for distinguishing the genuine from the fake. He offered his tutoring to the ones with the truest heart, encouraging them towards humanitarian activities with his selfless and simplistic approach to life, or giving them opportunities to work from his store.

He never took any notice of the publicity surrounding an individual, nor of their reputation, nor was he swayed by the crowd following the latest fads. If he felt that someone was out to impress, or that their main focus was on money, he tended to steer clear of them, believing that such characteristics were a block to long-term effectiveness and success.

He chose to assess people more by way of 'sounding out

their hearts' for their readiness for service. In his opinion, service should be the prime concern and goal of everybody's life; indeed Joe felt great joy in being of some help or service to anyone who approached him, whether it was by imparting some helpful philosophical pearls that would help to awaken a person's spiritual growth, or by guiding them towards their next step in life.

Although sometimes people came away from him feeling a little tired and confused by his deep thoughts, they would always return after taking time to think and make sense of what he meant, keen to thank him for his guidance, ready to drink again from his cup of wisdom.

People never seemed to get bored of Joe – his spirit of celebration and heartfelt gratitude seemed to rub off on people. He certainly revelled in the excitement of all the interesting things that kept happening in his life – he was always birthing new creative ideas and concepts that resulted in him experiencing a myriad of wonderful events, such as those that often took place at his store.

Often they were spontaneous but simple celebratory parties, or mystical talks, or mystery guest appearances to which his friends from his spiritual community were regular attendees, drawn by the exotic and varied nature of the activities. They all enjoyed the back-drop of romantic, antique, mystic and creative materials scattered around the store, the zealously collected treasures from his travels to far-flung reaches of the globe.

He had been to places such as Egypt, India and Rome to swell his collection and expand the choices available to visitors to his store. Each item told its own tale of intrigue and ambiguity, which visitors never tired of enquiring about. The gem stones were particularly popular, with their attractive rainbow hues and magnetic pull – as if reflecting the many-faceted character of the charismatic and popular store-keeper, Joe.

Donna however never seemed to be much of a people-person to him. She was rather self-involved and dare he say it, rather mean-spirited. She knew that helping others was necessary in as far as she would always expect that there would be something in it for her, some personal gain. His friends had always been made to feel unwelcome in their house; she seemed to feel uneasy in their magnanimous presence, as if unsettled by some mysterious challenge to her ego.

Donna made no bones about how she felt with respect to Joe's interests; he'd been on the receiving end of many an insult and patronizing comment, meant to belittle his beliefs as being nothing more than daydreaming.

He felt sorry that his ways irritated Donna so much. He took a portion of the blame for the break-up squarely on his shoulders – better to take responsibility for one's own actions than to blame others. He knew full well that the mind was like a knife – if you mishandled it, it could hurt you and others. In hurting Joe, Donna was unaware of how little control she had over her own mind at the moment.

Sure, knowing the truth could be sad, since it was often different from our desires. But the journey in seeking truth should be an adventurous and joyous experience.

Yet he had an inkling that the break-up with Donna had all been triggered by some sort of personal calamity she was having, that it was just a phase she was going through – perhaps even some form of personal transformation. As a result, he felt it was best to go with the flow of the separation; to give her the space that she needed to sort out her feelings and her predicament in her own way. Fortunately his capricious sense of humour helped him to see the funny side of this apparent mid-life crisis.

In truth he still held a candle for her. Plus, his heartfelt bond with his boy would forever tie him to Chris and his mother, no matter what happened in their lives. Perhaps this was why he was reticent to move on with his relationships; with that bond to Donna still in place, in reality any other woman was likely to find it tough to reach his heart.

His friends had gently voiced their concerns about Donna and her rather unyielding critical nature, taking his side (as friends often will in times of marital conflict), yet he always defended her – as was his way. Joe was a man of nobleness and honour, who never liked to hear a bad word said about another.

Despite his lingering support of his ex, his friends had cajoled him into the idea of dating again. He had good-naturedly opened the door of his heart just a fraction to let in a young, intriguing lady he had met when sourcing items for his store.

Nevertheless, in his heart of hearts, he knew he would never make a full commitment to this lady, as long as there was a chance of reconciliation with Donna. He could forgive and forget the fights, the insults, the criticisms, the exclusion, for the sake of his unconditional love for his boy and the possibility of rekindling the love he had once shared with his ex-wife. He knew that when you love somebody deeply your mind may harbour some fear of losing them, which adds more meaning and flavour to your relationship. Like a black spot on the bright moon, a slight sense of insecurity makes the love brighter.

If she were to ask him tomorrow to come back, would he do it? Perhaps, sometimes he felt like they had grown too far apart now, yet his spiritual understanding led him to believe that love is a connective force, an attractive mystical force; the only force that can unite broken relationships – and indeed the world. With that love still present in his heart, who knew what could happen?

A roosting bird called loudly through the open window, interrupting Joe's incessant flow of thoughts. Joe opened his eyes; he saw that the sun had sunk down leaving his meditation room in gathering darkness. He decided to give up his meditation practice for today, as his monkey mind was far too active to cooperate. He heaved himself up off the floor, straightening his loose white clothing and folded his yoga mat away into the corner.

4

Christina Larkin – Concerned Grandmother

Chris had always been fascinated by the Moon and although his mother, Donna, did not encourage its discussion, he did find a muse in his Grandma Larkin; Christina Larkin was the inspiration for Chris' name. She saw in him a spark of her own son Joe's brilliance, passed down to the next generation, ready to be fanned into a flame of flowering magnificence.

Ever-encouraging, this wonderful septuagenarian with shimmering eyes – reflective of tantalizing tales untold – would visit the boy and his parents often in the years before the break-up.

She had a very special relationship with her grandson, as is so often the case. Grandparents bring the gift of years of wisdom and freedom of reduced responsibility for the care of the child. When coupled with the tender enthusiasm and innocent spirit of the grandchild, some kind of mysterious magic seems to happen – as if the relationship is an alchemic gift from the Universe itself – such a love sought is a perfect love given, no strings attached.

Chris was an incredibly sensitive child; when he was five years old, he would often cry, sobbing and sighing as though he had lost something. He would stand at his window gazing out, as though wishing that the sun would disappear to allow the stars to shine.

On one such occasion, Chris' parents had exhausted all ideas of finding how to soothe him; unable to console him, they had even called in the doctor, who had pronounced him fit and healthy, well looked after, well fed, well entertained, such that even the medics were at a loss as to what was wrong.

They had called up his grandma in desperation. Christina Larkin had come to visit her grandson; on finding him in such a terrible state, she had calmly plunked herself down beside him at the window and gazed out with him into the ether.

Immediately, his sobs had subsided, as if she had come to his rescue. He had leant up against his grandmother's side as if she were a shady tree that sheltered him from the scorching sun.

His parents had looked on in amazement.

His grandma had gently begun to speak, to recount adventurous tales – stories of heroes and explorers. She had begun with Vasco DaGama and had wended her way through history to more modern times, the boy hanging on her every word. As she reached her tale of Neil Armstrong, Chris' silvery eyes had nearly popped out of his head.

As she had described the astronaut's first steps on the Moon, Chris had suddenly broken out of his muteness, springing question after question at his grandma;

'Will you please talk more about the Moon, Grandma? Where did it come from? What is it made from? How did it get there? Why is it so bright? Why does it only appear during the night? Why is it so cool? Why can't I visit it?'

She had slipped on her glasses to be able to 'hear' him better and attend to his questions. He had certainly many more questions than that, but at such a tender age he had been unable to frame the questions in his developing brain, nor find the vocabulary in his limited library of terms to describe the thoughts he was having.

Yet his brain and mind were clearly budding into a beautiful scientific curiosity of 'what, how, where and when, why so'? These were fundamental questions; the pillars of society's conscience, rising out of mankind's consciousness and reaching for the skies from humble, deep grounds, similar to the foundations laid by those responsible for Man's ever-developing technology.

So it was with Chris and his grandma – they had spent many a cosy time together; sometimes Chris would just listen to her, munching on her baked treats. She would come armed with tales to tell and songs to play, often with a moon theme, like 'There's a Silver Moon on the Golden Gate' – a song penned by Tobias, Rothberg and Meyer for the opening festivities of the City's wonderful suspension bridge completed back in May 1937. (He often played this soothing tune to help him sleep at night, dreaming of his grandmother strolling up and down the Golden Gate bridge arm in arm with his now-departed Grandpa Larkin, serenading her under the moonlight.)

As Chris grew older he asked deeper and deeper questions, which his grandmother tried to keep up with. Yet the boy's mother always intervened. Mid-conversation, Donna would charge in, expressing her disapproval, calling a time-out, with warnings of bedtime or study time, to which he always said, "I am studying Mum, leave me alone with Grandma." He would plead with Donna, but she had such a sword of discipline; she would simply slash anything that got in her way.

Sure, Christina knew that Donna had her own childhood issues; perhaps because her father had controlled her so much, she inflicted the same on her son. Perhaps she was borderline obsessive; there is sometimes a thin line between disciplining a child and controlling, slowly injecting or insinuating one's desires into the child's mind, in order to feel some desperate fulfilment; a parenting practice that is mediocre at best.

Many parents get caught in this trap, but Christina had always tried to avoid it with her own son, Joe. She was acutely aware of this fine line between caring, disciplining and controlling, and many times she had observed with concern as Donna seemed to stray over that line into the darkness of control.

Christina remembered all the times she had heard Donna emotionally blackmail Chris (and Joe, for that matter) with an uncomfortably subdued tone and strictness, 'If you don't listen to me, you won't get what you asked for'...or some other mild threat.

Eventually Chris would half-heartedly agree to end the conversations, making his grandma promise him that she would come again and continue her story. Sometimes he would also insist that she couldn't go home.

Yet home Christina had to go, as with Donna constantly breathing down her neck, she felt increasingly uncomfortable in their home. The atmosphere compromised her space and her freedom. No, it wasn't the place for her.

As much as she loved Joe and her grandson, when the arguments began she had visited less and less. When Donna cruelly divorced her son, she had made Christina feel so uncomfortable and unwelcome there that she felt even less inclined to visit. Donna would often make excuses about the boy needing to work on his studies, or would tell Christina that he was sick so she couldn't come to visit.

Christina realized that what had transpired was good in one way; everyone has to live their life the way they want to. Her son was better off without Donna; he was free now to do what he wanted to with his life.

However, poor Chris was always on her mind. She was saddened that he had been left – to all intents and purposes – alone, without understanding relatives that supported him and accepted him the way he was. What was to become of him?

5

Chris changes with the faces of the Moon

Over the course of the month, Chris continued to spend many evenings staring out of the window at the gradually waning then waxing moon, caught up again in its silvery presence, enjoying its changing faces and phases, marvelling at its decreasing and increasing brilliance.

As the days passed, he felt an increasing buzzing sensation in his ears, when suddenly one day a surprisingly acute level of hearing manifested. Noises that to most people were normal, he found unbearable. He had always been quite sensitive to loud noises, but now even quieter sounds seemed overbearing. He struggled at school with the loud chatter of his classmates and took to wearing ear plugs to keep out the majority of the sounds.

At home, he was driving his mother mad, constantly telling her to stop shouting at him, when in fact she was only speaking normally. When he tried to sleep at night, the tick of his alarm clock was so intense that he hid it in a cupboard.

Yet his hearing was not the only thing that seemed to be affected. As the two weeks passed, he found himself noticing more and more visual details on things, like patterns on the bark of trees, or wrinkles on people's faces, or fingerprints on the ends of people's fingers.

Bright Moon

Waking up one morning, he reached for his glasses which usually sat by the side of his bed, but realized he could actually see quite clearly – in fact far better than he had ever been able to before, such that he didn't even need to wear his glasses any more.

More intrigued than perturbed by all these experiences, he noted down all the changes in his notebook, as any good scientist would. Excited by the changing results he saw, he decided to perform some experiments on himself, to monitor the rate of the changes. At school he would test whether he could read smaller and smaller writing, first on the board, then in other peoples' books. This was his daytime activity, but when evening came, he was drawn ever more towards the widening face of the night-time Moon.

He found himself singing songs to the Moon, with the Moon, about the Moon, writing down more facts about the Moon onto post-it notes so he wouldn't forget a single thing about it. It was almost as if he had fallen in love with the Moon; it was sharing his life as any loving companion would.

Sometimes he was aware that his mum had come into the room and was standing staring at him, an expression of deep concern etched on her face, but he was so involved with his trance-like activities that he barely acknowledged her. Unable to get a response from her son, she usually left him to it, departing from the room with a sigh, muttering 'mooning about again,' leaving Chris to his beautiful reverie.

6

Donna wonders if Joe can help

Donna stirred the sugar into her steaming frothy Cappuccino, her work absent-mindedly thrown down on the kitchen counter-top – a legal case she was working on about a couple's divorce. Her mind wandered as she gazed out of the window down the path to the yard and the exotic rose apple tree. Her eyes rested on the bench beneath its bowers, sparking a memory of young love; of cuddles with Joe as they surveyed the stars together at night – newly-weds enrobed in the shimmer of deep-felt adoration for each other.

Everyone loved Joe, even Donna in the beginning. What did she love about him then? Perhaps she was drawn to his creativity, his artistic nature, his friendliness, his enthusiasm or his unfailing optimism. No-one seemed to care about the world and humanity as he did. So what went wrong with their relationship? Who can ever answer such a thing? Though happy at first, perhaps she was increasingly irritated by his popularity, his ever-growing circle of friends and well-wishers, the endless phone calls and home visits from his spiritual clan. It can make a woman feel quite insecure to have the limelight stolen away from her.

Yes, he was passionate about helping other people, but she firmly believed that charity should begin in the home and, if in all his services to humanity – on this eco-committee and that environmental rally – he had no time for helping his own family, then where was the sense of it all? He didn't even seem to have the basics in place of providing for a family, let alone knowing how to help around the house.

As for all his spiritual talk, she couldn't understand what all the fuss was about. All the unity consciousness ideas that he bandied around meant nothing to her, nor did all the talk of love and spirituality ring true for her, especially when it came to bringing up their son. Love might well bring people together, but it doesn't get the dinner cooked, or get the homework finished, or do the ironing for you. Nor does it get your child educated.

She believed that Joe didn't care what became of his son. He didn't seem to have an ounce of ambition in his body and she was very concerned that this would rub off on Chris, leaving him with no direction or goals in life. She felt like strict discipline and structure were the best way to bring up a child to give them any chance of a successful life. Joe never seemed to push Chris in any way, which to Donna was tantamount to neglect. To her, love meant strict control and structure; she believed that unconditional love should be like an umbrella whose handle should be disciplined love.

Consequently Donna felt like she was the only one who had Chris' best interests at heart. Without her firm hand and imposed structure and routines, she believed he would drift into a dream world, at risk of never achieving anything with his life.

Perhaps this was a source of her bristly, critical nature, insecurity flowing from her own damaged inner child, squashed by years of enforced formal structure from her father. At heart perhaps she was rebelling against this conflict, sub-consciously aware of her own truth – that she was good enough just as she was and that Chris similarly was a perfectly created being, with his own gifts and life path to live out.

Sometimes it was as if she had lost sight of the miracle of family, of the wonder of unconditional love attached to bringing up a child. Perhaps one day these truths would emerge from her daily consciousness, so she could be aware of her true nature and feelings, but at this moment they were well hidden from her.

For now, she had a sense of relief that Joe and his chaotic influence were more or less gone from her life. She was relieved not to be distressing any more about what he was up to. Whether she worried that he was forming some new strange religious cult, or whether he was involved with another woman – perhaps some spiritual nymphet he'd picked up on his rallies – she had always felt concerned that he would do something to turn her life upside down. In all fairness, he had never actually given her cause to doubt his loyalties - this paranoia was purely in her own mind as a result of her insecurities.

But that was all over now; he could do whatever he liked and she didn't care. Order and calm had been restored to the household.

She sometimes wondered how she might feel if he remarried, but usually she pushed that thought to the back of her mind – surprised at the wave of tearful emotions it stirred in her. She reached for a tissue to wipe away the tear that coursed over her flushed cheek.

Her thoughts turned to Chris. He had had another bad night, calling out and crying, yet when she had gone in to see him, he had barely been able to speak to her, uttering only;

'Noises, I can hear noises!'

She had been unable to get him to explain any more. He could only stare out through the window over the bay, as if absorbed in some other-worldly thought. After many failed attempts, she had finally settled him back into his bed, drawing the curtains on the moonlight that was flooding his bedroom and eventually he had dropped off to a fitful sleep.

He had gone to school that day, but only after some considerable negotiating. She knew deep down that he wasn't happy there. She remembered the ill-fated party they had held for his 11th birthday, where she had seen for herself just how unpleasantly his classmates treated him.

Truth be told, she was really worried about him; worst of all she felt like she was losing him. He had stopped asking her questions; although they had always irritated her at the time, now that he was barely speaking to her at all – apart from telling her to be less noisy or to turn down the T.V. – she felt the loss of their closeness like a painful twinge in her heart.

She wished more than anything that he would open up to her again – even to ask his questions – anything rather than these bizarre behaviours. Anything – did she really mean that? Would she even consider that Joe might be able to help?

The reality was that Chris had always got on better with his father, and perhaps now that he was growing up, he needed Joe more. Donna was realizing that much as she appreciated the structure in their Joe-free household, Chris was behaving more and more strangely without his dad's interaction. Despite her resistance to the idea, she was leaning towards the conclusion that he probably needed to see his dad.

Joe would be able to talk to him, to find out what was going on in Chris' head – all these eccentric behaviours that

Chris was exhibiting were beyond her; the over-sensitive hearing, the staring, the withdrawal, the singing and talking to himself. She had to admit that she needed some help.

Yes, perhaps it was time for her to invite Joe back into Chris' life, to let them spend a bit of time together. Perhaps that would help to draw Chris out of his shell again, to bring his old self back to her again. She baulked at the idea, unsure if she could bear to have Joe near her or Chris again, but perhaps it was the only way to find out what was wrong with Chris.

With a level of resolve, she picked up the phone.

7

HOLLY AND JOE INTERRUPTED

Joe was working in his store. Reaching for a round laughing Buddha statue, he placed it carefully down on the wide expanse of an antique oak table, price label in hand; ready to tie its string around the bulging neck of the ebony icon.

Having respectfully circled the Buddha's head with the string, as if awarding it a medal, he gently dusted it with a soft brush and placed it back on its shelf, next to the brightly painted serene figure of the great Ganesh, the elephant-headed Hindu god figure whose trunk curled majestically round onto its abundant belly, its almond eyes serenely gazing out, as if all-knowingly surveying the wondrous sight of the store. Joe nodded at the statues, acknowledging the essence of what they represented and said a little prayer to himself in gratitude for everything that he now had.

A lilting voice wafted from the back of the store – 'Honey, where do you want to put your Hanuman figure?'

Joe's eyes sparkled in response – it was so good to have Holly around. She made him feel happy again, full of hope and energy.

'Can you bring him over to me, Hol, I want to put him right here next to Buddha and Ganesh. I think he'll feel right at home on this shelf.'

'Sure, honey,' she laughed. Her laughter tinkled like a running waterfall and coursed out of her frequently, as if she could barely contain the joy that kept on bubbling out of her in a perpetual flow of happiness. Others would regard her and wonder what she was taking, wishing that they too could drink from the same cup.

He turned to watch as Holly breezed into the room carrying the statue. She had wavy, auburn hair that bounced around her and fell into a fluffy cloud almost down to her waist. Its golden highlights glinted like rays of sunshine and shimmered in a dancing display of light, as if her hair had a life of its own. She rarely tied it back, preferring it to be 'au-naturel' allowing it to create an ever-changing, flattering frame to her face. Holly brought sunshine into his life and a much-needed steadying hand to balance his spontaneous outbursts of activity.

He remembered the first time he had met her, sitting next to her at an auction. She had smiled brightly at him and he had felt himself falling into the emerald pools of her eyes. He had introduced himself and asked her what pieces she was interested in at the auction. She had explained that she was an antiques dealer, with a specialty in acquiring items of a spiritual nature. The moment he had spoken with her, he had felt right at home; soon they had found much in common with each other. They had bid against each other during the auction for several interesting spiritual icons, but each time Joe had given way to allow her to succeed in her bids. Afterwards they had chatted happily together in the café about their exotic travels in search of hidden treasures to bring back to America.

Although he had been in no hurry to start dating again, the words of his friends had echoed within his head; 'Get back on the dating horse, Joe. There's plenty more fish in the sea...' Before he'd even realized what he was doing, he had invited Holly to join him at a forthcoming 'New Age' exhibition he wanted to attend. She had willingly joined him, both of them keen to seek out new treasures for their work, and much to their amazement he had ended up giving a talk there himself. She had been so enraptured by his words that she had asked him out on a date the next day. They had been together now for a few months and they were clearly very good for each other.

Despite technically being available for dating again now that his divorce had come through, deep down he knew he was still entwined with his family and his ex wife, but the new relationship was certainly helping him to move on in many ways.

Holly reached up to the shelf, auburn hair cascading down her back, tiptoeing to get high enough for Hanuman to be placed gently down in his rightful place next to Ganesh and Buddha.

She turned her emerald green eyes to Joe's. His heart skipped a beat as he stared into their healing pools, gazing like a man drinking in life itself. She smiled at him in such a way that the whole room lit up. When she smiles, it's as if she spills her love and light around her, thought Joe.

They gazed fondly at each other and giggled at the shared excitement of the new acquisition for Joe's store. Their giggles were interrupted by the sudden sound of Joe's mobile phone ringing. Joe reached into his pocket and drew out his iPhone, the lit-up backdrop photo of a star nebula obscured by the name of the incoming caller.

'Donna?'

His surprised response was met by a moment's silence on

the other end of the phone. Then as if a floodgate had been opened, Donna's words tumbled out one after the other.

'Joe, please, it's about Chris – you've got to help him. I'm really worried about him. He's not right. He's just not himself.'

Joe's eyebrow shot up in amazement. He was not expecting her to ask him for any kind of help given their frosty relationship.

And yet Donna had opened the door of her heart just a fraction to let him in, because Chris' welfare was suddenly more important than her pride.

'Joe, I need you to come round and see Chris. You need to talk to him and see what's going on with him. He won't speak to me. Will you do it?'

'Donna, what's happened? Is he alright? What have you done, why won't he speak to you?' blurted Joe.

'Joe, don't start. It's just that I don't think he wants me to know and you've always been better at getting him to open up than I have. Will you come – only for a short time. I don't want you upsetting him.'

'Donna, of course I'll come. You know I'll help. He's my boy too, after all.'

He could feel Donna's palpable relief over the line. He knew this was a big turning point for their family, he'd been excluded for such a long time and yet something had happened and Donna had decided she needed him again. His confusion was clouding his thoughts as he looked up and saw Holly's pained eyes staring back. This was going to be really tricky, he thought, but he knew he had to be there for Chris.

'When do you want me to come, Donna?'

'Today, at 4.30 after school.'

'I'll be there'. The connection went dead; Joe turned off his phone, sliding it back into the pocket of his pants.

He looked up but Holly's watery gaze turned away.

'Holly, I'm really sorry, but I need to see what's up with Chris. It sounds like something's wrong. I think he needs me. I'm going over there in a bit, so I need to go and pick up a few things first. Are we still on for dinner later?'

'Sure. Come to my place, I'll cook.' She smiled at him, but it belied her real feelings of anxiety that he was going to Donna's. 'See you later.' She leaned forward and kissed him gently goodbye. Joe waved cheerily and apologetically.

'Later' he uttered as he sped out the door.

8

HOLLY RECALLS FIRST DATE WITH JOE

Holly finished arranging the items on the shelves in the store and surveyed her work languidly. The display looked great, but somehow she had lost her enthusiasm; her mind was elsewhere – away with Joe.

Holly had always known that Joe had a young son, but they had never been introduced. Besides, Joe had minimal contact with him, so she had always been able to appease her slight misgivings about Joe's 'baggage' due to the fact that his son and ex-wife remained absent from Joe's life.

However, this phone-call had come like a bolt from the blue and her somersaulting stomach gave away her feelings of concern about his distracted attitude. Yes, he had assured her that he was divorced and available, but Holly was keen to have an uncomplicated and traditional relationship. Whilst the ex-family was only vaguely in the background, she had felt fairly comfortable in building up a relationship with this wonderful man. She had surprised herself how quickly she had fallen head over heels in love with him, and wasn't sure if her heart could take it if he was ever to show interest in a reunion with Donna.

She remembered the first time they had met; her heart skipped a beat as she revisited in her mind the time they had gone to the 'New Age' exhibition together. She had happily accepted his invitation, telling Joe that she was keen to hear the speakers on the poster, but all the while aware of her very strong attraction to this kind, gentle man.

She had sat nervously with him in the hall, feeling like a school girl with a crush. She had been most surprised and delighted by the numbers of people that had come up to Joe during the course of the evening to chat with him. He seemed to know nearly everyone there and seemed to be very well thought of.

They had both been surprised by a sudden turn of events that day. Whilst waiting for one of the speakers to come on stage, there had been some considerable confusion amongst the organizers. It turned out that one of the speakers – a Robert Langton – had been delayed due to a traffic accident whilst hurrying to the event. Robert was a good friend of Joe's and had often given talks at Joe's store, but he had phoned to cancel his slot, unable to make it.

One of the organizers had approached Joe, on Robert's suggestion, to ask if he would like to stand in, well aware that Joe was also a mover and shaker in the 'New Age' world. Joe was of course unprepared, however – known for his spontaneity – he had willingly got up on stage, with the rapidly conveyed brief to talk on the topic of 'The growing New Age culture'.

Holly had watched with anxiety and excitement, worried on his behalf that he had been put on the spot, but awed to see that he had happily accepted. She was incredibly keen to hear what he would have to say.

She remembered that he had stood for a minute in silence, smiling at the whole audience, as though greeting everyone individually with his hauntingly magnetic silver-grey eyes.

Holly's stomach had churned, imagining that he was at a loss for words, however his calm, steady breathing that she could hear down the microphone was controlled, balanced and rhythmic – not the breath of an anxious person, but the breathing of a centred and connected person who was just taking everything in their stride.

She had felt like he was assessing the room, taking everything in, tuning into the audience – it was a mystical sensation almost. Yes, he had reminded her of her idea of a mystic in fact – yet he had never claimed to be a mystic. He had never claimed to have anything special to offer people, yet here he was on stage, extending his presence out to the audience and welcoming everyone there – without even uttering a word.

Hiding behind her cloud of auburn hair, Holly had sneaked a peek around the spacious brightly lit room – the audience was on the edge of their seats in anticipation, the atmosphere electric. The organizer had introduced Joe as an author, philosopher and facilitator, mentor of healers and owner of a very successful New Age store. She still remembered how her hair had stood up on the back of her neck as she watched Joe standing there, cutting a dashing muscular and lean figure in his casual jeans and T-shirt. As he began to talk, he surprised everyone there with his eloquence and insight.

He had started with a brief history of so-called New Age culture, but quickly drew people in with his evocative descriptions of where he thought it was all heading, describing his ideas of the existence of higher realities which challenged the realities most of us see in our physical world.

The entranced audience had clapped appreciatively, clearly having taken Joe pretty seriously for a drop-in speaker. Holly had been enthralled; her eyes had been opened to the depths of his wisdom. She had felt herself falling for him in a big way; her appreciation of him was obvious to all with eyes.

Her open and loving nature was an excellent balm for Joe's wounded heart. He had grown from strength to strength in his loving acceptance of what had happened in his previous relationship, making him ready in some ways to move on completely in fact.

Yet she had always sensed that he still maintained a deep connection with his family, and so when the phone-call from Donna was received, Holly's confidence in their future started to falter.

She had sensed a shadow coming towards her relationship with Joe. She even had a guilty conscience, because she had traditional values when it came to relationships, so any hint of a bigamous allegiance occurring was unacceptable in her eyes. Despite the official divorce papers, Holly knew that heart bonds were stronger. Holly's love for Joe went so deep, that she could not bring herself to stand in the way of his reunion with his family, were it to be in the cards. Family should come first.

9

Chris and Joe reunited by the cosmos

Chris threw down the moon book he was reading - his father, Joe, was due any minute. His head throbbed with all the questions that welled up in his mind. He couldn't wait to see his dad again. It had felt like an eternity since he had last seen him; so much had happened to Chris, but whenever he had asked his mum any of these questions she would become snide and would walk away, muttering; 'Waste-of-time daydreaming never got anybody anywhere.'

His hackles rose at the thought and his ever-growing frustration with his mother was hurled across the room in the shape of his left trainer. That's why he'd stopped asking her questions - she just didn't understand him, but his dad did!

His mother had given him the good news about his dad visiting when Chris got back from school; he was itching with excitement.

He heard the doorbell ring downstairs; his heart skipped a beat in anticipation of seeing his dad. As he grabbed his sweater he threw himself out the door and hurtled down the stairs in a clatter of excitement and expectation.

His mum was already giving his dad the third degree, yelling 'What time do you call this? I said 4.30!' and 'You've got half an hour – tops. You can go out in the yard but no further, got it?'

In her nervousness, Donna already seemed to have forgotten that it was her that had invited Joe to come. Joe was serenely weathering the storm – a radiant expression of anticipation shining on his grinning, bronzed face.

'Donna, you look lovely, have you done something new to your hair?' He smiled, eyeing her perfectly coiffed blonde mane and her accurately applied make-up. She pursed her lips at him in annoyance and turned to yell for Chris, but he was already there.

Joe's silver-grey eyes fell on Chris and he spread out his long welcoming arms ready for a bear hug. Chris threw himself headlong into his tall dad, nearly knocking over his mum in the process.

'Hi there buddy! How are you? It's so good to see you!' His dad's woolly sweater felt warm but too ticklish and smelled of incense and whisky – a heady combination with his elated emotions.

Chris' silver eyes shined brightly as he burst into his list of questions like a rocket off a launch-pad.

Donna appeared relieved to hear Chris open up.

'Whoa there, kiddo!' His dad's hearty belly-laugh was a sound for sore ears. He tousled his son's shaggy golden curls with his great hand. 'Hold your horses, son. I can see you're feeling better today! Let's say hello first, then we'll go and sit down under the rose apple tree in the yard, O.K.? Then you can fire away with all your questions to your heart's content!'

They happily wandered arm-in-arm out into the yard, Chris chatting excitedly over the fading sound of his mother's grating warnings of time.

They sat together on the wooden bench, in the shade of the spreading branches above. Joe crossed his white cotton-clad long legs and Chris nestled up close to his dad's ticklish jumper, warming his spindly arms around his lean, muscular belly. The bench was marked with dates engraved by Chris since he was a child, each one marking a Full Moon he had observed. They fell silent for a minute, as if drinking in the moment.

His dad glanced across at the sundial over by the pond, noting the lateness of the day by the shadow on its face – a poignant reminder of how everything seemed to be driven by time. A thought popped into his head – something he had read once, that he recalled as he smelled the sweet blossom scent wafting down from the tree above their heads;

'Time affects all that is visible, but not the invisible spirit of our being.'

He chuckled as he wondered whether his spirit would ever age and grow white hair like he had noticed in the mirror whilst shaving this morning.

He always loved this rose apple tree – it was the same type of tree that Lord Buddha was said to have sat under to contemplate and reach a state of enlightenment. He stared at its magnificent white spiky flowers which reminded him of star bursts.

Chris was desperate to ask his questions, but equally he was immersed in the happiest, warmest feeling he had ever recalled as he sat reunited with his father.

Still, he needed to ask the questions before they burnt a hole into his feverish mind.

'Dad,'

'Yes son?'

Chris launched into a breathless torrent of questions, which tumbled out of him like a powerful waterfall;

'Why do I feel like I am drawn to the Moon so much? Why do I feel like the Moon is speaking to me, and that I need to speak to it? Why am I hearing strange noises? How come I can see things now that I used to need glasses or a magnifying glass for? Why do I keep thinking strange ideas about things that I've never even read about?'

His dad took a sharp intake of breath at these unusual questions, gazed into the boy's eager spectacle-free eyes and marvelled at their depth and radiance. They seemed brighter somehow, as if reflecting an even more silvery quality than he remembered. He wondered if he had ever really noticed their true colour behind the glasses Chris had always worn before.

Chris seemed different in other ways too. He suddenly seemed so grown-up, so sure of himself, full of questions and yet so present, not absent-minded like he often used to be.

Confused, yet excited somehow by his son's thoughtful questions, he pondered for a while; he remembered the day that his precious boy was born.

Chris' arrival had been around midnight as a Bright Moon was shining in the sky. His birth had occurred at a tough time for him and Donna - with both of them unemployed at that point, money was tight.

Prior to Donna's pregnancy they had relied on her intermittent wages to pay all the bills. Fresh out of law school she had taken what work she could find as a locum lawyer, working short contract maternity cover for other lawyers to gain experience, but she had struggled with relationships at each firm, getting herself into all sorts of arguments with the bosses, as her feisty and uncompromising nature bubbled over.

Suddenly she had felt unwell, tired all the time and emotionally unstable, and things started to fall apart for her. Donna had been admitted to hospital after what seemed like a mini-breakdown. Her employers had been less than supportive, demanding that she get back to work immediately or lose her job.

Yet under investigation at the hospital, Donna and Joe were pleasantly surprised to find that she was carrying a child and was already 10 weeks on – the baby probably went undetected by her for some time as Donna actually thought she was unable to have children after a riding accident when she was a teenager. Still, the news was a blessing to the young couple, and they were more than happy to accept this miracle into their lives.

However, after her employers found out that she was pregnant, they didn't renew her contract, claiming all sorts of reasons other than the stark truth that they just didn't think a mother-to-be would be able to give them the hours and the commitment that they demanded. So the young couple had struggled on with no money coming in and Donna got increasingly mad at him for not being a responsible husband and getting a proper job.

Then there was the incident that occurred to Donna early on in her pregnancy. A mentally unstable lady visited her at home, scaring Donna half to death with crazy premonitions she had experienced about Donna's child. Joe hadn't believed Donna or the crazy old lady at the time, dismissing the event as pregnancy anxieties and the mad ramblings of a senile woman. Yet now some premonition was stirring within him, perhaps something that could help them to understand what had been happening to Chris; he felt an urge to discuss Chris' birth date and its astrological significance.

He took a breath and started to try to solidify the strange ideas forming in his head.

'You know how all the planets in our solar system are continually revolving around the sun?'

'Oh yes! I know the names of all the planets Dad! There's a way to remember from the first letters of this daft phrase; Make Very Easy Mash Just Squash Up New Potatoes. So here we go; there's Mercury, Venus, Earth, Mars, Jupiter, Saturn, Uranus, Neptune and Pluto – although Pluto is no longer considered a planet of course!'

'Yes, son, you're such a bright little guy! Well, at the exact time you were born…'

'It was a Bright Moon, wasn't it Dad! It was the 20th of February 2000. I think it was about midnight so the Moon was at its zenith!'

'Exactly, kiddo; at that exact time, at that Full Moon, each of the planets in our Solar System were in a particular position relative to the Earth; I guess they were in a pretty auspicious arrangement that night when you were born, because look at all the amazing things that are happening to you now. Your mother and I, we both thank our lucky stars that you came to us.'

Chris breathed heavily for a moment as he thought about these words; his mind raced as he wondered what it all meant. His train of thought was broken as his dad began speaking again.

'Now listen to this bit son, this is the really cool part; each planet can exert an influence on you to a different degree, depending on how close the planet happens to be to Earth at the moment of your birth. So some planets will be closer and more influential on you than others.'

'Wow, Dad. I know the Moon isn't a planet, but do you think the Full Moon was influencing me?'

'Yes, son – I think it probably was. The Moon can definitely affect us too. You know, I've looked at your astrological birth-chart; I have to say that it's a pattern I've never seen before. I don't really know what it means. But I can tell you what I think. I think the Moon had such a great presence and exerted such a great influence on you that night you were born, that it's made some kind of permanent connection to you that you can tap into whenever you want to.'

'Really - but why are all these things happening to me now? Why didn't they always happen to me right from when I was born?' Chris' silver eyes gazed curiously up at his dad.

'I don't know son. I just know that something seems to have triggered a connection between you and the Moon. Why else would you be so obsessed with it? It's not only the Moon that affects you though; I know it was the Full Moon that everybody saw on the night of your birth, but you know all the planets are still there even if you can't see them?'

'Yes, Dad – but we can see some of them, can't we? Do you remember that night we looked at the stars together and I pointed to that really bright one in the sky...you said it wasn't a star, it was a planet; it was Venus...'

'I do remember, son.'

His mouth transformed to a wistful smile, as the memory of that special night spent together with his son filled his mind; he saw a picture of them lying together on the grass gazing up at the stars and felt such warmth in his chest, remembering the feeling of love he had for his special little boy, the gift of family and sharing intimate times together...

Almost instantly this picture was erased by a harsher one; a picture of conflict and horror as he replayed in his mind the fight with his wife when Chris had turned 11 years old, the argument which was to tear his life apart, to turn his world upside down. In his mind's eye he replayed Donna's cutting words ...

'You're a waste of space and a loser! You have no idea how to be a good father. Chris needs stability, he needs certainty and routine. You wouldn't know routine if it jumped up and bit you! I can't stand the sight of you a moment longer. Get out, leave us both alone. Don't you ever set foot in this house again! Don't even think about trying to see Chris...he doesn't need you and I don't need you!'

He felt a sudden pain in his chest as he recalled this traumatic memory, as if someone had shot an arrow into his back piercing him all the way through his heart, out to the front of his chest. For a long time after that he'd been ostracised by his family, left out in the cold; left to pick up the pieces and restart his life.

Yet here he was, reunited with his son; he felt a mixture of feelings. Although he had at last been allowed back into their lives, the time he was allowed to spend with his son today was controlled and rationed as if he was some kind of criminal – a prisoner with limited visiting time.

It was as if he was being punished by Donna; but for what? He had only ever showed them love and tried to take care of them – albeit a little impractically he had to admit. He knew he had his faults; he knew he didn't have a regular job or income when he was still with Donna. He knew he was a bit of a daydreamer, with his nose always stuck in a book; but hey, who doesn't have their faults? Surely the fact that he still loved them both was the most important thing? Plus he was bringing in money for them now from his work at the store, so she couldn't complain about that? She'd kept her house in the break-up and she was doing well with her work now she had found a good legal firm to work for. She seemed much more settled these days; things had certainly moved on.

It seemed a miracle that Donna had given way sufficiently to let him see his boy again; such precious time together, such sad sweetness, but every second treasured and milked for all it was worth. He was grateful now for any relationship he'd been allowed to resurrect with his son.

In the beginning, when he'd first tasted the poisonous bite of rejection, he'd retreated to the safety of solitude, spending many whisky-soaked evenings seeking solace in the sweet numbness of alcohol-induced anaesthesia. Yet even behind the bars of his prison of rejection, he was touched one night by a profound thought; 'sometimes when we are lost, we need inspiration and guidance from others who are journeying smoothly with confidence and clarity.'

He knew then it was time to break out of his self-imposed solitude and reach out to his closest friends, who willingly took him under their wing. As the words of sorrow and abandonment flowed out of his heart, his friends gently soaked his words and in well-meaning, light-hearted laughter and philosophical banter. Their words rang in his head:

> **'Let a thousand people dislike you;**
> **there is always one who likes you...'**

> **'Don't expect other people to understand you. It's up to**
> **you to try to understand them...'**

'Those who criticize you and trouble you, are the ones who sculpt you into a beautiful idol...'

It was as if the light inside, that seemed to have been snuffed out by Donna's cruel words, had been switched on again.

Suddenly, he was aware that Chris was staring intently at him, an anxious expression in his eyes. He shook himself, as if to shake away a dark cloak of feelings that forever threatened to suffocate him, were he to let them.

Realizing he had been silent for some considerable time, that his face was wet with sorrowful tears, he cleared his throat and tried to resume where he had left off.

'Sorry, kiddo. It's just that it's hard sometimes. I miss you so much, but I know that you're there even if I can't see you...'

'Yeah, I know Dad. Like the planets. I miss you too. I miss our talks.'

Chris reached out and wiped the tears away from his dad's face. Joe's heart swelled and he suddenly felt like everything was going to be alright.

'I love you Chris. You know, son, love is a funny thing; it's like a thread, it weaves us together. No matter if we can't always be together, love keeps us connected – our minds, our bodies, our spirits – everything stays connected. All we really need to be together is to keep on loving each other no matter what.'

Chris' silver eyes were shining in the fading evening sunlight, then suddenly the floodgates were opened and the tears were flowing down his rosy cheeks like a waterfall, as if all the sadness was pouring out of his eyes, and welling from his heart.

'S-s-s-sometimes,' he sobbed 'I really hate her, Dad...'

'Listen son, you're bigger than that. Mum loves you too, you know? She thinks she's doing the right thing. She thinks she knows what's best for you and her.'

'She doesn't know anything, Dad! She doesn't understand. Sometimes I just wish she would leave us alone!' Chris' words came out in stabs, as if he was trying to hurt her with his words.

'O.K., O.K.,' he soothed as Chris' fury rolled over him. 'That anger you're carrying around is pretty destructive, you know? You'll only end up provoking her like that, you need to calm down and understand why she's doing this. Do something more constructive with your feelings, alright? Channel your anger into something more productive than wishing your mother away. Write your feelings down. While you're at it, write down all of those questions you've got. I might not be able to answer them all but if you keep a note of them, you might find some answers one day. You might end up finding out something really inspiring...'

His dad wrapped his arms around Chris' heaving shoulders. They stayed locked in their embrace as if the world around them had dissipated, as if there was only ever the two of them and their love that existed.

Donna had come out to see what was happening; she stared at the father and son embracing and felt the old intense jealousy strike her heart again, making her forget why Joe was here. She was angry that Chris wouldn't open up to her like he would to his dad. She felt the old pangs of loneliness and exclusion roll over her in a suffocating wave. She saw red – how dare Joe waltz in here after all this time and steal her son away from her like that? Lost in her little world of self-inflicted pain, she yelled at Chris and Joe.

Their reverie was broken by Donna's harsh words cutting through the balmy evening air.

'Right that's it. Time's up. Come on Chris, get in the house. Joe – it's time for you to leave.'

She charged down the path towards the tree like a warrior with a blade intending to wound their enemy; Chris' dad jumped in shock, releasing his arms from his clinging son's shoulders. He held his hands up as if the ferocious words she was brandishing at him were like an imaginary weapon. He'd clearly outstayed his welcome and his usefulness.

'Dad, please no, you have to stay!'

'Kiddo, I'm sorry, you have to listen to your mother. This is just the way things have to be right now.'

'Come on Chris – get away from him now. Your father has to go.'

Donna reached for Chris' hand and tugged him harshly away from his grieving father. Chris sobbed and felt like retching. Surely things didn't have to be like this. He loved his dad and his dad loved him. What more truth do you need than that?

As if reading his son's mind, his dad stood and said;

'Truth doesn't lie on the horizon or beyond the stars, son; it's right here in your heart. It may have been eclipsed today, but it will emerge again like the morning sun...'

With that he raised his hand to wave a remorseful goodbye and took off down the driveway towards his car.

'Poppycock!' shouted Donna down the street, hurling the

word after him like a sharp stick meant to maim and wound. Donna's heart contracted in pain as if the stick had whirled round in a Boomerang-like fashion and pierced her heart.

In the midst of her suffering, as she dragged Chris' sobbing body up the path back to the house, a sudden strange thought seemed to hit her.

> **'Words expressed out of anger are like bullets. Bullets can be surgically removed, but not words...'**

As she sent Chris upstairs to his room, she slammed the door in frustration. She sat in a heap on the sofa, sobbing with heaving shoulders until there was nothing left in her to come out. Then she realized that she still didn't know what was wrong with Chris; she'd just thrown away her chance of finding out. Worse than that, she'd ruined her chances of getting close to Chris. She was struck with a terrible sense of regret for her behaviour.

She held her head in utter despair – 'Damn my impetuous anger and my stupid insecurities,' she wailed to herself, unaware that the more you become possessive of someone, the more you portray your insecurities and feelings of inferiority...

10

HOLLY VOICES HER FEARS

Holly was reunited with Joe after his visit to Chris and Donna's house.

They were sharing dinner at her antique-adorned apartment - she had created a beautiful candle-lit table, scattered with flower petals and confetti stars. She had cooked his favourite meal for him – vegetable bhuna curry, with naan bread and chutneys. Holly placed his meal in front of him, but he barely seemed to notice. She sensed that he was very distracted; she felt a sadness seeping through her veins.

Joe stirred from his thoughts of Chris, picking up on Holly's emotional heaviness. On asking her what was wrong, she decided it was time to get some things off her chest. Sweeping her auburn waves away from her troubled face, she reluctantly voiced her fears.

'Joe, I'm really worried that you might still be attached to Donna,' her emerald eyes gazed at Joe's surprised face. 'It's completely understandable,' she added kindly, 'I'm only thinking of you, Joe. I'm just worried that if you still have a chance to make things up with Donna, being with me might be a barrier to your family getting back together?'

'I don't understand why you're thinking this way, Holly!' exclaimed Joe sadly. Holly grasped for the right words, her beautiful face unusually pained.

'Look, you may not even know it yourself Joe, but you may still have feelings for Donna. After all, she is the mother of your child. If you do still have feelings for Donna, then for me to be with you at the same time would be completely morally unbearable,' she blurted out.

Joe gazed into her troubled green eyes and felt a sudden sense of doubt - what if she was right? But he couldn't lose this wonderful woman.

'Listen Holly, you do understand that Donna and I are divorced, don't you? I am legally and officially a single man.'

Although Joe tried to convince her that she was being irrational, Holly just couldn't shake this idea from her mind.

Joe persevered, 'You know Donna was really unpleasant to me when I went over. There's no way she wants me back anyway!'

Yet he had been unable to lighten her heart on this matter, so they shared an uncomfortable evening together.

II

JOE HAS DINNER WITH HIS MOTHER

In need of a friendly face and someone to talk to with all this relationship upheaval occurring, Joe had invited his mother to have dinner with him at a local restaurant.

She was a wise and sympathetic woman and Joe adored her; her body was starting to appear aged but she was still very active. She was rarely confrontational, preferring to allow others to go their own way and learn from their own mistakes. She was most understanding towards those who acted from the heart, and although she gave traditional guidance, she was modern and broad-minded in her thinking.

A good listener, she had a most endearing characteristic created by her desire to really understand what others were telling her; when she wanted to hear better she would remove her glasses as though her eyes and ears had interchanged their roles as senses.

Christina had an interesting take on the notion of fashion. She was often tightly dressed to help her to feel young, yet she wore flat simple shoes as her feet and joints were often painful. Unable to stand for long periods of time, she usually sought out the comfort of a chair to rest her aching legs.

A compassionate woman, she often worried about the well-being of the family and all her acquaintances. This emotional exercise maintained her vitality and enthusiasm, keeping her going even as she watched others of her generation slowly decay.

Mother and son chose a cosy corner of the beautifully decorated Italian-inspired eatery and sat down.

Joe observed his mom's bright face; although Christina showed some signs of ageing, her face was well behind its years, perhaps due to her timely and disciplined attention to eating and sleeping and her rare indulgence in revelry. Today he wanted to treat her to something special.

'So what do you fancy to drink today, Mum - champagne?'

'Someone's feeling flush! No that's far too expensive, dear. A sparkling mineral water would be just fine thank you.'

'Alright Mum,' chuckled Joe. 'How about food, are you hungry?'

'Oh yes, dear – I can always eat a mountain of food in a place like this, I adore Italian!'

Donning her glasses, Christina eyed the menu thoughtfully. 'Hmm, I think I'll choose this creamy pasta with vegetables – it sounds lovely' - she smiled appreciatively at her son, removing her glasses and letting them dangle on their chain around her neck. 'So how is it going at the store, Joe? Is business going well?'

'Pretty good actually, thanks Mum. I'll be able to pay back your loan soon. We have a whole new batch of figures in stock which I just adore, and I think I might actually be quite gutted when someone comes in to buy them – they seem so at home on those shelves!'

Christina laughed – she was delighted to see her son so happy. His bronzed face appeared healthy and vital. His mood certainly seemed to have improved over the last few months as he had followed his heart back into the world of healing and spirituality.

'Holly found the figures – she's so good at sourcing stock for the store. She has a real knack of knowing what will sell and what has a good feel about it.' Joe crossed his long legs, baring his brown slip-on shoes.

Christina raised her eyebrows at the mention of Holly – she'd not yet been introduced to her, but had a feeling that she was doing wonders for her son's emotional welfare.

'When am I going to meet this wonderful girl, Joe?' she teased, silvery eyes twinkling behind her glasses.

Joe seemed a little uncomfortable, but he was saved by the waitress waiting to take their order. They offered their choices to the pleasantly smiling girl, who pottered back to the noisy kitchen.

Christina pressed home her question a second time, hoping to get a positive response, but she was to be disappointed.

'Well, I'm not sure I'm ready for that Mum; as a matter of fact, things have been a little rocky recently between Holly and me. Also, I have something to tell you.'

'Oh?' asked his mother keenly, unsure where this conversation was going. She placed her glasses carefully back on her nose in order to 'hear' him better.

'I went to see Donna yesterday.' Joe sat back in his chair, waiting for the fall-out.

'You did? What on Earth made you do that?' asked Christina, peering in surprise at Joe over the top of her glasses. She was in no hurry for her son to get embroiled back into that poisonous relationship again, but she knew she needed to keep her feelings on that to herself.

'Actually, she asked me to – more to see Chris than her really,' explained Joe, carefully.

'Well, that was unexpected!' exclaimed Christina, aware that Donna forbade most contact with Chris since the divorce. 'How is the little fellah?' she asked affectionately.

'He's doing alright, I think, but he's really missing us,'

'Well of course he is! That Donna has a lot to answer for!' she said angrily.

'It's not just that; he's been having a bit of a strange time hearing unusual sounds, but both his hearing and his eyesight have remarkably improved.' Joe seemed worried, and Christina reached out across the table to hold his hand.

'Well they sound like positive things darling! What's the problem?'

'Donna thinks he's not well. She says he's been acting a bit strangely; she can't determine what's wrong, but he told me that he's been talking to the Moon again.'

'That's nothing new, Joe! We know that he's always loved the Moon; he has a hundred and one stories about it, which will all feed his incredible imagination.'

'I know, Mum, but he just doesn't stop staring at the Moon – it's as if he's lost interest in anyone or anything else!' Joe ran his long fingers through his chestnut brown hair in distraction.

'Well dear, people often become immune to the beauty and goodness around them. We become tempted by things that lie in the distance. We often adore them, perhaps until they are reached and realized. I'm sure he will grow out of it soon.

'You know, with both of us evicted from his life so suddenly, I don't think it's any surprise that he's reacting badly. It's not like Donna has a very understanding relationship with Chris - she's always telling him what to do, or what NOT to do. She just doesn't leave the kid alone. I bet he's desperate for a decent conversation with someone; he's turned the Moon into a surrogate imaginary friend or something.'

'Hmm, I can see that, but why the strange sight and sound symptoms?' asked Joe, unsure.

'Well I don't know about that, but you'd better make sure that Donna takes him to the Doctor's to get his eyes and ears checked out. It's probably nothing – he's growing up after all; all sorts of things start to change around his age. I remember when you were 12 and...'

'Alright Mum, don't embarrass me!' begged Joe, laughing.

'We'll leave that for another day, then!' she joked. 'See if you can get Donna to agree to me seeing him. I'll have a chat with him. I miss him so much – it would be lovely to spend some time with my best grandson.'

'You mean your only grandson!' laughed Joe. 'I'll see what I can do, but Donna was already yelling at me after one visit, so I doubt she's going to speak to me again so soon,' said Joe, wistfully. 'I miss him terribly, Mum!'

'I know you do, son. I'm so sorry.'

Christina clasped Joe's hand and squeezed. She spotted

the waitress wiggling towards their table balancing a silver tray laden with domed plates. 'Hey, let's eat. I'm ravenous!' she smiled.

May

Full Moon: 8.36 am on May 5th

12

Chris is entranced once more by the Full Moon

Chris had been furious with his mother for breaking up his meeting prematurely with his dad. He'd begged his mum to let him see his dad again, but she had stubbornly refused, still embarrassed by her loss of composure during their last meeting.

Chris fell back into his introvert ways, as if resorting to a familiar rut. He now refused to speak to his mother most of the time.

He had been obsessively staring out of the window again. He had attached new lenses to his telescope; with updated components, he was getting a much better picture of the Moon. This way he felt much closer to it, almost as if he was actually living on it and able to glide over its surface, soaring over its rifts and valleys, its craters and its 'seas'.

Now that the Moon was full, he just stood staring at it. He was absorbed in its beauty, his awareness so far away from where he was physically standing, it was almost as if he had actually been transported to the Moon and he was somehow melded with it – mind, body and spirit. He felt light, almost weightless.

Bright Moon

He became unaware of his surroundings, or of there being any boundary between him and other objects. It was as if he had melted into oneness with everything around him. He felt filled with light, but the light wasn't just in him, it was him. His eyes shimmered with a silvery glow. He felt such bliss and relaxation. He felt ready to sleep.

In a trance he walked over to his bed and lay down. He enjoyed the best night's sleep he'd had in ages.

13

CHRIS WAKES TO A TERRIFYING EXPERIENCE – HIS FIRST VISIONS

The sun peeped through the curtains of Chris' bedroom, sending fingers of light to search around the room. They rested upon Chris' eyelids and he began to stir. As he came to, he became aware of the strange yet familiar sound buzzing in his ears, yet today it seemed louder than ever – more like waves rolling in the ocean. He remembered his dream had been about sailing on a boat under the moonlight, with the waves crashing on the nearby rocks.

He lay still in his bed, with his eyes still closed, listening to the noise, trying to understand what it was. There was a definite pulse to it, a coming in and going out of the sound, almost like the blood pumping around the body when you place your hands over your ears, but much louder and higher pitched. His heart was actually racing.

He began to open one eye – carefully peeling the eyelid to reveal a little light. Immediately his sight was filled with minuscule ovoid shapes and wriggling wormy structures. He gasped in shock, shutting his eye tightly closed again. What on Earth was that? He must still be asleep, yet his heart was beating faster than a racehorse's feet pounding round a track. The sound was ever-present; he felt significantly overwhelmed. What should he do? He decided he needed to know more about what he had seen; he breathed deeply, trying to calm his nerves sufficiently to open his eyes again.

Timidly, he unfurled both eyes; the jiggling clumping shapes danced in his vision. He began to shake uncontrollably. He had no clue what was happening to him. He was certain that something had gone terribly wrong. What was wrong with his eyes? Were they making these strange shapes, was he creating them himself, or was it an illusion? Perhaps he was dying? He clamped his eyes shut again and furiously rubbed them with the palms of his hands, hoping to eradicate every trace of the strange shapes he was seeing. He tried again, but again his sight was met with dancing wiggly shapes that filled his vision. He heard a scream; then he realized it was emanating from his own throat.

His scream was one of pure terror; it rang piercingly through the house, reaching his mother's ears in the kitchen. She froze at the sound, alarmed, aware – as any mother is – that this was no ordinary sound she heard, but a portent of something most sinister. Her legs carried her swiftly up the stairs to where the sound was coming from – Chris' bedroom. Her heart was pounding fast as she hurled the door open wide to see her son writhing and screaming on his bed.

'Chris! Chris! Oh my God, Chris, what on Earth is the matter?' She grabbed him around the shoulders but he shook her off with behemoth strength - he was screaming uncontrollably.

'Chris! What's happened? Tell me, son. What can I do?' she wailed, deep blue eyes wide in fright.

He opened his eyes but he did not seem to be looking at her. He seemed to be looking straight through her. He screamed even louder. Then he shouted out.

'They're all over you, Mum! You're covered in them!

They're everywhere! Oh my God, what are they?'

'What are you talking about?' she wailed.

'There are little creatures wriggling all over you, Mum.'

She stared down in shock, but she could see nothing out of the ordinary, wherever she searched on her body. She could only see her neat blouse and her tight black skirt. She turned back to Chris, and he was pointing at her with an agonized expression on his face.

'They're right there, Mum! They're little monsters or something. They're writhing all over you!'

She gasped in horror, unable to see what he could be talking about. Her stomach twisted in angst as she realized he was terribly unwell.

'Chris – honey, really, there's nothing there! I can't see anything sweetie!'

'Mum, you're not looking properly! I swear they're all over you and they're ALIVE!'

She tried again to hold him, reaching for his hands to calm him down. As he followed her gaze to his own hands, he started to scream again.

'Mum, they're on me too!' His face was a picture of terror and confusion. Donna began to cry. This was all too much. She knew he hadn't been himself, but really this had gone too far. She needed help.

'Chris, I'm going to get you some help. Wait there. I'll be as quick as I can. You'll be just fine, son.'

With that she threw herself down the stairs at break-neck speed to seek out the phone.

She turned over cushions and newspapers in her search, with the sound of Chris' racking sobs reaching her down the stairs. Finally she located the phone, and with trembling fingers, she dialled 911.

'Emergency services, what is the emergency?' answered a voice at the end of the line.

'Please, you've got to come quickly. It's my little boy. He's really sick. I don't know what to do. Please help us?' Donna burst out.

'Yes of course ma'am. What seems to be the problem?'

The emergency operator calmly responded.

Donna struggled to find the words. 'My son, he says he can see little creatures all over him and me. He's hysterical.'

'Ma'am, I'm not sure I understand? Has he taken anything? Does he seem to have a fever?'

'N-no, I mean, I don't know actually,' stammered Donna.

'Well, ma'am, perhaps you can try to check his temperature and if it's really high, call your doctor?'

'Um, O.K....' she hesitated, 'I'll try.'

The operator asked a few more key questions before deciding that no response seemed necessary. Donna went back up the stairs via the bathroom cabinet to fetch a thermometer, to check on Chris.

'Honey, I need to take your temperature.' Donna approached Chris with the thermometer.

'No! Don't touch me Mum!' screamed Chris in a horrified voice, observing the wiggling ovoids all over the thermometer and his mother's hands.

'Chris, I need to see if you've got a fever,' Donna explained.

'You can't touch me, Mum!' He nervously backed away from her up against his headboard. Donna gave an exasperated gasp.

'Well, have you taken anything, Chris?'

'No!' He yelled.

'Are you sure, honey?' she questioned.

'Yes, Mum – please just help me!'

Donna sighed – she didn't know what to do. She ran back downstairs and called 911 again.

'Emergency services, what is the emergency?'

Donna tried to explain the situation better this time.

'My son, Chris, he's only 12. I think he might have a really high fever or something, but he won't let me touch him to take his temperature. I'm really worried about him. He seems terribly sick. Please send an ambulance?'

'Where is he at the moment, is he somewhere safe?'

'Yes he's in his bedroom.'

'Good. Has he taken anything, drugs or something toxic?

'No he hasn't.'

The emergency dispatch operator asked several more questions, before requesting the address and phone number for the house. Donna relayed the information as clearly as she could, but her voice was quivering.

'We'll send an ambulance out to you, it should arrive in about ten minutes, ma'am; try to stay calm.'

Donna sobbed down the phone. 'Please, just get here quickly...'

She put the phone down and ran back upstairs to Chris, who was staring wide-eyed around the room in horror.

'Mum, they're everywhere! They're all over the surfaces! They're in my water glass, all round the rim, they're crawling all over that apple core over there...oh my God, Mum, what are they?

She tried again to comfort him, reaching out to hold his shoulders, but he wouldn't let her touch him. They stayed like that – trance-like and shaking – until the sound of the doorbell cut through their horror ten minutes later.

14

Paramedics arrive to help Chris

Donna ran to let in the two paramedics – a man and a woman.

The man was tall and burly, but friendly-looking. Donna noted his badge; it read 'Brian'. Strong and muscled, he was built to heave even a weighty person over his shoulder. Donna could imagine that his build either provoked ego-challenged individuals into attempting to fight him, or else his size advantage instantly sucked the fight out of them like a deflated balloon. His closely-shaved head was a nod to the skinhead generation, (although he would argue that it was purely for practical purposes).

The woman was shorter with a very kind face. Donna clocked her name badge – 'Sarah'. Her glossy raven hair was geometrically styled and shined almost as brightly as her intensely polished shoes. Donna eyed Sarah's beautifully manicured nails that were short and practical but painted bright red like precious rubies. Her long lashes framed deep brown compassionate eyes that smiled and twinkled as she introduced herself. Bedecked in her paramedic uniform she cut a striking figure which commanded attention as she walked into the house, all long and leggy and authoritative.

Donna invited them in and showed them upstairs, as

Donna gabbled out what had happened. The male paramedic nodded his understanding at Donna and asked her not to worry. They crowded into Chris' small bedroom, picking their way round the space rocket models and the planetary paraphernalia. Brian carefully approached Chris, but the boy's eyes widened in horror.

'The creatures, they're all over you too!' screamed Chris at the paramedic, who stopped dead in his tracks in surprise. 'They must be spreading! Stay away, you'll get hurt! Don't come near me!' screamed Chris.

Brian, an avid fan of horror stories, was never short of a few chilling tales of his own to tell when requested to speak about the nature of his job. Yet this scenario was a new one to him; he was surprised how the hairs on the back of his neck were standing up.

'Kid, I don't know what you're talking about, but it's all going to be O.K. My name's Brian and this is my colleague, Sarah. We're going to help you, but you need to help us first. Please will you let me examine you?' asked the male paramedic calmly. His bright piercing blue eyes were kind and surprisingly gentle. Brian slowly reached forward with gloved hand towards Chris' wrist, ready to check his pulse. Chris pulled away, shivering – his wide eyes staring at the gloved hand that seemed to be alive with a blanket of writhing creatures.

'Please, don't touch me!' yelped Chris. Sarah came forward to intervene, smiling kindly. Her raven hair fell forward over her face as she leaned towards Chris. Donna had the impression that this lady's efficiency was unrivalled, that she let nothing get in her way. Indeed, once set in motion, she was a whirlwind of action, a blurred image of fast-paced competence. Brian knew Sarah was not someone you would quibble with on a dark (or light) night, as her loyalty and compassion for the vulnerable made her a model of maternal fieriness; a mother tigress fighting for her endangered cubs. Yet if required she could switch instantly into the sweetest, most feminine and delicate of ladies.

'It's Chris, isn't it? I'm Sarah. I can see that you're a big fan of space rockets. What's this model here?' Sarah picked up a model to pass to Chris, but he began shouting again.

'No, put it down!' She hastily placed the model carefully back in its place and, undeterred, tried a different tactic.

'Alright Chris, maybe you need to calm down with some deep breaths, to a count. How about we imagine we're a rocket and do a countdown to take-off together with deep breaths in and out? Breathe slowly in – ten, nine – breathe slowly out – eight, seven – breathe slowly in – six, five – slowly out – four, three – slowly in – two, one, blow it all out and take-off into a starry night sky!' she smiled kindly at him. 'There, feeling better?' Chris nodded.

'Listen, Chris, I need to check you over so we can get you sorted out. Please, let me take your pulse,' she said gently. She reached forward with her gloved hand to take his wrist, but Chris began to panic once more.

'No, no, no! Leave me alone! They're all over you too!' Chris' ramblings were confusing the paramedics. Brian and Sarah withdrew to the doorway to confer, then nodding in agreement, Brian called over to Donna.

'Can we have a word with you outside please, ma'am?' asked Brian, empathetically. Donna followed them out of the door.

'Mum, don't leave me!' shouted Chris in terror.

'It's alright Chris, I'm right here. I won't leave you honey. I just need to speak to the paramedics a minute.'

Donna joined Brian and Sarah outside the bedroom. They were quietly discussing Chris. Although Brian's skills as a paramedic were clearly honed and efficient from years of experience, he also fancied himself as a bit of a detective, with a nose for sniffing out facts and secrets from his patients that helped him to fill in the holes of what had happened as he arrived at the scene of an incident. Yet even Brian was puzzled by the strange symptoms that Chris was presenting with.

As Donna arrived, Sarah gently questioned her on his medical background;

'Does Chris have any history of diabetes?'

Donna shook her head.

'How about mental health issues, has he been diagnosed or treated for anything like that?'

'No!' exclaimed Donna, her eyes wide.

'Is it possible he might have taken anything, or been drinking?' Sarah could see that her last question had upset Donna, who vigorously denied that he was a druggie.

'Alright,' she soothed, 'how about allergies?' to which Donna shook her head miserably.

Sarah asked a few more key questions, but was abruptly interrupted by Donna;

'What's wrong with him?' she blurted. Brian glanced over at Donna with an apologetic expression. He looked back at Sarah with his eyebrows raised in question. Sarah knew Brian well enough after a long working relationship with him to read his mind. Despite Brian's obvious doubts about what he was about to suggest next, Sarah nodded to him to continue.

'Now ma'am, he's clearly very distressed, so we're unable to get close enough to him to find out what's wrong. I'm sure we need to take him into hospital for a proper investigation into what's going on with him, but I'm afraid as he's not being very co-operative, we need your help to get him there.' Brian was willing Donna to understand.

Donna breathed deeply, and with wide eyes filled with anxiety she replied; 'O.K. what do you need me to do?'

Brian gazed gently at her with his blazing blue eyes and quietly and apologetically explained that she had to do whatever it would take to get Chris in the ambulance.

'He's only 12 so I'm afraid it's not up to him whether he goes or not,' shrugged Brian. 'I'm a big guy, so I'm more than capable of lifting him and carrying him there over my shoulder' he laughed 'but it's always best if the patient consents and goes under their own steam.' He winked good-naturedly at Donna.

She knew he was only joking but, with a sigh, she walked back into Chris' bedroom and sat down on his bed.

'Darling, you're really sick, you need help. You need to go with these kind people to the hospital. They can help you there.'

'Mum, I don't want to!' complained Chris.

'I know, honey. I know this is all really scary for you, but you have to trust me on this.' Donna tried to win him over, but was unsuccessful.

'Mum, no, I won't go!'

She sighed, and glanced over at the dresser, spotting the

photo of Chris and his dad standing together, hand in hand. She paused for a moment, thinking.

'Chris, will you do it for your dad?'

For a moment, Chris' silver eyes appeared a little calmer.

'Mum, where is he? I want Dad.'

She gazed tenderly at her suffering boy; she knew what she had to do.

'Honey, I'll call him. We'll get him over, O.K.? Don't worry; it's all going to work out just fine.'

Chris' heaving sobs seemed to dissipate a little and he nodded. Donna went to make the call.

15

DONNA ASKS JOE FOR HELP

Joe was drinking coffee with Holly at her apartment whilst discussing their relationship, when his phone rang; he picked it up. They both saw Donna's name flashing on the display; they glanced at each other, an expression of apology from Joe and a look of pain from Holly's emerald green eyes, as if Donna contacting Joe was proof that her doubts about their relationship were founded.

'Joe, it's me, Donna.' Her quivering voice gave away her distress.

'Donna, what is it? What's the matter?'

'It's Chris. He's really sick. He's really gone crazy this time and I don't know what to do. We've got the paramedics here, but he won't go with them. He's screaming about monsters crawling all over everyone. What's wrong with our little boy, Joe? I'm really scared...' she sobbed uncontrollably down the phone.

Joe thought for a moment, trying to take in the words. After a slight pause, he said;

'Donna, I'm on my way. Hold on.' With that he pocketed his phone, grabbed his coat and car keys and ran for the door without saying goodbye. Holly watched his retreating figure in sadness, the door banging behind him. She peered wearily and resignedly into her skinny Latté.

What could she do? His family was really important to him, but he could have at least said goodbye. She glanced up as she heard the door open again – it was Joe's head peeping round.

'Holly, I'm so sorry. It's Chris – he's really sick. I have to help him. I'll see you later, O.K.?'

Holly weakly smiled back at him and nodded her agreement, but even her wavy auburn hair seemed to have lost its bounce.

'Yes of course, Joe. You do what you've got to do.'

Joe smiled his handsome grin and blew a kiss in her direction, which she playfully caught in her hand, but she sensed all was not well.

*

Joe came bounding up the stairs – three by three – and leapt into Chris' bedroom. Running over to his son he stopped dead in his tracks as he saw Chris sobbing on his bed. Chris looked up on his arrival and his sobs began to cease.

'Da-ad,' he sniffed, 'You came!' Chris sighed in relief.

'Yes, son, I'm here for you. What's going on? What's the matter?'

'I can see m-m-monsters everywhere, Dad!' Joe tried to stroke Chris' tear-dampened blond hair out of his reddened eyes, but Chris pulled away, spotting more wriggling monsters on his dad's hand. 'Oh NO! LOOK! They're on YOU too! They're moving around all over our bodies and I can't get away from them!'

Chris pressed his palms into his eyes and rubbed hard, trying to wipe away the horrific visions.

'Son, I don't know what's happening to you, but I'm sure it's happening for a very good reason. We don't know what it is – it's some special thing that we don't understand, but until we get to the bottom of it, no-one can help you.'

Chris stared desperately at his dad; the words seemed to be sinking in.

'I'll come with you Chris, but we need to go to the hospital – the doctors will know what to do for you.'

Joe's soothing tones had an almost hypnotic power to them.

Chris seemed confused and unsure for a minute, but he slowly nodded his agreement.

'Come on kid, let's get you ready. Will you get dressed?' asked Joe.

'No Dad, I don't want to.'

'Sir, it's alright, he can come to the hospital in his pyjamas,' said Sarah, encouragingly.

The paramedics ushered them all down the stairs, into the ambulance. Chris started to climb in without assistance, but stopped in horror as he surveyed the inside of the vehicle. It was teeming with the strange life-forms; they were everywhere, on every surface and in every nook and cranny. He turned to his dad, who encouragingly put up his hand in a thumbs-up position. Chris shuddered and resignedly climbed into the ambulance, cautiously crouching down as low as possible so as to touch the bare minimum of surfaces, and closed his eyes tightly to shut out the horrific visions.

Joe and Donna sat beside their shaking son, with Sarah close at hand, uttering calming words. Brian skilfully negotiated the sharp corners of the angular San Francisco streets, picking their way past the cable car routes towards the hospital. Even though Chris was calmer with Joe there, he reacted hysterically when Sarah tried again to check his vitals, so she settled with keeping a close eye on him instead.

The ambulance screamed down the streets, over the busy swarming highway towards the San Francisco Wharfside General Hospital, its lights flashing to warn the other road users of its impending arrival. Driving up to the imposing concrete main building, the ambulance screeched to a halt and the paramedics rushed to wheel Chris' trolley off the back into the hospital entrance, their actions carried out like a smooth, well-practised dance.

'Mum, Dad, I'm scared!' said Chris, anxiously.

'It's O.K. son, we're here. We won't leave you,' soothed Joe.

16

CHRIS GOES INTO HOSPITAL

As the paramedics skilfully negotiated the crowded entrance-way they caught sight of a ginger-haired gangly Junior Doctor, ready on-hand to deal with the case after a warning had been phoned ahead.

Sarah rattled off her report to the lanky doctor at break-neck speed, shouting over the noise and never breaking her racing stride as she and Brian hurried Chris' trolley through the hustle and bustle;

'This is Chris, aged 12. He's complaining of hearing voices and seeing strange things, difficult to calm him down, G.C.S. 15 throughout. No previous conditions relating to this, unable to do any obs. Mum and dad travelled.'

The doctor nodded his understanding, his ginger hair flopping into his eyes, acknowledging Donna and Joe as he ran alongside, trying to match the paramedics' rapid stride.

'Hi Chris, I'm Dr. Calloway, resident physician. We're going to take care of you now, please try to relax, everything is under control.' Chris eyed the gawky doctor warily.

As he was wheeled towards the Emergency Room, Chris cried out in terror. The place was teeming with the creatures. Every light switch, door and person he clapped eyes on was covered in an ever-moving blanket of tiny beings. They seemed to know he was there and eerily even seemed to be watching him.

In the chaos of the Emergency Room, nurses tried to gather medical and insurance information from the family, but Chris' alarmed cries were creating disruption. He was gathering copious attention.

Chris was quickly wheeled to a cubicle. He timidly opened his silver eyes and let out a blood-curdling scream.

'I want to go home! I can't stay here! The creatures are everywhere!' he yelled. The paramedics tried to restrain him on the trolley as he yanked himself up in an effort to escape.

A consultant rushed over, tripping a little over his unfeasibly long shoes. The big-footed man introduced himself.

'Ma'am, sir – I'm Dr. Holmes, consultant paediatrician.' The man twiddled his brightly coloured bow tie as he eyed the gibbering skinny boy. 'Who do we have here?' said Holmes genially to Chris, beckoning a hovering nurse to assist. Nurse Kathy Harries swiftly glided over as if she was on roller-skates. Holmes pulled the curtains discretely around the bay, as Chris was deftly transferred to the bed by Nurse Kathy with the help of the paramedics, but the physical intervention was met by loud remonstrations from the terrified boy.

'Don't touch me!' yelled Chris to the nurse from his bed. She raised her painted eyebrows above enormous blue eyes and tutted, as if to say 'don't mess with me kid!' She waggled her long-nailed finger at him, but all Chris could see was weird scurrying monsters swarming on her hands. He screamed in terror.

'Chris, it's alright, they only want to help you!' soothed Sarah gently. 'Listen, they'll take good care of you here. Your mum and dad are right here with you too. Take some deep breaths and try to calm down. Remember your count-down to take-off? Breathe in – ten, nine...'

Turning to Donna and Joe she wished them luck with Chris. The parents thanked the paramedics profusely for their help.

Dr. Calloway sputtered his update.

'This is Chris, he's aged 12. He's complaining of hearing voices and seeing strange things – possibly psychotic delusions. It's been difficult to calm him down – he's very agitated and scared, G.C.S. 15 throughout. No previous conditions relating to this, unable to do any obs. Mum and dad travelled with him. I suggest we may need to administer a sedative before we can carry out any tests?' The gawky-looking doctor turned to Dr. Holmes for approval.

'Thank you Dr. Calloway, I'll take over from here.' Dr. Holmes turned on his boat-like feet to Donna; 'Ma'am, if you have already given your consent to routine testing, I may need to administer a sedative to your son. He's clearly very upset, but we won't be able to examine Chris whilst he's refusing any contact.' He twiddled his bow-tie as he waited for Donna's response.

Donna was clearly undecided and blurted 'I don't know what that will do to him.'

Calmly, Dr. Holmes explained what the sedative would do, such as help Chris to feel sleepy and relaxed, allowing the medics to examine him.

With a reassuring glance from Joe, she was able to nod in agreement. Dr. Holmes rattled out various questions to

Donna about Chris' medical history and state of health, allergies and height and weight, then deciding his course of action, Dr. Holmes shot his instruction across to the hovering nurse;

'Right, Nurse Kathy please get me some oral midazolam.' She glided away to get the medication, muttering her thoughts on the weirdly acting kid to anyone in earshot. Turning back to Donna, Holmes calmly and quietly posed more questions about Chris' medical background;

'Now ma'am, does your son have any history of mental illness?'

'No, no nothing like that,' wailed Donna.

'Any heart problems, strokes or seizures?'

'No, none of those.'

'Is it possible he might have taken anything, or been drinking?'

'NO! I already explained that to the paramedics!' shouted Donna.

'O.K. ma'am, I'm sorry, but I need to check. We will need to do a drugs screen anyway in case that's what is causing his strange visions. We intend to carry out tests to find out what's wrong with Chris, but I have some concerns that there may be some mental health issues concerning the visions that are clearly disturbing your son. I would like to ask for an opinion from the paediatric psychiatrist.'

Donna gasped and turned her anxious face to Joe. 'Oh Joe, what's wrong with our boy? This is awful! I don't know what to say...'

Joe took her perfectly manicured hand and rubbed it

gently, soothingly. 'Donna, I don't know what's wrong with him any more than you do, but the doctors here are really great and it won't do any harm to check out all avenues of enquiry. They may rule out any possibility that he has mental issues and find it's all just some silly virus or a fever or something. Try not to worry.'

Donna nodded her agreement again, his tall, strong presence surprisingly comforting to her.

'Thank you ma'am; we'll do our best for him,' said Dr. Holmes, reassuringly. 'In the mean-time, please just wait a little over to the side so we can give Chris the sedative.'

The medical team carefully approached Chris, explaining what they were about to do and how it would affect him. Chris resisted but Joe encouraged Chris to cooperate until they were finally able to administer the sedative. His parents talked soothingly to him whilst the sedative took effect. After a few minutes, Chris' terrified face started to take on a softer expression and his rigid muscles relaxed.

Various medical observations, tests and scans were carried out whilst Chris was under sedation and although Donna and Joe never left his side, Chris insisted on keeping his eyes closed throughout. He was still very aware of the eerie noises reaching his ears. They whispered and pulsed away insistently. The boy's mind was racing as to what could be going on.

Eventually he was left alone by the medics to rest, falling into a fitful sleep as his anxious parents remained, brooding at his bedside.

17

Dr. Holmes calls in the psychiatrist

Holmes was a bit of a clown – a characteristic that was reflected in his comedic repartee with both parents and child patients alike and in the unfeasible length of his shoes. On occasions he had played on this persona, dressing up in a clown suit to entertain the children on the wards, or walking around with a water-spraying red and white-spotted bow-tie that he used to cheer up the sick crying children. He had even been known to secrete his comedy bow-tie into dull and tedious meetings to lighten the atmosphere.

His colleagues could be entertained by it only for so long, but it was sometimes hard to take him seriously as a doctor when he continually clowned around like a buffoon. Sadly it covered up for a darker side of his personality, which left him feeling empty and depressed at the end of the long days in the hospital.

He was sure that there must be more to life than this. His ever-present five-o'clock shadow which was nearing on messy stubble was his signature facial wear, a sign of his tiredness which he tried to mask with his child-like humour. His brightly coloured waistcoats and ties were often adorned with comic-book characters to cheer up the children (and perhaps himself) but his sad eyes often held a far-away lost expression of one who is searching for answers and not yet found any enlightenment. The deep shadows under his eyes were a dead give-away that this hard-working dedicated soul was in need of some serious recuperation.

The boy's strange symptoms and behaviour had puzzled Holmes. They had found few previous medical notes as the boy had never before been admitted to hospital. The family physician notes confirmed that he was up to date on all his vaccinations.

Apart from occasional visits with typical childhood coughs and colds and recent hearing and sight test referrals, there was nothing significant to report. Holmes felt he should investigate the possibility that it was a mental health issue.

He decided to call in his colleague, Dr. Barnes. The psychiatrist arrived at Dr. Holmes' request, anxious to see the boy. He slunk in with stooped shoulders and stared round the room hunting for Holmes. Barnes was a grey man – both in pallor and character, indicative of a poor digestion and clogged liver, with puffy indistinct facial features. Pockmarks were scattered randomly over his grey skin almost as if he was permanently scarred from frequent self-inflicted incisions of sharp wit. He had a persistent cough, which accented many of his sentences as if he was always trying to bark for people's attention. He seemed somewhat lacking in compassion for someone who was supposed to be in a caring profession, often with an almost unsympathetic tint to his perspective. He was quick to judge and slow to forgive. His thin lips were tight and unemotional, reflecting his 'take-no-prisoners' attitude.

Spotting the brightly coloured bow-tie, Dr. Barnes marched over. Holmes stuck out his hand to firmly shake Barnes' damp hand, but swiftly moved his hand into the Vulcan greeting of Spock from Star Trek, his favourite T.V. show.

'Greetings, Captain!' he quipped. Barnes ignored the childish gesture, with a certain disdain.

Coughing sharply, he plunged into the case at hand;

'So Dr. Holmes, what has the boy told you so far?' queried the grey-faced psychiatrist.

'Well, Dr. Barnes, he seems afraid to open his eyes and is claiming to hear whispering voices which he is unable to interpret. It may be some sort of psychosis perhaps. I also suspect he might be exhibiting signs of a phobia. When he opens his eyes, he sees some kind of 'micro-cosmic world' – I don't know, perhaps he is delusional. Anyway, three good reasons to suspect that he may need a psych consultation, which means it's over to you!'

'Hmm, that's most intriguing indeed. What exactly can he see?' asked Barnes, scratching his pock-marked face in surprise.

'Well, he can see things normally around him, but he can also see some kinds of tiny creatures – he says that they are odd-looking wiggly worm-like creatures but he can't really figure out what he is seeing. He is clearly upset by them and sees them everywhere – on people, on surfaces and all over himself. He has even asked to have himself covered up with a surgical gown and to wear an eye mask so he doesn't have to see the creatures.'

Holmes tapped his lengthy shoe distractedly against the floor as he waited for Barnes to comment.

'And the other tests – have they showed anything unusual?' queried Barnes with a confused expression on his pitted face.

'Blood tests, L.F.T.'s, U.'s and E.'s, B.P. and temperature

seem normal, no sign of any illicit drug use, no cardiac issues, no physical signs of injury and I see no signs of any infection or fever. I suppose if we rule out other options, it may be a brain infection, in which case we may need to consider a lumbar puncture test. However, his heart and respiration rate are slightly raised and we are not so sure about the scans – we suspect we may need a more in-depth brain scan to see if there is some sort of abnormal activity going on there. I think I need more input from the neurologists on that one. I'm going to call in Dr. Krefeld.'

'Alright, well please let me know when he has woken up? I can come straight over to assess him. Meanwhile I'm going to speak with his parents to see what they have to say.'

'Yes of course Dr. Barnes.'

Barnes sought out Joe and Donna. Chris' parents nervously eyed the pallid psychiatrist as he approached. Drawing them to a side room and closing the door gently, Barnes questioned them about Chris' behaviour, his mental and emotional stability and whether he had experienced any traumatic events recently. Donna could only think of Chris' obsessive thoughts of the Moon, his withdrawal and slight social issues with his peers at school. Barnes noted the edginess between the couple with a somewhat judgemental perspective, tightening his lips into an even thinner line.

'Thank you – I have no more questions for now. I'll speak to Chris when he wakes up,' barked Barnes coldly.

He departed swiftly; Donna heard him cough sharply as he closed the door on them, leaving the estranged couple to wallow in their angst.

18

Psych consultation with Dr. Barnes

The boy stirred and opened his eyes, lifting his eye mask – perhaps forgetting what he would see. He gasped and cried out for help. His mother reached over and fitted the eye mask back into place for him, nestling the elastic into his curly golden mop of hair. He was dressed in a smooth white medical gown, with a biologically resistant outer layer and a surgical mask covered his nose and mouth.

The ever-present Nurse Kathy acknowledged his waking with a cheery 'Hello, sleepy head! I'll fetch the doctor to see you now.' She fluttered her long false eyelashes and glided away.

Moments later, the paediatric psychiatrist arrived with Dr. Holmes, to speak with Chris.

'Hello Chris, my name is Dr. Barnes. I wonder if I could please have a chat with you. You don't need to take off your eye-mask, if you would feel more comfortable that way?'

Chris shuffled uncomfortably on his bed. Donna and Joe piped up;

'It's alright son, we're here too. Say hi to the nice doctor.'

'Hi' he muttered, wrapping his spindly arms around his

knees in a protective pose.

'Chris, I wonder if you could tell me more about these creatures that you have been seeing?' asked Barnes in a tangibly sarcastic fashion.

'Well, they're everywhere, wherever I look. They're all sorts of shapes and sizes, some are round, some are like worms and they seem to be dancing around – sometimes they are splitting in two, so somehow there seem to be more and more all the time. It's terrifying. I don't know what they are.' Chris' voice was rising in pitch just talking about them.

'Hmmm, I see,' said Barnes, who plainly didn't see at all. 'Dr. Holmes tells me that you are hearing some voices too?'

'Yeah, they're sort of like voices, although somehow more like whispers or waves on a sea shore.'

'Right, I see. Have you heard these voices before Chris? Are they telling you to do anything?' Barnes was leaning in his grey face towards Chris in a rather sinister way. Donna shuffled nervously in her plastic chair and looked ashamedly round the busy ward to check if anyone might overhear them. She clocked Nurse Kathy standing in close proximity with her big flapping mouth wide open.

'Well, I have been hearing some really strange things recently and although I can't make out what it means, I do feel like they're trying to tell me something...'

'Hmm, I see,' replied Barnes in a tone that implied disbelief. His lips were thinning again.

Dr. Barnes barked a few more pointed questions to assess Chris' mental and emotional state. Observing how the parents were sat so far apart barely speaking to each other, his lips thinned to an almost invisible line. He decided to check something that was bothering him;

'Chris, are you happy at home?'

Chris shuffled even more uncomfortably on his bed. Donna threw Joe a dark look.

'Well, I miss my dad since he left. Mum threw him out after they argued at my birthday, and I never get to see him anymore – but he's here now!' He threw a big smile in the direction of his father, who also sat uncomfortably in the other cheap plastic seat beside the bed.

'Hmm, that's very interesting...' Barnes tapped his pitted chin in thought then added 'So, are you doing well at school?'

'No not really, all the kids hate me and they bully me all the time,' said Chris miserably.

'I understand, Chris – that must be very upsetting for you.' Barnes took a sideways glance at the boy's perfectly turned out mother who was frowning, then threw in a personal question. 'Do you get on with your mum?'

'Well no, not really. She doesn't listen to me and she really doesn't understand me. She won't let me see my dad and she always yells at him,' said Chris truthfully.

Donna grimaced, and her deep blue eyes began welling up with tears. Joe looked across at her sadly.

'Right, Chris, that will be all for now,' announced Barnes, who had heard enough. 'I'll let you get some rest and come and see you again later.' Chris nodded dejectedly. Barnes turned back to the parents. 'Thank you, Mr. and Mrs. Larkin.'

'Um, that's Ms. McKenzie actually,' muttered Donna, her annoyance piqued.

'Hmm, apologies' replied Barnes, coughing loudly.

Dr. Barnes walked away, raising an eyebrow at Dr. Holmes, beckoning him over. Once they were out of earshot, the psychiatrist reported his opinion to Dr. Holmes;

'I'm not sure what's going on here but I recommend you keep him under full observation. We may need to transfer him to the psychiatric ward if you find no other medical issues. He's clearly traumatized over his mother and father's separation. Perhaps he has fallen into some sort of psychotic delusional experience as a cry for help, but it isn't cut and dried. I am wondering about paranoid schizophrenia, but I need to do more tests and assessments. His isn't a classic case. You're sure there is no sign of physical abuse?' asked Barnes, brow furrowed.

'Nothing we could find,' said Holmes, raising his eyebrows towards his great shock of hair.

'And there is nothing in his records about excessive injuries so I don't think it's that, but he does seem excessively anxious about something. I'll be back with more tests soon. Maybe consider getting in social services should you spot anything suspicious going on with the mother and father,' Barnes tapped his nose knowingly and not a little meanly.

'Thank you, Dr. Barnes. I may call Family & Children's Services to get some advice,' whispered Holmes discretely.

The medics parted company, leaving the estranged family to themselves. Donna and Joe looked uncomfortably at each other, suspicious of the turn that had been taken in the whole investigation. Were the doctors trying to lay the blame at their door? Could it all be their fault? Was Chris really that affected by their divorce? It was a bitter pill for them to swallow, but they both felt incredibly upset.

Nurse Kathy came bustling in to offer Chris dinner, but he refused to take anything, claiming that it was teeming with creatures and unfit to eat. She raised her heavy false eyelashes to the sky in frustration. Now he wouldn't even drink from the water jug at his bedside. The nurse muttered to herself as she resentfully set up a drip to keep him hydrated – amongst copious protests from Chris.

Joe and Donna sat in vigil at Chris' bedside, each lost in their own guilty thoughts, staring out of the window into the night sky at the Full Moon that had risen overhead, as Chris fell into another fitful, exhausted sleep.

'I'm going to take my break now; I'll only be ten minutes, but when I get back why don't you go out and catch some fresh air while he sleeps too? Taking rest is the queen of all therapies, you know; he'll be just fine.' Nurse Kathy glided away, and Donna and Joe stiffly stood up and stretched.

19

KATHY SPOTS THE REPORTER

Down in the cafeteria, Nurse Kathy reached her slightly podgy hand over and took her Café Americano from the woman serving behind the refreshment counter, the diamanté on her varnished nails sparkling as they curled around the polystyrene cup.

Spotting her friend Shelly, a fellow nurse from another ward, Kathy carried her drink over to her table, wiggling around the randomly placed plastic plants that littered the room. She plonked herself down in the seat opposite her colleague and let out a manly whistle that rang shrilly around the packed cafeteria.

'Phew you wouldn't believe what a nut-case we've got in the ward today, sis!'

'Go on, tell me,' laughed Shelly.

Shelly had known Kathy for many years and knew that even though Kathy could go hungry all day and not touch a scrap of food, her unbridled hunger for the latest news of people was enough to raise her excitement and energy.

Shelly gazed at Kathy's big, wide pouting mouth from which many secrets had already spouted over the years, in a torrent of gossip, unable to stem the floodgates of confidences. It would take but a look of curiosity from someone for her to pass on what she knew. She often stirred up trouble for the doctors in the hospital as she spilled the beans about discussed diagnoses even before they had been confirmed.

Although her legendary mouth was on the large side, her ears were small, which to Shelly ironically matched Kathy's poor listening skills. Her moistened clear skin reflected her inability to hold on to festering information, preferring to pass it straight on to someone else to lighten her load. Shelly sensed Kathy was about to unload again.

'Well there's this kid who came in today, who claims he can see all these weird creatures everywhere – all over the hospital, in all the food and drink and all over us!' exclaimed Kathy, fluttering her long false eyelashes in dramatic aplomb.

'What! He sounds completely crazy!' The nurse's companion, Shelly, had eyes the size of saucers. Kathy leaned her slightly ample frame forward conspiratorially, a blonde curl falling over one baby-blue eye.

'I know – and he can hear all sorts of sounds too – voices or something.'

She sat back, with a knowing expression on her round beaming face as she revelled in her gossip. The wayward curl shuffled back into place with the others, which seemed to sit like an oddly misplaced hat on the top of her large head.

'Oh boy, poor kid – he's not been taking something has he?' asked Shelly, rubbing her bulbous nose as if it were itching. Kathy nodded, half in agreement.

'You would think so, wouldn't you, but he's clean. His mum and dad seem a bit flaky though – my guess is the poor kid has had a rough ride at home and he's flipped.' Nurse

Kathy wiggled the coffee stirrer round at her temples to depict madness.

'Ah well, he's in the best place for that, then – we've got all the nut-cases of San Francisco holed up here, so I'm sure they'll sort him out real soon.' Shelly took a sip from her Cappuccino and sighed.

'It still gives me the creeps, though, you know? He's absolutely convinced he can see these crawling things everywhere; I'm feeling real itchy just thinking about it!' Nurse Kathy started scratching all over. 'I just hope it's not contagious!' giggled Kathy, glancing over at a nearby table occupied by a hunky-looking guy with a laptop who was staring at them over his glasses. The curly-haired man turned away quickly, shut his laptop and reached for his phone, walking quickly out of the cafeteria.

'Who is that?' asked Kathy, puppy-dog eyes following the man's departure.

'Some reporter guy, I think,' replied Shelly, cautiously. 'I've seen him hanging around the hospital. You wanna be careful around those guys. You never know when they might make up some story about what we do here and get us stuck in another law suit!'

Nurse Kathy sighed and finished up her drink with a loud gulp and a smack of her enormous lips.

'Right – that's my break over. It's time for me to get back to the crawly kid. See you later, Shell.'

She left Shelly to sit a while longer and Kathy rushed off back to the ward, dreaming about hunky reporters and exclusive interviews. She wondered if she might be able to make some money from giving him a story. She was pretty skint at the moment, and needed to supplement her income to pay her way in this expensive city.

20

A Reporter phones a scoop in to his editor

The reporter that had attracted the nurses' attention was rushing round the corner to a deserted alleyway, calling his boss, desperate to discuss the scoop he had overheard the nurses discussing. He got through to his editor and rattled out his idea.

'Sir it's Kevin here – I think I might be on to something. There's some kid in the Wharfside General who seems to be a bit wacko, seeing weird creatures and hearing funny voices. Reckons he can see them wriggling all over people in the hospital.'

'Sounds like he's whacked out on drugs to me, Kevin!' retorted his boss, irritated. 'There's nothing newsworthy in that! Unless you're gonna tell me he's some kind of celebrity?'

'Nah – I doubt it, but what if there's something in it and it's some sort of contagious outbreak of a virus or something that gives people weird visions? Or aliens! I want an exclusive if there's any truth to it.' Kevin shuffled from foot to foot, excited at the prospect of a juicy story.

'O.K. Kevin, you've got 24 hours. See what you can come up with on this and report back to me, but you'd better not be wasting my time. Oh and next time, don't call me so late!'

'Thanks, boss – sorry. I won't let you down.' Kevin ended the call and headed back along the lamp-lit streets towards the hospital to carry out some research.

Kevin was ambitious but lacked integrity; logical but often missed the point. Neither fully-shaven nor trimmed, his facial hair was sparsely grey, as were his tightly curled locks. One had the impression that he should be handsome, his profile even worthy of drawing were one an artist, yet his face had become care-worn and cold, lacking in vitality.

His eyes were often half-closed behind his thin-framed spectacles, reflecting his frequent disbelief of people's words. Often eyeing others over the top of his glasses, he frequently unnerved those he questioned as they sensed his suspiciousness. To him doubt was necessary and enjoyable, preferring to use it to seek the truth of a situation rather than to believe everything that crossed his path.

Beneath the lidded looks he had intense darting eyes belying his ever-sceptical nature. Although this prickly persona made others wary and uncomfortable around him, he felt that it did however serve its purpose in his career, as if it created a golden scoop for the truth. Many a time he had used his long, sharp, almost fox-like nose to sniff out facts, and the juicy tit-bits of information which would lead him to a great story. If the complete truth was elusive, he was content to seek it as far as he could.

However in his search for truth, his mind seemed more prominent than his heart, which had receded under the influence of painful experiences and scepticism, as if faith's bright spark had been all but snuffed out, leaving him lost in the dark seeking answers. Yet he was not seeking for the light and until he did, he was unlikely to illuminate those dark areas of his soul thirsting for inspiration and love.

When required to attend some formal occasion, he would choose to be smartly dressed – albeit in a rather old-fashioned way – but otherwise he preferred casual dress that allowed him to slink around unnoticed in corners. His jackets always hid a secret pocket from which he could discretely acquire a notebook and pen – a throwback to older reporting traditions in the ever-advancing world of digital technology. Thus, he was ever-ready to jot down a tasty tit-bit of information even if he was without his laptop. He usually carried a stretchable bag too, into which he loaded numerous books, files, papers and documents. Even if he was weighed down with this bag slung over his shoulder, he was capable of a cowboy-like quick-draw reaction to his pocket to grab his notebook and gold pen.

Kevin enjoyed his job – it was a natural progression for him to go into journalism as he had turned somewhat cynical about life following his mother's severely poor health.

He used to be very close to his mother. Although she continued to hold a very strong faith in God and believed that God would bring her through this illness, he was less inclined to agree any more as he had watched her decline over the years. Having to see her suffering and in pain for such a long time had really been hard on him. He couldn't see how such a God could be a good character, letting people suffer like she had.

He had been brought up by his parents to follow his religion staunchly – as had his brothers and sisters, but his mother's dwindling health led him to choose not to believe in anything invisible, as this was the only rational approach a person could take.

Nor did he choose to blame God therefore for what had happened. No, for him, there was no God. Everything that happened to people was down to their own doing rather than providence or divine intervention.

Let his family continue with their prayers and their penitence – if they believed that it helped them. He knew his girlfriend Merry would chastise him for his coldness, but that was just the way he was.

He stepped through the sliding doors of the hospital just as an attractive couple came out. They were discussing something strange and his ears pricked up. He hung around the entrance pretending to hunt for his phone, staying in earshot of the chatting couple.

'Donna – these visions, none of us know what they are, but the doctors are going to help Chris. He says he can see these things on all of us – who is to say that he can't? Has he ever lied to us? The voices too, perhaps they are real and he is tuning into something that no-one else can hear, but whatever they are caused by, to him they seem real, so we just have to support Chris and tell him we believe him otherwise he'll think that we're ganging up on him.'

'Joe, that's easy for you to say! What if there really is something wrong with him mentally? How will I cope? He's always been such a sensitive boy, but I never expected any of this! Why can't he just be normal? Why can't we just live a normal life?'

'Listen Donna, I know we've had our differences, but that boy means the world to me, and I will stand by you and Chris as much as you will let me. I'm here for you, alright?'

Kevin just about caught their words over the howling sounds of the ambulances, and stored the data in his memory banks, including the names and faces. This sounded promising for his story. He was about to head back into the hospital, when a doctor called over to the couple;

'Ms. McKenzie, Mr. Larkin – will you please come back inside? Your son is awake and wants to see you.'

Kevin grinned – Bingo! He had surnames to work with. He watched as the couple shared a brief hug, and went back inside the busy hospital. Ready to rock 'n' roll with his research, Kevin headed to the cafeteria with his laptop ready to connect and see what he could find out. He ordered a Café Americano; he was ready for an all-night vigil.

21

CHRIS MEETS THE NEUROSURGEON

Donna and Joe rushed up to E.R. to find their son surrounded by doctors.

'Chris, are you alright? What's the matter? What's going on?' asked Donna fearfully.

'Mum, is that you?'

'Yes Chris, Dad and I are both here.'

'Nothing to worry about, Ms. McKenzie' said Dr. Holmes. 'We've just invited some more specialists to take a look at Chris.'

'So do you know what's wrong with him?' asked Joe, wearily.

'Sorry Mr. Larkin, I'm afraid we don't seem to be making any progress on a diagnosis, so we may need to carry out more tests.'

'What do you mean more tests?' exclaimed Donna, impatiently. 'He's been here for hours and had more tests than you can shake a stick at. How can you not know what's wrong with him yet?'

'Donna, please calm down, they're doing their best,'

soothed Joe.

'Well what if I don't want to calm down?' she was about to hit fever pitch.

Dr. Holmes expertly tackled the anxious mother, well-practised in dealing with fearful relatives;

'Ms. McKenzie, please. We have more specialists here who would like to take a look at your son, and they may be better placed to help him. We would like to carry out some more brain scans, to help us get to the bottom of this.' Chris began to cry. Donna tried to reassure Chris but he was clearly distressed at the thought of this.

'Well, alright,' said Donna, 'but I'm beginning to think that you don't know what you're doing, and he'd be better off at home with us, because all you're doing is frightening him!'

Dr. Barnes chipped in.

'Listen, ma'am, we'll carry out the scans as quickly as possible, and when the results come back, we will discuss the best course of action; whether it's to keep him here, or to have him moved to our psychiatric unit.'

'You're not keeping him in any nut-house, I can tell you that for nothing!' cried Donna, alarmed. 'He's just got a bad case of flu or something that's sent him delirious!'

Another medic stepped in.

'Hello Ms. McKenzie, Mr. Larkin. My name is Dr. Krefeld. I'm the consultant neurosurgeon.' They eyed the new doctor warily. He was smartly dressed, in a tailored waistcoat with a pocket watch. His silver-striped hair made him appear quite distinguished and respectable. 'I realize that you are feeling very frustrated and anxious for your son's welfare, but please believe that I'm as keen to get to the bottom of what's happening to your son as you are.'

'I suggest that we scan Chris' brain, to look for anything unusual and when we get the results back, we will be in a much better position to say what might be happening to him. In the meantime, you must be feeling very tired and perhaps in need of a good meal inside you.'

Dr. Krefeld turned to Nurse Kathy with twinkling eyes;

'Can you order these lovely people some food for when they get back from the scans, please?'

The neurosurgeon turned to Donna and Joe with a glint in his eye, saying;

'Listen, I know the food isn't great here, but this one's on me. Please don't worry about your son; he's in the best possible hands. I'm sure we'll find out what's happening to him. He's clearly a very special boy; we need to explore all the possible causes for these strange experiences.' He rubbed his goatee beard thoughtfully.

Noting the different approaches of the medics, Joe smiled wryly to himself at the more sympathetic words of Dr. Krefeld and – aware that a noble person has few complaints and more compliments about others – he felt he was willing to trust this guy. He nodded his encouragement to Donna. She was also clearly won over by the surgeon's kindlier ways and grudgingly nodded her agreement to the tests, appeased by the neurosurgeon's obvious compassion and honesty.

'Chris, I'm sorry honey, but you're going to have to go back in the scanners, but we'll be right here with you every step and you can keep your eye mask on so you don't have to see anything, O.K.?' Donna squeezed Chris' hands reassuringly.

22

Chris goes to the scanners

Chris was wheeled on his trolley through the hospital corridors. He felt the trolley bump to a halt and he raised his eye-mask to see where they were. They had stopped at the lift and Chris' eyes widened in horror as the porter reached for the button to call the lift.

'Don't touch that!' Chris mumbled through his sedated haze.

'What on Earth is the matter? I'm just calling the lift!'

'Shush Chris, try to keep calm,' soothed Donna.

The porter pressed the up button and as the lift announced its arrival with a ping, the doors opened wide, allowing Chris to be wheeled into the box of terrors. His eyes darted this way and that, eyeing the teeming clumps on the buttons, on the floor, on the walls and on the other people in the lift. Chris shut his eyes and began to cry.

'It's alright Chris, you'll be fine, the doctors will help you,' soothed Donna.

The porter pressed the button to the first floor – and Chris shuddered as he saw the creatures wriggle under his touch. He quickly slid the eye-mask back over his eyes to hide the horrible visions.

The lift lurched upwards and the inhabitants' stomachs – left at Ground Floor – eventually caught up with them as they stopped at Floor One.

The doors slid open and Chris was delivered to the scanners. His mother and father waited nervously for him outside.

Chris anxiously waited in the M.R.I. room, his ears deafened by the regular banging sounds that the machine was emitting. He felt his trolley moving; he peeped out from under his eye-mask to see what was happening, just in time to see the rotating drum of the scanner in front of him, with its yawning great hole ready for him to slide into – like some kind of astronaut entering into a tiny spaceship.

He spotted swarms of moving creatures all over its surface and quickly pulled the mask back over his eyes. He felt very anxious, but he remembered what his dad had said. He had promised Chris that they would take a trip to Florida to see the N.A.S.A. space centre as soon as he was better; this thought made him deliriously happy, despite the frightening experiences he was currently having.

As he felt himself gently moving through the machine's tunnel, he pondered what it must feel like in a rocket ship in space. He pictured himself stepping out onto the Moon's surface and tried to name all the planets and stars that he knew in an effort to stay calm inside the machine.

Soon it was all over; the boy heaved a sigh of relief. The whispering noises had been all but drowned out by the noisy machine, which had seemed somewhat of a blessing. However as soon as he came out of the room, away from the noises of the scanner, he could hear the whispering noises all over again.

Bright Moon

He was wheeled back to E.R. via the torturous lift with his mother and father anxiously glued by his side.

23

Medics draw a blank

'So, Dr. Krefeld, what do you make of that?'

Dr. Holmes and the neurosurgeon were poring over the functional Magnetic Resonance Imaging results on an iPad; picture slices of Chris' brain that when put together gave them a 3D picture of his entire brain and its activity. Holmes rubbed his hand through his shock of hair in consternation.

'Well, Dr. Holmes, I can't say I've ever seen anything like it before. I can't see any kind of pathology, so I think he's on safe grounds with respect to tumours; I don't think he's likely to need any kind of surgery. However I've never seen this kind of neural pattern of brain activity before. Combined with the E.E.G. results, I'm not sure I can make head or tail of it.'

'The electrical activity is off the charts and seems to be inducing a high level of magnetism. I'm going to need to research this one. He seems to be pretty healthy, to be honest, but this brain activity is certainly puzzling me. There are connections going on there that I've never witnessed before.'

Krefeld tugged his hand in disquiet through his badger-like striped hair. 'Let me trawl Medline to see what medical research I can come up with, alright? I'll email the medical library too to see if they have any ideas. I have to say, I'm quite excited. We may be onto something completely new!'

'Well I'm inclined to think that with no pathology there, we've narrowed it down to some sort of mental health issue, with him showing various characteristic symptoms of paranoid schizophrenia, however various associated tests have all come back as normal, so I'm quite puzzled myself.'

Dr. Holmes rubbed his stubble-covered chin, deep in thought. 'Perhaps we should try a different tack. Maybe we need to bring in an eye specialist?' pondered Dr. Holmes.

'I don't see why not, we need all the help we can get!' admitted Krefeld.

'I'll see to it. Thanks for your input Dr. Krefeld. Keep me updated if you get any ideas.' Holmes shook the neurosurgeon's hand affably.

'No problem – I'd better let the parents know where we're at.'

Krefeld made his way over to Chris' bed.

'Ms. McKenzie, Mr. Larkin – we've got the scan images back; thankfully they show no sign of any growths or tumours. I have however seen some rather unusual brain activity which is rather puzzling. I would like to have more time to research this as it's a pattern I've never seen before.'

Donna glared at him like he was dirt on her shoe. 'Good grief, you doctors are all the same! You don't know anything, do you? You've no idea what you're doing! Well I can tell you for sure that you're not going to go poking around with my little boy a moment longer. He's had enough, and so have I.'

Chris began to cry as his mother yelled at the medics.

'You see what you're doing to him? I want to take him home right now!' demanded Donna.

Joe tried to restrain her as she seemed like she was about to hit someone.

'Come on Donna, calm down. He's doing his best!'

'Well Ms. McKenzie I'm very sorry that you feel that way. You have to understand that you would be discharging Chris against our wishes?' warned Krefeld.

'What about our wishes? I want him out of here!' she yelled.

'I understand your feelings Ms. McKenzie. Let me consult with my colleagues and I will get back to you,' soothed Krefeld.

Donna started to pack up their belongings – desperate to get back to some normality again. Chris seemed calmer and very happy that he might be going home. He even peeled the eye-mask off – encouraged that they had found nothing seriously wrong. He began to observe around him, with a more scientific approach, feeling a greater sense of curiosity about his unusual senses.

Yet the strange sensations seemed to be fading. He peered out of the window over the San Francisco skyline, his eyes drawn by the beautiful pinky golden sunrise. Another day had dawned and suddenly he felt like everything was going to be alright.

'Mum, I'm feeling a lot better now,' he smiled. 'I'm sorry... can we go home?'

Donna smiled back encouragingly.

'That's great news Chris, you don't need to apologize. The doctors can't find anything wrong with you, isn't that great?' she said, heaving a huge sigh of relief. 'Perhaps you just got yourself all worked up and upset over something – it happens sometimes. You mustn't worry. Let's get you out of here, shall we?' she winked.

Krefeld was huddled with Holmes and Barnes by the nurses' station, as they quietly discussed their options.

'The mother is adamant that she wants to take him home...what do you think, Holmes?'

'Well, we haven't got to the bottom of what's going on with this case, but to be honest, as all the test results have otherwise come back as quite normal and social services don't seem to think there is any issue here, he is probably safe to go home. Perhaps that's what he needs right now. What do you think, Dr. Krefeld?'

'I agree that none of the tests signify cause for danger, even if I can't work out the meaning of the unusual patterns in his brain scans. Plus he seems much better, so if Dr. Barnes agrees too, then I guess we can let him go home, but we'll have to get the parents to agree to bring him back in for more tests if they notice any change in his condition.'

'How can you be so sure he is stable?' sputtered Barnes. 'He says he's feeling better now and his strange symptoms are decreasing, but what if they come back? He's been showing signs of paranoid schizophrenia as far as I can tell, but until we can confirm this one way or another, we can't treat him. I'm not convinced he should be allowed to go until we know what we're dealing with.'

'Alright Barnes, we'll see if you can persuade the mother that it is in her son's best interests to stay,' said Krefeld, passing the challenge over.

Barnes stalked over to Chris' bed and spoke fervently with the parents, trying to persuade Donna that Chris needed further observations. Chris watched as they battled over his care, observing his mum heatedly arguing his need to get home and his improved temperament, but it was soon resolved, as Donna stuck to her guns. She took Barnes' contact details for future reference, agreeing to bring him straight back to the psychiatric department for further assessment if he experienced any more symptoms. She signed the discharge papers and gathered up her family to leave.

'Do take care of yourselves and remember, we're here to help if you need it,' said Krefeld as the family hurried away.

24

KEVIN OVERHEARS MEDICS – MORE FUEL FOR HIS STORY

Kevin was prepared to wait all night if necessary for a whiff of more gossip amongst the hospital staff and his patience was rewarded. He whiled away several hours of coffee drinking in the hospital cafeteria, carrying out searches on the boy and his family as people milled in and out around him.

Then, just as the sun was rising and he was about to give up, two medics came in to the cafeteria chatting earnestly and sat down close by to Kevin's table.

'Well, this case has really stumped me, Dr. Barnes. I can't work out what has caused that poor boy to see creatures everywhere, yet it sounds like he is able to sense some kind of bizarre micro-cosmic world. None of the tests seem to reveal any abnormalities apart from the brain scans; his brain activity is certainly most unusual.'

'I wonder if we will get to see him again. Perhaps another E.E.G. would have been helpful. I have located an eye specialist – Edward Baines. His name came up when I was researching eye abnormalities leading to extra-acute visual capacity. I might give him a ring just to see what he thinks.' Krefeld sipped his coffee thoughtfully, mulling over the strange occurrences of the night.

Kevin strained to hear the voices drifting over from their table, whilst trying to make his presence as inconspicuous as possible.

'Well I can't see that it can be anything other than psychotic delusions, Dr. Krefeld. Perhaps he should have started a course of anti-psychotics to set him straight.'

Barnes rubbed his pockmarked grey skin and gulped down his drink, which he followed up with a huge bite of a sticky raspberry doughnut.

'Dr. Barnes – don't be such a cynic!' countered Krefeld, combing a hand through his silvery striped hair. 'I know a large percentage of the cases we get here are psychiatric in nature, but it's not the answer to everything. The boy has no history of mental illness, nor does his family and he's not taken any recreational drugs, so you have to admit that the brain scans pose a real conundrum.'

'It's almost as if he is making new neural connections that wouldn't normally happen and this is leading him to be able to see and hear things that others can't.'

'Dr. Krefeld,' sputtered Barnes through a spray of doughnut, 'you've always been a philosophical kind of guy, haven't you, but you can't possibly believe what you're spouting? He's just a kid having a hard time at home I reckon.'

'You saw what his mother was like – a bad-tempered crocodile would have been easier to handle than she was! See what social services come back with.' Barnes accentuated his scathing report with one of his barking coughs.

'Suit your-self, Barnes!' laughed Krefeld good-naturedly. 'I'm not ready to write this one off to mental issues. I've got a gut feeling there's a lot more to this case than meets the eye – if you'll pardon the pun!' He laughed and polished off the dregs of his coffee, wiping the remains from his facial hair. 'The kid's gone home now anyway, so we may never know – it's over to the family doctor now. Come on, let's finish our shift.'

They stood up to leave, Barnes stuffing the last of his doughnut into his mouth; Kevin sank lower in his seat to avoid detection. His ears were practically popping off the side of his head and the hairs were sticking straight up on the back of his neck. He knew a good story when his fox-like nose sniffed one.

As he wondered if he could get either Krefeld or Barnes to be interviewed, he spotted his way in.

'Can I get a Latté, please?' Nurse Kathy swiped the coffee from the lady and turned to idly cast her curious blue eyes around the cafeteria in search of a friendly face.

She was rewarded with the gaze of the hunky man she'd seen in there earlier. His chiselled face broke into a mischievous smile, as he beckoned her over;

'Join me for a chat?' he called, smoothly. 'I could do with some company.'

She looked him up and down, noting the smart suit, the expensive glasses which gave him a distinguished air of intelligence and admired his tightly curled hair which reminded her of a Greek god. She thought that he seemed pretty harmless. He might be loaded, plus she was in need of a pick-me-up after the night she'd had. She smiled back at him and wiggled over to his table with her drink, settling herself into a plastic seat opposite his.

'Why not,' she smiled. She unconsciously fluffed her blond curls on her head to revive their bounce.

'Hi, my name's Kevin,' he stretched out his big hand to shake hers. As she proffered her slightly pudgy hand he grabbed it and kissed its back in a somewhat romantic gesture.

Kathy giggled and withdrew her hand in mock affront to cover her overly large mouth in false modesty.

'Nurse Kathy Harries, I presume?' Kevin raised his eyebrows inquisitively, staring over his glasses.

Kathy giggled again, 'How did you know?' she asked, fluttering her lengthy false eyelashes.

'Your name badge is quite a give-away!' teased Kevin, pointing at her uniform.

Kathy raised her big blue eyes heavenward. Taking a well-earned sip from her steamy cup, she checked him out, noting his laptop and mobile and his 6am shadow over his manly face.

'So, you're a reporter, right?' It was time to check out his credentials.

'Sure, how did you know?' he laughed.

'Your laptop, mobile and very forward demeanour are quite a give-away!' countered Kathy.

'Hmm, touché!' Kevin replied, raising his large palms in surrender. 'So, how was your shift?' asked Kevin nonchalantly.

Kathy stirred more sugar into her Latté and tapped the stirrer on the edge of the cup.

'You wouldn't believe the day I've had!' Kathy's enormous blue eyes were round like saucers, ready to tell this attractive man about her bizarre deluded young patient.

'Why don't you try me?' challenged Kevin, grinning cheekily.

25

CHRIS GOES HOME AND JOE CHECKS IN WITH HOLLY

After the traumatic hospital experience, Joe had driven Donna and Chris home.

Happily ensconced in the safety of their house, Donna had assured Joe that she would be able to take care of Chris from there, but she promised to call him if anything else happened. Chris had clung to his dad in the hope that he would stay, but Joe had bid them farewell, assuring Chris that he was only a call away if he needed him.

He had turned back to see son and mother hugging, which encouraged Joe greatly. He felt a warm glow in his heart as he saw his family pulling together.

Joe's first thoughts on leaving Donna were of Holly. He needed to see her and felt a pang of guilt that he had been away from her for so long, but it was not something that he could have helped considering the circumstances.

He wondered how she would react to him after he had spent so much time in the company of his ex. He decided to phone her.

'Hello,' her voice sounded dull and strained.

'Hi Holly, it's me, Joe. How are you?'

There was silence for a moment; Joe could sense a hint of awkwardness in the air.

Eventually she replied, saying 'Oh hi Joe. How have you been? I haven't heard from you for ages. You haven't answered my calls.'

'Holly I'm so sorry. It was Chris. We had to take him into hospital for a while and you know what hospitals are like about banning mobile phones.'

'Oh,' she said in a small voice. There was silence. Then, 'Well, is he better now?'

'He seems much better thanks, but it was touch and go for a while. There's something very strange going on with him, that's for sure; no-one seems to know what's causing it.'

Holly was quiet again, and then in an even smaller voice she ventured 'Were you with Donna?'

Joe was taken aback by this question. Of course he had been with Donna; she is the boy's mother after all. Yet why did he suddenly feel guilty?

'Listen Holly, I need to see you. Let's talk. Do you fancy meeting for dinner at our favourite place?'

She agreed to meet him, but Joe sensed that Holly was troubled.

26

HOLLY VOICES HER DOUBTS

At the coffee shop, Joe threw his jacket over the back of his chair, ordered a Latté and settled down to wait for Holly, who arrived dejectedly half an hour later.

'Holly, what is it?' he asked, his concerned gaze boring into hers.

'I'm fine Joe. Just tell me what happened at the hospital, please? Is Chris alright?' she appeared a little evasive, with a hint of sadness around her eyes, as she sat down and ordered herself a skinny Latté.

Joe explained everything that had happened. Holly was most supportive in her discourse, but Joe could sense that a distance had developed between them. It was true – she was convinced in her mind that Joe and Donna should and would get back together. It seemed almost inevitable; energetically, she was preparing herself for the worst.

'So do you think that you need to see them again?' asked Holly, green eyes boring into him as she implored the answer to be no.

Joe looked confused by this question, unsure whether she was inquiring after his personal feelings. He pushed his large hand through his floppy chestnut brown hair and continued carefully;

'I did promise Donna I would help out with anything that she needs. Chris seems much better when I'm around, so yes, I guess it's likely that I'll be seeing them again.'

Holly turned her face away to hide her eyes; they were stinging with tears.

'Hey Holly, what's up?' asked Joe kindly, stroking a wave of Holly's auburn hair out of her face.

'I think you know, Joe. Your family needs you; your loyalties should lie with them now. But I can't share you like that. I'm so sorry, but I'm afraid I'm going to have to call it a day. I hope Chris gets better and you can see him again, but I don't think I can see you anymore.'

She choked back her emotions as the tears welled from her emerald eyes. This was one of the hardest things she had ever done.

Joe gazed sadly at her and nodded. 'I see,' he said with resignation, yet in his heart of hearts, he knew that she was right. He had sensed that he still had feelings for Donna; although he was very happy with Holly, she was right that if there was any chance that he might get back together with Donna, then his loyalties should lie there, for the sake of Chris.

He took her hand kindly; with a deeply sad expression in his eyes, he kissed it gently.

'Holly, you are such a wonderful woman to put my family first like that. I'm so terribly sorry that I have caused you so much pain. You will always be a special person to me, but maybe I don't deserve you. Although this pains me to say, I'm sure there is someone out there with less 'baggage' so to speak, who will be much better for you. I leave it to you to move on and will respect your decision.'

Holly sobbed and pulled away, covering her distraught tear-stained face with her hands.

'The edge of sadness is the beginning of realization that leads to enlightenment,' he whispered. He stood up, reaching for his jacket. Turning back to Holly, he asked hopefully;

'Friends, at least?'

Holly peered down at her tepid skinny Latté. Although it hurt her to say it she nodded faintly, muttering 'Yes Joe, always.'

He smiled at her and blew her a kiss, sweeping out of the door on his long legs in a cloud of hopefulness and spiritual assuredness.

Holly looked down dejectedly as the door banged shut behind him. Her auburn waves closed around her face like a curtain closing after the final act of a play.

She sighed painfully into her drink and wept.

27

KEVIN RELEASES HIS FIRST STORY

The door swung behind Joe as he walked away from the lovely Holly. What a blow it was to lose her, but he knew how important it was to her to have no ambiguities in her relationships. He couldn't truly say with all his heart that he could commit to her when there was any chance of reconciliation with his family, so although his heart weighed heavily in his chest, he knew it had been the right decision, considering his situation then.

He wondered how he could make things right for Holly and he dearly wanted to keep her friendship and their special bond, even if he couldn't give her exclusive rights to his love. He mulled over how he could maintain a professional working relationship with her too without causing her more grief. She deserved far more than complete abandonment, and he vowed he would find a way to help her in some way.

As Joe wandered onto the street, his eyes were drawn to a newspaper in the stand outside. Startled, he noticed his son's face staring out from the front page. He grabbed the paper, and read the headlines.

'BOY SEES ALIENS IN SAN-FRANCISCO HOSPITAL'

What is this rubbish? Joe read on, and was horrified to see that some reporter – what was his name?

Kevin Masters – had created a sensationalized story out of his boy's terrible experience.

Joe threw the paper back at the stand and stalked off, annoyed that the media needed to prey on others' difficulties. He vowed he would contact this man and set him straight. He thought of Donna, how was she going to take it when she found out about this? He decided he'd better warn her, thinking he could break it to her gently.

*

'Donna, hi; it's Joe. How are you?'

'Joe! We're doing great thanks. Chris is so much better. He's slept well and he's eating again; I think he's going to be just fine. How are you?'

'Um, I'm alright, I just needed to tell you something. Please try to stay calm,' Joe predicted she would explode when she heard the news.

'What is it? What have you done?' asked Donna suspiciously.

'No, it's not me!' laughed Joe, 'not this time anyway! I'm afraid there was a leak about Chris and his stay in hospital. Some reporter has released a rather sensationalized story about what happened.' Joe waited for the reaction, breath held anxiously.

'What do you mean 'sensationalized'?'

'Um, they said Chris had seen aliens in the hospital...'

'What? That's ridiculous!' shouted Donna. She ranted for a full five minutes; Joe held the phone away from his ear to protect his villi. Mercifully, her landline phone rang, prompting her to give up her tirade.

'Donna, I'll sort it out, O.K.?'

Joe's words were left suspended in the air as he realized she had already hung up.

28

DONNA IS HARANGUED BY MEDIA

'Who's calling me now?' muttered Donna to herself as she stomped to her home phone.

'Yes?' she answered curtly.

'Hi, is that Donna McKenzie?' asked a drawling woman at the end of the phone.

'Hmm, who's this?'

'This is the Tribune. I read your son's story in the paper and I wondered if I could do an interview with him?' Donna's brow furrowed in annoyance.

'You've got to be kidding me! That reporter stitched him up good and proper; he spouted all sorts of rubbish about aliens! Get lost!' she shouted down the phone.

Many more people called over the following days, eager to get a take on the story, perhaps to get a glimpse of the boy who'd seen the alien creatures in the hospital. Some people saw it as an excuse to dredge up their own mad-cap stories about aliens. The papers were alien-obsessed as others got on the band wagon.

Irritating as it was to endure, the family's story was however soon old news; the papers pushed on to new ideas.

*

Donna had kept Chris at home for a few days to be sure that he was improving. She worked from home to keep him company, reading to him to help distract him from his strange symptoms – in between fielding phone calls from exasperating busy bodies.

Within a couple of weeks, Chris was feeling much better. His strange symptoms had gone, all the strange noises, all the unusually acute vision experiences had dissipated, such that he was back to wearing his glasses. Everything externally seemed to have pretty much gone back to normal, apart from a residual ability to sense a greater awareness of objects – as if he had a better appreciation of all that was around him.

The world seemed a much more complicated place than he had ever perceived before and yet bizarrely, also much simpler – he had a greater sense of the magical and clever network of goings on that underlay and connected everything.

Despite this strange sense of awareness he felt, he was able to pick up his usual routine life again, but the transition back into school had been somewhat fraught, as many local families had read the cynical news report about his time in hospital, which had done him no favours in terms of his reputation for eccentricity. Many children taunted him about his experience, but he tried to block them all out; he was still very much caught up in his own world of sensory experiences. How could he not be affected by what had happened?

He stared out of the window of his classroom and

watched the leaves waving in the trees, marvelling at how old the trees were, wondering whether they held wisdom in their roots about the nature of the world. His gaze fell out of focus between the branches. Suddenly he noticed a kind of glow emanating from around the branches of the trees. It looked a little like a silvery luminous blanket that covered every surface and lit up the tree in all its glory. Pleasantly surprised by the beauty around him he continued to stare in awe at the bright colours of Nature that seemed to declare its stronger presence. His reverie was interrupted as he heard his science teacher yelling out his name.

'CHRIS!' He turned to stare at his teacher, hearing the rest of the class giggle; he realized that the teacher had asked him a question and was pointing at an ovoid picture on the white board. Chris couldn't believe his eyes! It seemed remarkably like some of the shapes that had crowded his vision during his time in hospital! His jaw dropped; he was unable to say anything.

His teacher's eyebrows shot skywards; 'I'm waiting...' the tall skinny man uttered impatiently.

A carefully aimed rolled up ball of paper sailed across the classroom and hit Chris squarely on the back of his head.

'Wake up alien boy! Are you seeing funny creatures again?' taunted one of the boys. Others in the class sniggered, but Chris was barely aware that they were laughing. He was too absorbed in his train of thought. What was that picture? What had he been seeing in hospital? Another kid's hand shot up and the lanky teacher sighed.

'Please pay more attention in class, Chris!' he muttered with frustration. The teacher turned his bald head to the keen ginger-haired child whose hand was now waving furiously in the air like a fluttering flag. 'Yes Hannah. What are we looking at?'

'Sir, it's a bacterium,' cried Hannah enthusiastically. Chris' eyes had widened in surprise. So, was that what he had been seeing in his 'visions'; but how?

The teacher congratulated the flame-haired girl; 'Yes, well done Hannah.'

Hannah turned to smile kindly at Chris, her feline-green eyes silently apologizing. 'A smile means so much to someone in agony', he thought.

Chris nodded his thanks to her, surprised and pleased by this display of camaraderie, but also very grateful that he may have identified the source of his recent disturbing visions.

His mind was racing for the rest of the school day, which ended with Science Club. This was his favourite school activity; although he wasn't exactly sure he could call his fellow members friends as such, they certainly had a certain degree of empathy for him in so far as they shared the same obsessive interests about matters of science.

Ensconced amongst a huddle of fellow science explorers sat at a hub of computer terminals, Chris was able to blend in with the crowd. He felt a certain unspoken acceptance here, without even having to interact directly with the others.

He took advantage of his time at the Club to surf the internet, seeking some sort of understanding of his bizarre experiences, his recent visions and what the shapes he had seen could possibly be.

Thinking that he might have received a clue in class today, he typed in the word 'bacteria' to the browser, setting the computer to work to find some answers for him. Deep in thought, his eyes widened as he found images of bacteria, like the rounded blob shapes of M.R.S.A. bacteria – Methicillin Resistant Staphylococcus Aureus – and other micro-organisms. Although they were all different shapes, he had to admit that they bore a striking resemblance to the many strange shapes he had been seeing!

What an amazing revelation! What if he really was able to see micro-organisms? How on Earth was that possible? How could the eyes be able to see such minute things? He read off the size data against each picture. His mind boggled at the numbers he read, numbers with so many zeroes after the decimal point that they needed special nomenclature to represent them; 0.0000006m was immensely difficult to get your head around, yet 0.6×10^{-6}m was not much better. 0.6 μm was a neater, shorter way to say it, μm representing micrometer.

He was used to such number manipulation after all the time he had spent playing with his telescope, but that worked with numbers from the opposite end of the spectrum – from the vastly immense to the infinite. This was a different matter; numbers on a microscopic scale, used to measure a micro-world of life that most people are barely aware exist.

Suddenly he felt a tickle on his cheek. He turned to find Hannah peering over his shoulder at his screen, the tufts of her bright orange fiery hair brushing his face.

He jumped, losing his glasses off his nose, but she just giggled. 'I see you're doing your science homework!' she grinned.

'Um, yeah, sort of,' muttered Chris shyly. Peeking at her out of the corner of his eye he thought she was small for her age, but he knew she had a personality larger than life. Her wayward orange locks stuck out from her head like flames, matching her feisty fiery nature. Her feline green eyes blazed with an inner determination which tended to protect her from the usual taunts of the other school children who found Science Club members geeky and incomprehensible. Her freckles jumped out at onlookers, distracting them from her rather untamed eyebrows. Her dress was conventional – safe, even – yet scanning her all the way down to her feet revealed a pair of clumpy Doc Martins, which suggested she would boot anyone into touch who pushed her too far. She continued to stare at Chris, who coughed in embarrassment.

'You know, my dad knows all about this stuff. He's a microbiologist; he's always going on about bacteria, viruses and strange microscopic worlds of alien-like creatures. Maybe you have something in common with him,' she said astutely, raising her bushy eyebrows up towards her ginger mop.

'Really?' pondered Chris. Perhaps this was someone he could talk to after all. He decided to pursue the topic with Hannah. 'Yes, I think that might be what I was able to see when I had to go into hospital.'

'Honestly? Not aliens then?' questioned Hannah, astonished, emerald eyes round like plates.

'No, I don't think so!' laughed Chris. 'Does your dad know how bacteria move? Or how they behave?' His silvery gaze was bright with excitement.

'Well, sure, he knows all that stuff. You should meet him. He'd love to talk to you about it!' Hannah blushed and peered down shyly at her clumpy boots.

'Why don't you come over after school sometime?' she was shuffling nervously from side to side, feet clomping noisily on the wooden floor.

'Um, sure, I'd love to,' whispered Chris, fairly in shock.

'Great, I'll let you know when's good.'

She smiled again and wandered back to her computer terminal. As an afterthought, she turned back and added, 'You know, I missed you at school. I'm sorry you were sick. I hope you're feeling much better now.' She smiled kindly, her freckles bunching up into bigger brown spots. She picked up her coat to leave, then turning to face him, she added; 'Don't worry about what the others are saying, Chris. They don't understand. They're just jealous – or pea-brained!'

Chris laughed and waved goodbye, his heart lifted by this unexpectedly positive encounter. Sitting back in his seat, pushing his glasses up his nose, he whistled to himself, somewhat taken aback by this surprise invite. He wasn't used to other children being so friendly to him, but he realized that Hannah had always been very kind to him in class and at Science Club. She would often stand up for him when the others were trying to make fun of him.

Ain't that funny! He thought. *'Let a thousand people dislike you; there is always one who likes you'* - he made up his mind that he would go to her house, even if only to meet her father and see what he could find out about bacteria.

He shut down the computer and headed home.

June

Full Moon: 4.11 am on June 4th

29

CHRIS IS DRAWN TO THE WAXING MOON

Over the next two weeks, Chris was drawn again to watch the widening face of the Moon out of his window. As it waxed from evening to evening, he was increasingly aware that his vision and hearing were changing once more – growing more acute.

His rational scientific brain was intrigued by the symptoms. For a second time he noted the rate of changes in his notebook, but this time it was coupled with an increasing nervousness, as it all seemed too familiar; he was certainly not keen to go through another frightening experience of strange visions again.

He continued to research the microcosmic world online, keen to seek out any accounts of other people experiencing such visions, but every day, his senses were heightening and his attraction to the waxing Moon was ever more persistent.

30

Donna notices Chris is acting strangely again

Chris' mother kept a close eye on him; she noted he was getting increasingly agitated and he had taken to walking around without his glasses again. She questioned him on this aspect; he insisted that his eyesight had improved so he didn't need his glasses. Donna was sceptical at first, but realized he wasn't bumping into anything without them, so he must be seeing more clearly.

She mentally noted that she should call the family doctor for an appointment.

She found Chris increasingly sensitive to noise around him, so she patiently tried to speak to him only in a quiet voice, keeping the T.V. turned down low at all times. Yet as she settled down to watch T.V. in the evenings, she found herself increasingly able to hear his evening monologues, his Moon songs, his mutterings and his cries.

Concerned once more, she rang Joe for a reassuring word of comfort.

'I'm sure he's fine,' said Joe amicably, 'but if you're worried maybe I can help? Perhaps Chris is feeling a bit unsettled still and needs more stability? Maybe I should come round and spend some time with you guys as a family again? If you're ready to spend more time with me, that is...' said Joe, hesitantly.

Donna was quiet for a moment as she considered his offer. She wondered if she would like that, but she decided that she wasn't prepared to let Joe back into their lives that way, in case things didn't work out again.

'No, I don't think I'm ready for that yet, Joe, but thank you.'

'You know, I'll come over any time you or Chris need me; just call. Your happiness is my happiness,' he added shyly.

Donna had smiled warmly to herself, for the first time in a long time.

Joe felt that the best way to handle his relationship with Donna was to play it gently, to offer her whatever support she wanted but to leave everything up to her. He put no pressure on her, suspecting that she needed to feel in control of things, so he stated his position and then left the ball in her court.

They ended their conversation on good terms. Joe was ready to move on with Donna, and he had stepped towards making peace with Holly, buying her a beautiful sculpture for her apartment as a thank you for her ongoing support.

Holly had agreed to still help out at the store from time to time and continue to source stock for him, but they agreed to maintain a strictly professional relationship for the sake of her aching heart. Yet Holly knew she would always care for Joe and couldn't help but watch in trepidation as he risked his heart at the hands of his feisty ex-wife.

*

Bright Moon

The Bright Moon insistently beckoned through the bedroom window; Chris was pulled once more into its seductive presence. He stared longingly at it; his mind drifted effortlessly up, up and away into the night, up into the heavens. It was as if he was traveling to the Moon in a bubble. He was being drawn along a ray of moonlight directly to its source.

He basked in its silvery wisdom and relaxed into bliss. His energy levels were shifting and his consciousness was rising to a heightened state of awareness. He was once more transported to a world of unity and a loss of all boundaries. His sense of self had dissolved and he was one with the Moon and 'All that is'.

Sometime later as his mother climbed the stairs to bed, she heard a beautiful tune coming from Chris' bedroom. She realized that he was gently singing to himself. She smiled at its haunting beauty, popping her head round the door to see him planted in his window seat, basking in the moonlight.

Her stomach twisted in a pang of fear, thinking how much like his dad he seemed in that meditative pose. She was shocked by a sudden feeling of déjà vu. This was how it had all started last time, she worried.

She gently guided Chris away from the window, settling him into bed without any resistance from him. His face was radiant, relaxed and glowing. She kissed his forehead, and tousled his curly golden locks, willing him to have a good night.

31

2nd Bright Moon event

Chris awoke abruptly with noisy whispers ringing in his ears. He peeled back the curtains of his eyelids; his vision was filled with the strange wiggling creatures again! He screamed and shouted out for his mum, the same bloodcurdling scream that sent chills of horror down his mother's spine.

She rushed upstairs to find him writhing around on the bed again, screaming about the strange creatures being everywhere. He was rubbing his eyes trying to rub the creatures out of them; he refused to open them so he wouldn't have to face the horrific sight again.

'Honey, I think you're just having a bad dream!' she soothed, trying to hug him gently. He shrugged her away and cried 'Don't touch me Mum, they're everywhere!'

'Are you sure, Chris? Just try opening your eyes again for me, son – I bet it's just a really nasty nightmare.'

Chris tried to slow his breathing and screwed up his courage to take another peek, hoping that he had indeed imagined it, that the illusion would have vanished. Gingerly, he opened one eye to a slit, but again he could see the creatures writhing around. In horror, he clamped his eyes shut again and vowed not to open them again. *'This world is crazy',* he thought. *'This is surely not just my imagination? If these things are real, and they really are micro-organisms, then we really aren't alone – there are so many micro-beings everywhere! Is it just here in my house, or is it outside too?'*

He cried, turning to his mother with heaving shoulders.

'Mum, please take me to the window, I need to see if they're outside too.'

She led him carefully over to the window; he very slowly and bravely peeled open his eyes. Peering anxiously down into the garden, he saw the vegetation was overrun with minute creepy shapes; he gasped in awe.

'Mum there are micro-beings everywhere! They're all over the garden too!' he exclaimed, horrified.

'Micro-beings, what do you mean, Chris?' asked Donna, shocked.

He turned to stare at her in horror. Wide-eyed he said,

'Mum, you're covered in them again. They're all round your mouth and your nose, Mum; I'm so scared, what's happening to me? Why is this happening again?'

Donna was weeping, her rising panic was unbearable.

'Chris, please try not to worry. I'm going to get help for you.'

32

DONNA CALLS THE PSYCHIATRIST AND JOE

Donna clambered downstairs and turned the kitchen upside down hunting for the card with the contact number on for Dr. Barnes, the psychiatrist.

She definitely couldn't see these strange creatures that he was crying about, and was seriously concerned for his mental health. Although worried that she and Joe might end up labelled as bad parents and Chris as God-knows-what, Donna needed medical help for him. She ran for the phone and dialled the number on the card, immediately reaching her intended destination.

'Dr. Barnes speaking,' uttered a serious voice at the end of the phone.

'Um, hello Dr. Barnes; it's Donna, Donna McKenzie, Chris' mother.'

'Hello Donna, how are you?' he said, surprised, remembering the Rottweiler-like woman's fast exit from the hospital last month and her scathing comments about their diagnostic capabilities.

'Dr. Barnes, it's Chris, he's getting those visions again; I don't know how to help him!'

'Alright Donna, will he let you bring him in to us? I can have a bed waiting for you here,' coughed Barnes.

'I don't know, Dr. Barnes, I'll try.'

'Do what you can Donna; bring him straight to the psychiatric ward. I'll have him admitted.'

She hung up, called work to arrange some time off and ran to gather Chris' things together, aware that it could be another long stay for him.

'Chris, I need to take you in to hospital.'

'No, Mum, I don't wanna go! That place is crawling with creatures!' Chris was adamantly stubborn.

'I know son.' Donna knew that she had only one course of action. 'Do you want me to call your dad?' she smiled encouragingly at him.

The thought of seeing his dad was a huge incentive. He hesitated, weighing up his options, then quietly negotiated; 'I'll go if Dad goes.'

Donna nodded her agreement and went to phone Joe.

With his eyes clamped tightly shut, Chris was able to tune in to his other senses. Chris was gob-struck by the sounds that crowded his ears. The pulsing and whispering of a million voices were washing over him; he was overwhelmed by the rush of communication that was however completely garbled to his ears.

He rocked himself gently, holding his ears with his palms to soothe their overload.

33

Chris goes back to hospital

When his dad arrived, Chris was able to describe what it felt like to him, in a slightly less panicky way. Chris explained that the only relief he had from this burden of bacterial sight was either when he shut his eyes, or when he watched the sky. Joe encouraged him into his car, guiding him there blindfolded and with ear defenders.

Donna, Joe and Chris sped through the angular streets, past the cable-cars and hilly roads towards the freeway. Joe pulled up outside the hospital and they carefully guided Chris to the psychiatric ward, gathering whispers and stares from people as they walked.

Donna overheard two nurses standing at the lift, who clearly were unable to contain their curiosity;

'There's that crazy kid who was in last month raving about alien creatures invading the hospital!' whispered one to the other – rather too loudly.

'Oh yes!' said the other, hiding her smirking face, 'I wonder what he's gonna say this time? We've all been hypnotized by aliens from another planet and are being turned into zombies!'

'Sure! I can see the headlines now!'

The nurses hurried away, sniggering; Donna's face burned in shame, wishing she hadn't heard them. They arrived at the psychiatric ward; Dr. Barnes was waiting for them, with Dr. Holmes and Dr. Krefeld, the paediatrician and the neurosurgeon. They all announced their presence to the blind-folded boy, who was still not brave enough to look at anyone.

Joe removed the ear defenders so Chris could hear them speak. Dr. Barnes cleared his throat with a sharp cough.

'Well Chris, let's see if we can help you shall we?' said Dr. Barnes. 'First of all, can you please take off your blindfold and open your eyes for me?'

'No, I don't want to,' said Chris, shaking at the rush of sounds that had overloaded his ears.

'Come on Chris, let's stay calm and help out the doctors so they can help you' said his dad, kindly. 'Courage, son – I'm right here.'

Chris slowly nodded his agreement, bravely peeling off the blindfold, but as he carefully opened his eyes he was once again distraught to see the masses of wriggling minute creatures that filled his vision. He panicked and cried out, but he held his eyes open for a little longer and saw the shapes more clearly. They were bustling around in clumps and some were dividing in two creating more and more of the wriggling creatures. It was a thoroughly macabre sight yet strangely fascinating if he could just bear it. But he couldn't. He clamped his eyes shut again and shook his head.

'Please, no more' he begged. Barnes' lips thinned tightly.

'Chris, I think we need to help you calm down again. May we give you a sedative for that?' asked Dr. Barnes.

Donna and Joe nodded their agreement on his behalf, and answered another list of questions from the medics. Nurse Kathy slid forward with something in her false-nailed hand. Chris' eyes were tightly shut as she carefully administered the calming drug.

His muscles began to relax; he felt more at ease. He was able to lie back on a bed in Bay Two.

34

CHRIS MEETS EDWARD THE EYE SPECIALIST

Chris reluctantly allowed Nurse Kathy to bustle around him checking his blood pressure and so on. Then he went through another psychiatric assessment with Dr. Barnes.

Presently a new man arrived at his bedside. Donna observed the stranger with distrust, taking an instant dislike to his strange appearance; it reminded her of a lollipop; an overly large head resting on a stick thin body. Oversized and out of proportion with his lean frame, his head appeared sufficiently large to house the brain of a genius.

'Hello Chris, my name is Dr. Baines, but you can call me the eye man!' he chuckled to himself, amused by his weak joke, which matched his weak-looking appearance.

Peering through his enormous glasses with his contradictorily tiny eyes, he observed Chris like he was an insect under a magnifying glass.

'I'm here to examine your eyes, to see if there is anything unusual going on. I wonder if you can please open them for me.'

'Don't touch me!' shouted Chris, terrified.

Baines jumped in shock, sending his heavy glasses

plummeting downwards. Pushing his hefty dislodged glasses back up his angular nose, he cleared his throat.

'Young man, unless you open your eyes, I will be unable to examine you. If you would like me to help you, then I suggest you open them right away! If you are happy to continue in this fashion with these strange optical visions then please feel free to keep them closed.' He stood patiently by Chris' bed-side; certain Chris would give in soon enough.

Chris had to agree that he wanted help with these frightening visions, so reluctantly he opened his eyes, cringing at the rush of movement in his vision.

Dr. Baines leaned forward, uttering conspiratorially, 'I knew you would see sense! Get it? See?' He chuckled good-naturedly at his feeble joke and began his examination, experiencing considerable difficulties with Chris' co-operation.

'Chris usually wears glasses for his short-sightedness, but he has been going without recently, saying that he doesn't need them,' explained Donna.

Baines raised his eyebrows in surprise. He checked Chris' distance vision, asking him to read out the letters on his chart. Chris struggled to open his eyes and made a supreme effort to focus on the letters, reading them out one by one all the way down the chart to the minuscule letters right at the bottom.

'Hmm, well I agree that there seems to be no sign of myopia now, which is bizarre. You say he usually has a prescription for short-sightedness?' questioned Baines, perplexed.

'That's right,' mumbled Chris, struggling with the influx of wriggling movement around him.

'Hmm, well let me try a couple more tests. Chris, please close your eyes?'

Chris clamped his hands back over his eyes, relieved that he could shut out the disturbing visions at last. Baines suppressed a snigger and asked him to open his eyes again. Chris removed his hands but did not want to see the creatures again so he kept his eyes clamped tightly shut.

There followed a comedic discussion between Baines and Chris as the ophthalmic expert struggled to get co-operation from his distraught patient. Baines stifled a hysterical giggle as the boy continued to argue the toss about whether his eyes should be open or closed.

As the boy's lack of co-operation signalled that he had clearly finished his examination, Baines explained to the family that he could not see anything else particularly unusual about the boy's eyesight, apart from a certain silvery glaze to his eyes.

He recommended antibiotic drops for the boy that he tried to put into Chris' eyes, but Chris wrestled with him, fending him off. Giving in, Baines turned to Donna and Nurse Kathy.

'See if you have better luck with this,' he said. 'Administer to his eyes three times a day.'

Donna nodded her agreement.

Turning to Chris again, Baines said;

'So Chris, what is it exactly that you claim you are able to see?'

'Well sir, I can see little creatures. They're all over everything; on the surfaces, on your face, on your clothes!'

Dr. Baines stifled a laugh. 'Really; they're on me, eh? Aren't I the lucky one! Don't shout or we'll all want them! Well I hope they go away soon, son.'

Chris could clearly sense Dr. Baines' disdain and realized he was not being taken seriously. He decided to tell him something a little more personal;

'Well, sir, they're swarming all over that cut on your face,' he said, pointing at a shaving nick on Baines' chin. 'They look like ovoid shapes, or little gel capsules that wriggle around or clump together. Sometimes they split in two until there are more and more of them.'

Dr. Baines laughed again, but also seemed more interested. 'Splitting in two, you say? Like they are dividing?'

'Yes, but multiplying in number,' replied Chris.

'Do you mean like bacteria do?' queried Dr. Baines, quizzically.

'Yes, like bacteria. I think maybe they look like bacteria.'

Chris was nodding enthusiastically, happy that someone had mentioned the word that he also had on his mind; someone appeared to finally be listening to him.

Dr. Baines was intrigued, as the boy had explained a feature of bacteria that was unmistakably distinctive.

'How old did you say you were, Chris?'

Chris told him his age; Edward Baines raised an eyebrow in wonder, uncertain for a fleeting moment as to whether a boy this age could be making up such a story after all.

However, reason overtook fantasy and with no evidence that the boy was telling the truth, he shrugged his shoulders in dismissal, telling Chris just to revisit his regular opticians to get his lens prescription updated, as his glasses were clearly too powerful for him.

Edward reported to the other medics on his way out, explaining he was none the wiser about the boy's visions, as there didn't appear to be anything very unusual that he could pick up about his eyesight in the prematurely ended examination he had managed to carry out. After giving them the run-down of Chris' possible infection, his prescribed medication and his likely change of lens prescription, he pottered away back to his office, muttering that it had been a strange old day.

As he left the building Baines overheard Barnes the psychiatrist confiding to a colleague;

'Chris is clearly delusional, possibly some form of psychosis or schizophrenia. I must say I feel sorry for the parents; he's a real piece of work. I think he's leading them a real merry dance. I guess they played their part in all this though with their strange behaviour at home. It's usually the way in my opinion; you can put it down to blood chemistry but there's always a trigger and I blame the parents.' Barnes' thin lips compressed together as he concluded his judgment.

'Well, let's see what Krefeld says, but I'm inclined to agree, I've never heard such a strange story in all my life – it's enough to make your ribs split with laughter!' said his colleague, belly-laughing his way to the vending machine, walking right past the erstwhile implicated reporter, Kevin, who was trying hard to seem like he wasn't listening.

Baines felt inclined to agree with the gossiping medics, but something didn't quite sit right with this whole case. Perhaps because of his beliefs about eyes, he had a different perspective on the possibilities for unusual eyesight and visions. His mind was ticking over the possibility that there was some bizarre brain connection causing Chris' visions, but as he had no evidence, he decided for now to put today's strange goings on down to the Full Moon. Hospitals were always rammed with crazy kooks on Full Moon nights – everyone knew that.

Meanwhile Nurse Kathy was attempting to get the antibiotic eye drops into Chris' eyes.

'Please try to stay still for me, Chris!' she ordered, as Chris wriggled and complained.

'Open those eyes a little for me – come on, you can do it!' Kathy bit her big lip as she struggled on.

'Come on darling, these drops will help you! Please try for Mommy and Daddy?' pleaded Donna. Chris sighed and made an almighty effort to peel back his eyelids just a crack. He could see wiggling creatures around the outline of his lashes, but Kathy was well-practised and lightning fast, dropping in the medication before he was able to clamp his eyelids shut again.

'Well done darling!' praised Donna.

'Try to open and shut your eyes for me a few times, Chris?'

Kathy hovered impatiently, fluttering her own long lashes in demonstration.

Chris fluttered his eyelids but he could see the strangest of scenes – the creatures were writhing around on his lashes, wiggling faster and faster, as if they were agitated, then their movement slowed down. Suddenly they stopped moving altogether!

Surprised, Chris opened his eyes wider, but the influx of

wriggling creatures out on the surfaces of everything else he surveyed shocked him. He placed his hands over his eyes and rubbed. Opening them a little again, the wriggling creatures could again be seen on his eyelashes, writhing faster, then slower and then stopping dead. What on Earth was going on?

35

Kevin gathers another story

Kevin couldn't believe his luck. It had been a month since he'd had that last fantastic scoop and here he was again with a sequel forming in his mind's eye. He hurried to his favourite seat in the hospital cafeteria. Opening his laptop, he quickly noted down his latest ideas gleaned from casting his radar towards the gossiping medics.

His editor had been delighted with the last story about the alien-spotter. Kevin had ridden on the back of its glory for a full 48 hours, but after that it was just old news. Since then, he'd been scraping around for another blinder to take its place. Yet here he was ready to resurrect the story, searching for a twist that would sell it afresh.

As he feverishly typed he caught movement at the side of his eye, followed by a little squeal in his ear.

'Hi Kevin, long time no see!' oozed Nurse Kathy, as she confidently plunked herself down in the seat opposite him.

Kevin scraped himself off the ceiling, forcing a smile in the nurse's direction. His brain was whirring swiftly, as he worked out a plan to get his story twist.

'Well hello gorgeous, we meet again, how's it hanging?' he reached for her manicured hand, which she happily gave up to him to receive a kiss on its back.

'Pretty good thanks. That was an awesome story you wrote last month! It was all over the hospital, not to mention the rest of the city.' Kathy whispered enthusiastically, beaming her approval at him with her big flapping mouth, not least because he'd slipped her a few dollars for the exclusive. With her menial income in mind, she gave him another tip-off faster than a rat up a drain pipe.

'You'll never guess who is back on the wards...' she winked conspiratorially, leaning in to whisper Chris' name.

'No! Well that's very interesting! What have you got to tell me?' probed Kevin encouragingly.

Kathy decided to gamble and play hard ball with him – she shrugged nonchalantly and slyly peered over at him, saying;

'Well maybe something, maybe nothing...it all depends...' she held her long false nails before her as if inspecting them in a bored fashion.

Kevin was ready for this diversion – he'd heard it a thousand times before with informants that had enjoyed their first pay-off, but always wanted more. He threw his next comment at her equally as casually;

'Well I always find that more exclusive conversations take place in more exclusive surroundings, perhaps with an exclusive glass of champagne in one's hand...' he fixed his bespectacled gaze on hers and smiled provocatively.

Kathy was taken off guard and, flustered, she gabbled;

'My shift finishes in a couple of hours; I'll be all yours...'

'Well, meet me at Smyth's as soon as you knock off; if you make it worth my while, I'll even get the check,' Kevin tapped his sharp nose knowingly.

Kathy realized he would be after an even juicier story than last time, so she nodded her understanding, quaffed her Café Americano and slipped away ready to gather information about Chris.

36

CHRIS POINTS OUT MICRO-ORGANISMS IN THE HOSPITAL

Meanwhile upstairs, Krefeld was keen to order more tests for Chris. He was ashamed to hear the others making fun of this poor boy, feeling Chris was getting short shrift from them. He couldn't believe that they were so dismissive of the young boy – after all it was their job to uncover all possible causes for medical imbalances. He for one was determined he would try to get to the bottom of this case. He owed the boy that at least; he was well aware that all cases like his should be taken very seriously, as any abnormal behaviour, brain activity or body functions could lead to a serious medical situation.

He prepared the boy to go back down to the scanners, enrolling Kathy to help him as she rolled breathlessly into the ward after her break. Chris was dressed in the special protective surgical gown and this time wore goggles too, to help him feel more at ease. Krefeld questioned Chris again on what he could see. Chris was able to reply in a rather more matter of fact way this time;

'I see strange creatures; they seem very eccentric and odd-looking, almost beautiful. I see many different shapes; cylinders, balls and spirals and so on. They wiggle and split in two and when I spoke to Dr. Baines he thought I might be seeing bacteria.'

Even Nurse Kathy's small ears pricked up at this comment. He thinks he can see bacteria, eh? This might be her juicy snippet for Kevin. She moved in closer to make sure she could hear properly, sidling up to change the water in Chris' jug.

'I can see them on your shirt, on your hands, on your glasses, even there on the table. Can't you see them? Look over there at the equipment being wheeled out of the ward.'

Chris pointed at some machines on a trolley, being pushed to surgery by a porter.

'What is it? It's just machines Chris,' said Krefeld, bemused.

'Well, they're all over the machines too. I can hear their sounds.'

Kathy's blue eyes were nearly popping out of her blond head. She coughed and tried to disguise her shock, covering her cavernous mouth with a podgy hand.

Krefeld glanced at Chris' parents with concern. 'What do you mean, Chris? The machines aren't on, so they can't be making sounds.' Krefeld pushed a large hand through his silver-striped hair in consternation.

'No, not the machines; I can hear the creatures, sir. It's like they're talking to each other, and I can hear them.'

'Well, what do you think they are saying, Chris?' asked Krefeld, intrigued.

'I don't know, sir. I can't make it out. It's a bit like white noise really, you know when you're trying to tune one of those old analogue radios to get a station that you want and you hear all that crackling sound in-between the stations?'

'Sure, I remember those old radios!' beamed Krefeld.

'Well, it's like that; I sometimes wonder if only I could tune into the station perhaps I would be able to hear what they are saying!' said Chris somewhat whimsically.

'Well kid, I wonder what tune they would be playing?' smiled Krefeld affectionately at the boy.

'My guess is it would be 'Going Loco Down in Acapulco,'' muttered the porter who had overheard their conversation.

'Hey Carter – quit that tittle-tattle and come over here with your trolley!' shouted Krefeld to the porter who was still in earshot. Carter grudgingly trundled the equipment towards Bay Two.

'Here, Chris, take a closer peek at these bacteria you say you can see. You know we wash everything down ready for surgery, don't you? We have to disinfect everything before it can go into any surgical environment? I don't think it's likely this stuff has any germs left on it,' Krefeld challenged.

Chris bravely peered at the equipment; he shuddered as he watched the tiny creatures crawling all over it. He began to describe their shape and their movement and their behaviour, trying to tame his racing pulse by pretending he was just observing another science experiment.

Krefeld's eyebrows were rising to the ceiling. Bizarrely enough, the boy seemed to be describing something which reminded him very much of the hospital's nemesis – M.R.S.A., or Methicillin-Resistant Staphylococcus Aureus. This was a deadly strain of bacteria that was running rampant in many hospitals of the world following wide-spread use of antibiotics over the last few decades. This 'super-bug' M.R.S.A. had cunningly adapted to not be affected by current antibiotic therapies. Whenever it struck a vulnerable patient, it had a tendency to cause terrible infections and sometimes death.

Nurse Kathy was aware of this bug too – it had been the subject of many nursing meetings in their efforts to keep the hospital hygienic – but she didn't believe Chris; she just thought he was making it up. She stifled a giggle.

Well aware that this strain of Staph was also highly resistant to extreme temperatures and most of their detergents, Krefeld shifted his weight nervously from foot to foot.

'I see, Chris. That really is something to think about.' Krefeld's brain was running faster than a prize race horse around a track. He turned to the porter, whispering something under his breath.

Carter's jaw dropped; he exclaimed 'I've already had it cleaned!'

'I don't care, Carter. Please do it again – better to be safe than sorry.' Krefeld nodded at the porter to get on with his job. The disgruntled porter trundled the trolley back where he came from muttering obscenities under his breath.

Chris was elated that someone was listening to him at last, and was finally taking him seriously. However observing around him he noticed all the staff and patients were smirking and giggling at him. He glanced over at the bed next to him in Bay Three, where a young man sadly lay, looking gaunt and depressed. The man caught Chris' eye.

'Don't you take any notice of that lot, kid; they've got nothing better to do all day than laugh at our misfortunes. You just stick with me kid, I'll see you right.' The man blew his nose onto a tissue and reached over to place the slightly bloodied tissue on his bedside table.

Chris' eyes nearly popped out of their sockets. The tissue was covered in minuscule round balls, looking a little like tiny versions of the mines that used to be left in the ocean in World War Two to catch unsuspecting submarines. Chris whispered to Krefeld what he could see on the tissue.

Krefeld's eyes also popped out of their sockets, as the boy was describing something that sounded a lot like a description of a virus. He went over to the man's charts to check his details, but found no mention of any virus, only that he had been prescribed anti-depressants. Unsure what it all meant, he walked back over to Chris, who was gently rocking with his eyes closed and his hands over his ears.

Feeling sorry for Chris, Krefeld slipped the boy a pair of ear plugs before sending him on his way to the scanner with Nurse Kathy.

Krefeld headed back to the desk, just as Barnes appeared with some blood test results. He headed Krefeld off at the pass, hoping for a second opinion, as he was going to be very sad delivering this news to the patient in Bay Three if the diagnosis was indeed correct.

Krefeld scanned the results and gasped.

'Are you sure these are the right results for the young man over there next to Chris' bed?' asked Krefeld.

'Sure am – it's a rotten deal for him, but do you agree, this man has been infected with H.I.V.?' Barnes observed Krefeld sadly and Krefeld nodded his stunned agreement. The man next to Chris did indeed have a virus – he was tested as H.I.V. positive. Chris had been right after all.

37

KREFELD PUZZLES OVER CHRIS' BRAIN SCANS

Chris was relieved to have blocked out the majority of the sounds with the ear plugs that Krefeld had kindly given him. He was still aware of a strange sensation in his head though, as if the sounds were still able to penetrate his mind even without the benefit of blocked ear canals, but it was much less disturbing, pleasantly lulling almost.

When questioned on his sleep patterns, Chris revealed that he often spent a lot of the night awake, whether staring at the Moon, or just thinking deeply about all sorts of questions. The medics wondered whether his poor sleep patterns were contributing to psychological disturbances in Chris, so they set up further brain tests to observe what happened to him.

He had undergone more M.R.I. scans and an E.E.G., for which he had endured many electrodes being placed all over his head. Then he went back to the ward with his mum and dad to await the results.

Krefeld was poring over an 'iPad' with colleagues; he was scratching his goatee beard with a rather puzzled expression on his face. Eventually he came over to Chris' bed;

'Hi Chris, how are you doing? We've got some test results back which I'd like to tell you and your parents about.'

Joe and Donna glanced nervously at each other, but Chris encouraged him to continue.

'Your brain scans again showed some unusual magnetic activity. The brain wave patterns from your E.E.G. showed a particularly regular and unusually slow level of activity, with predominantly 'alpha' and 'delta' waves from the lower frequency end of neuron electrical wave activity.'

The family stared blankly at him. Krefeld explained;

'I would usually associate this pattern with a particularly relaxed state of mind which most of us know as meditation.'

They nodded, registering some comprehension.

'We also spotted occasional spikes in the gamma region. Gamma brain waves are sometimes produced during times when the brain is processing information at a high level, or experiencing bursts of precognition and higher states of consciousness. During this state the waves pulsed coherently over the brain at a frequency of about 40 cycles per second.'

'What does that mean?' Joe and Donna had held each other's hands in concern.

'I'm sorry, but I don't know. It might mean that Chris' brain is functioning in such a way that he can achieve different states of consciousness, which might be something to do with why he is having these unusual experiences.'

They watched as their distinctively unrelaxed boy was placed under the influence of more sedatives to help him sleep.

As Chris succumbed to the medications, he watched his parents with a widening grin on his face, pleased to see them so close. He hadn't seen them like that for a long time. Chris gazed out of the window and saw that the Moon had risen in the sky, with a small chunk of it disappearing to shadow as it had entered its waning gibbous moon phase. He sighed, as relaxed as he had ever been in this hospital, and he fell into a deep sleep, with his parents watching protectively over him.

38

KATHY MEETS KEVIN TO SPILL THE BEANS

Nurse Kathy had finished her shift and was tottering on scarlet stiletto stilts out of the hospital to catch a taxi. Jumping to the front of the queue, she hailed the next approaching car and punched out her instructions impatiently to the driver.

'Put your foot down!' she yelled, as they were pulling away far too sedately for her agenda. She didn't want to miss her meeting, her free champagne and her pay-off.

She had butterflies in her stomach as they tore through the streets, a tell-tale sign of her certain guilt. She knew she would get into big trouble if anyone found out it was her that had spilled the beans to the reporter, but the frisson of excitement she felt at the thought of her misdemeanor was more than enough to help her push her guilt to the back of her mind. She pulled out a compact from her Leopard print handbag and checked the scarlet lipstick on her large lips.

The taxi pulled up, and she threw some dollars at the driver as she exploded out of the car. Running into Smyth's, she tripped over the door step in her blind haste. Flustered she picked herself up off the floor, pushing the misplaced blond curls back out of her blue eyes, and searched desperately round the dimly lit room for her companion.

The little tables were occupied by a variety of couples engaged deeply in conversation, which created a low murmur of sound. The room was draped in twinkling fairy lights, creating a glow by which she could scan the faces sat at the tables. She finally spotted the curly-haired reporter seated in a dusky corner; she waved gregariously at him.

He smiled slightly awkwardly and watched the fairly diminutive blonde totter towards him. She was wearing a very tight 'bling-wear' dress covered in diamanté – perhaps not the best choice for a woman with her bulky figure. She was draped in thick, flashy jewellery, and wore 'bling-rings' on her sausage-like fingers. The latter were also adorned with patriotically decorated and impractically long false nails. The whole package screamed 'look at me!' It was indeed difficult not to.

'Do take a seat' offered Kevin, charmingly, standing and kissing her hand again in greeting.

'Can I get my champagne now – I'm gasping!' sputtered Kathy, plunking herself down into the chair. Unperturbed by the forward request, Kevin nodded.

'Sure, I'll order for you,' Kevin turned to a waiter and clicked his fingers. The waiter hurried over and he directed the waiter to fetch two glasses of his best sparkling champagne.

Equally as keen to get what he wanted, Kevin complimented Kathy on her eye-catching outfit, which in truth was a little too gregarious for his tastes however she had obviously made an effort with her appearance.

They chatted awkwardly for a minute until the champagne arrived. Kathy nervously grabbed her glass and drained it faster than Kevin could blink. It proved to be just the lubricant necessary to ease out her story.

Bright Moon

Kevin listened carefully, noting her sceptical references to bacteria and their sounds with some incredulity, but she had done her snooping well, so he gave her what she wanted.

39

BAINES RECALLS HIS BIZARRE CONSULTATION

Edward Baines – the ocular specialist – had, from a very early age, been incredibly passionate about eyes. In his teens it seemed a natural progression for him to focus more on the study of eyes, leading him to become an eye surgeon.

He couldn't leave his glasses, even for a moment; sometimes he even forgot to take them off in bed. His exotic, beautiful wife Meschall had given up reminding him and chastising him about it. She was long suffering; as soon as he entered the house, rather than asking about how his wife or his twin children were, he would embark on another eye-related story. Sometimes she found it funny, but most of the time his wife would shut her ears, close her almond-shaped eyes and shout 'Will you stop it!'

After his encounter with Chris, Baines came home laughing, baring his exceptionally white teeth, as though he was challenging dentists with their brightness. A stickler for eating plenty of raw fruits and vegetables, his enamel was clearly naturally enhanced. (This was evidently not a genetic inheritance from his father, who had appalling teeth.)

His beautiful bubbly daughter enjoyed hearing people laugh; she bounded into the room, long raven-black hair flowing behind her, to ask him what he was laughing about and to see if she could share in the joke.

She had all the patience in the world, unlike her mother; she listened intently to him, her large brown eyes gazing intently at her father.

Without disclosing the identity of the patient or any details of his condition, he couldn't resist sharing with his teen daughter the bizarre nature of his recent consultation with Chris. Edward explained that he had asked a patient that day to close his eyes, but that the patient had closed them with his palms. When he had asked the boy to open them again, he had taken his palms off but had still kept his eyes closed.

His daughter had giggled with him, bronzed face turned upwards to her dad, curling round his feet like a cat as he sat on the sofa. He continued his story, pleased to have an avid audience in his daughter;

'I said to the patient – not without a certain authority – "could you please open your eyes?" Then my patient said, "I can't see," so I said to the patient; "You won't if you don't open your eyes!"'

'Then my patient said "I opened them when I came in, but then you asked me to close them."'

'I tell you, it was all I could do not to laugh out loud! Then when I wanted to pour some drops into his eyes, he resisted with all his might as though it was a judo competition. It was so funny!'

He had laughed for a long time with his daughter, his humongous head rolling and his enormous glasses slipping off his nose. His daughter was delighted whenever he spent time speaking to her, even if it was only about work. She would hang on his every word, keen to encourage his attention.

He often came home thinking about the families of his patients. He would compare them with his, especially how some husbands seemed to have compassionate and empathetic wives, yet Edwards's wife Meschall was so bored with him and his stories and made no bones about telling him. She spent a lot of time out with her friends venting her frustration. She found that he had very high expectations of her and the rest of the family, yet he gave little back.

He was hardly ever affectionate towards them; he only spent time with them on his terms, when he felt inclined to, but he would lose interest in his family quickly, preferring to bury his nose back in another book.

Though he had found nothing abnormal in his examination of Chris, his interest in the boy's situation had piqued – not least because of his fascination with extra acute vision capacity of the eye.

He decided to do some reading and research around some evolutionary ideas ticking over in his head. His daughter sighed, watching him reach for a book. She knew that was all the interaction she would get for tonight with her dad.

40

Medics discharge Chris

After an uncomfortable night sleeping in chairs by their son's bedside, Joe and Donna were keen to hear good news from the doctors that morning about his state of health. Indeed Chris awoke with a much-reduced level of noise in his ears and the visions had again dissipated.

After various test results had been discussed amongst the puzzled medics, they had to admit that this was no classical case. Barnes was still suspecting some form of psychosis, despite the test results indicating otherwise.

The symptom pattern combined with the test results followed nothing listed in the I.C.D. – the 'International Classification of Diseases', so the medics were unable to provide any diagnosis once again.

The puzzled medics had to admit they could find no logical reason for Chris' ability to hear what appeared to be the sounds of bacteria and other germs, and to be able to see them with his naked eye.

He was given a final examination by the doctors. Then, with a clean bill of health, he was given the all-clear to head home, with the proviso that the family stayed in close contact with the medics, reporting in regularly about Chris' state of health.

41

KEVIN'S SECOND STORY GOES PUBLIC

As Joe and Donna arrived home with Chris, they were greeted by a herd of reporters with microphones and camera crews. One reporter thrust a newspaper in Donna's hands and a camera in her face as she stepped out of the car onto the front lawn, saying;

'Your son is big news again, ma'am; this time we understand that it's not aliens, it's bacteria that your son can see.'

Donna stopped in her tracks, flummoxed by the ambush. She stared in horror at the latest sensational headlines about Chris, splashed all over the paper she was clutching. Feeling under duress, Donna climbed back into the car, turning to Joe for guidance.

Joe scanned the ridiculous story and, stepping purposefully out of the car, he took the limelight, comfortably breathing himself into a relaxed and centred space from which to answer the reporter's questions. He concluded that it was better to give them the truth than to be at the mercy of some over-imaginative writer who was out to exploit Chris' difficulties.

Chris hid his face, hunching down as small and inconspicuously as possible, whilst Joe fielded the questions with confidence and purpose.

Chris listened to his father's deep voice emanating from outside the car;

'My son Chris seems to be experiencing a temporary ability to see things on a microscopic scale. He seems to be able to see what appear to be micro-organisms. He also seems to be able to detect their sounds.'

The reporters went into a mad frenzy of questions, but Joe put up his hand for quiet, and continued;

'The doctors are working hard to understand what is causing Chris' experiences, but we have no answers as yet. If there is anyone out there who has had any similar experiences or thinks they have any information that would help us to understand what is happening to Chris, please contact me via the news channel.'

The reporters burst into another loud competition for questioning; but again Joe raised his hand;

'There is a reporter out there called Kevin Masters who has written two sensationalized and somewhat ridiculous stories about my boy. Please, Mr. Masters, I ask you to come forward and speak to us directly for a more accurate version of events rather than broadcasting made-up nonsense that makes Chris sound like some deranged lunatic.'

The news crews lapped up his words and graciously thanked Joe for his explanations, repeating his plea for help down their cameras to the viewers.

As they wrapped up and departed, Donna and Chris crept back out of the car and gave Joe a hug.

'Thank you so much Joe, I couldn't have done it without you,' she smiled warmly.

'You were awesome, Dad!'

Joe grinned – it was good to be back in the warmth of their good wishes again. They hastily ran into the house before any more visitors could ambush them.

42

FALL-OUT FROM NEWS REPORT

The news reports had bounced around the neighbourhood, and the family had received a mixed response – some people had been horrible, taunting Chris with accusations of mental instability, whilst others had heralded the news with optimism and support, offering empathetic but mostly unhelpful stories of distant relatives who could see a whole plethora of bizarre visions.

Kevin had seen Joe's challenge on the news and, never one to miss an opportunity, he took up Joe's offer to meet up and discuss Chris' experiences to help him get a more balanced view on the story. Sceptical as Kevin was, he went with a negative attitude, thinking that he would be facing a fight, that whatever Joe would have to say would be irrational and potentially add more fuel to his sensational fire, but Kevin was not prepared for Joe's gracious but determined intention to have the record set straight.

Joe invited Kevin to his store and right from first contact, he put Kevin at ease with his respectful and honourable charm, his evident good wishes towards Kevin surprising the usually suspicious man.

Joe talked him round to seeing the humanity in Chris' situation, helping him to accept that although he may not believe everything that Chris was claiming to see and to hear, the experiences for Chris were very real. He suggested that Kevin opened his mind to the idea that Chris may be telling the truth. This would throw a different light on his story-telling perspective.

Joe was able to persuade Kevin that he would get much more benefit from telling the truth of the story in a compassionate way. He was sure that people would respond better to a more humane style; a more fact-driven style. His icing on the cake was an offer to exclusive rights on Chris' story if Kevin was able to deliver true researched facts about Chris' experiences from a more supportive perspective.

Kevin was slightly taken aback, thinning his eyes in suspicion but weighing his options; he surprised himself by choosing the offer of exclusivity. It would herald a whole new way of working for Kevin, who was more used to underhand sneaking around, but he had to admit that he really liked this family, plus the story had certainly caught his interest.

At the risk of losing out he shook hands with Joe, accepting his generous offer. The men parted company with smiles, planting the seed for a new friendship.

43

Alternative therapy

Donna tried to shield Chris from the media attention as much as she could, and she was keen to help him get back to some sort of normality as quickly as possible, so she was somewhat distressed that Kevin had been asked to interview Chris. Joe fought his corner, explaining his decision to contact the reporter;

'I know you don't understand what I see in him, Donna, but listen – *goodness is not merely in the mind of the perceiver; it is really in the heart of everyone.* I think he just needs an opportunity to work with us so he can see how much Chris has to offer; it may prove to be advantageous to us in the end.'

Donna grudgingly agreed to try, so at the risk of Kevin going back to his disruptive story-telling, they somehow developed a working relationship which allowed Kevin to spend time with Chris.

Chris imparted his version of events to Kevin soulfully but factually. Kevin was pleasantly surprised by the boy's extensive knowledge. Confused as he was about Chris' experiences, his curiosity helped him to quell his rationalism and scepticism sufficiently to gather the facts in a neutral, impartial manner.

Unsure what the future held for Chris, Kevin respectfully backed off after he'd collected enough material, not wishing to upset Joe whom he found to be a most influential and respectable character.

Following his release of a written apology to Chris and his parents, Kevin published a more compassionate version of events, requesting help from readers to support Chris and his family. Having finally gained the family's trust, they promised to contact Kevin first should any further developments arise with Chris.

As soon as Chris felt he had recovered sufficiently, he was eased back into school and Donna was free to get back to work amidst much attention from her colleagues.

All the media hype put Donna on edge however, so at the first opportunity, she had invited Joe round for coffee and a chat about Chris. Joe jumped at the chance and came bounding round like a puppy.

'I'm still really worried about Chris,' she confided, absent-mindedly stirring her Cappuccino for the umpteenth time.

'It's not that I'm ungrateful for the help we've had from the hospital, it's just that we never got to the bottom of why he's had these strange experiences. What if it happens again? How am I going to manage it, especially if it keeps on happening? I can't deal with it Joe, I don't like our little boy being so abnormal. Why can't they find out what's wrong with him?' She started to weep, the tears streaming in little rivulets over her pale cheeks, creating slight imperfections in her otherwise perfect make-up.

Joe leaned over and wiped them away, taking hold of her manicured hand.

'Listen, Donna, I'm here for you. I'm sure it's all happening for a very good reason, and it's all going to work out in the end. Have you considered that what's happened might be a blessing in disguise?'

His grey-silver eyes looked encouragingly into Donna's. Joe had spent many a sunrise in contemplation on this matter. His meditations had led him to the inkling that Chris' experiences were part of his life's journey and carried more spiritual weight than anyone was aware of, but he suspected it was more than his life was worth to mention any spiritual meditation to Donna – she would likely chew his ear off!

'Goodness, no Joe! How can you say that? Poor Chris, how many other little boys have had to go through this sort of experience? No, I wouldn't wish this upon anyone. I have to find another way to help him.' Joe flinched from her rebuke, but as she was already riled, he took his life in his hands and decided to reveal more of what was on his mind.

'Well I'm inclined to think that no matter what we manage to explain or establish through scientific means, there is more to this than meets the eye. I truly believe that the fulfilment of our life potential is possible only through spiritual experience. I think this is somehow what is happening to Chris,' said Joe, cautiously.

'Who knows, but I do think it's time I look elsewhere for help. Let's see if we can find someone who knows a different way of treating this kind of thing.' She seemed determined in her decision that Chris' experiences were something to be battled to the end.

Joe sighed, recognizing that she was not going to give up on this idea for anyone, and thankful that he still had his ear.

'Can we consider some form of alternative therapy then,

Donna?' suggested Joe tentatively; he was greatly involved

in this field, but well aware of Donna's disdain for their practices. To his surprise, she nodded her consent.

'Well I'm pretty desperate at the moment. Much as I don't rate what those guys do, I have to admit that the conventional methods have not given us any answers. Who would you recommend?' she asked kindly to Joe, squeezing his hand as if acknowledging that they were moving into his field of expertise; she was gracefully allowing him to contribute.

Joe was flattered and delighted.

'Perhaps we could start with hypnotism to see if Chris can reveal any answers himself and we can take it from there. If it turns out to be something that is manifesting from his own psyche, if there is some sort of underlying emotional trauma issue that needs addressing, I can recommend Emotional Freedom Technique, which might help him to release whatever negative emotion he is hanging on to. Maybe we could try some acupuncture too – that might help to release any blockages in his energy systems that are causing imbalance.'

Donna nodded her consent, somewhat confused by all these ideas, but prepared to try.

'Alright then, I will make some appointments with the therapist guys who work at the store – they're all really good healers; we'll see what transpires.'

Donna leaned forward and kissed Joe gently on his bronzed cheek, grateful for his input and support.

Joe touched his face in delighted surprise. He was equally surprised by his instantly tender reaction; he returned an affectionate kiss full on her perfect lips with a big chuckle.

Though enchanted by his kiss and his infectious giggle,

she playfully threw a spoon at him.

'Watch it, you! Don't push it!' she laughed.

Joe gathered his things and left to sort out the appointments, turning to blow one more kiss at Donna on his way out. She playfully caught it in her hand and blew one back, just like Holly used to.

He caught his breath, but he realized that things with Donna were moving on, and he wasn't putting up any resistance. He sensed a stronger connection forming between them, a more heartfelt and truthful communication, with less judgment and criticism. He knew that love must contain heartfelt emotions and mind-full awareness; then that love can bring forth peace, health and progress – Joe's hopes were raised, Donna was giving him a chance.

44

CHRIS MEETS THE ALTERNATIVE THERAPISTS

Chris entered the therapy room hand in hand with his mum and dad. It was small but neat, with few adornments and a rather clinical feel to it. In the corner of the room, an oil burner dispensed aromatic scents around the tiny space. The hypnotist asked Chris to lie back on the couch and close his eyes. He began by counting backwards from ten to one, asking Chris to relax with each count; Chris complied, keen to find out more about his experiences.

Under the expert guidance of the hypnotist, Chris fell into a calm reverie. He was able to imagine himself floating through a moonlit sky under a blanket of stars, on a cloud of starlight and sparkling stellar dust.

The hypnotist gently questioned him as Chris explored his cosmic environment, describing what he saw. After some considerable time in the trance, Chris was brought back to the reality of the neat therapy room, slowly counting up to ten, until he opened his sleepy relaxed eyes and smiled happily at the white-coated therapist and his parents.

'Well, what did you find out?' Chris asked the therapist curiously.

'I can't find that there is anything in particular that is wrong. You seem to be a very happy, well-rounded little boy with an extremely curious nature and a thirst for knowledge. You talked me through a very beautiful scene which made us all feel quite relaxed as a matter of fact. We found nothing sinister there, although you did mention you could hear some voices that you didn't understand. You also explained a great deal about micro-organisms that you could see and how they behave.'

The hypnotist turned to Chris' parents and shrugged his shoulders, in a rather stumped fashion.

'I'm not sure I can see anything here that needs to be treated, as he seems to be very adapted to this idea that he can see micro-organisms. In fact it's almost as if he has integrated them into his psyche. I'm not sure that it is actually doing him any harm, so I would suggest that you're better off leaving the idea there for fear of – as it were – upsetting the apple cart.'

'What do you mean?' asked Donna, a little annoyed. 'Why can't you just put him back under and tell him to stop all this nonsense so he doesn't go through this again?'

'Well, ma'am, I'm not sure that would be in his best interest. There are times when certain ideas have become firmly integrated into someone's psyche and personality such that were you to try to remove them, they might cause a great deal of psychological damage. I would rather not put your boy through that so I recommend that you don't put him at risk with that approach.' He crossed his arms, striking an immoveable pose to reflect the fact that his opinion was not to be swayed.

They left, with Donna muttering angrily to herself that it had all been a waste of time.

Joe tried to soothe her annoyance, passing her a calming chamomile tea. She accepted gracefully and sat sipping as

Joe went around the store and the therapy rooms with a spray bottle of flower essences.

'Hmmm, that smells lovely, Joe!' gushed Donna. 'What is it?'

'It's a Space Clearing Spray – it helps to clear out old energies that might be hanging around.'

She smiled sweetly at Joe; Chris grinned from ear to ear.

'Can I have some of that for home?' Chris joked. Joe tousled Chris' curly golden locks and threw him the bottle.

'That one is on the house!' he laughed. 'You need all the help you can get, living with Ms. Grouchy here!'

Donna threw a mock annoyed look in Joe's direction then burst out laughing – her tinkling laughs were music to their ears. It had been a very long time since they had shared laughter together; it felt really good, as if it was clearing the air between them, raising their energies as well as their spirits.

As they joshed with each other, the acupuncturist came breezing into the store.

'Hi Joe, how are ya, my mystical buddy?' she grinned. She threw a poster down on the table. Donna observed Betsy warily. Tall and slender, with greying hair in a bob cut, Betsy wore half-moon glasses which she peered over to observe others, or they hung on a chain around her neck. The glasses made her appear a little austere to Donna, though with her close acquaintances she was warm-hearted and approachable.

In Donna's experience, Betsy was often forthright with her comments, especially if she disagreed with her. Betsy's blue-green eyes could pierce right through you like her acupuncture needles, as if she could intuitively read you like a book. She had long fingers which appeared deft and delicate enough to handle the hair-thin acupuncture needles carefully and sensitively. She wore a tight tailored jacket, tweed skirt and flat pumps, giving her an overall professional look. Joe's face lit up – he and Betsy were good friends.

'Hi Betsy, it's good to see you! What's that you've got?' asked Joe, pointing to the poster.

'It's a poster about tonight's talk in City Hall. Would you mind putting it up in the window?' she asked. 'You know we have regular speakers on a Friday night to talk about spiritual matters, well this one's gonna be a real eye-opener.' Betsy raised her eyebrows conspiratorially over her half-moon glasses. 'You may have seen him on T.V., or heard him on the radio? He's a modern-day yogi and he can blow your mind – why don't you come along? He's right up your alley.' She paused as she spotted Donna sitting rather awkwardly in the corner hugging a cup to her-self.

'Oh, hi there Donna,' she said casually. 'Long time no see. How's it going?' Betsy well remembered how badly Donna had treated Joe and his friends. She was rather taken aback to see her here with him again, aware of their rather acrimonious divorce.

'Hello, Betsy,' managed Donna, weakly.

'What brings you here then?' asked Betsy mischievously.

'Um, well I'm here with Chris, he's had a session with the hypnotist as he's not been very well recently,' she muttered, embarrassed.

'Oh I see, you've turned to the Dark Side have you?' she joked, loving every minute of this moment of victory.

Joe stepped in to defend Donna. 'It was my idea,' he explained. 'As it happens I don't think it's been much help today, but I was wondering if we could book a session with you too?' he queried.

'Why sure you can, Joe! I'd do anything for you and little Chris here'. She peered over her glasses appreciatively at Chris, who smiled back. 'I'm free now if you are?'

Chris knew Betsy from his occasional trips to his dad's store. He liked her very much. He nodded, as did Donna, rather reluctantly, who asked to stay outside for this one, excusing herself with a fictional needle aversion.

Betsy and Joe went off to perform the treatment for Chris, whilst Donna was left alone in the store. She picked up the poster that Betsy had left on the table and idly read it.

It seemed to be some kind of spiritual talk, which usually Donna would avoid like the plague, but something inside her registered an interest in the speaker. She felt drawn to the idea of meeting him. Perhaps he was the sort of person who might have some different answers about Chris' predicament. She certainly felt like a different approach was needed, as she was still very much in the dark about the whole thing. She made up her mind to try to go, but she felt strangely nervous about it. This was new territory to her; she felt like she was not confident about going alone. She decided she would ask Joe to accompany her. She would need a babysitter for Chris – he was nearly old enough to be left alone but with all this strange stuff happening to him, she thought it would be safer to have him watched.

Before long, Chris emerged from the treatment room smiling cheerfully. He seemed very relaxed and was chatting easily with Joe and Betsy. Chris spotted his mum and came over to give her a big hug. Her heart swelled with joy – he hadn't done that for a very long time!

'Oh Chris, you seem happier! Thank you, Betsy. How did it go?' she asked shyly.

'Well we tried a general energy balancing treatment then I worked on his ear and eye meridians to see if that would make any difference. Keep an eye on him and see if you notice any changes. He is welcome to come again any time you like.'

She removed her half-moon glasses and smiled at Donna encouragingly; Donna felt relief. She plucked up the courage to ask about this evening's talk.

'Sure, you can come along if you like!' said Betsy, somewhat surprised, but pleased. 'Why don't you come together?' she grinned at Joe, aware that the energies between the divorced pair seemed to be mixing more healthily these days. 'It's free of charge. I hope we see you later – I can introduce you to a few more people, Donna.'

Betsy breezed out of the store. Donna felt a great sense of relief that things were flowing so well between her and Betsy after their history of rather awkward conversations, and decided that she wasn't so bad after all. She wondered what she'd made such a fuss about, unaware that when we interact with others, sometimes much of their behaviour, attitude and response towards us are due to our own influence on them. The world and its people may not change as you desire, but you can change yourself.

'So whaddya say?' Donna grinned at Joe. 'Do you want to go?'

Joe was slightly confused by these sudden changes of heart he was experiencing in Donna, but he definitely liked what he saw.

'Donna, I would be delighted to escort you tonight.' He grinned, handsomely, then added rather cheekily, 'so is this a date then?'

Donna stared shyly at her neat feet, then up into his grey-silver eyes. 'Sure,' she nodded, blushing.

'We'll need to find someone to sit with Chris though – I daren't leave him alone at the moment.' Donna anxiously twiddled her long golden hair.

'I can ask my mother if you like?' suggested Joe cautiously – aware that Donna's relationship with Christina was far from amicable at the moment. 'She'd love to see him – it's been a long time,' he added persuasively.

Donna hesitated, but Chris had overheard and interrupted;

'Please, Mum, I really miss Grandma Larkin! Please ask her, I really want to see her!'

Chris' silvery eyes were piercingly imploring; Donna struggled to say no to his 'puppy-dog eyes' look.

'Well, alright then, I guess that would be fine. You can call her, Joe.'

Joe grinned impishly and Chris bounced around the room ecstatically, curly blond locks flapping around his face.

Joe and Donna continued to gaze happily at each other, lost in their own little world of mutual appreciation. Chris grinned to himself. This was great! Suddenly he felt a little awkward in their presence; he quietly slipped to the book shelf and sat down to read out of the way, while his parents mooned over each other.

45

DONNA LETS CHRISTINA IN

Christina was shocked to receive a phone-call from Joe. She'd kept up to date with Chris' welfare via Joe's regular calls, but she was far from expecting an invite back to the family home.

Anxiously she gathered her things together, but she reasoned to herself that Donna must have had a change of heart during all this upset with Chris, so she allowed herself to feel the tingling sensation of excitement that heralded her reunion with her beloved grandson.

Joe came to pick her up, and they travelled in a wave of excitement to Donna's. On arrival, Christina gingerly pressed the bell, trying to contain her rising exhilaration. Her arms were bursting with goodies – peace offerings for Donna and indulgent reunion gifts for Chris.

Donna opened the door and smiled coyly at Christina – her mixed feelings plastered all over her face. Donna however had decided that her poor son's suffering should put her own misgivings firmly into perspective. From the outset, she was determined to be nothing but pleasant and welcoming towards her mother-in-law.

Her positive outlook was rewarded with a surprisingly big hug from the septuagenarian, who was delighted to be stepping back over the family threshold. Chris bounded towards his grandmother and they embraced warmly and lingeringly, as if making up for lost time.

Donna was startled by the warm glow that emanated from her heart as she observed the moving reunion. She felt a sudden pang of guilt for the deprivation of family time that she knew Chris rightfully should have had.

These new sensations revealed a more compassionate view that had sparked a light in Donna's heart, like a tiny flickering and vulnerable flame. She vowed to try harder to bring the whole family back together, accepting for the first time the part she played in the sorry breakdown of their family's relationships.

After much excited chatter and busy checking of what Christina might need during her stay, Joe and Donna confidently left the house, arm in arm, thrilled at spending an evening alone together and anticipating a thought-provoking evening.

46

YOGI GIVES A TALK AT CITY HALL

Donna and Joe arrived at the magnificent City Hall, locating the meeting room within five minutes of the start of the talk. They entered the small cosy side room which held a smattering of different people from various walks of life. There was a buzz of expectation in the air, a sense of hopeful excitement and eager anticipation.

They picked their way through the rows of plush chairs, finding a pair of seats together, somewhere near the exit, just in case Donna felt too uncomfortable and decided she wanted to leave. The room was gently lit with glowing side lamps that splayed their golden light across the ceiling, and there was a comforting aroma of exotic essential oils floating in the air. They spotted Betsy near the front, ushering people to seats and setting up a microphone. She saw them through her half-moon glasses and waved cheerily.

They settled themselves down in their chairs and a gentle hush descended on the room as the yogi entered, his presence filling the space. The crowd respectfully stood, as the yogi walked up to the stage. He stood silently before the audience for a minute or two, with his eyes closed, feeling the vibrations of the people in the room and sensing everyone's mixed expectations. When he opened his liquid brown eyes, he searched the room until his eyes met with Donna's. Their gazes locked for a moment and Donna felt as if he somehow recognized her, as he nodded and smiled in her direction.

He motioned for everyone to sit down. He guided everyone in a brief group meditation, to help everyone connect with each other's consciousness. Donna glanced warily at Joe, raising a sceptical eyebrow, but he smiled at her encouragingly, whispering that she had come this far and it wouldn't hurt her to try.

As if sensing Donna's feelings of anxiety, the yogi looked over at Donna and encouraged her to take some deep breaths, explaining that they were purely relaxing, learning to just be with each other, with no judgment or expectations of any kind.

Donna closed her eyes and heard the stippled breathing of the audience around her come into a regular, deeper and more synchronized pattern with each other. She suddenly felt very tired, as if the last few months of worry had all suddenly gotten on top of her. She was concerned that she might fall asleep by mistake, so she kept pinching herself. Then as her breathing slowed, she felt more at ease. She was able to feel a deeper sense of calm and her vitality rose.

When the yogi slowly encouraged them to open their eyes, Donna was almost reluctant to, but she did so and turned to smile at Joe, who squeezed her hand.

The yogi began his talk with a general discussion about life and its synchronicities, urging the audience to remember incidences in their lives when they had found an event happening that could have been a coincidence, yet somehow seemed much more significant, as if it was meant to happen.

Donna pricked up her ears, thinking of the way she had found the poster about tonight's talk and the deeper feelings that had stirred in her heart that made her sense the significance of the event. She wondered at the processes that had taken place in her to do such a thing, as it was so out of character, yet it felt so right for her to follow the internal signs to come along.

The yogi went on to discuss the inter-relation between all people, the way that sitting together quietly, meditating if you like, could bring people's thoughts, awareness, consciousness into some sort of alignment with each other's. That sense of connection that people then felt lay in this shared consciousness that underlay the Nature of all living entities – not just here on Earth, but also out in space, throughout the cosmic world.

His words drifted through Donna's mind in a surprising way – she thought that her reasoning mind should reject all that this unusual but charming man was saying – and yet they somehow made sense to her today. She was beginning to understand what he meant, and – to her surprise – found herself nodding sagely to his words along with the other enrapt members of the audience.

Joe turned to smile at her, thoroughly glowing with joy that Donna was sharing such an experience with him.

Donna smiled back, her deep blue eyes bright with wonder and renewed hope. She felt a certain uplifting in her mental attitude too, which made a very pleasant change to her usual feelings of anxiety and annoyance.

The yogi continued, brown eyes twinkling;

'We are all inter-related with each other and also with the planets and the outer environment. Each element and each entity has some connection with us, having a tremendous influence on us. However this effect does not only occur one-way. We also sometimes can have an influence on other entities, provided that we become intuitively and subconsciously aware of this fact. Rarely, there can even be instances where – by virtue of some past life influences combined with perfect coincidence and synchronicity – our consciousness can actually make a huge leap, unfolding certain superhuman abilities in our bodies, such as microscopic vision, or a very high degree of sensitivity to other life beings, such as trees and plants and micro-beings.'

Donna jumped, startled by his words. The yogi looked over at Donna and gazed openly towards her with his liquid brown eyes. She felt like a deep chasm of space had opened in front of her, almost as if she was stepping off a cliff into the chasms of the Grand Canyon. She felt like she was floating, suspended in space, with a great sense of dizziness overwhelming her. Those words – did she really hear him say that? It shocked her and yet she felt sure that he had known the questions of her heart and had brought them out of her consciousness, and had delivered the answer without her even saying a word.

She was shaking – this was such a bizarre experience. She turned to Joe to see if he had heard it too, but he just smiled at her. She decided that she needed to find out more from this man, so she sat forward, listening carefully to the rest of his words. As he drew the talk to a close, Donna felt like she was riding on a wave of hopefulness and renewed strength. The atmosphere was electric and she felt the general sense of euphoria that was shared between all the people present. There was a ripple of applause as the yogi left the stage, bowing his thanks to the appreciative audience.

As they sat quietly soaking up the words and basking in the beautiful lilting music being played in the background, Donna decided she needed to converse directly with the yogi.

'Joe, do you think I could meet him? I'm sure he knows something that might help us understand what's happening to Chris.'

'Sure, why don't we ask Betsy to introduce us?' he replied encouragingly.

They made their way over to the stage where Betsy was packing away equipment, her spectacles swinging wildly on the end of their chain. Spotting the approaching couple, she grasped the swinging chain of her glasses, and straightened her tweed jacket.

'Hello you two!' she said with a friendly smile, helping them feel at ease to ask their next question.

'Hi Betsy, that was really amazing. Isn't he wonderful? I so enjoyed his talk,' enthused Donna.

'I told you it would be awesome, didn't I? I'm really glad you were able to join us tonight.'

'Betsy, do you think I could see him for a moment? I'd like to ask him a few questions.' Betsy raised her eyebrows in surprise, replacing her half-moon spectacles to take a closer look at Donna as if she couldn't believe what she was hearing. Observing Donna's resolved expression, Betsy nodded in acceptance, her grey bob swishing around her face.

'I'm sure that would be just fine, Donna. Follow me and I'll introduce you.'

They respectfully approached the yogi who was sat in a smaller candle-lit side room. He turned to greet them with a friendly smile and handshake. Donna thought he seemed ageless, with a classically noble face. His dark shining hair was carefully and neatly styled back over his head. He wore smart clothes that gave him a most professional air. Betsy told him their names and explained that Donna would like to see him for a moment. He nodded and they made their way to a quiet corner by the window. As she felt the breeze playing gently through the open window on her flushed face, Donna began to explain to him what had been happening to Chris and how upset she was about his strange symptoms. She reminded the yogi of his words concerning micro-beings and super-sensitivity. She asked whether he thought that this might be what was happening to her son.

The yogi sat in contemplation, gazing deep into the starry sky through the wide open window, feeling the breath of the breeze gently touch his skin. Then he closed his eyes for a moment, as if to hear some internal message. Then taking a deep breath, he leaned forward to whisper something in Donna's ear.

Donna's bright blue eyes widened and they seemed to reflect a certain sense of clarity. She smiled a faint yet hopeful smile as she met Joe's searching gaze.

47

Donna and Joe take a romantic walk

Joe and Donna strolled hand in hand through the verdant park, listening to the gentle rustling of the leaves in the trees and enjoying the warmth of the balmy summer's evening as they slowly sauntered their way to Donna's from City Hall. They could hear the melodic chatter of birds coming to roost in the treetops. The distant sounds of busy city life were far enough away for them to feel like they were in some quiet countryside scene.

'So how do you feel now Donna?' asked Joe, happily.

'I feel much more positive now; it's all thanks to you!' she gushed, squeezing Joe's large warm hand appreciatively.

Joe grinned sheepishly, smoothing his other hand through his brown hair.

'Listen, Joe, I know things have been pretty tough between us over the last few years, but I really feel like all this business with Chris has helped me to see what's important in my life. I've really begun to appreciate the importance of family and sticking together. I can see how much Chris means to you. You've been so kind and so helpful with all this business. You've really shown me how much you care about both of us.'

Joe felt a little tingle of excitement growing from within and wondered what was coming. Donna's gratitude seemed to be melting away her bristly attitude, revealing her heart's truth. Joe knew that gratitude was one of a few noble qualities that can bring inner peace, joy and appreciation to life, helping to create a close connection to the heart.

'I've been thinking, Joe. It's clear that Chris has been really missing you and his grandma. It really hasn't done him any good not seeing you both. He's so much happier when you're around. I was wondering, what do you think about staying at our house again just to see how things go, at least until we get Chris better?' Donna peered shyly up at Joe through her long eyelashes, like she used to when they first got together, as if layers of built-up hardness and veneer had been removed.

Finally, in her vulnerability, Joe could see her true nature shining through. With this natural demeanour it was as if she had become everything that belonged to Nature; her honest beauty had been revealed. His heart stirred, recognizing a deep love for Donna welling up inside.

'Wow, Donna, I don't know what to say. Are you sure about this?' asked Joe, somewhat surprised by her sudden change of heart. He couldn't help but remember all the acrimonious arguments, but he couldn't deny that Donna seemed quite different with him these days. It was as if she was somehow blossoming and opening up to him again. *There's nothing like a little forgiveness, appreciation and gratitude to help a relationship get back on track*, he pondered. Who would have thought it?

'Why don't we just try it for a little while?' asked Donna, sensing his hesitation. 'We can always lay down some ground rules about domestic routines – we don't need to be rich to be neat and tidy,' she smiled wryly; 'I could even introduce you to the washing machine and the dishwasher!' she laughed cheekily.

Joe liked this new lighter-hearted banter; he felt hopeful that their relationship stood a chance. Perhaps reconciliation was on the cards.

'Well, I guess I could make their acquaintance for the sake of the greater good!' he joked back.

They reached out to each other and hugged warmly and appreciatively. Life felt good; their united front was a positive intent to support each other through this family crisis, no matter what.

48

CHRIS MEETS A MICROBIOLOGIST

Chris was feeling much better, all his symptoms had dissipated and he was enjoying having his dad around again. His mum was a lot happier and his dad was pitching in with all sorts of things around the house, generally trying to be what is commonly known as a 'new man'.

Joe discretely discussed with Chris some of the experiences he had been having. He advised that Chris needed to spend time in contemplation to see what answers he could uncover. He didn't want to rock the boat with Donna, so it seemed wiser that in these early days of reunion, he should go lightly on the big spiritual and philosophical discussions with Chris. They each did their own research without being too obvious about it, trying to keep their activities under Donna's radar.

Back at school, Chris had been keeping his head down so as to attract as little attention as possible from the other children, but they continued to taunt him whenever they could. Thankfully school vacation was round the corner, so Chris decided to use his time at the last Science Club of the summer semester wisely. He researched on the Internet for more information about the creatures he had seen, following up his hunch that they could be micro-organisms. The more he looked, the more convinced he was that he truly had been witnessing a microscopic world of bacteria and other germs.

Relieved to be back in an accepting environment after receiving a mass of taunts from most of the students at school, he settled into Science Club with considerable relief.

Bumping into Hannah again, bright green eyes and orange hair blazing, she reminded him of her invite to tea, set for that evening – a little celebration for the end of the semester and beginning of summer vacation. Chris shyly accepted, but not before she quizzed him about his latest school absence.

Chris wasn't sure for a moment whether to trust her, as most of the other children just made fun of him, having heard about his other-worldly experiences in the news.

Yet she had always been kind to him; his instincts told him that she had his best interests at heart. Strangely he felt like he was much better able to assess people's intentions these days. It was almost as if he could sense whether someone was building him up or trying to attack him somehow. He observed her guileless, freckled face and her clear but quizzical green eyes. Sensing only friendly curiosity, he decided that she was on his side, and so began to impart some of the experiences he had been having.

Hannah's emerald eyes were round like saucers. She couldn't believe what she was hearing. She asked if he would be prepared to speak to her dad about it. Chris hesitated but agreed. They jumped on the school bus together after Science Club and headed towards her house.

On the way they chatted easily about all things microscopic, barely noticing their surroundings they were so deep in conversation and before long, they reached their destination.

Her father, Dr. Cousins, opened the door as they arrived home. Hannah introduced them both, as Chris peered shyly at the scientist. He was a serious-looking character, with round glasses nestled in his curly ginger hair, which was much more controlled than his daughter's, yet one could see that it had the potential to break out into a massive shock of fire-like tufts were it not frequently tamed by the barber's scissors.

Dressed in a white lab coat, he appeared like someone who spent a lot of time peering down a microscope – which was indeed what he did all day at work, staring at slides of bacteria and other micro-organisms as part of his microbiology research, often continuing his work late into the night at home in his study, which doubled-up as a makeshift lab.

Chris greeted Dr. Cousins respectfully.

'Come on in, don't be shy, take a seat' said Cousins genially, pointing to the black sofa in the spotless lounge. Hannah giggled and plonked herself down next to Chris, grateful for the feel of the cooling leather on her hot legs.

'Does he always wear a lab coat at home?' whispered Chris into Hannah's ear.

'Oh yes! I know it's odd but I'd rather he wore that than the hideous clothes he chooses when he goes out. I just die with embarrassment every time!' she whispered back. Chris stifled a chuckle.

In fact Cousins was rarely seen out of his starched white lab coat, yet if ever his clothes were espy, they were eccentric in nature, to the point of hilarity. Hannah chastised him if ever his bright garish Hawaiian shirts were on show, in case her friends might witness his appalling dress sense. She frequently told him he should grow up and wear something more his age, yet Dr Cousins had never left behind his student mentality, preferring a good night out at a Hawaiian-themed student bar that sold cut-price watered-down beer to a night at a stuffy wine bar any day!

'So Chris, it's nice to meet you at last. I've been hearing a lot about you, young man. Let's take a good look at you shall we?' Dr. Cousins was scanning the room for his glasses.

'Dad, they're on your head again!' Hannah chuckled and turned her freckled face to Chris, shrugging apologetically for her father's absent-mindedness. Chris grinned – he liked this family very much.

'Oh yes, of course!' smiled Cousins. He reached up into the tight curly ginger locks and, un-plucking his glasses from the orange nest, he placed them snugly on his nose. He was unable to see down a microscope whilst wearing his glasses and since he spent most of his time staring down an eyepiece at wiggling microbes mounted on glass slides, he resorted to wearing his glasses on top of his head most of the time.

Consequently he often was heard rooting about looking for his glasses, or asking if anyone knew where they were, forgetting that they were safely placed on his head. Hannah loved to tease him about this, well aware that his head was filled more with science and ideas than practical thoughts of how to take care of his possessions.

'I'm intrigued to hear more about this micro-world you say you can see.' Dr. Cousins peered carefully at Chris through his glasses, as if trying to assess and classify him like one of his samples.

Chris proceeded to explain his recent experience, describing the physicality and behaviour of the small, wriggly creatures that covered every surface he looked at, comparing them to the mines in the ocean used in World War Two to catch submarines.

Dr. Cousins' eyebrows were raised in astonishment. 'Well Chris that must be most surprising for you.'

'To say the least, sir,' nodded Chris.

'I can't say it's easy for me to understand this son, but what you're describing does sound a little like bacteria and viruses, but it doesn't make any sense, because of course they're so minute that we have to use special equipment called scanning electron microscopes to see things on that small a scale. It's just not possible for our eyes to detect something so tiny.'

Cousins was clearly somewhat sceptical, but remained open to discussion.

'I can't explain it, sir, I don't understand it either, but what if it really is what I can see? Can you help me?' pleaded Chris.

'Well I don't know what I can do really,' said Dr. Cousins thoughtfully, peering into Chris' pleading silver eyes.

Goodness me, he thought to himself, *what an unusual colour his eyes are!* After some minutes, he made up his mind how to proceed.

'Perhaps you'd like to see some pictures of micro-organisms to see if you recognize anything?'

'Oh yes please!' chorused Hannah and Chris together. They turned to look at each other and giggled.

'Come with me,' beckoned Hannah's dad, leading them to his study. It was stuffed with scientific equipment. The shelves bowed under the weight of microbiology reference books.

They spent a pleasant couple of hours poring over books, pictures, slides, microscopes and research papers. Cousins was increasingly astounded by the reactions from Chris, as the boy recognized various strains of bacteria from their visuals. Cousins helped him to put a name to them all. When Chris let it slip that he could also hear their sounds, he froze in astonishment.

'I'm sorry? You can actually hear them?' he questioned feverishly, his ginger eyebrows almost squashing into his curly locks in surprise.

'Yes, well I think I heard them during the times I was having the visions, but I didn't really know what they were saying. I could tell that they were communicating, but I couldn't understand it,' said Chris dismissively, scratching his skinny arm.

'Goodness gracious, Chris, this is just breath-taking! I'm writing a paper at the moment on communication systems of bacteria; I had a hunch that it was possible that they could be passing messages to each other, probably by way of viral release, but for them to be making actual sounds is really quite phenomenal. I can't think how they do it either, or how we could possibly measure it – it's a complete conundrum.'

Chris' silver eyes were shining – it felt so good to find someone he could talk to about all this who wasn't completely dismissing his experiences. Hannah was equally spell-bound, and he felt she was proving to be a strong ally and friend. He grinned at her and she grinned back, freckles bunching on her rounded cheeks, each feeding off the other's excitement.

'Well Chris, I think all this needs to be properly investigated. I would love to help you. Perhaps we could speak to your doctors and your parents and see what we can do? Plus I really think it's essential that we find out more about these sounds you can hear and find a way to crack the codes of their communication. Imagine if you really can hear microbes, how incredible it would be for mankind to find out what micro-organisms are saying?'

Chris was spellbound by this man's vision; he had to agree that it was an exciting thought, but for the moment he didn't have a clue how he was going to do it, or even whether he was going to experience the microbe encounter again.

He then had a sudden thought – 'Dr. Cousins, do you know anything about the Moon?'

Cousins appeared confused again.

'It's just that I've always had this fascination with the Moon. I spend a lot of time observing it and – weird as this may seem – both times that I've had this experience of the microbes, it's happened the morning after a Bright Moon.' Chris stopped dead in his question, as Cousins was gazing strangely at him.

'Well son, I've no idea about that. My specialty is microbiology, certainly not astronomy, but you've made me think of someone who might be able to help you. I met him at University; he went into the field of astrobiology. Maybe there's some kind of connection here, but I can't say I have a clue what it might be. I'll call him to see if he has any ideas.'

Chris nodded enthusiastically. They were interrupted by a call from Hannah's mother to join them for dinner.

49

Hannah discovers an interest in the Moon

Chris expressed to Hannah that she and her family had offered the first sign of real empathy and practical help in this whole saga. Hannah had promised to help Chris, offering to research what she could about the Moon. With this in mind, she found herself drawn to seek out the Moon in the night sky after Chris had gone home.

Although she was a big fan of star-gazing, she had to admit that she had not paid too much attention to the Moon before. Secretly she wondered if perhaps she also might gain some sort of insight or special powers from staring at it. The thought filled her with excitement and her green, feline eyes blazed with exhilaration.

She gazed out into the night sky from her bedroom window, seeking the Moon's location. The city sky was flooded with light pollution, so it was tricky to pick out many stars, but the Moon's partial orb was fairly easy to spot through the trees of the park. She stared at it in wide-eyed wonder, pondering what secrets it might hold, and drifted off with her thoughts.

50

Bacterial connections

Chris was too elated to go to bed when he got home. He felt he had to share his positive experiences with the Cousins family with his parents.

'What do you think it means?' he asked after describing all the micro-organisms he had been able to identify in Dr. Cousins' pictures.

His mum looked horrified, but his dad appeared very thoughtful. 'Son, perhaps you have been given some sort of gift. Perhaps the Universe is trying to pass on some sort of message through you.' Joe had an inkling that this may be the case since he'd heard the yogi's talk and from his recent meditations.

Donna seemed seriously unnerved, shuffling on the sofa. 'Joe, I'm not sure you should be filling his head with such scary fantasy nonsense. How can this be a gift? If anything it's more like a curse. Whatever it is it seems alien to me and I'm not comfortable with it. We still don't know whether there is something seriously wrong medically, do we?'

'Mum, I feel fine!' exclaimed Chris, in frustration.

'Son, try to stay calm. Your mum is just worried about you; that's all.' Joe turned to Donna.

'Listen Donna, I know you just want to protect him, but what if there really is some bigger meaning behind all this? What if there really is some special message that Chris might be able to deliver to the world through a special gift? You heard the yogi – he said it might be possible for people to get a special connection to micro-beings through meditation.' Joe appeared suddenly very curious. 'You never did tell me what the yogi said to you.'

Donna was even more uncomfortable now, and she got up to make a Cappuccino. Chris and Joe followed her neat figure to the kitchen.

'Well?' asked Chris demandingly.

'Well alright, but I don't think you should necessarily take him seriously,' she conceded. The others gave her a persistent stare. Donna squirmed for a bit, and gave in;

'He said that if Chris really was having these experiences, then he should try to learn from them. He said the best way to learn was to meditate on the micro-beings, to tune into them, to try to pick-up what they were saying.' Donna was avoiding their feverish gaze.

'Mum, why didn't you tell me before?' yelled Chris. Then more thoughtfully he added; 'How do I do that anyway?'

Donna was silent for a long time, anxiously stirring her coffee. She was fighting her massively strong instinct to protect her son from all this madness, but Chris and Joe were pressing her to answer.

'Look Donna,' said Joe soothingly but firmly, 'I believe that each of us has an individual destiny, which is something that we write with our choice and individual freedom. It's our birthright. You might not like what is unfolding for Chris, but sometimes we just can't change things. It is up to Chris and Chris alone.' Joe glanced at Chris, who was nodding furiously.

With a big sigh she conceded, saying;

'Well, the yogi said that you could visit him and he would teach you.'

Chris stared in disbelief. 'He did? Well, let's go!' He got up to get his coat.

'Don't you think we should try more therapies first?' she countered.

Joe stared firmly at her; 'Donna, I know you want to protect him, but if this is his destiny, then you mustn't stand in his way. We all want answers don't we?'

'Oh alright then,' she sighed reluctantly, 'but Chris, you'll need an appointment first honey. He's a very busy man,' she added weakly.

'I'll organize it,' said Joe and reached for the phone.

51

CHRIS MEETS THE YOGI

Summer vacation was in full swing; mid-summer's day had come and gone and Chris and the yogi were finally meeting. Chris felt a very strong sense of excitement in the pit of his stomach. He and his Dad had located the yogi's beautiful residence set in plush gardens and, having driven up the winding gravel drive and parked, they were excitedly entering the reception, which was decorated with beautiful paintings, statues and framed quotations.

Chris was like a cat on hot coal – his eagerness to see this yogi with his own eyes was only surpassed by his curiosity to answer his burning questions. What would he look like? His father had spoken much of the mystical abilities that people could achieve through meditation yet how would such mystical presence manifest in a human being?

An exquisitely dressed, exotic-looking lady with brown almond eyes was seated on the floor arranging a beautiful array of tropical sweet-smelling flowers into a golden vase. She turned her bronzed face and smiled up at them.

Announcing that they were here to see the yogi, she gracefully stood and guided Chris and Joe along a corridor lined with compelling artwork through to another room. As Chris approached the room with his dad, he felt a sudden surge of energy. He reached to open the door but it swung open before he could touch it.

As the door swung open Chris was finally able to see the real-life yogi in person. He felt butterflies in his stomach as he tried to take in the man's appearance. Clothed in comfortable loosely flowing white attire from his neck down to the floor but with bare feet, the yogi appeared ready for a martial arts encounter.

Chris wondered if he would be expected to join in – perhaps some kind of fight on a mat would ensue. He cast his eyes quickly around the small room and realized that there would be no space for such a physical encounter, although he did spot two long green mats lying side-by-side overlooking a glass door that lead out to a beautiful veranda, steeped in luscious flowers that were lit by twinkling fairy lights.

He realized that there was a hush in the room apart from the beautifully lulling and hypnotic waves of gentle music that rolled into his ears from a sound system secreted in a corner. He noticed the sweet and heady scents of jasmine and pine reach his nostrils; the wafts of aroma floated from flickering candles placed at certain points around the room.

As he eyed the yogi intently, the stillness of the man's presence emanated deeper currents which, like an electrical charge, created an unseen but palpable field around him, drawing Chris towards him like a powerful magnet. Chris crept forward, sinking his pumps into the deep soft carpet, edging ever closer towards the yogi.

Chris observed the yogi's noble features, which reminded him of faces chiselled on statues dedicated to people of great wisdom. He was barely able to perceive the man's stature as his presence seemed to extend out way beyond his actual physical body, inviting thoughts and illusions of a much taller person. He was unable to determine the yogi's age, as he seemed to have an almost timeless appearance, as if he always was and always would be the same – a classically handsome face – neither old nor young. Yet when he began to communicate he encapsulated an incredibly child-like demeanour alongside an eternally knowing gracefulness.

'Chris, Joe, how wonderful to see you,' smiled the yogi, beckoning them over to a seat. They shook hands, embraced and the yogi closed his eyes for a moment. Sitting quietly together Chris felt surprisingly calm and peaceful. His gaze surveyed the room and he noticed a statue of Hanuman and Ganesh on a shelf, which made him smile – recognizing the similar figures from his father's store. He caught his dad's eye; Joe was also smiling in recognition. Chris gazed through the window and spotted the Bright Moon resplendent in the sky. Hello old friend, he said in his mind.

The yogi opened his eyes and saw Chris gazing at the Moon.

'She's a beautiful being, isn't she? You know, it says in the ancient Vedic scriptures that the Bright Moon fuels our desires to manifest what is in our heart. Tell me, Chris. What is in your heart? What is it that you seek?'

Although Chris was not sure whether he should treat the yogi as if he was an awesome and important figure, perhaps like a prince or something, his mind was laid at rest by the yogi's welcoming and friendly gestures, inviting free and easy communication on an equal level. Chris gazed back at the yogi, drawn into the deep question and a contemplative mood. He closed his eyes without thinking, shutting out all the outward distractions. He stayed in this pose with the Bright Moon's cool rays shining onto his face, until a thought popped into his head.

'The truth, sir; I seek the truth, I seek answers to all sorts of questions, like why we are here and who made us. Why do I have so many questions, sir?'

He eased into a conversation with the yogi with surprisingly little difficulty, finding him most approachable and likeable.

The yogi smiled kindly at Chris and clasped his hands together in silent thought. Eventually he began to speak;

'We seek answers as if they are some kind of fuel to us, Chris. The physical body needs nutrition. The mind needs peace. The heart needs love. The inner self needs truth. Only then can we have true health. Yet an inquisitive mind gains only knowledge of the world. An accepting heart however gains knowledge of the self through mystical and spiritual experiences.'

'You see, the mind itself is a question. Heart is an answer. Our spirit is an experience. Yet our mind is just an extended entity of the deeper consciousness within us. As the tail is to the comet, so is the mind to deeper consciousness in the sky of our spirit.'

'Often though, when we become occupied asking questions, we may miss the whispers of answers emerging from within. You see there is a super-sensor, a deep-seated self beneath everything we feel, think and talk about. This embodies the impenetrable formulae, codes and secrets of Nature and the Universe, just as genes in the body carry information about our ancestors.'

'If we can learn to access this part of ourselves, the answers start to come. Many complex questions have simple answers. Some simple answers spark remarkable discoveries and inventions.'

Chris was staring wide-eyed at the yogi in fascination. The yogi's voice seemed to sing with a bell-like clarity, conveying both warmth and compassion. His wise words were like nectar to Chris' hungry ears. Whilst conversing, Chris sensed a deep and intensely strong bond with the yogi, as if they were so much on the same wavelength that he was almost inside Chris' head, enhancing Chris' ability to voice his questions.

His thoughts wandered for a moment – was the yogi actually able to predict what he would say next? Was he able to predict what was round the corner for Chris? What about prophecies for the world and its destiny?

Realising that these thoughts put him off kilter, he reined them back in and concentrated on forming his burning questions concerning his experience with the microbes.

Before he could even form his words, the yogi cut straight to the heart of Chris' doubts;

'What do you feel when you hear the sounds of the micro-beings?'

'I feel confusion and fear,' shuddered Chris. The yogi nodded again.

'Doubts are like harmful bacteria. Clear them immediately; otherwise the mind may become infected. What if you opened up to a state of complete relaxation? You can try something called meditation to help you relax and calm your thoughts. It's a way to tune into yourself and see what's beneath all of your mind's chatter. Do it with me Chris and then we'll see what answers you get for yourself. You see, all the answers you seek are within you already, and meditating is a way to help you discover them.'

Chris hesitated. How could meditating with your eyes

closed be any more than just a sneaky way to get some sleep? He turned to Joe for reassurance; Joe nodded his encouragement.

'Its fine Chris, you know I meditate too, don't you? You'll love it, and you'll feel just great afterwards. It's just like I've told you before.'

Chris had always asked questions all his life, but he had never found anyone who could truly answer them, yet now he had suddenly reached an epiphany – the yogi had said that Chris could answer his own questions! Was that really true? How could it be true? Weren't all answers to be found in books, or on the internet, or in the brains of clever people? It didn't make any sense.

Yet somewhere inside him he knew he must try the meditation to prove to himself that the yogi's words were true. He knew this was a leap of faith, and he knew that he had to take the leap if he wanted to move forward in his baffling situation.

The yogi slid over two mats for them to sit on. He laid them side by side and sat on one of the mats cross-legged, indicating for Chris to do the same on the other mat. Chris looked enquiringly at his dad, who smiled and nodded again. Chris shrugged and took the leap. He sat down on the squishy mat with his legs crossed and back straight just like the yogi, who then guided Chris through a meditation sequence, during which the yogi placed his hands on different energy centers of his own body, breathing deeply then singing special sounds at each point. Chris copied the hand positions and the sounds – they seemed to cycle through four different sounds, and each one was connected with the next by humming.

At each new sound, Chris was guided to place his hands at

points higher and higher up his body, starting with the soles of his feet, then the backs of his calves, the knees, the thighs, the base of the back, the solar-plexus, the abdomen, the heart, the shoulders, the elbows, the hands placed together in a prayer-like position, then moved to the throat area, to the mouth, to the nose, to the cheeks, the ears, the eyes, the forehead, the crown of the head; finally they completed the hand movements in another hands together prayer position.

The yogi explained that the sequence allowed their attention to be moved like a bubble to each energy point of the body, allowing the whole body to be noticed and included in this state of conscious awareness.

The yogi then instructed Chris to lie down on his mat and relax with his thumb and forefinger touching together. He demonstrated, closing his eyes, lying still. Chris wondered if he had fallen asleep and looked across at his dad quizzically. Joe gestured for him to copy the yogi, so he did as instructed and lay down on his own mat.

Soon Chris was immersed in a blissful state of relaxation and almost felt like he was floating. He stayed like this for an unknown time, then – stirring – he slowly raised himself up to a sitting position.

The yogi also stirred and sat up, smiling kindly.

'How do you feel, Chris?' he asked.

'Wow, I feel just wonderful, like a new person!' laughed Chris.

'As flowers blossom in sunshine, so does the inner self blossom in silence,' explained the yogi. 'And if I were to ask you again what you think the micro-beings are communicating, what would you say? Don't think, just say.'

Chris blurted out a word – 'COOPERATION!'

The yogi smiled and nodded. 'Well done. I recommend that if ever you feel the sensations of the micro-beings again, that you employ this technique, to see if you can meld your consciousness with them. You may well receive some answers to the questions that you have.'

'You mean I can actually communicate with them?' uttered Chris in awe.

'On the outside we are individuals; but deep within we are all one family in the home of the Universe – yes, even micro-organisms. When we realize and experience this, our connections become re-established and stronger.'

'I still don't understand – surely they can't speak, can they?'

'Thanks to Nature, we are not confined to words alone for communications. Gestures, emotional vibrations and even silence add to the whole of communication. Do not fear, Chris, you are just experiencing a different way of communicating.'

Chris appeared a little disturbed;

'No-one will ever believe me though when I say I can communicate with them, will they?'

'Truthfulness should not dwell silently within you. Especially when challenged, it should be expressed clearly and with a spirit of confidence. Otherwise you may be perceived as being untruthful.'

'Hmm, no pressure then...' muttered Chris.

'Fear not, Chris; you are a gentle warrior with the power of love; mind as a sword, heart as a shield, smile as a command.

Whatever we creatively imagine does exist somewhere in the Universe. This is because our imagination cannot be entirely different from the nature and content of the Universe.'

The yogi gestured for Chris to stand; they stretched and yawned.

'Thank you so much,' said Chris, 'I will practise this every day. May I ask you about this technique you've shown me?' He glanced over at Joe. 'My dad has told me about yoga where you stretch into different positions on a mat whilst breathing deeply and relax into a meditation, but yours is different. Why do you make the sounds and touch at different points?'

'Well, let's speak about sound first,' said the yogi. 'Self-generated sounds are one of the most powerful centring, clearing and healing tools that we can employ. Some sounds are considered sacred, often those that have the most healing effect on our bodies.'

'Do you mean like mantras?' asked Chris, with shining eyes. His dad had spoken of these.

'Yes, Chris. The sounds set up vibrations which reverberate throughout your body, but each vowel and consonant sound particularly affects specific parts of the body and different vibrations help to clear your energy centres, or chakras. Think of it as helping to clear blockages, which are basically caused by uneasy thoughts and beliefs.' The yogi was staring intently at Chris to see if he understood, then added;

'Most people find it difficult to clear their minds of persistent thoughts, but the sounds are also helping you to distract your mind away from thinking.'

'I can see how that might be useful,' said Chris, 'I quite often get stuck in a thought pattern; usually it's to do with persistent questions. My mum says I never stop thinking of new questions. Sometimes I can't sleep because my head is so filled with thoughts.'

'You can try this meditation method before you sleep – you might find it helps you,' smiled the yogi kindly.

'As for the touch points,' added the yogi, 'they are each important energy centres and you are effectively setting up an energy circuit by touching each point with your fingers and palms, which emit a certain healing magnetic field, helping to bring your awareness, or consciousness to reside in each point.

'When you have completed the whole touch cycle, you have brought many of the most important energy centres into balance with each other, helping your whole energy field to be more balanced, connected and harmonious. This helps you to be more aware of your infinite self, the part of you that is connected with the Universe, or Source energy – or God as some might say – your connection with all the answers to all the questions that have ever been asked, or will ever be thought of.'

Chris' eyes were popping out of his head. This was amazing stuff he was hearing and he couldn't wait to get on this journey.

He felt a surge of empowerment course through him, an inner-knowing and a sense of calm and serenity that he had never before felt. Imagine having a direct-line to God! Imagine having access to more answers than you could get from any supercomputer ever built! My God, that was awesome! Was this something everyone could do, or just him? He didn't know if this made him someone special, or just very lucky to have found this mystical knowledge. What questions would he ask? What was he going to find out about these micro-beings? Would he be able to talk with them, to 'cooperate' with them as he had sensed during his meditation? What on earth did that mean? Where would it all lead him and why?

The questions were backing up and he laughed inwardly, vowing to get started with this meditation as soon as he got home, to see if he could discover some answers before he drowned in a sea of queries!

He felt a sort of divine pull, a sense of fulfilment in all this, as if it was meant to be this way. Some of the puzzle pieces were finally fitting into place. He grinned at Joe, who was beaming back at him, fit to burst with pride.

'I call it an adventure in self-discovery,' smiled the yogi, 'because the more you go inwards during these meditations, the more you find answers to all those questions that you have and the more you find out about yourself.'

'This is a spiritual path, Chris. Spirituality is a gracefully adventurous inner journey and a silent battle for balance between the logical mind and the loving heart. As you journey into the inner realms of your consciousness, your presence becomes vast and spacious. All artificial barriers and boundaries break away, inviting abundant peace and serenity into your being.'

'When you reach the level of the heart, your personality changes and your uniqueness shines through. Your spirit becomes recharged and now you are more than just an ordinary human being – you have become a special cosmic being. You discover new spiritual laws that give you access to miracles and unexplained phenomena that do not fit with our current physical laws.'

'Is that why I have been having these terrifying experiences?' asked Chris in sudden concern.

'Like a flower, the heart has many petals of emotion. Experiencing these awakens the body's potential. Otherwise we remain as partially-blossomed humans. Don't think of these experiences with a purely scientific, sceptical mind – think of it as a spiritual experience. Science may encourage us to think deeply, but spirituality inspires us to become profound.'

'So what about Chris' experiences with the micro-organisms,' interjected Joe?

'Yes! Can you tell me anything more about why I have been seeing and hearing them?' Chris was questioning urgently now.

'I think you must already have somehow linked in with their consciousness. If you spend a great deal of time in contemplation on an object, it opens you up to the underlying essence of the object.'

'But I haven't been thinking about micro-organisms!' exclaimed Chris.

'What have you been thinking about?' asked the yogi.

'All sorts of things, but mostly the Moon I guess.' He gazed out of the window at the Bright Moon peeping through the clouds. Its light was stippling the clouds creating an effect like shaded and highlighted cotton wool across the heavens.

'Then you have connected with a cosmic consciousness, Chris! This carries the consciousness of all beings – large or minuscule – their essence from the dawn of time to the end of the Universe. Your radio has tuned into that of the microcosmic world, young mystic!'

'Awesome...' Chris' silvery grey eyes shined brilliantly and his face had taken on a new strength as he adjusted to this expanding information.

'I suggest you don't speak to everyone about this, son. Not everyone is ready to hear this sort of information. You however are well on your awakening journey. Your abundant questions and contemplation have bought you the grace to reach this point. You are finding your own answers. I suggest that you notice how such things happen in your life, how things come to you as you request them, how synchronicities happen around you. You may be surprised by what you notice.'

The yogi put his hand on Chris' shoulder.

'Each of us is bound to grow and evolve at some point. There is an individual time for everyone within the Universal time. Apart from our responsibility and accountability for our own growth and expansion, evolution and growth do not result only from the will of human beings, but are the imperatives of the Universe.'

'Enjoy your adventure, Chris. The Universe is waiting for you to say yes to it!'

Chris felt a shudder down his spine, as if he had experienced some sort of déjà vu. He was feeling most light-headed with all this unusual talk. He decided his head could take no more of this mind-blowing information, asking his dad if they could go home now. Joe nodded and they bid farewell to the yogi, thanking him profusely for his wise words.

'Goodbye Chris, Joe; may the Universe go with you.' They smiled at each other and parted ways.

As Chris and his father left the room, Chris turned back to cast his eyes one last time over the scene, observing the ever-shortening candles' feverish glow that cheerily and comfortably fought back the night-time darkness, casting flickering shadows on the walls, reminiscent of girls dancing beautifully in celebration. The candlelight reflected back off the glass of the veranda door and he caught sight of the yogi's reflection – he was staring intently at the Full Moon.

Chris smiled inwardly; he was well aware of the Moon's intense attraction. He was content to have found someone else who understood her passionate allure.

July

Full Moon: 11.51 am on July 3rd

52

CHRIS PREDICTS ANOTHER BRIGHT MOON EVENT

'It's bed-time for you, my clever mystic!' laughed Joe as he bundled Chris upstairs to bed. Joe settled his son under the bed covers and kissed his forehead.

'Sweet dreams, Chris,' he smiled to his son, tousling the boy's curly hair.

Chris smiled back, but he was aware of the strange sounds rushing in his ears again.

'Dad, I think it's happening again...' he anxiously grabbed his dad's hand.

'Alright son, we'll briefly try your new meditation before you go to sleep. I'll do it with you.'

Chris sat up and they arranged themselves side by side, cross-legged on the bed, running through the various touch points, breathing deeply and singing the sounds that the yogi had showed them. As they completed the cycle, Joe settled Chris down into bed for the lying down part of the meditation and kissed him goodnight again.

'It's all going to be fine, son, relax into sleep now.'

Joe closed the door behind him and went to tell Donna what had happened.

53

3rd Bright Moon event

Chris woke early, the sun's rays heating his face through a crack in the curtains. He stirred and reached over to the bedside cabinet for a drink to quench his raging thirst. Through the haze of his sleepy eyes, he saw a vague movement. Then the images developed into a clear structure and appearance. He was able to make out the shapes of the bacteria floating in his water; he spat out the water in disgust.

'Mum, Dad, they're back! The bacteria are back! They're everywhere!' he screamed.

They bounded up the stairs and threw open his bedroom door, to see him wildly running around his bedroom. Donna's legs weakened and she leaned up against the wall at the threshold for support. Chris ran towards his mother to hug her but stopped short as he noticed many more microorganisms on her tailored dress and on her porcelain skin.

'Chris you need to calm down, son!' soothed Joe. 'Can you hear them too?'

'Yes Dad, I can hear them. It's like they're talking to me!'

'What are they saying?'

'I'm not sure Dad, it's still garbled, but I'm really scared.'

Donna grabbed an armful of his clothes from his drawers.

'Let's get you to the hospital again,' she stated decisively. 'We need the medics to check you over to see if they can cure you.' She was scouting around the bedroom as she talked, collecting a bagful of his belongings to take with them.

'But Mum, I don't wanna go! They don't help me there!' he wailed.

'Now listen, Chris, what's happening to you just isn't normal. We need their help to take this all away. I can't bear to see you so upset. I just want my little boy better!' she was crying.

'Please wait Donna! The yogi said that Chris might be able to communicate with the micro-organisms, so why don't we let him try?' begged Joe.

'I'm not waiting around here for you two to do some odd meditation thing when there could be something seriously wrong with Chris. No, we're going to the hospital and that's final.'

Donna whisked down the stairs to phone Dr. Barnes, who agreed to admit Chris again for observation.

54

MEDICS QUESTION CHRIS ON WHAT HE CAN SEE

Back on the psychiatric ward at the hospital, Chris was ensconced in a side room, with extra hygiene protection. The neurosurgeon – Dr. Krefeld, and Dr. Barnes knocked on the door to see the boy.

'Well hello Chris, we meet again!' uttered Dr. Krefeld with a friendly grin. 'Are you ready for us to carry out some more tests on you? We would like to check your brain activity with another head scan, do an E.E.G. to check brain wave activity, get your eyes and ears checked over again.

'I'd also like you to meet a new gentleman, Professor Callows, who will come in this afternoon. He is a professor of neural-psychology from the University of San Francisco. He might have a different perspective on things that could shed more light on what's going on here. I'm sorry that you have to go through all this Chris, it's just that we are really trying to understand what's happening to you so we can help you.'

'I know sir, that's alright,' smiled Chris encouragingly.

He was trying to keep his eyes open a little more, aware that the micro-beings were everywhere, but trying to deep-breathe his way into a more relaxed state, so he felt less threatened by the bizarre sensory input. He was able to watch as Ward Sister Sue bustled in and efficiently checked his blood pressure, temperature, heart and respiration rate and extracted a few blood samples. She grinned cheerily at him and he was able to smile weakly back at her, despite being able to see the wriggling bacteria all over her gloved hands.

'There you go, mate. All done, and if you carry on being this good, I'll see if I can sneak you a doughnut up from the cafeteria!' grinned Sister Sue mischievously.

Chris giggled but couldn't resist asking her to make sure she removed her gloves and washed her hands before she picked up his treat.

Sister Sue's eyes rose to the sky and she shook her head in a mock affronted way, then she bustled off, yelling instructions at the other nurses as she passed them.

She was a formidable woman with impeccable hair and a knock-out smile to counter her killer put-downs. She stalked the wards like an alpha lioness, her stunningly huge eyes like radar that picked up anything out of place or in need of her attention. Though her nurses were unlikely to challenge her, those that dared to soon learnt that it was more than their job was worth, as her lashing tongue would strip them of their ability to speak, let alone stand up for themselves. She ran a tight ship and she was the best captain the doctors could wish for. Behind the scenes she let her guard down and revealed her golden heart and her infectious sense of humour which always helped to dispel the heaviness of a difficult day at the hospital.

Chris watched her departing, strict figure and lay back on his pillow thinking about delicious doughnuts. He wondered if she believed what he said about the microbes. Chris thought he should try to explain what he had found out with Dr. Cousins about the micro-organisms he had seen last time, in case this would throw any light on the puzzled medics' perspectives. He was aware that they seemed to be split into different camps at the moment – many were still sceptical, but some were just neutral, trying to empathize and deal with whatever they found. One or two were really helpful and supportive, showing that they believed what he was saying and wanted to look deeper.

He decided to talk to Krefeld, who seemed like an approachable, affable kind of guy. When Krefeld next came to check Chris over, he was accompanied by the grey-faced Barnes and Sister Sue.

Chris explained to the medics that he had received some help from a friend's father who was a microbiologist and he had been able to identify several micro-organisms from pictures. The medics' faces were a picture, Krefeld appeared awestruck, Sister Sue was open-mouthed and Barnes was smirking.

Dr. Krefeld was intrigued; he asked for details of the microbiologist, to see if they could consult with him. Chris gave his name; Dr. Krefeld recognized it as someone who had been trying to speak to him that week.

'I'll invite him in to discuss this with us,' said Krefeld resolutely. 'What can you see now?' he asked Chris curiously.

'Well, I seem to be able to see the same creatures, but more clearly than last time. For instance over there on the door I can see a chain of round blobs; I think Dr. Cousins said that sort of micro-organism would be called streptococci.'

Eyebrows were raised around the room. Sue turned to stare nervously at the door Chris was pointing at, aware of the serious health issues implicated with that particular bacteria; not on MY ward, she thought defensively.

'The sounds are becoming clearer too,' said Chris almost apologetically, seeing the strained expressions on the medics' faces.

'What does it sound like, son?' asked Krefeld kindly, stroking his goatee beard warily.

'Well, it's kind of like music now; some of them make nice soft music, while others just seem to make a low grumble or groaning sound.'

'Alright Chris, well we'll get onto those eye and ear tests right away and see what comes up. You just take it easy for a while. I hope you like this new room we have here for you now? Cosy, isn't it? We thought you might appreciate having a little more privacy with all this upheaval going on.' Krefeld winked at Chris and sent Sister Sue off to arrange some tests.

Krefeld and Barnes left Chris alone with his parents. The troubled family looked at each other anxiously.

'Here we go again,' said Joe.

55

BAINES EXAMINES CHRIS AGAIN

Edward was called back into the hospital to examine Chris. He scurried in, enormous head wobbling on top of his match-like skinny body.

Although Edward had taken things casually with the bizarrely behaving boy in the beginning, he had had the chance to do some background research on his symptoms. This guided him with his next round of tests, as he peered into Chris' eyes through his humongous glasses.

Now that he had the chance to examine him again he took the boy's visions more seriously and he was becoming increasingly intrigued by Chris' apparent abilities.

He wanted to be around the boy, especially when he was starting to get his visions, to find out whether his eyes physically changed, but frustratingly the spontaneity and irregularity of the vision occurrences made it difficult for him to examine the boy at the time of his visual transformation. Yet he was able to notice that the eyes of the boy became radiant with a sort of silvery glow in conjunction with his visions, which was something that he couldn't explain, especially as he saw no other signs of impaired eyesight.

Questioned by Donna on the state of Chris' eyesight, Baines was unable to offer anything new to assuage her fears.

Donna was prepared to mount another attack on the latest useless medic, but Baines rallied with his stock comment to riled patients;

'Doctors are only human, you know!'

56

MEDICS, SCIENTISTS AND PHILOSOPHER MEET TO DISCUSS CHRIS' CASE

Krefeld tracked down Dr. Cousins, the microbiologist that had assisted Chris. He invited Cousins into the hospital to discuss Chris' case, and was joined by Holmes to hear what Cousins thought of Chris' claims.

In his brief encounter with Chris, Cousins concluded that the boy seemed to be able to accurately describe different micro-organisms without the aid of magnification equipment. Aware of the scientist's excellent research credentials, the gathered medics began to waver in their opinions, although the whole scenario was still unbelievable to their logical minds.

Since the medics were not yet totally convinced, but still healthily sceptical of Chris' highly irregular abilities, Cousins pleaded with them to witness first hand Chris' accurate visions. With much muttering and disbelief, they moved the meeting under Cousins' direction to a sunlit microbiology laboratory at the top of the hospital. Chris was invited to join them to take part in an experiment which Cousins hoped would convince the medics of Chris' microscopic visual abilities.

Chris arrived in the lab and saw the waiting medics, backlit by the huge windows through which streamed the afternoon sunshine. He saw the fluffy clouds slowly waft by in the deep blue sky, before turning to observe the microscopes that sat almost expectantly on the bench. Cousins greeted him affably and Chris returned his grin with mounting excitement. This moment was crucial for getting everyone on Chris' side.

Cousins set up an experiment to show Chris describing what he saw on different slide specimens with his naked eye. The gathered medics watched in awe as time after time his visions were checked through the microscope with Cousins concurring that Chris' descriptions matched those of the micro-organisms on the slide. The excited chatter in the room rose to fever-pitch as more medics were invited in to observe the experiment.

Those that still could not believe what they saw could be true wanted to give Chris extra tests in case it was all a huge set-up. They ransacked the laboratory for every sample slide that they could find; each one was put under Chris' nose, but every time, Chris was able to successfully describe the microbes.

Eventually, with no more slides to test, the medics sat back – mouths agape in stunned amazement. The sun streamed its glorious rays of golden light through the windows of the research lab, as if heralding the dawn of a new discovery. The light splashed its presence over the room, reflecting in a dazzling display off the surfaces of the safety screens which housed the microbial experiments. What did all this mean? The evidence towards Chris' visions being that of real micro-organisms was stacking up.

Chris smiled triumphantly at the astounded medics, the light creating a beautiful glow around his head. 'The microbes want to cooperate with us...' he announced, feeling it was time to pass on this revelation.

Stunned expressions adorned the faces of the silenced medics. Unable to process this information, many of them simply dispersed from the room. They had seen and heard enough. Krefeld however came over and placed his hand on Chris' shoulder. Unsure what to say about Chris' announcement he just acknowledged his ignorance about it;

'Well my boy,' said Krefeld affectionately, 'you've got some incredible talent there son. I can't say I understand it and I don't know why it's happening to you, but let's just say for now that we've seen enough and we will continue to monitor you to find out more about your visual abilities. Why don't you head back down to your ward and have a rest for a while. I'll be down to see you again later.' Krefeld smiled in awe at the boy, straightened his waistcoat and gestured for a nurse to accompany Chris back to his bed.

Turning to Holmes, he said 'Well that puts the cat amongst the pigeons! What do we do now?' Holmes gazed down worriedly towards his long shoes, racking his brains for an answer.

'It seems pretty clear that he really can see microbes without the aid of any magnification equipment. That clearly raises all sorts of questions about how that is possible. But also moral questions about whether he should be protected from the media and from exploitation;' Holmes stroked his garish bow-tie thoughtfully. 'Plus I don't know what to make of his last comment. What did he mean when he said the microbes want to cooperate? Is he really hearing messages from them or is he making a wild leap from experiencing all these strange visions?'

'Goodness knows – it leaves me even more confused,' said Krefeld. 'Right, well I propose that we get our heads together with some key specialists to brain-storm what we know, what we still need to find out and how we proceed.

It's crucial that we handle this sensitively. Of course we still don't know whether he is in any kind of medical danger, so we need to keep him under observation and monitor his vital signs, then maybe we can discuss some observational experiments to monitor his brain function.'

They listed who they thought would bring some helpful ideas to the table and dispersed to organize a meeting.

Some time later, the specialists were gathered together in the Board Room. Present were Krefeld, Barnes the psychiatrist, Cousins the microbiologist, Holmes the paediatric consultant, Baines the eye specialist, Callows the Professor of neuro-psychology from San Francisco University and a psychologist specialising in cognitive science, from a private institution in New Jersey. Also present were various other key doctors, psychologists and even a philosopher, an expert in phenomenology, who had contacted the hospital after hearing about the boy in the news. His specialty was cosmic consciousness.

The specialists sat around the oval table, sipping sparkling water from expensive crystal glasses as they listened to a summary from Krefeld. Dust danced in the streams of light that shone through the impressive windows as the sound of the excited chatter in the room rose noisily.

Having kicked off the meeting with a general discussion about what might be happening to the boy, views were divided amongst the room as to whether this was some sort of medical anomaly or whether in fact Chris was experiencing some sort of attuning to a different sort of consciousness. They agreed that his senses appeared to be functioning optimally.

Baines chipped in with his results of the day; 'I see no evidence from the eye examinations of any abnormal activity, except that the boy's pupils were greatly dilated, his prescription has changed again and the silvery film or glow was present on his eyes like last time he was admitted.'

Baines confessed that he couldn't explain these effects, but he felt an urge to mention his theory that we have the ability and a system in the body which could create extraordinary effects on vision, such that we can literally see the most distant objects without the help of any devices.

Wobbling his enormous head in a nodding movement, he explained that he had been involved with plenty of research exploring how emotions play a role in expanding and contracting the pupil and how tears can change vision, but he couldn't see how emotions were at the root of the unusual behaviours of Chris' pupils at the moment.

Pushing his glasses back up his nose, he proffered that more evidence was needed about Chris' brain activity, to see whether unusual neural connections might be responsible for his visions.

Krefeld then stood again, straightening his waistcoat to report on Chris' brain scans, sharing that the boy's brain waves appeared to be very relaxed and uniform, mostly registering in the alpha and delta brain wave range, similar to that found during meditation, but with regular gamma spikes which he associated with high levels of information download.

Callows, the Professor of neuro-psychology, had been intrigued to hear this, and began pacing the room as he spoke of his research into the effects of different states of consciousness on brain wave patterns. Callows, evidently in need of a belt, was tripping over his sagging trouser legs then hoisted them back over his waist to reveal his brown strappy leather sandals. He had fine wispy blond hair, a sparse almost non-existent moustache and pale skin that appeared almost transparent.

Callows shared that he had done some research into the effects of different states of consciousness on brain wave patterns and wondered if a change in consciousness might have initiated Chris' unusual brain wave pattern. His previous research had measured the brain wave activity of Tibetan monks during meditation and compassion states and found that they had similar prolific gamma wave spikes in the 25-40Hz range.

Krefeld interjected, 'Callows would you be prepared to investigate Chris' case officially? As you already have expertise in this area of brain wave measurement, you'd be ideal to have on the case.'

Callows nodded his agreement good-naturedly, flapping his wispy fine hair in a static, shimmering display. 'I would need to check brainwave data from Chris daily and cross-check with when the boy was having his experiences against when he wasn't, to eliminate any coincidental changes.'

'That should be achievable with the parents' consent,' Krefeld mused.

Dr. Barnes interrupted; 'I suspect the boy registers on the autistic spectrum; I believe he exhibits Asperger's Syndrome characteristics, do you think this might affect his brain wave patterns?' His thin lips closed tightly together.

'Hmm, I'm not sure. We know that meditation may change brain wave patterns anyway. I've read some research about the benefits of meditation in cases of autism and Asperger's; it seems to help with creating brain connections necessary to make new associations and improve cognitive function,' explained Callows. 'Often key brain connections are not as well-formed in some autistic patients, creating issues for them with recognition of facial features and body language interpretation. It was proposed in this research that anything that helped form these connections might improve the patient's integration into society.' Callows was pacing and tripping over his trousers again.

Krefeld diverted the conversation; 'I do believe that the neural connections in Chris' brain seem surprisingly prolific and plastic, which means they would be easily remoulded.'

Callows nodded his head of wispy hair in agreement; 'The brain should be the most changeable organ in the body; you can expect around 1.8 million new connections to form per second in normal growing kids, but these connections only form according to experience exposure. Habit behaviour typical of autistic spectrum patients only deepens existing connections, which is a bit like getting your-self 'stuck in a rut'. It lowers your capacity for new connections.' Callows heaved up his sagging trousers once more.

'Yes but clearly Chris' neural connections are indicating a rate of exposure to new experiences far beyond what would be expected!' exclaimed Krefeld in awe.

The psychologist from New Jersey chipped in. 'Is there any evidence of other cases in the records similar to Chris?' But no-one was able to recite any. They admitted that this was a unique case and that they needed to understand what was special about Chris that might have created such an outcome.

The psychologist explained a little about his specialty; 'I've also come across cases where individuals have been deep contemplators – yogis, mystics and monks. They were able to change their brain wave activity by their meditation and reported experiences of unusual connections with the Divine, some kind of spiritual ecstasy that led to certain revelations.'

He smoothed his dark hair and folded his long arms.

The philosopher nodded; 'It reminds me of the well-known tale of the Eureka moment in the bath, when Archimedes had his revelation.' Some of the others had blank expressions on their faces, so the philosopher elucidated.

'Whilst lying in the bath, Archimedes noticed that the water level had risen up after he got into it, then he realized that the volume of water displaced must be equal to the volume of the part of his body he had submerged in the water.'

The subsequently-entitled "Eureka effect,' the philosopher explained, 'was the sudden unexpected realization of the solution to a problem. In this case, lounging in the bath was the everyday equivalent of mystical contemplation!'

The other medics nodded as the penny dropped. He continued;

'Don't forget about Newton; he was deep in contemplation beneath an apple tree when he felt an apple hit him on his head. This lead Newton to suddenly intuit the information needed to postulate the model for gravity. He was able to explain that gravity brings the apple perpendicularly down to the ground, but it also kept the Moon from falling towards the Earth and the Earth from falling towards the Sun.'

The philosopher went on to explain how each individual's Eureka moments build onto humanity's current world-view;

'However this world-view manifests itself in any particular moment in time has a knock-on effect to how humanity's belief systems are created. World-views have changed; once the Earth was seen as the centre of the Universe, but then when the sun was discovered by Aristotle to be the centre, it created what was known as the heliocentric model of solar motion. This created big changes in the religious world. Man was no longer seen as being central to everything. They realized that Man was just a cog in a much greater system, a much less influential being in the Universe.'

The listeners started to nod.

'These days we have a much greater knowledge of cosmic consciousness, interplanetary influences and micro-organism behaviour. I think that's why Chris is having these experiences.'

Cousins cut in here, his glasses nestled in his curly ginger locks; 'I agree; the information Chris has been able to recite fits beautifully with current knowledge about micro-organisms. Furthermore, Chris has even been able to explain things about their communication and behaviour that I as a researcher have not been able to prove, but have suspected for a while. It's almost as if Chris is tapping into some unknown pool of knowledge which has up until now been just out of reach of the world.'

The psychologist got very excited at this point, unfolding his long arms and gesticulating wildly; 'Yes, I believe that there is a cloud of information that we all could potentially access, if only we knew how, which would answer every question that we could think of. I'm sure that's what the mystics and the saints and the philosophers were doing when they were deep in contemplation. When they emerged from their prayers or meditations, they had unlocked some key to a doorway that opened into a storehouse of records, containing all the information that man could ever wish to know.' His dark hair had shaken itself into a spiky array through all the wild gesticulations. He smoothed it back down self-consciously.

Cousins stood up excitedly and interjected; 'Does anyone actually believe that Chris is able to do this? Because if he can then the possibilities it could open up for the world in the field of microbiology could be phenomenal, it could change everything. We could get insights into dealing with micro-organisms that could help wipe out illness!'

The room erupted into a wave of chatter, as the specialists discussed the possibilities.

Dr. Holmes, the consultant paediatrician broke through the noise to speak up on Chris' behalf.

'Please calm down everyone. We have to remember that Chris is only twelve. We must work with discretion and respect for the boy and his parents. How do we intend to proceed from this point?' He clutched his bright bow-tie as if threatening to squirt water on the unruly audience. The medics composed themselves and gathered their scattered thoughts into a practical plan.

Callows and Krefeld discussed a daily observation program that would allow them to gather brain wave and neural activity data. Krefeld added that they hadn't yet called in a sound expert to discuss Chris' aural symptoms.

The psychologist wanted to spend time interviewing Chris about his meditation experiences. Krefeld nodded his agreement.

Cousins asked if he could set up a research project which involved close collaboration with the boy to determine how micro-organisms communicate. He also offered to bring in his astro-biology colleague to discuss if there might be any connections between Chris' experiences and his obsession with the Moon. 'You see Chris has spent much of his life obsessing about the Moon and observing it whilst in deep contemplation. Maybe this is the connection with the psychologist's ideas concerning cosmic consciousness,' he said, tapping his temple knowingly.

Baines had been rubbing his enormous forehead with a bemused expression on his face. 'If this all points to Chris actually being able to see micro-organisms, then we need to get to the bottom of how he is able to do it, which would lead us into a very exciting new field of optical research.'

The others nodded in agreement.

'You see, I have a theory that the body has evolved from being effectively like an enormous eye. I believe that one day, humans may develop to be able to see if necessary without eyes, were the eyes to be disabled, but I believe that evolution has for now somehow lost its track.'

The others were startled at this idea, asking Baines to clarify his thought processes.

'You see the eye is an extension of the brain – albeit an immensely complicated and elegant work of evolution. If the mind was somehow disconnected from the eyes, then the person would no longer be able to see, even if they were still "looking".' He laughed; the silence in the room was reminiscent of tumble-weed scenes in a cowboy film but he continued regardless.

'My theory is that if a human's eyes were disabled, then the other organs in the body – including the brain – might be able to gather momentum in their functions, their abilities, or their evolution, to be able to partly take over the function of the eyes. My side-line research aimed at finding how the body could contribute to the development of the eye's visual capacity and focus.' He playfully joked, his glasses slipping down his nose; 'My ultimate ambition is not to need glasses, or surgery, or lens implantations at all in order to improve one's eyesight, but to reach a position whereby all such artificial interventions are unnecessary.'

Another line of thought concerning the collection of photons had been troubling Baines. 'Photons are the little 'packages' that light come in from the Sun,' he explained. 'I have another theory that if we can learn to cultivate our brains to gather photons during the night, we may even develop the ability to see at night almost as well as we do during the day. Of course,' he said, 'one could never stare at the sun to gather its photons directly, as it would burn one's retina and permanently damage one's eyes.'

This lead him to another cosmic thought that had popped into his head, remembering that he had noticed the Full Moon had been out the first night he had examined Chris, and that it was out again this time round that Chris had been admitted as well.

Baines explained this to the others and described to them that Moonlight was simply reflected sun and starlight. 'This means that Moonlight is simply reflected photons, albeit providing light at a much lower intensity to sunlight, which is why humans are unable to perceive colours properly in the Moonlight.' He illuminated how it was thus possible to look for longer amounts of time at the Moon than at the Sun. He wondered if somehow Chris' brain might have been capturing the extra photons reflected off the Moon's surface during his Moonlight meditations, which he was putting to use in some unexplained way to enable him to see better. Baines however was still unable to explain the mechanism of how Chris was able to see objects down to a microscopic scale.

He went on to argue that this might be an example of where evolution might be taking the human race. The others were awestruck by this idea, but questioned why other people didn't display the same abilities. Baines explained that he didn't claim to have all the answers. Indeed, even with all his research and reading, he felt like he had only been able to confirm that he knew nothing, that whatever he thought he knew yesterday was likely to be disproved today.

'Listen!' he said, eyes wide. 'Consider the path evolution has trodden so far; the first life-forms on Earth were single-celled organisms, which evolved to be able to sense light, developing sensors that detected light's presence. These sensors then developed into eyes on stalks, then ultimately into modern eyes, but each stage seemed to describe an evolutionary path towards the development of eyes and other senses to greater and greater sensitivities, in order to experience life 'out there' more accurately. So why', he questioned, 'shouldn't evolution continue to try to develop our senses in that same trajectory?'

The listeners stared quizzically at the bespectacled genius.

'I suspect that for all its good, science draws people away from Nature and naturalness, making us lazy due to all our 'conveniences' and modern appliances that make us feel artificially comfortable. I think they only divert Nature away from its natural ability to evolve us as humans. Maybe we might even be held back from evolving our senses because we have intervened in evolution's progress with all our so-called modern advances.'

Dr. Barnes spoke up, breaking the spell of entrancement created by Baines' futuristic visions; 'I don't believe any of this evolutionary poppy-cock. I'm not convinced that any of Chris' visions are real. I suspect it's just some kind of unpredictable mental reaction Chris is having to the mass hysteria that hits San Francisco on Full Moon nights.' Barnes eyed the others pessimistically, his grey face a picture of disdain.

Brought back down to Earth by Barnes' cynicism, the others in the room pondered popular culture's common beliefs that abounded concerning strange experiences and behaviours on Full Moon nights.

Baines admitted that he had also suspected some kind of Full Moon-driven lunacy, but now he felt that there was much more to this case than met the eye. He then broke into fits of laughter his enormous head wobbling as he guffawed. The others just looked on, bewildered.

Krefeld decided it was time to bring the meeting to a close, reminding the group that they needed to have some practical ideas about what to do next for Chris. The specialists agreed their next steps on the case, and finished up their drinks ready to continue with what had proved to be a most unusual and enlightening day.

August

*Two Full Moons: 8.27 am on August 1st and
Blue Moon 6.57 am on August 31st*

57

CHRIS HEARS A MESSAGE IN THE FLOWERS

As it was the summer vacation, Chris had agreed with his parents that he would stay in the hospital under observation for a while, to see if the various specialists could spot any unusual patterns in his physiological processes. Donna had good medical insurance for Chris through her employment contract so thankfully his medical costs were covered. Joe and Donna dropped in and out of the hospital as and when they could around work commitments.

He also received lots of other visitors – Grandma Larkin came regularly to spend time with her favourite grandson, bringing lots of baked treats and a good ear to listen to all his concerns. Confused as she was by his experiences, she remained open-minded and supportive, ready with soothing lunar stories to ease his troubled mind. They would sit side-by-side, snack in hand, sharing scintillating and inspiring thoughts.

He would nuzzle into her side as if she were protecting him from the storms around him, then she would hug him tightly, encouraging him to follow his heart and hunches, assuring him that it would all work out in the end. Their renewed relationship was a great help to Chris, who had missed her enormously.

Hannah came often too. One day she popped in to see him with her dad, Dr. Cousins. Her ginger-flamed hair was partly obscured by a large floral offering that she was clutching in front of her. To Donna and Joe's surprise and delight, she had brought Chris a big bunch of beautifully scented flowers, which had cheered him up no end, although he had struggled a little when he had noticed that the flowers were swarming with bacteria. Strangely he also could detect sounds coming from the flowers; the noise they produced was somehow soothing and pleasant, like harmonious notes.

He suddenly felt really vitalized and vibrant, as if picking up some sort of beneficial vibration coming from the flowers. Somewhat distracted by this bizarre phenomenon, he tried to focus back on Hannah's words.

Hannah sat on his bed, swinging her Doc Martin–clad feet, as she chattered cheerily for a while about the Moon research she was doing with some other Science Club members. They were meeting regularly at her house to discuss their findings. Buoyed up by this lovely visit, he asked if she would visit again soon. With a cute wrinkling of her freckled nose, she promised she would.

Dr. Cousins told Chris they had the go ahead to work together on his microbiology research. Chris raised his eyebrows at his parents, who happily nodded their permission – although Donna was a little wary, hoping that Chris would not be exploited. Chris however had no such doubts, declaring that he was very much looking forward to this discussion.

They were interrupted by Sister Sue; Chris was due for more tests and no-one was going to argue with the formidable Sister. Hannah and her dad waved goodbye. Chris grabbed the flowers as a Hispanic-looking porter arrived to wheel him towards another treatment room, and asked if he would also take him to get a vase and some water.

Chris was feeling pluckier and he was prepared to observe what was going on around him, so as to take part fully in this mass experiment on him. He carried his notebook and pencil with him ready to jot down anything unusual that he noticed.

Traveling past a trolley he noticed a patient in extreme agony. The nurses were fussing around him unable to soothe the poor man's pain. Suddenly he heard a rushing noise in his ears.

'Wait!' he shouted to the porter, who stopped pushing him in surprise.

'What's the matter? Are you in pain?' asked the dark-haired porter with concern. Chris had closed his eyes and was sinking into the rushing sound that filled his ears. A thought flashed into Chris' mind – *'breathe in the flower scent'* – it seemed to say! Then his mind was filled with doubts. Where are these sounds coming from? Are the microbes speaking to me? Is this how they want to cooperate with me?

The yogi had said he had to clear his head of any doubts if he was going to communicate with them. He breathed in slowly and steadily, trying to calm his mind. As he breathed in, the flower perfume from the bouquet he held rushed into his nostrils. As the aroma exploded into his awareness, he felt a sensation of elation and lift. Wow, that feels great, he thought. Is this perfume like some sort of medicine? Do the microbes want me to help the man get well with the scent of these flowers? Bizarre as the thought seemed, it wouldn't go away; he felt a very strong urge to carry out the instruction. Opening his eyes, he plucked a flower from the bunch and held it out towards the patient, stammering;

'Please, take this flower and hold it under your nose.

Breathe in its scent. I think it will help you to get better very soon.'

The nurses scowled at Chris, shooing him away from their patient in annoyance. They smirked at each other as they rushed the patient away on his trolley in contempt. He was taken to a private bay.

'What did you think you were playing at?' asked the porter incredulously. 'You could have caused a serious problem getting in the way like that! That man was in a lot of pain; he doesn't need any loco ideas about sniffing flowers like a hippy, he needs medication!'

Chris felt very embarrassed, but he couldn't shake the thought from his mind that he had been right. He focused in on the flowers and gazed between the petals, which seemed to give off a wonderful glow. The whispering rushing sounds came again. He closed his eyes and tuned into the sound; he was sure he could make out the words 'breathe in the flower scent' again.

He decided he would try again later to deliver the flowers to the man when he got the chance. It seemed like a long shot, but he had to try. 'Los chicos' muttered the porter with contempt and pushed Chris' wheelchair off in annoyance to get his tests done.

After his tests had been completed and Chris had found a vase for his flowers, he returned to his bed to get some sleep.

The nurses offered him a sleeping pill, but he refused;

'I won't have a problem sleeping this time, thank you,' he smiled. Still thinking about the sick man and the message from the flowers, he pretended to settle down into his bed for the night. He said goodnight to his parents, who kissed his forehead, tousled his blond locks and departed for home to get some rest. As he waited for the coast to be clear, he stared out of the window at the Bright Moon up in the sky. It was drifting in and out of the clouds. He felt its hypnotic call to him. Resolved, he knew he had to act on the message.

When he was certain that no-one was looking, he clambered out of his bed. Sinking his feet into his slippers and popping on his dressing gown, he sneaked out into the corridor, carrying a flower plucked from his vase. He crept around the bays until he spotted the same patient.

The man was still groaning in pain, clearly still quite distressed.

Chris approached the man and smiled compassionately. The man gazed up sadly and broke into a feeble smile – 'Hello kid, is that for me? How kind you are.'

'Yes, it smells beautiful; I think it can help you if you smell the flower.' Chris gazed shyly at his slippers, certain that the man would just laugh at him, but he didn't. The man gently took the stem and weakly lifted it to his nose, giving it a sniff.

'Ah yup, you're right, kid, it smells wonderful, thank you.' The man smiled and his gaunt pale cheeks seemed to redden with a more lively hue. The machines by his bed showed a steadying of heart rate and blood pressure, much to the nurse's surprise who had come over to check up on the disturbance.

'Kid I feel great!' exclaimed the patient. 'What did you just do? My pain has gone! I can't believe it! I don't understand; it's like a miracle! I feel healed – what did you do, pray for me or something? Was it some kind of magic? Was it God? Please, just tell me!'

Stunned by the sudden improvement, the nurse called for extra assistance; Nurse Kathy – back on shift – came running.

Chris smiled shyly at the patient and shrugged. 'I'm sorry, I don't know. I just had a really strong feeling that you needed to smell the flowers, that's all.'

Chris tried to go back to his bed, but the man wanted to talk more with him. Chris ended up telling him more about his recent experiences, whilst the thriving patient was checked and re-checked by the stunned nurses. Chris even talked a little about what the yogi had told him. The man was enthralled and promised to tell the doctors on the ward round what had happened.

Nurse Kathy had heard all she needed to. She shooed Chris to his own bed, flapping her unfeasibly long varnished nails behind him, warning him to get some sleep before she rang his parents. She tucked Chris in tightly, checking all his vitals before she settled him down to sleep.

Nurse Kathy grinned to herself. *I'm going to dine out for months on this story*, she thought.

58

Nurse Kathy spreads the news

Kathy was keen to spill the beans again about Chris' latest exploits. She had to tell someone and fast so as soon as she went on her break, she scuttled to her locker to find Kevin's number. She rooted around in her leopard-print bag for her mobile. Locating his contact details, she pressed 'call' and crossed her fingers.

'Yes?' Kevin answered curtly, causing Kathy to draw a sharp intake of breath.

'Hey, I've got a lot to tell you! Oh and I'm feeling pretty thirsty' she fished, hoping he would bite.

Kevin's thoughts were racing; it must be more news about Chris. He'd promised the family that he wouldn't create trouble for them; his conscience was pricked, but at heart he was still a reporter, so what else could he do but gather the news, especially when it kept falling in his lap?

'I can meet you at Smyth's at ten tonight,' he snapped shortly, the guilt weighing heavily on his shoulders.

'You're on' she replied, her big flapping lips drawn into a great beaming smile. 'Have my champagne ready for me!' she flirted, plumping her blond curls with her talons and eyeing her reflection in the mirror on the back of the locker door.

He hung up; she reached for her lippy to apply a thick scarlet layer on her pouting lips.

59

CHRIS IS IN THE SPOTLIGHT

News spread fast of the mysterious healing event in the hospital – with a little help from a reporter with shaky principles, a loose-tongued nurse and a grateful patient. Joe and his family read the latest sensationalized version of events by the persistent reporter and sighed at his propensity to cause trouble for them.

'A leopard can't change its spots...' uttered Donna dismissively. Joe was particularly disappointed that Kevin had gone back on his word but, rather than dismiss him for a lost cause, he held out hope that Kevin would soon become aware of his misguided behaviour and change his ways. Chris remained neutral, showing his increasingly non-judgemental nature.

The medics were astounded at what they heard about the apparent healing. Chris was subjected to rigorous questioning from some, but ridicule from others, who continued to be sceptical. Chris' parents agreed that he could extend his stay in the hospital throughout the summer vacation to allow the scientists to really get to grips with what was happening, to explore all the possible options for his symptoms.

He underwent test after test; the medics and researchers logged their results over time to seek any patterns concerning his brain's neural activity, or its wave activity, or his eye and ear function. They began to plot fascinating cyclical changes, which seemed to coincide with symptom occurrence and seemed to rise and fall in a monthly sequence – almost as if his symptoms were occurring in conjunction with the waxing and waning of the Moon.

This possible lunar link led the scientists to seek out more answers from the astrological community. First they consulted with Cousins' colleague, the astro-biologist, who spoke with fervent interest about the occurrence of micro-organisms in space and on other planets.

They then called in the assistance of an astrophysicist from NASA who expressed an interest in the case. However even this clever man's intelligence was stretched trying to understand this conundrum. He was able to teach them all more about the presence of certain elements on the Moon, speaking about the analysis results from the rock samples taken from the Moon's surface. He was also able to elucidate about the influence of the Moon on the Earth's gravitational pull. Yet when it came to explaining why the Moon appeared to be influencing the boy and this boy alone on the whole of the planet, the scientist was completely stumped, claiming it to be completely crazy.

They were too late to call in the expertise of the recently deceased British astrologer Sir Patrick Moore, who had hosted the world famous B.B.C. T.V. program 'The Sky at Night' for many decades and owned the maps of the Moon's surface; he had clearly known its intimate details better than most. This man had had an interest in the science fiction aspect of the Moon's mystery. They wondered whether he had experienced any such stories in his lifetime.

Chris stayed in the hospital over a few Moon cycles in all, regularly practising his special meditation that the yogi had showed him – sometimes with the other yoga participants at the Wellness Centre in the hospital – and he continued to watch the Moon through the hospital windows.

He observed it waxing and waning over each month of the summer, noting that his visual and auditory symptoms increased and decreased in sync. He continued to claim that the symptoms were caused by micro-organisms, and as the symptoms continued to recur, he found himself becoming more accustomed to the experiences, better able to handle them.

One day, Chris spotted a doctor about to give a shot of penicillin to a patient. Chris interrupted him, imploring the doctor not to use that particular needle as it was covered in germs that were likely to endanger the patient's life. This doctor was one of the sceptics and laughed at Chris, telling him to mind his own business.

The doctor had persisted with the shot, eyeing the boy contemptuously out of the corner of his eye. The poor patient had passed away within a couple of days, which had surprised many medics as he had only visited the hospital for a routine operation. Some thought the outcome was just coincidence, whilst others were in the camp that increasingly believed that there was something in the warnings that Chris was giving.

Other events triggered similar split judgments about the boy's abilities. One patient was similarly about to receive an injection from a syringe that Chris claimed was dangerous. Again the doctor ignored his advice and the patient ended up in Intensive Care, bleeding heavily.

On another occasion, the boy came across a gaunt sickly patient who was about to eat a piece of fruit without washing it; Chris noticed it was covered in harmful bacteria.

Assuming they would make the patient sick, he shouted out to the man not to eat it. The man froze in shock and then put the apple down, not sure what to make of the strange command, thinking perhaps he had taken the boy's fruit by mistake or something.

Chris was then suddenly overwhelmed by noises in his head, which he couldn't understand. He closed his eyes and breathed deeply, trying to connect with his inner self as advised by the yogi. Suddenly he could hear voices in his head. It was as if he had been tuning his radio antenna and instead of just hearing the white noise of random signals, he was suddenly picking up a radio station. He could understand the language that was spoken, yet it wasn't people, it was micro-organisms! Chris knew that they were communicating from the piece of fruit!

Startled, he stopped in his tracks and stared at the apple. The patient appeared even more disturbed and offered the fruit to Chris in supplication, concerned that Chris was about to flip out on him in some kind of psychotic fit.

Chris took the apple by the stem, where there was minimal bacterial coverage. He stared intently at it, tuning in to the beautiful sounds emanating from it, which became words that he could hear, which seemed to say;

'Shashanka, take us, use us, we are on humanity's side. We can help you. Why are you humans so ignorant that you do not know the remedies? We bacteria have descended from another source from deep space. We do not comprehend how human understanding functions.

Human vocabulary is insufficient to communicate the subtleties of feelings that we experience, so humans seem superficial. We do not know how to name the planet that we came from using your language;

all we know is that we are here.

Maybe you are the only human at the moment who can be a bridge to communicate between humans and our world of bacteria. Now is your chance to use us; just let us come into contact with the man just for a split second and we will enter his system and overpower the demonic germs he has in him.'

Chris felt dizzy and wobbled unsteadily on his feet. Dr. Holmes and Nurse Kathy were on duty and came rushing over to help steady Chris, asking him what was the matter. He was in shock, but he felt compelled to act on this message he had received directly from the bacteria. He gazed up at the patient, who was staring wide-eyed and nervously at Chris.

'Please, get a taste of this apple! It's not garbage, it is a life-saving piece of fruit,' said Chris urgently to the man, whose eyebrows were now raised heavenwards in confusion.

'Try! Please try!' implored Chris. 'It will help to combat the bad germs in your body which are making you really sick!'

Nurse Kathy put her pudgy hand over her great mouth to stifle a giggle; 'Do you think you're Harry Potter or something?' she said sniggering.

Chris fought back his embarrassment, persisting with his appeal to the patient to eat a piece of the fruit. Confused, the patient glanced enquiringly over at Dr. Holmes, who tugged on his bright bow-tie, shrugged and said,

'It's just an apple, one of your five fruits you're supposed to eat in a day. I can't see why you shouldn't eat it.'

The patient nodded weakly; he was too sick to argue. He reached over to take the apple and pressed it to his lips for a bite.

After chewing the sweet apple for a few seconds, his cheeks seemed to fill out and become rosier. His glazed eyes cleared and his oxygen saturation improved. His renewed vitality positively oozed from every pore. The patient grinned from ear to ear and leapt out of bed to hug Chris.

'Son, you're a miracle worker. I can't thank you enough! I feel like a million dollars!'

'It wasn't me sir, it was the bacteria!' countered Chris, embarrassed by the show of affection from the grateful man.

'Whatever you say kid, you're the boss!' the patient was dancing around the room with the nurses, who were giggling and smiling, despite their confusion.

60

CHRIS TUNES IN TO THE SOUNDS OF THE MICRO-ORGANISMS

This event triggered Chris to take more notice of the sounds coming from the bacteria and over the following weeks he fine-tuned his antenna to be able to interpret the different sounds emanating from different micro-organisms around him. Having identified the unique sounds of the friendly bacteria that helped to heal the man with cancer, he was better able to detect where they were around him.

Hard as it was for him to keep seeing the micro-organisms everywhere, he was gathering courage daily in opening his eyes to detect them, aware now that some of the bacteria were potentially life-saving and others were harmful. Strangely they seemed to emit different types of sounds. The micro-organisms that seemed to intend good to humanity expressed beautiful harmonious sounds, whereas those that were intending harm sounded harsh and grumbling.

Using this knowledge, Chris would seek out those with harmonious sounds, and wherever he found them, he would dare to open his eyes and identify what the micro-organisms were crawling on. One occasion he felt sure he could detect the harmonious sounds again coming from the other side of the room. He nervously peeped out trying to focus in on the sound and spotted a surgical spoon on a tray. He picked up the spoon and took it to a patient, who was similarly suffering from cancer. He begged the patient to lick the spoon; the desperate terminally-ill patient eagerly did so. Again the nurses around the patient were laughing contemptuously, but the patient rapidly improved, finding great relief in his symptoms.

61

THE POWER OF MUSIC

Chris was gathering more and more experience identifying sounds with different micro-organisms, but sometimes the incessant noise proved too much for him. He needed to drown out the sounds to get some sense of peace. His dad bought him an 'Tablet-Gadget' to help cancel out the sounds; this led him to make another interesting discovery.

One day when he was quietly listening to the music on his bed, a female patient came up and tapped him on the shoulder. Chris jumped in surprise. He pulled out the earplugs to hear what the girl had to say. Instantly his unprotected ears were filled with a harsh groaning kind of sound; he was repulsed to see the girl's arms were covered in strange-looking bacteria, which were rapidly multiplying on her angry inflamed skin.

'Excuse me, but what are you listening to?' asked the girl inquisitively. Chris tried to tear his eyes away from her arms to focus on what she was saying.

'Um, Coldplay – a British band that I like,' he said distractedly. The girl smiled, but she didn't go away. She just stood there scratching her swollen eczema-covered arm. Chris wanted to escape from her, but instead he swallowed his aversion to the teeming bacteria and offered her a spare

Bright Moon

surgical gown from his drawer to wear, suggesting it was to keep her warm, but actually it was to cover her arms. She accepted, slipping the gown over her clothes and covering her arms, helping Chris feel more at ease in her company.

'I can't sleep, my arm itches too much,' she said sadly, scratching away under the sleeves.

'Would you like to hear some music?' asked Chris kindly. The girl nodded enthusiastically. Chris took the earplugs and popped them into the girl's ears. She smiled, her pretty face lighting up. She began to bop around; Chris laughed. They shared a happy dance together – a blessed relief from the serious life he had been leading recently.

When the album finished, the girl asked if Chris had any other songs.

'Um, not really; I only have this meditation one that my dad downloaded for me, but I don't know if you'd like it.'

'I don't mind, can I hear it?' asked the girl enthusiastically, her wide hazel eyes imploring.

'I guess so,' said Chris, rotating his finger round the button to select the meditation album.

They had an earpiece each, sitting together side by side on the bed. The album played many different tracks each with various instruments creating harmonious and relaxing sounds, which sent Chris and the girl into a trance-like state.

As the music came to an end, they tugged out the earpieces and sighed happily, with a big grin on their faces. The girl suddenly laughed a tinkling sound of pleasure.

'What is it?' asked Chris, curiously.

'My arm; it feels much better, it's not itching so much

anymore!' she was smiling from ear to ear, her hazel eyes clear with relief.

'I guess we took your mind off it with the music!' laughed Chris.

'Maybe, hey look – it's less red!' she cried. The girl had pulled the gown sleeve up and was showing Chris her arm. It was still eczema-covered but appeared a little less 'angry'. Chris swallowed his revulsion and noticed that the bacteria he had spotted earlier were only moving slowly. They also seemed to have stopped replicating. He listened carefully, but the harsh groaning sounds of earlier were much weaker now. Why? Was it something to do with the music? Were the bacteria somehow affected by the music?

The girl smiled at him; 'My arm feels a lot better, you know. I think I could get some sleep now. Thanks, I had a lot of fun. See you later!' and slipped away back to her bed.

'My pleasure, see you later,' he said. He was delighted for her, but puzzled. He tried to work out what had just happened. Was it just coincidence that the inflamed arm had improved, or had the music somehow helped her?

He knew that the harmonious sounds from the music had blocked out the groaning harsh sounds of the micro-organisms crawling on the girl's arm. Yet when the music had stopped, he realized that those harsh sounds had nearly gone and so was the worst of the itching and the redness on the girl's arm!

He could only conclude that the multiplying and wriggling bad bacteria had been partially responsible for the acuteness of the girl's skin symptoms. He wondered if the beautiful music had somehow cancelled out the effects of the bad micro-organisms; in their apparent neutralization her symptoms had been able to improve.

If this was true, it was a real turn up for the books. Chris needed to talk to someone about this revelation. In the meantime, Chris put his scientist hat back on and decided to do some more experimenting – after all, it was pretty boring stuck in hospital all the time, he needed something exciting to do.

Chris decided he would visit patients that seemed to have the harsh groaning sounds emanating from their bodies. He would play them the meditation music and see if they began to feel better. He took his Tablet-Gadget around the ward and offered to share the music with various patients. Much to his delight and awe, each patient that listened to certain tracks seemed to experience some sort of cancelling out of the disharmonious sounds and an equivalent improvement of symptoms.

'Curiouser and curiouser!' quoted Chris, as if he was submerged in the story of Alice in Wonderland.

Realizing that some tracks seemed less effective at helping the patients, Chris wondered what was different about the healing tracks. He decided to ask his dad during one of his visits, as Joe was a huge music fan.

62

Sound healing

They sat together on the bed listening to the tracks. Joe, delighted that Chris had sparked an interest in the healing power of music, picked out the sound of a violin in common to each of the healing tracks. He knew that stringed instruments had a similar quality to the human voice, but wasn't sure what was special about a violin. He suggested that they spoke with his sound healer colleague from the store to glean more information.

Chris agreed this was a great idea, and a couple of days later, Joe brought the sound healer – John Silverman – to the hospital to visit Chris.

Chris watched as Silverman approached. He had an almost other-worldly air about him, and was light on his feet, walking towards Chris as if dancing on his toes. Silverman was indeed a silver-haired man, whose long straight hair was scraped back into a ponytail, accentuating the proportions of his enormous ears.

Silverman had noticeably large ears for a man with such a small head and eyes, as if he had evolved a fantastic sense of hearing at the expense of his appearance. These fine auditory appendages clearly brought him much pleasure as he was invariably absorbed in a sea of music or sound from his Tablet-Gadget, which he never turned off, although he conceded to turn it down in order to converse with Chris.

'Hello Chris,' he boomed. His voice was intense – a deep luscious voice which emanated from somewhere deep within him. It reminded Chris of a fine theatrical actor who could project his voice to the very back seats of the auditorium, yet it also carried a healing quality to it; a timbre of believability and comfort, as if he could transport the listener to far-off lands of paradise and peace through his meaningfully spoken words.

From the first meeting, they hit it off magnificently, as if they were on the same wave-length. Chris excitedly chattered about different patients that had seemed to get well after listening to specific tracks, explaining that the violin sound was present in each one of them.

'Chris, what you're reporting – about certain sounds having healing qualities – is exactly the science that I use in my job as a sound healer,' uttered Silverman with his deep bass voice. 'All life is based on the premise that its matter is vibrating at various frequencies. Right from the beginning of time, life was brought into existence by sound – the Bible says that The Word of God was the instigator for Genesis.'

'We can say that matter vibrates at an optimum frequency but if that frequency goes off-tune, then in humans for example this can manifest as disease. Yet it only takes an immersion in the correct frequencies for that matter's resonance to be entrained by natural resounding frequency back to its optimum vibrational state. This helps the body to shake off disease.'

He passed an earphone to Chris so that he could hear the sacred-sounding choral chants playing on his Tablet-Gadget. Chris listened to the eerily powerful music, entranced. He felt it resonate through his body down to his feet; his entire being shook in a sea of sound.

'Music is a fantastic way for humans to immerse their bodies in beneficial sound waves; the human voice is one of the most powerful ways to do this – especially if the sound is self-generated,' explained Silverman in his liquid tone. Chris nodded enthusiastically, passing back the earphone.

'Wow – that's what the yogi taught me! I perform a singing meditation to help me tune in!'

'There you go! You're already helping to heal yourself. Stringed instruments do have similar sound wave patterns to the human voice and similar expression through vibrato, so I'm not surprised that the patients' health improved when they heard the violin.'

'If I had my way, all hospitals would be housed in resonating concert halls like cathedrals, which immerse the patients in healing music. How much more pleasant would that be than being cut open, or irradiated, or given hideous medication that made you even sicker.'

'You can say that again! I'd much rather listen to beautiful music, or make beautiful music!' exclaimed Chris.

'There are lots of people that understand these principles now – but they are nothing new. Ancient cultures and civilizations used this sound entrainment knowledge long ago to heal their people. All we are doing is remembering how to do it again, in our culture.'

'This is amazing! Are there other instruments that have a healing effect?' asked Chris, intrigued.

'Sure – many of them were used by the Ancients, because their shape was important for setting up the desired vibrational and sound wave effect. There is an Indian instrument called a Veena and a Flute of China. Each of these are also specifically effective for healing. I think there are also various Native American instruments, such as flutes. There are Aboriginal Didgeridoos, ting-shas, singing bowls, medicine drums and many more – mostly from the Ancient civilizations.'

'They're all different examples of instruments that have been used to change energy by clearing energetic blockages and entraining cells and perhaps brain waves too into a more healthy optimum vibrational state. Think 'coherence' – the cells are all 'singing to the same hymn sheet' and therefore are much better able to communicate with each other on similar wavelengths.'

'Each instrument, however, might have a different effect in a different part of the body or energy field, due to its specific vibrational frequency. Our voices are capable of shifting all our blockages – we can use different vowel sounds and different pitches to shift them, but it's particularly effective if the sound is carried on a conscious wave of intent. We can intend healing, wholeness, peace, love, compassion – all such intentions create a beautiful brain wave pattern that somehow interweaves with the sound. The sound helps to deliver these patterns into our body cells and helps them to remember a more healthy structure and vibration.' Silverman smiled.

Chris and Joe were floored by this conversation, but Chris was keen to continue, dying to get to the bottom of his experiences.

'Why do you think the music is doing something to the micro-organisms in and on the patients?' asked Chris.

'Well, microbiology is not an area I know much about,

but perhaps micro-organisms also respond to vibration and sounds. Perhaps on a very fundamental level, it's the bacteria actions that are changing in response to the sounds. Harmony somehow soothes them into a less harmful state, a more melodious state, where they are having a less negative effect on the patient, but I've never done any research on sound and microbes.' Silverman fell quiet as he pondered these ideas. It could certainly open up a new research area in the sound healing field.

'I'd like to talk it through with a bacteria specialist,' he finally said.

'I'm sure Hannah's dad would love to do that!' said Chris excitedly.

'Well let's do it!' said Silverman. Joe nodded, and promised to set up a meeting.

'Why don't you show me your sound meditation, Chris?' asked Silverman.

'I'd love to!' grinned Chris.

The three of them sat on Chris' bed and, much to the surprise and amusement of the nurses, they began to sing their way through the 'HREEM-GREEM-GLAUM-GLAHA' meditation.

63

WHAT CAN THE MEDICS CONCLUDE FROM ALL THIS?

The fall-out from these bizarre events was immense; the fruit-eating patient was a case in point.

He had been admitted to hospital requiring surgery and chemotherapy for a particularly aggressive cancerous tumour, yet following the apple incident, his test results showed a complete reduction of the cancer; he went on to make a full recovery. Similarly the patient that had licked the spoon was found to have gone into remission.

Although many medics were reticent to believe the results they were finding, it became increasingly difficult for them to ignore the regular healing events that seemed to be occurring and the miraculous test results that came back proving that people really were getting better after following Chris' advice.

Yet without a valid explanation for why these miracles were occurring, the medics felt unable to communicate to the patients what was happening, uncomfortable admitting that the healings were occurring by means outside of the clinically trialled drugs of their profession.

Meetings were held, in which confused medics discussed the ethics of what was occurring. They decided that the F.D.A.

– the Federal Drugs Agency – would have to be informed. But without using drugs, what was there to tell them?

64

Researchers look at bacteria

Under Dr. Cousins' direction, scientists were sent to research about beneficial micro-organisms that were capable of combating disease-causing micro-organisms; they dug out research which was currently underway in the world with what was known as 'friendly bacteria'. They were so called because they were naturally present in the human body, and provided beneficial protective action for the human immune system.

Such beneficial bacteria included the exotically-named lactobacillus acidophilus and bifidobacterium bifidum strains.

They even found that such bacteria were being clinically trialled in hospitals in the U.K. and U.S.A. – albeit for less severe illnesses, but the friendly bacteria were shown in the trials to be helpful against harmful bugs such as Escherichia coli, Noro virus and M.R.S.A. Certain progressive and forward thinking nutrition supplement companies were utilizing this research to expand the sales of friendly bacteria products, known as probiotics; they were already getting magnificent results in the fight against all sorts of diseases.

There was even research evidence to support the concept that getting an effective balance of friendly bacteria in the gut was beneficial in helping to prevent various types of cancer. Startled by their findings but buoyed up by their scientific evidence they were better able to accept the results which Chris seemed to be getting with his intuitive advice about micro-organisms.

Some experts felt that Chris' visions of micro-organisms were a sign that the hospital was invaded by a new infectious outbreak; they warned the Hospital Board that they might be in for a tough ride if this were to go public. Experts were called in from the Centres for Disease Control and Prevention in Atlanta to assess the situation, in case there was potential for a Public Health threat.

This triggered off a massive investigation into the hospital and its hygiene policies.

As the healing events continued to happen, various medical staff started to change their attitude towards Chris' abilities, until gradually, most of the doctors, surgeons and medical directors in the hospital were prepared to consider that the boy's visions were in fact the genuine article.

His abilities to interpret the sounds from the micro-organisms seemed to be developing over all this time. It was as if he was able to communicate with them in their own special language. He found it hard to explore this idea with most of the scientists, but Cousins came in regularly to discuss his findings. They shared many scintillating discussions about the ways the micro-creatures might be communicating, which Cousins proceeded to investigate through his research.

Buoyed up by a conversation with the sound healer – Silverman – Cousins was keen to explore the current studies of microbiology on sound waves. Cousins delved into research that showed microbial cells may communicate through various physical means, not just via sound, but also via electric currents and electromagnetic radiation; specifically infra-red and visual light in the form of photons. This physical signal communication seemed less well understood compared with the chemical sensing techniques many researchers usually focused on.

Some of the sound wave communication between bacteria was shown to increase or regulate bacterial growth. More excitingly, a coherent collective vibrational mode was reached when all the cells were 'in tune', which could amplify the signal.

In terms of Chris' ability to hear the sounds of microbes, Cousins wondered how a human could tune into this sort of communication, to be able to 'hear' what microbes were 'saying'. He didn't think that human ears were built to be able to physically hear such ultra-low frequency sounds.

Then he wondered if bacterial communication with Chris may be more to do with thought waves – like E.S.P., or Extra-Sensory Perception – but he felt out of his league in terms of explaining how a brain could act as an antenna for such signals, especially as brain waves are at a much lower frequency. He needed to research much more about whether bacteria emit waves in the same frequency range as human brain waves, but this was not his field.

He also found that there may be some similarities between the way that both humans and microbes inter-convert physical signals for their communication networks. In a manner analogous to the inter-conversion of sounds and electric signals in fixed telephone lines, research indicated that microbial cells might be polarized by incoming sound waves of the correct frequency to control the flow of electrons and electric currents generated or received by the cell and vice versa.

Intriguingly, some of the research showed that microbe sizes and visual light wavelengths correlated, showing perhaps how light photons may be involved in the way micro-organisms 'spoke' to each other, by sharing or downloading information.

As the proof stacked up for microbes communicating through sound and other physical means, the other medics became keener to get on board.

Chris regularly astounded Cousins with his ability to describe micro-organisms in terms of their appearance, communication, growth and behaviour, such as division, mutation and reaction to anti-microbial drugs – all without the aid of a scanning electron microscope. He could draw micro-beings and Cousins would help him to identify them. This miracle stirred Cousins' excitement and wonder; he reported back his finding to those medics that would listen, such as Krefeld and Holmes, prompting numerous discussions to work out how Chris was able to do it.

Cousins called in extra help from the Department of Microbiology and Immunology at the University of California, San Francisco. Their heated discussions led to excited enquiries about how this knowledge and insight could be used to help answer some of the world's questions about germs and viruses. They discussed whether they would be able to share these ideas with the Centres for Disease Control and Prevention, in the hope that any new insights could assist the world with battling infectious diseases, or preventing outbreaks. Surely funding would be available for more research into this; they just needed to find the right open-minded scientists to carry out this ground-breaking research.

65

A NEW PARADIGM FOR HEALTH

The research question led Chris' medical team to contact new specialists in the field of psycho-neuro-immunology, including a psychologist from Harvard – Dr Kelso – whose specialty was treating the person rather than treating the disease.

Dr Kelso had a full, rounded figure, smiling face, welcoming kindly eyes and a lilting gentle Irish accent which as a combined package brought to mind the description of an 'Earth Mother'.

In a meeting in the sun-dappled hospital Board Room with the 'psych' specialists on Chris' case, Kelso was able to explain a relatively new paradigm in Western medical thinking that encouraged a complete change of perspective from focusing on the disease to having a vision of potential for health. She explained that disease may be triggered by having negative thoughts and beliefs, which seemed to cause a glitch in the body's natural healthy operating system, such that it veered from a state of optimum health and regeneration to one of compromised health and mutated or impaired regeneration – i.e. disease.

As the medics sipped from their sparkling crystal water glasses, enrapt with her words, she likened the healthy state to one of harmony and optimum function, explaining that this state was encouraged by the presence of love and heightened conscious awareness of the oneness of all beings, from individual cells and micro-organisms up to more complicated bio-systems such as humans.

The dust particles in the room lit up, dancing in the shafts of sunshine streaming through the large open windows. The pleasant tune of a songbird drifted through from the trees outside.

Krefeld stroked his goatee in contemplation for a moment, then asked her how this idea could be applied to real-life patients. Kelso laughed – a full-bodied chuckle that brought smiles to everyone's faces. She took a sip from her cool clear water and continued, explaining that patients came to her with so-called splintered personalities, because they had issues with certain facets of their character, such as their anger, or guilt. Patients often entered a state of denial about that part of themselves, thus creating a blockage and cutting off a vital part of their whole energetic system.

She stopped as she noticed the medics' confused expressions. Remembering that this was not a well-known Western idea for many conventional medics, Kelso's eyes scanned the room as she searched for a way to depict her idea. Spotting a white board, she grabbed a marker and swiftly drew out a picture of a person, drawing circles around specific parts of the body and labelling them with emotions, linking the liver with anger, the gall bladder with resentment as examples.

She drew lines of energy meridians over the body, drawing large crosses at the specified organs, showing how the emotions had created a blockage in the energy network, which forced an energetic imbalance within the body, which could lead to a diseased state.

Some of the medics were nodding indicating they were starting to understand. Kelso pushed on, explaining that if the patient could come to terms with these denied parts of themselves, then they could rebalance their energetic system, removing blockages and returning flow and harmony to their body once more. She rubbed out the crosses on the diagram and showed arrows of energy flow around the body.

Barnes was slow to catch on; his scepticism seemed to be clouding his understanding. He threw a sarcastic comment in her direction, which she countered deftly with an offer to explain in more simple terms that a child might understand. Barnes frowned, but Kelso pursued the child-like illustration. She joked that the idea could be represented by the fairy tale story of Snow White and the Seven Dwarfs. Barnes coughed sharply in embarrassment, his usually grey complexion turning a subtle shade of pink.

Kelso smiled kindly at him and continued. To her, she explained gently, each dwarf represented the different characteristics or facets of a person's mind; conceptualized into a separate dwarf body, they were likened to splinters of a person's split personality. In the fairy tale, as Snow White drew the Dwarfs together and cared for each one, she brought an unconditional love into the Dwarfs' home, bringing harmony and acceptance. In her lilting Irish accent, Kelso explained that Snow White's uniting loving force represented the heart of the person with the split personality, which had the power to embrace all the split personalities back to a whole and healed state, creating a heightened awareness and energetic harmony.

Barnes, unable to connect with the discussion, left the meeting prematurely, shaking his pallid puffy face with lips tightly held in resentment. Turning back he eyed the smiling faces of the others chatting round the table, excitedly discussing the new paradigm. He coughed a loud barking cough, as if demanding that they notice his dramatic exit, but no-one noticed. He shut the door on them all disgustedly, grimacing as he felt the all too familiar sharp pain in his side.

66

EXPERTS DISCUSS THE ROLE OF MICRO-ORGANISMS IN HEALTH

The recoveries witnessed in the hospital catalysed a series of meetings between a widening group of experts, including neuroscientists, physicists, philosophers, psychiatrists, eye specialists, alternative therapists, microbiologists and psychologists. They discussed the recoveries witnessed in the hospital and how micro-organisms could possibly have helped.

The experts had gathered in a meeting room at the hospital; the atmosphere was buzzing with excitement and curiosity.

Krefeld kicked off the discussion with a question for the assembled group.

'Thank you all for coming today. You know that we have gathered to discuss Chris McKenzie and to acknowledge that various medical events have occurred in the hospital in conjunction with Chris' intervention that we have been unable to explain scientifically. My main focus would be for us to discuss the possible role that micro-organisms might have had in these events, as Chris claims that the medical advice he gets comes from the bacteria. So I'd like to ask you all what your opinions on this matter might be?' Krefeld surveyed the room, meeting the eyes of each individual.

'Are you asking if we think that bacteria can truly be intelligent enough to offer us medical help?' Barnes appeared uncomfortable.

'That is a good place to start' encouraged Krefeld with a smile.

'Well, my first question is to ask how intelligent could bacteria actually be?' Barnes seemed to be in his usual cynical mood. 'If bacteria really are intelligent, then where do they carry their intelligence, as they don't appear to have a brain?'

Krefeld countered this with another question;

'I think that what has happened clearly demonstrates that bacteria could have a depth of knowledge that we cannot comprehend, indicating a very real intelligent presence. This poses a different question that lies in the field of neuroscience. If they have no brain but are still intelligent, does this mean that the brain is not essential to a being having intelligence? What is intelligence? Is it an effect of consciousness, or a self-contained, interactive and self-developing energy of information?' He rubbed his goatee beard thoughtfully.

'Well I think that is a very likely hypothesis,' agreed the psychologist, but Barnes was clearly riled by this thought;

'I don't know about any of that, but what I don't get then is, assuming micro-beings actually are intelligent – and I'm not convinced yet that they are – how do micro-beings have the ability to comprehend more than what we know? We are so much bigger than them and so much more evolved, surely?'

Krefeld grinned at Barnes;

'Well I'm not sure you could argue that evolution point,

as bacteria and other micro-organisms have been around a lot longer than we have, but I agree that intelligence can't therefore be contained within a brain. I think it must be a bit like a separate entity – like 'The Cloud', perhaps, that makes wireless broadband available for information download away from home.'

The psychologist chipped in; 'Well, if intelligence is a separate entity – perhaps like electricity – then it needs a base for it to develop in its own way.'

Barnes was still fighting the sizeist point; 'How could such cleverness manifest in minute viruses such as H.I.V.?'

Krefeld was showing signs of frustration – his eyelid was flickering as he answered;

'As we've just said, it can't be to do with size – the quantum or quantity of matter – otherwise such intelligence couldn't exist in such tiny beings.'

The psychologist interjected, sensing a disagreement in the air;

'In my understanding, intelligence seems to be an automatically evolving entity; it is happening on all levels of life, from the micro-world to the macro-world. Perhaps if intelligence is like a cloud, it is somehow shared between all beings?'

The acupuncturist jumped into the conversation, keen to encourage this line of thought;

'I wouldn't be surprised if that was true! Many religions speak of the oneness of everything, so why not the oneness of intelligence; the mind of God, if you like?'

'Well I'm not religious, and I don't believe in a bearded man in the sky who controls everything, but this does make me wonder if the Universe is simply a massive intelligent being?' The psychologists' eyes were shining with the overwhelming thought.

Barnes scoffed at this idea; 'Well, where do we humans fit into that model then? What happens with our intelligence? I'm sure I'm not controlled by any other entity – I make up my own mind and thoughts and I couldn't know everything that I know without a lot of hard work learning from books and research!'

Cousins felt it was time to get in on the conversation and steer it back to the micro-organisms. Finding his glasses nestled in his ginger curls, he placed them on his nose and flicked through his notes. Much of his research and discussions with Chris had led him to postulate some quite revolutionary hypotheses about their behaviour and how it may link with ours as humans. He cleared his throat and began to speak.

'Maybe we are simply splinters of organic matter, like individual cells or germs, making our own mind and interpretations within that massive intelligence. If we compare this behaviour with that of micro-organisms, it's like that of single-celled organisms working alone. Yet they don't ever work entirely alone. They can adapt to work together by creating clusters or communities that work together as a wholly functioning unit, for the good of the community, but how do they do that? They somehow tap into each other to make a joint decision on their behaviour, so is this a sign that they are sharing intelligence, or that they are being influenced by something outside of the community, a bigger entity, a bigger intelligence that controls them all?'

'If you're going to start talking like that, then what's to stop us thinking that maybe our bodies are just an encased environment for a bunch of germs, that there are cultures out there that are controlling us.' The acupuncturist had added this last idea into the room, but it had landed like a hand grenade.

Each person round the table was now shuffling nervously, staring anxiously at each other.

'This is getting a little bit eerie now! It's like some sort of extra-terrestrial science-fiction movie; next you'll be saying that the micro-organisms are some kind of alien creatures that are here to take over the world!' Barnes said sarcastically, but the others laughed nervously.

'Well micro-organisms have a pretty good track record for how they run their lives – they know how to adapt and mutate to become indestructible, so let's hope they are on our side!' Cousins took a sip from his water glass, while the others contemplated their next question.

'Why are some bacteria and viruses indestructible?' asked Krefeld, curiously. Cousins was ready with his answer;

'Micro-organisms have been around ever since the beginning of life on Earth, so they have had a very long time to learn how to protect themselves. Single-celled organisms were the very first life-forms to develop on Earth 3-4 billion years ago. In the Precambrian Eon, all organisms were microscopic, so for most of the history of life on Earth its life-forms have been on this microscopic scale. Bacteria, algae and fungi have been found in 220 million year old amber fossils, dating from the Triassic period, showing similar morphology to today!'

'Some are able to survive even at significantly high temperatures or freezing temperatures, aren't they? How do they do that?' Krefeld was stabbing the table with his pencil at every syllable.

'Micro-organisms can reproduce rapidly and bacteria can freely exchange genes through conjugation, transformation and transduction, even between completely different species. This enables them to evolve really quickly as they swap genes and mutate to survive in new environments proportional to environmental stresses. However as cells cluster into bigger organisms called eukaryotes – we humans are a eukaryote species by the way – they may become less adaptable. Dinosaurs were possibly not very adaptable because they were so large. Perhaps we should beware of what happened to the dinosaurs...unless we learn to adapt like micro-organisms do, how can we possibly expect to survive through all the environmental stresses we are placing on the planet at the moment?'

The room fell silent as they considered this apocalyptic idea. Cousins observed their reactions then added;

'As I said, microbes are incredibly adaptable. Scientists have found them in most habitats on Earth, even at the poles, in deserts, geysers and rocks. Extremophiles are the micro-organisms that have adapted to survive at extreme temperatures, salinity, pressure, radiation and acidity or alkalinity, which leads us to suspect they may survive on other planets.'

'Are you saying that they came from another planet? Is that the connection Chris has with the Moon and micro-organisms?' asked Krefeld incredulously.

'Well I don't know, and I couldn't tell you who would know such a thing. Perhaps my astro-biologist friend would have something to say on this?' pondered Cousins.

'If they have come from another planet, is there an extra-terrestrial language, community and culture associated with these micro-beings?' asked the acupuncturist curiously.

'Yes, and if so, how can we communicate with them?' considered the psychologist.

'Would they really listen to us?' asked Barnes sceptically.

'I wonder, what is their awareness of us? What must they think of us humans?' questioned Krefeld. 'After all, aren't we just a mountain of bacteria?'

'You could say! We have more than 1000 billion microbes per square meter of skin, and even just in shaking hands, we pass on 34 million microbes.' Cousins humorously offered his hand to his neighbours to shake; each made a mock disgusted face.

'We've talked about intelligence of micro-organisms, but what about their consciousness? If each of these billions of micro-organisms is a source of consciousness, what effect does this mass of consciousness have on us?' The psychologist was wide-eyed, appearing a little overwhelmed.

'Well I can't begin to imagine! When you put it like that, it does make me think that they can't fail to at least influence our consciousness.'

Krefeld was studying the confused expressions of the other experts, feeling slightly giddy in the head trying to comprehend what this all meant.

'Perhaps it actually is our consciousness,' postulated Cousins. 'Perhaps our self-awareness is simply the collective consciousness of the trillions of bacteria we have in our bodies?' He was aware that he had just removed the pin from the proverbial hand grenade, and watched the faces of the group pass through various emotions – horror, incredulousness, anger, dismay and epiphany. The atmosphere in the room was electric.

'Is this the reason that we don't have much control over our bodies?' asked Barnes, interrupting the moment to voice his thoughts.

'You speak for yourself!' laughed Baines, who had been listening carefully to the whole discussion, quietly taking it all in. The room erupted into laughter, which helped to disperse some of the nervous anxiety that was pervading the atmosphere. Krefeld stepped in to take back control of the discussion.

'Well I don't know about that – our bodies come under the control of our brain, and the different parts of the brain control different activities – some are conscious and others not.'

'I don't think we need to worry,' said Cousins. 'Certain French microbiologists believe that we don't submit to bacterial control until our brains instruct the micro-organisms to act – albeit unconsciously. They may even act in our favour, to symbiotically create some sort of cell clearance via an illness so as to let the body start again in its cell regeneration, preferably with a healthier construct program in place.'

'That would fit with Alternative Medicine ideas,' said the acupuncturist. 'For instance both Naturopathy and Chinese Medicine philosophy support the idea that illness serves as a beneficial re-harmonizing tool when mal-adaptation has created an imbalance in the system. Illnesses and micro-organisms create a mini-explosion, a turmoil, which clears away some of the original problem – perhaps a mass associated with a perceived stress or emotional disorder. Such approaches have led people to understand that specific illnesses may be created by specific maladaptive and negative thought beliefs.'

The psychologist nodded; 'There is a great surge of new therapies available now to help re-frame these negative mental constructs – we would use Cognitive Behavioural Therapy, but I know there are others out there like Neuro-Linguistic Programming and Emotional Freedom Technique'.

'I think they all help the patient get to the root of their energetic blockages, which is also what I do with acupuncture, but without asking about the thought process.'

'So are we saying that microbes only activate themselves in illnesses when ordered to by the brain? That indicates a sort of psychic instruction program that triggers and controls their activation in the body.' Krefeld was playing with new ground here – and starting to feel a bit lost. Silence descended on the room as the experts struggled to figure it all out. The acupuncturist interrupted their thoughts;

'I know this is a bit of a curve ball idea, but is this all just a mystical question? What do religions and the scriptures say about all this?'

Krefeld reiterated the question, clutching at straws for answers.

'Isn't it true that micro-organisms weren't discovered until the 17th century when the first microscope was invented, so I doubt that anything was written about them before then,' said Baines.

'Well I thought that too,' said Cousins 'but Chris got me thinking about all this. He visited an Indian yogi guru a while back, who said some pretty astonishing things about people being able to communicate with micro-beings, so I began wondering what else there was in Indian teachings about this subject. Chris explained that he thought many things came to light through the yogi's meditations, but we wondered whether there were any descriptions of such beings in ancient Indian history.

'We looked them up with Chris and Joe, and actually from what we can work out, they were first spoken of centuries ago, in 6th Century BC in the Jainism religion, based on teachings by a guru called Mahavira. This guru had led a pure life and spent most of it in deep contemplation, until suddenly he attained a profound understanding about the nature of all things. He went on to teach about his understandings and through his cosmology teachings he revealed that microbiological creatures were living in earth, water, air and fire.'

The group was entranced. Cousins straightened his lab coat and continued;

'Jain scriptures actually described sub-microscopic creatures called 'nigodas' which had a very short life span and lived in large clusters within plant tissue and animals. They were pervasive throughout the Universe. They believed that these lowest forms of life had little hope of release by self-effort. Jain tradition said that when a human being rose to the state of the Supreme Abode, located at the top of the Universe ready to live a liberated existence in omniscient and eternal bliss, another being from the Nigoda realm was given the potential of self-effort and hope.'

Cousins stopped, noticing a glazed expression had appeared on everyone's faces, apart from Baines.

'It reminds me of Star Wars' said Baines, his eyes shining behind his enormous glasses. His apparently flippant comment created a ripple of laughter around the room, but he defended his comment; 'I know it's only science fiction, but it's a surprisingly similar story. Do you remember? Let me look it up to show you!'

Baines pulled out his phone and found a web page that

described the philosophy behind the Star Wars story.

'Look, it says here that the Jedi from the Star Wars stories spoke of 'midi-chlorians' – an intelligent microscopic microbe-like life form that lived symbiotically inside the cells of all living things. When present in sufficient numbers they enabled their host to detect the pervasive energy field known as the Force. Higher 'midi-chlorian' counts were linked to potential in the Force.'

The others were laughing now, anxieties lessened by the memory of film fantasy world. Baines continued;

'One character was even believed in the story to have been conceived without a biological father by the midi-chlorians. The microscopic life-forms were also said to continually speak to their hosts, telling them the will of the Force. One Jedi character explained to his pupil that when he learnt to still his mind, he would hear the midi-chlorians speaking to him.'

'Well there you go. That's where the quiet meditation and contemplation bit comes in! That's what Chris does when he stares at the Moon!' Cousins was getting very animated.

'But why does Chris seem to get his visions only after the Full Moon day? What influence does the Full Moon have on all of this? What is it associated with? Perhaps there is more information about that in the scriptures too!'

The acupuncturist chipped in;

'I don't know anything about the Vedas apart from this quote from the Rig-Veda:

Truth is one, the sages speak of it by many names.

But I did a little training in Ayurvedic Medicine, and that system supports the idea that each celestial body in our solar system has a meaning to us – a specific purpose if you like. Each one represents a different part of us. Let me look up what it says about the Moon...'

There was a low chatter in the room whilst the acupuncturist brought up information on her phone.

'Right, here we go; the Moon is said to control our mind and hands. The Moon stands for the symbol water. The entire content of our body is in direct control of the Moon. The Moon is also the supreme controller of our mind and all its effects are related to psychiatric diseases as well as freshness. The Moon is responsible for pain management in our body, pains being of two types; due to lack of water, or excess of water. The first occurs when the Moon is closest to the Sun (New Moon), the second during Full Moon. Did you say that you thought Chris had characteristics that may place him on the autistic spectrum?'

'Yes – I think he may have Asperger's Syndrome, but that is the least of his concerns at the moment,' added Krefeld.

'Well it says here that autism is known in this system as the lunar disease, and that Meditation is seen as very beneficial to calm a hyperactive nature associated with the autistic spectrum. Symptom cycles are reported here to follow 27-day patterns, because the Moon hyper-stimulates the Central Nervous System.'

'That's fascinating, but is it supported by Clinical Evidence?' questioned Barnes, sceptically.

'I'm not finished with the midi-chlorians story!' Baines interrupted; 'Some Jedi in the Star Wars story worked with the 'midi-chlorians' to assist them in their healing work. The 'midi-chlorians' served as organelles – specialized structures – within all living cells, comprising a collective consciousness among them. They were isomorphic – all having a similar form – on every planet that supported life.'

'That's the all-pervasive Universal theory of intelligence then!' laughed Cousins.

'They tested for them in red blood cells,' pointed out Baines, tapping his enormous temple knowingly.

'Right, so are we saying we have to look at Chris' red blood cells again?' laughed Krefeld.

'Would that be such a crazy idea?' questioned Cousins. 'After all I believe that haemoglobin in red blood cells is the same porphyrin macromolecule as chlorophyll in plants. The only difference is what it holds in the centre – one holds iron, the other magnesium. So perhaps the role of chlorophyll in collecting photons from sunlight to transform into energy can somehow be linked with the role of haemoglobin as some sort of photon transformer...?'

Cousins could see Baines was jumping excitedly in his seat at the mention of photons.

'That might need more research...' pondered Krefeld.

'Yes, and I'd love to look into it!' enthused Baines. 'What if there really is some truth in the Star Wars story? It gives me the creeps; it's so similar to what's happening now! In the story there was a prophecy about a Chosen One, with a high concentration of midi-chlorians, who would bring balance to the Force.'

'Ah yes, young Anakin Skywalker in the movie!' said Krefeld, reminiscing. 'Don't tell me you think Chris is a Jedi! Get real! Come on let's bring this discussion back to reality and facts.'

Baines looked hurt.

'Well, if you want scientific facts, I believe mitochondria were the inspiration for the midi-chlorians. I remember learning at college that mitochondria are also organelles that provide energy for the cells, passed on via the female lineage. They are believed to have once been separate bacteria-like organisms that inhabited living cells and have since become part of them. They still have their own D.N.A., as if they are a completely separate life form.'

He surveyed the audience around the table with a conspiratorial expression on his face, nodding his gigantic head as if he had found the answers, hidden in the Star Wars story.

'It even says here that scientists have actually discovered a real bacterial presence residing within mitochondria and they were granted permission to call it midichloria mitochondrii!'

'Well, whaddya know? I'd better clue up on that one!' laughed Cousins, his glasses falling from his nose. 'You see, my friends? We are not as different from bacteria as you may think...! What do you say to all this now?'

Krefeld grinned, stood and straightened his waistcoat.

'I think we have fried our brains enough for one day. I do feel like we've got closer to the answer though don't you?' he gazed around the room and, although many faces appeared a little confused and pale, they nodded in agreement.

'I guess our next discussion should be about what do we do next with this idea? I'll leave that one with you.'

The group disbanded amongst a noisy chatter of animated conversation. This had certainly sparked some interesting ideas, but as Krefeld had highlighted, they needed to turn their minds to where these ideas could lead them.

Krefeld's thoughts turned to Chris. He was suspecting that the conclusions would lead Chris and his family to a rather difficult place and he wasn't sure how he could morally justify that for a twelve year old boy.

This was potentially going to turn into one tricky situation, something ground-breaking perhaps, but in this new territory they would need to make up some new rules... the wheels were turning and Krefeld wondered if this was going to be another giant step for mankind in its evolutionary journey.

He also wondered how the masses would be able to comprehend it all; he questioned if they needed to keep it all under wraps as much as possible to avoid inevitable fall-out at such mind-boggling ideas – after all, it was all just conjecture at this point.

67

COUSINS IMAGINES NEW PARADIGMS FOR EVOLUTION

Cousins was keen to explore some of these ideas that came out of the discussion. He wondered mostly about the equivalent behaviours of microbes and humans, and what could be learnt from their very successful communities and lives.

He was particularly enthused by the thought that single-celled organisms could be equivalent to individual humans; he pondered how they moved from this existence to a multiple cell community and why. He found out that there was a type of cell called an 'imaginal' cell, which was an evolutionary catalyst. Working within the community of other cells, these imaginal cells seemed to break the mould by imagining a new form for replication, which when passed to a critical mass of other cells, allowed the whole system to change in a metamorphosis process, which was likened to that of a caterpillar transforming into a butterfly.

He got very excited, wondering if specific humans could be the imaginal cells of the human community. Maybe Chris could be acting as such a cell, inviting in a new way of being for the rest of humanity. He pondered whether other people might be able to attain the same communication abilities as Chris had accomplished with micro-organisms, if they were to meditate enough on them.

68

Hannah initiates new ideas at Science Club

Hannah continued to show interest in her dad's work relating to Chris; they chatted one evening about his idea concerning imaginal cells and their relation to humans.

She vowed to take the idea back to her Science Club friends to see what the others thought. It was to start a great sweeping change in the children's attitude towards Chris, as each child – instead of thinking what a freak Chris was – embraced the idea that he had managed to achieve something amazing and revolutionary, which might be possible for others to do too. It certainly appealed to their sense of imagination – rich with ideas about attaining super-human powers.

With Hannah's input, a new blog was set up between Chris and their Science Club, whereby Chris was able to post answers to various members' questions and offer inspirational quotes such as;

'The body is like a time machine; you are the pilot, mainly in the cockpit of the brain.

With space outside, the soul inside, powered by consciousness, with wings of materialism and idealism, your thoughts create a constant thrust for you to experience the flight of life.

You cruise with little turbulence when you reach higher altitudes of awareness.'

'We do not know if we have been here before. We do not know where we will be next; but we know we have a life. If we can experience its wholeness, with acknowledgement, we may know our destiny in the cosmos.'

'Nothing is more satisfying to human beings than knowing and experiencing their inner selves.'

The quotes sparked many interesting discussions amongst the members.

69

SHARED INTELLIGENCE AND CONSCIOUSNESS

Cousins and Krefeld had both been chewing over all these new ideas every minute they could, intrigued to understand what it all meant. Bizarrely they had both come to similar conclusions at about the same time, and so decided to discuss their findings at a coffee shop suggested by Krefeld.

An hour later, Cousins and Krefeld arrived simultaneously at the coffee shop, greeting each other with a warm hand shake.

'You know, Cousins, I can't help but think of all the bacteria you're generously giving me by shaking this hand of mine!' joked Krefeld, wiping his hands on his waistcoat.

'Well, I only have the friendliest bacteria on my hands!' laughed Cousins warmly, wiping his on his garish Hawaiian shirt.

'Thanks for meeting me today,' proffered Krefeld, waving Cousins to a seat at a freshly cleared table in the busy coffee shop. The ginger-haired genius sat down.

'No problem. It's funny; I'd just had the same thought about speaking to you when you rang me.'

Cousins grinned at Krefeld and the two men's twinkling

eyes met in a shared gaze of mutual respect.

They both sat down and a rather hassled-looking waitress bustled over to their table. Each ordered a Latté and – revealing their impeccable manners – they offered to get the busy waitress anything that she would like to drink too. She smiled, transforming her troubled face into a beautiful and happy grin, and offered them a delicious cake on the house, which the men gleefully accepted.

The men settled to begin their conversation;

'You know, Cousins, I've been thinking about all this shared intelligence and consciousness idea. I'm not sure if I understand it correctly, but are we saying that everyone could tap into it?'

Krefeld rubbed his goatee beard as he thought. Cousins' eyes widened in awe behind his glasses.

'I've been thinking the same thing! We've been thinking that micro-organisms seem to be able to tap into this intelligence or consciousness but perhaps all living beings can, including humans. But what on Earth would that mean? If we could have access to any information we wanted about how to do things, wouldn't that mean that we would have untold power? The control that we would have would be exceptional. We could construct or destroy anything in moments!'

Krefeld was nodding, his eyes hooded with concern.

'I know; the sheer power would be remarkable. Yet we don't know everything, do we? We don't seem to know how to get this information yet. There must be a reason why we don't know everything?'

'Hmm – maybe we aren't meant to be the ultimately

intelligent beings in the Universe that we seem to think we should be. Maybe Chris is an exception to the rule though; somehow he has slipped through the net, affected by something from deep space perhaps, as my learned astro-biologist friend has suggested.'

'What is it about Chris though that allowed this to happen just to him?' wrestled Krefeld mentally.

'I don't know; perhaps it's just coincidence, or perhaps it's something deeper.'

Cousins stared out of the window. The waitress arrived with the drinks and cake; the two men thanked her profusely. Krefeld stirred some sugar into his Latté and continued;

'Chris has spent a lot of his life in deep contemplation as far as I understand it; perhaps that has somehow purified his mind? Made him more synchronized perhaps? His brain wave patterns certainly suggest that. Perhaps with the right frame of enquiring mind combined with being in the right place at the right time, he has coupled up with some deep intelligence that we can't yet understand.'

Cousins checked his spoon for cleanliness before immersing it into his drink.

'Well I can't work out if it's a general Universal intelligence or just that of micro-organisms that Chris has tapped into, or whether they are one and the same.'

'Anyway, how can micro-beings hold fundamental answers to all our diseases?' asked Krefeld in frustration, rubbing his hand through his silver-striped hair.

'They may know even more than that – they may know fundamental answers about all our problems and conflicts too. They may know the destiny of Nature, humans and the Universe for all we know! They have so many similarities to us – they have their own culture, their own communities and language, customs and habits, yet they do inter-depend on us too, so we are more linked with micro-organisms than we would care to think!'

Cousins had reached the zenith of his thoughts and – somewhat exhausted by all these mental gymnastics, he laughed and tucked into his delicious-looking cake.

Krefeld grinned and followed suit. 'Thank heavens for cake!' he laughed.

70

CHRIS MEETS A DYING WOMAN

Chris was pottering around the ward, stretching his legs, when he heard a faint voice. Thinking it was a microbial sound, he stopped in his tracks, but then he laughed at his error, realizing that it was just an elderly lady who was calling feebly – 'Kevin,' over and over.

Concerned, he approached the tiny frail figure.

'Are you alright?' asked Chris gently. The lady weakly turned her head and gazed over at Chris. He nearly fell back in horror as he spotted a large mass of microbes crawling around her mouth and nose.

Appearing distraught, the elderly lady very quietly uttered a few words.

'I'm so sorry, I can't hear you,' Chris reluctantly came closer; she beckoned him to come right next to her. Quelling his aversion for the wriggling bacteria, he put his ear near to her mouth; he was just able to make out her pleas above the rushing sounds of the microbes that filled his ears.

'I need to contact my son Kevin,' she whispered.

'Oh, I see! Have you asked the nurses to call him?'

'No number,' came her disjointed feeble reply.

'Hmm, what's his name, what does he do?' asked Chris, wondering if he might be able to help.

She whispered his name and occupation and Chris' eyes lit up. 'I think I know him!' he said excitedly, stunned at this synchronicity. He proceeded to describe the man he had in mind; she weakly nodded her agreement.

'Look, I can get his number to you, alright? Don't worry I'm sure you'll find him.'

The sickly lady squeezed his hand in appreciation then Chris heard a sudden voice in his head.

'She doesn't have long now. Her system is too weak. We are ready to do our work, but she is waiting for something before she will let us take over.'

Confused, Chris tried to ask a question mentally for clarification, but the voice only came back saying;

'There is nothing more you can do for her. She will soon be with us.'

Shivering with horror, Chris veered off to get the number.

On his return to the agitated lady, he sorrowfully pressed a piece of paper with her son's number on into her hand. He'd scribbled it on the back of a little verse he'd created and signed.

71

Kevin and Merry contemplate life

It had been a busy few weeks; Kevin needed some 'time-out'. He invited his girlfriend Merry out to the coffee shop after work one evening – the whole Chris saga had raised a lot of questions in his own mind, not least bringing him to think a lot more about his mother, perhaps because he had seen the closeness of Chris' family.

Normally he didn't bring up the topic of family with Merry, but he felt a great urge to discuss his mother with someone.

They sat together at a discrete table by the window, shadows flickering on their faces from the tea-light flame playing in proximity.

Kevin observed the raindrops spattering against the darkened pane, wending their way slowly in many different directions before running together into a gully at the bottom of the window, merging as one, each losing its own identity to become one bigger entity. His Americano cup lay untouched on the table as his thoughts wandered.

He turned to Merry, whose rosy cheeks shone with the warmth of the cosy coffee shop. Clothed in a flowing floral-print dress, she was nervously chewing on her full lip, anxious about how their date would go. Sipping her iced-tea and twiddling the ends of her long silky blonde hair with her delicate slender fingers, she eyed his features in an attempt to gauge his state of mind.

So often when they got together they ended up fighting, hurling insults at each other. Yet, to her relief, he seemed quite calm this evening, if very distracted. She watched as he pushed his thinly-framed glasses up his angular nose.

'I've been thinking about my mother a lot lately' said Kevin, almost absent-mindedly. 'I don't know why she is in my thoughts more now. I feel like I need to see her, but I can't get through to her; she doesn't answer her phone.'

With difficulty he combed his fingers through his tightly coiled hair as he tried to gather his thoughts.

'I even phoned one of her neighbours to see if they know anything about what she's up to, but they don't seem to know. She seems to have become quite an introvert'.

Merry's full lips turned upwards into a rare smile – her smile a silent song from a warm heart and an acknowledgement of his efforts to speak about emotional matters with her. It wasn't often he was able to open up to her; she knew how hard he found it. It made a change that they were speaking pleasantly to each other. She tapped her short lilac-painted nails rhythmically on the checkered tablecloth, as if unconsciously playing a tune on her beloved piano at home, as she pondered his unexpected words.

In a moment of revelation and compassion she wondered if perhaps his anxiety about his mother had been playing on his mind recently and that was why he had been so foul to her in the last few weeks. She sensed that there was more to his recurrent thoughts than he understood. Her gut instinct was that he needed to get this worry off his mind by going to see his mother – after all she only lived about four hours' drive away. He was very lazy though, so she guessed he just needed some encouragement to commit himself to the idea. She clutched the exotically coloured beads draped around her slender swan-like neck as she reached for the right words to diplomatically make her suggestions.

'I think you should go over to see her, Kevin. You're clearly very worried about her; until you know what's going on I don't think you will be able to relax'. Merry reached out for Kevin's large hand and curled her piano-playing fingers around his. For once, he didn't pull away; she felt glowing warmth around her heart at this rare expression of unity.

She bit her lip and continued earnestly, seeing her chance to open his mind;

'There might be a reason why you keep thinking about her, you know? She might be thinking about you too, in the same way. It might be some kind of sign, some sixth sense perhaps.' Merry was staring intently through Kevin's glasses into his eyes trying to connect with him; unusually he held her lingering gaze for a moment – as if tasting what she had just said, then broke away from her eye-contact and her touch in disbelief, his eyes narrowing, snorting as his logical mind registered the ridiculousness of her words.

He pushed his glasses up his nose with a sharp thrust of annoyance.

'You have to be joking Merry! Please don't start with all your New Age nonsense! You know I don't believe in any of that! None of it adds up; until I see it with my own eyes, I'm not prepared to believe in any old wives' tales about a sixth sense.'

Merry recoiled in horror as he continued his tirade.

'No, we have been given five senses for a reason. There is

no such thing as a sixth sense, so stop trying to confuse me with crazy ideas! What do you think you are, some kind of witch?!'

He laughed cruelly at her expense, his eyes half-closed in suspicion. She turned away sighing, saddened by his perpetual negativity and cynicism. She remembered a time when she had really admired him, but these days he really pushed her into a corner with his doubts and continual need for evidence. Sometimes she felt like he would never understand her, or accept her for who she really was. She bristled in response to his name-calling, prepared for yet another fight. Pushing her delicate hands against the tabletop she half rose up out of her seat, towering above him.

'Oh Kevin, you always see things in such a black and white way, don't you? You're just not prepared to look outside of the box or imagine new ideas, are you? You have such a gloomy view of the world, it's heartbreaking, you know?'

Kevin turned his broody face away and glared back out of the window into the blackness outside, but could only see his own frowning face reflecting back at him.

'The world isn't as bad as you think, Kevin!' continued Merry. 'Most of the time we can only see what we want to see.'

Kevin stared at his reflection and realized how old he appeared.

'You can turn things around, Kevin, if only you would try!' begged Merry, falling back into her seat. She tried again to get him to understand. 'You have to turn your mind upside down and tune into things, open yourself up a little. That way you can see beyond people and their words, beyond the objects around you.'

Kevin's saddened features took on an even more cynical expression, which Kevin clocked in the window's reflection. Boy, he looked 70 years old! The wrinkles were deeply etched around his disbelieving eyes; he felt a sudden wave of shock as he recognized the elderly features of his own father peeping back at him – a flashback of a face he hadn't seen for ten years since his father had passed away from a heart attack at the age of 70.

He remembered his father well – a deeply religious man who believed that a firm hand was required in the bringing up of children, so discipline was a major component of their family life. His father had been greatly against New Age ideas – Kevin had at least this in common with him.

His father and mother's religious piety had been the backbone of their childhood, with consistent visits to Church and Sunday school; his parents had expected Kevin would continue to be an active member of their church as an adult. However his cynical views of God born out of his father's death and his mother's illness had kept him right away from any spiritual involvement; his betrayed and hardened heart seemed to have firmly closed its door on any ideas of reconciliation there.

Merry reached forward to take his hand again, as if hoping this would help her to reach him with her words. Her silky hair brushed over his hand as she leaned in.

'Sometimes truth is hard to get at. It is the core of all that we see and experience. It is like the pulp of a coconut; you have to peel the coconut's husk, break the shell, then only when you can see and break it and taste it can you get the full essence of it.'

He said with a dry response, 'Oh please stop your philosophizing! You're so naïve and gullible, Merry! Do you think that attitude has got you anywhere? Look at how little you have achieved! You don't even have a proper job! Your last boss sacked you. You don't have a proper place to stay or even anywhere to keep your paintings and poetry'.

His harsh words rained down on her like stones; she withdrew her hand again, hurt, but she was not prepared to give in to him, throwing her golden hair back over her shoulder and retorting; 'Well at least I am healthy and happy! At least I know who I am! Everyone has their own stresses and expectations. Anyone can behave that way when things don't work out the way they want. If I let these things bother me, it means I have taken them to heart, that I have let them affect me. We need to take a leaf out of Nature's book, Kevin; take what you want from life, but only take what is really good for you.'

Her glistening emerald eyes betrayed the heightened emotions of her plea to Kevin.

'Look at yourself Kevin! Do you think you're in such good shape? Can't you see how drained you are? You keep roaming around, working incessantly, you're losing your hair, you haven't been sleeping properly, all because your energy is scattered all over the place!'

Kevin warily eyed his receding hairline in his reflection, acutely aware that there was an even greater patch of baldness on his crown.

'Why don't you just leave me and find somebody else to be your girlfriend?' gasped Merry in frustration. 'I don't love you because you have a reporting job. I think you have so much to give, but you need some inspiration, someone to understand you. You need love!'

Kevin needed no further reminders of his ageing features. He turned his back on his reflection to reply more gently;

'You need love as well.' Merry's strained features softened as she heard his kinder words.

'Everybody needs love, Kevin; whoever wants to give more, will get it back multiplied, but most people don't even realize that they want love in the first place.'

Kevin gazed into the distance as he considered her wise words; 'Merry, what attracted you to me in the first place?'

Merry managed a smile; 'Your honesty, purity and outspokenness; but you need a positive touch.'

He smirked, 'Well, there is nothing positive about the world. Look how many people are suffering, how many big players get away with their greedy acts. There is no proper justice in the world.'

The quiver in her voice revealed her emotions, 'You know what, Kevin? You need healing.'

Kevin bristled at these words. What did she know? Though he found this healing talk nonsensical, his heart was beating a little faster, as if changing its tune and a tiny part of his mind was peeking round the corner to see if she might actually be right...

72

KEVIN LOOKS FOR HIS MOTHER

Merry's words seemed somehow to have found their way into Kevin's heart. They had left the coffee shop and parted company on friendlier terms, with Kevin promising to think about what Merry had said. For the first time in ages, Merry had felt a glimmer of hope about their relationship.

After a somewhat restless night, tossing and turning as he fell in and out of a fitful sleep in which he dreamed about his mother, Kevin had woken abruptly, certain that she was calling his name. Shaking his head to clear his thoughts, he realized that he had only been dreaming; however in that moment when the dream had still felt so real, he had made up his mind to visit her.

He tried once more to phone her, but again there was no answer, so he dressed rapidly and grabbed his car keys and mobile ready to set out on his long trip.

The four hours' drive passed slowly for him, as he anxiously went over all the possible scenarios for why he hadn't heard from his mother. He tuned and retuned the radio stations to try to take his mind off his rising anxiety, but each song seemed to speak of loss and sadness.

He turned the radio off in frustration. What if she had died alone in her bed? That would be the worst possible outcome and too much for him to bear. His morose mood weighed heavily on him as he got closer and closer to her home.

Although he daren't dwell on the possibility that she had taken a turn for the worse, his guilt about not checking up on her sooner dragged his sorrowful heart through the mud. Facing up to this situation was one of the hardest things he had ever done.

After a painful journey, during which he felt like his soul had passed through a very dark tunnel, he pulled up outside her small apartment and sat in his car with the engine running, as if paralyzed by what he might have to face. He gathered up all of his courage and went slowly to her door.

He peeked through the window, but was unable to see any signs of life. It was dark inside, but there was no evidence of any fracas – just the usual neatness of his house-proud mother's lounge.

Reaching up to knock on the door felt like lifting a heavy weight, but gingerly he managed a small 'tap, tap' on the wooden frame. With no response forthcoming, he knocked louder on the glass pane.

With no answer again, Kevin's anxiety levels rose. Certain now that this silence portended bad news, he panicked. He ran next door to her neighbour's apartment and hammered wildly on their door, but again there was no answer. This place was beginning to feel like a ghost town.

Kevin suddenly spotted movement out of the corner of his eye. He turned to see an elderly lady slowly pottering her way towards him. Was this his mother? He focused his eyes on the small frail figure, but didn't recognize her. Yet she seemed to be heading for him; he wondered if she knew his mother, and waited for an anxious few minutes as she slowly wobbled her way in his direction.

Finally the woman was close enough to him to call out.

'Hey, you!' she uttered in a rather feeble voice.

'Can I help you?' asked Kevin, impatiently.

'Are you Gladys' son?' she asked.

'Ye-es', he said hesitantly, 'who wants to know?' asked Kevin, suspiciously staring at the silver-haired diminutive woman over his glasses.

'I'm Joyce, a friend of your mother's. I live in that block over there. I saw your car drive up and when I saw you get out and go up to Gladys' apartment, I knew I had to catch you before you left again. Thank goodness you've finally come. I've been worried sick about her, but I didn't know how to contact you.'

'Yes, I'm Kevin. What's happened to my mother? Where is she?' stammered Kevin anxiously pushing his glasses up his angular nose.

'You mean you haven't seen her at all?' asked the elderly wizened lady.

'No, I live in San Francisco. I haven't seen her for a long time, but I've been trying to call her this week; she hasn't been answering!' cried Kevin clutching his curls with rising fear.

'She's been really sick, Kevin. I've been trying to look out for her, but I'm not too well myself.' As if to illustrate her point, she coughed feebly. 'She was desperate to see you but I know she didn't want to bother you, with you being such a long way away and so busy and all. She said she was going to try to visit you. I warned her not to try to travel – she really wasn't well enough, but she insisted that she could catch a bus over to San Francisco and find you there. I begged her to call you first, but she said she threw your number out in the trash by mistake.'

Kevin's thoughts went into overdrive. He rubbed his temples near his receding hairline to encourage some clarity in his thoughts. At least this meant that she was probably still alive; he breathed a sigh of immense relief. Yet how could she think of traveling in her condition? And where was she now? She certainly hadn't been to his apartment, so where could she be? His sneakers squeaked as he shuffled uncomfortably.

The elderly lady interrupted his thoughts. 'I'd hoped she had found you alright, but it seems not. Thank God you came so I could tell you what's happened.' She lifted her stick and pointed it at him.

Kevin snorted – 'What's God got to do with anything? She wouldn't be in this mess if it wasn't for him!' He surprised himself with his sudden outburst; he realized he wasn't completely atheist after all – he was just extremely angry with God.

'Well son, you shouldn't go blaspheming like that! None of us would be here if it wasn't for God; He's looking out for your dear mother right now, even if you aren't!' she snapped, waving her stick angrily at him. She turned precariously on her heels and stropped off in as stormy a way as was possible for an infirm old lady. She muttered under her breath 'Kids today – they don't know the meaning of the word respect!'

Kevin stared after her, shocked by her response. His hands flew to his face as the colour drained from his cheeks. Dawning on him that this crotchety old lady was the only link he had to find out where his mother was, he decided to swallow his pride and go after her.

He paced down the corridor and caught up with the muttering old woman.

'Listen ma'am, I'm real sorry about what I said. I'm just really worried about my mum. Please help me. I need to know when she left.'

'Well, kid, she left about a week ago, so you'd better go and find her, hadn't you?' she said haughtily.

Kevin nodded humbly, mumbling his thanks to the old lady. He watched for a moment as she stumbled back towards her apartment, before hurrying back to his waiting car. Kevin drove off in a smoky cloud of burnt rubber and exhaust fumes, leaving the old woman muttering to herself.

73

KEVIN DRIVES TO THE HOSPITAL
IN THE MOONLIGHT

Unsure how he was going to find his mother, Kevin drove through the night back to San Francisco, the Bright Moon up above shining its eerie light onto the winding roads. He nervously watched its curious luminous face appearing and disappearing through the branches of the thick trees lining the roads, as if it was playing a game of lunar 'hide and seek' with him.

He had never liked the Full Moon – he always associated them with evil and horror movies. Many a time as a boy, he had been scared witless by evocative night-time scenes in movies, where the moon had always illuminated some horrific event. An American Werewolf in London had been an old favourite of many of his friends, yet that movie's terrifying story had left him pale with fear, carrying a permanent phobia forever more about people going crazy under the influence of the Full Moon. This was a most irrational fear of course – his logical mind told him that no such thing could possibly occur.

Whatever the truth was about the Full Moon – whether it was possible that it could have any effect on people or not – he suddenly felt a feeling of foreboding in his gut, which he put down to nervousness about werewolves. He muttered angrily at himself for having such irrational fears. He put his head down to drive the rest of the distance back to San Francisco, vowing to find his mother and do whatever it took to help her. Well aware that he had neglected her recently, the grumpy old woman had not helped his feelings of guilt; he swore to spend more time with his mother when he found her.

All this stuff going on with the boy, Chris McKenzie, had really distracted him from dealing with what mattered most – his family. He decided then and there that he would take a sabbatical from work as soon as he could arrange it with his boss, to make himself more available for his mother. He wanted to shake this heavy feeling he had; suddenly he found himself uttering a Prayer under his breath.

His questioning mind became like a bubble on water in the pool of emotions. An emotional thought occurred to him resonating throughout his being.

'We take life for granted. When we are on the verge of losing life, we realise its precious value whether of our own or somebody else's. What really clouds us from living a profound life?'

Surprised at this sudden change of heart, he felt certain lightness about his being for the first time that day. He smiled a wry grin to himself as he drove along; aware of the irony of what he was doing. Merry would be most surprised, as would his mother...

His mother had despaired at Kevin's loss of faith, but never failed to try to encourage him back to the loving arms of God. Many a time she had asked him to pray with her, particularly during the most difficult times of her illness, but he had always refused, claiming it was all nonsense and that God didn't exist. She had always reacted with sadness at his attitude, but her unerring faith had been a strange comfort to her throughout her suffering.

Yet tonight, here he was, offering his first small prayer for many a year back up to the Universe, in case there was anyone up there listening. Once he had started, it was like the floodgates had been opened; he couldn't stop – all his pent up concerns came gushing out in a long, ranting utterance of pleas.

'God, if you're there please help Mum and keep her safe. Help me to find her. I'm so sorry – I've been such a fool, I haven't been looking after her, I've been consumed by my work, but that's all going to change now, I promise, just please let me see her again, safe and sound. I'll do anything you want, just please help us.'

Kevin drove on into the night and just as he approached the twinkling lights of his home city, his mobile rang, making him jump a mile in his seat.

He pressed the button on his hands-free set to answer the call; a voice at the other end of the line said;

'Hello, is that Kevin Masters?'

'Speaking,' he replied, suddenly feeling tense again.

'Sir, I'm so glad we've tracked you down. This is Dr. Tanner of San Francisco Wharfside General Hospital. We have your mother Gladys here; I'm so sorry to have to tell you that she is seriously ill. I would advise you to come as soon as possible...I'm afraid that she may not have much longer.'

Kevin's heart nearly stopped, but with his mind on automatic, he replied;

'I'll be there as soon as I can.'

74

Kevin's farewell

Kevin abandoned his car in the parking lot and sped towards the hospital entrance with a mixed feeling of relief and concern – relief that he would soon see his mother, but concern at how serious her condition sounded.

Running past the abandoned trolleys along the corridor he felt like his legs were about to give way under him. As he stopped at the lift, he tried to focus his blurry eyesight on the button enough to be able to press it. His thoughts turned to Chris McKenzie and his reports of bacteria wriggling all over the hospital. Suddenly terribly anxious that his mother was exposed to all these bacteria, he pressed the button again and again with his fumbling large fingers in impatience.

The lift doors opened and he stepped into its cavernous mouth. As the lift jerked upwards, leaving his stomach somewhere down by his feet, he wondered at the coincidence of his mother arriving in the same hospital as Chris.

Kevin prayed that he would be there in time and, miraculously, he was.

Dr. Tanner greeted him warmly. 'Kevin, thank goodness you're here. I'm so sorry, we must hurry, your mother's condition is critical. Please come with me.' He escorted Kevin over to his dying mother's bedside.

Kevin froze as his eyes fell on a tiny figure hunched in a bed. Barely recognizing her shrunken features, Kevin stared at his mother's fragile body. Her gaunt face shocked him to the core.

Overcome with grief, he fumbled for her delicate hand and gently squeezed it, saying;

'Mum, it's me, Kevin. I'm here.'

Her moment was getting closer. She held out her other hand and Kevin realized that in it was a piece of paper, which he took. Giving Kevin a serious smile, she looked him in the eyes, but she was silent.

'Speak to me Mum!' uttered Kevin, despairingly. She said nothing but breathed her last breath, as though her spirit was waiting to leave straight after seeing him.

Kevin squeezed and squeezed her hand, as if trying to pump life back into it. Desperately he stared round at the hovering medics, crying;

'Isn't there anything you can do?'

But they shook their heads resignedly and sorrowfully, extolling their praises on her for having lasted so long as they closed his mother's eyes for the last time.

Kevin wobbled in shock and a nurse guided him gently to a seat. Sitting distraughtly in the chair, he suddenly became aware of the piece of paper in his hand. Unfolding it, he saw his own mobile number scribbled on one side. Puzzled, he turned it over and read a beautifully hand-written note, that seemed to be some kind of verse;

'Every gain comes with some loss.
We may not know at that time whether
we have gained or lost, but we will know later.

> *Some will regret the loss physically;*
> *For others it will be a spiritual realization.'*
> *- Chris McKenzie*

The tears rolled down Kevin's cheeks.

75

Kevin's new story

Kevin shakily rose to his feet and excused himself from the bustling scene of medics that were buzzing around his departed mother's body.

Mopping the tears from his cheeks, he stumbled around the wards, dazed – until he spotted Chris seated on a bed with his Tablet-Gadget.

Chris jumped when he saw the curly-haired man lurching towards him and, recognizing the troublesome reporter, he tugged his earphones out.

'You gave them my number!' blurted Kevin, gratefully. 'How can I ever repay you?'

Chris smiled shyly and shrugged. 'You can start by writing a decent story about me for a change!' he laughed. 'How is your mother?' he asked, quietly.

Kevin gazed down at his sneakers, filled with grief. Stuttering, he said;

'She...she passed away...' When Kevin looked back up his eyes were filled with tears; Chris was filled with compassion for Kevin's loss.

'I'm so sorry...'

Bright Moon

Suddenly Kevin's mood changed, and he blurted;

'Couldn't you have done something? Given her some of your special flowers or fruit or something?' His eyes were fiery with anger.

'I thought you didn't believe any of that stuff!' said Chris, taken aback.

Kevin averted his accusing gaze, muttering an apology.

'Anyway', said Chris gently, 'I think she was too weak. The bacteria told me she was too sick and was near the end, but she was waiting for something before they could finish their work.'

Kevin looked up, confused. 'Me?' he questioned, pushing his glasses back up his angular nose.

'Of course,' said Chris kindly. 'She loved you.'

'Oh...' He rubbed his hand over the stubble on his face. 'Can I come back and speak to you later?' he asked somewhat humbly.

'Of course, I don't think I'm going anywhere...'

Kevin wandered off in a daze to get some fresh air.

Standing by an open window, gazing out at the swaying trees in the hospital grounds, the gentle breeze playing on his tired face, he thought long and hard about Chris, about all the difficult things that had happened to him, about how badly he had treated Chris and how Chris had still helped him nonetheless. Kevin was also starting to realize how the loss of his mother seemed to have changed him and decided to amend his actions.

When he came back to Chris' bedside, he promised Chris

without a shadow of a doubt that he would no longer release stories that were cruel and untrue. Then and there he also pledged to Chris that he would help him in any way he could to find out what was happening to him. He offered his services to help Chris publicize his experiences in any way he wanted.

Touched by the reporter's sincerity, Chris agreed and they shook hands. Before their parting, Chris tried to write down some consoling thoughts about Kevin's recent bereavement on a piece of paper he had torn out of his diary. He passed the note across to Kevin.

'Sorry it's not a proper card or anything,' said Chris, shrugging. Kevin took the note, scanning the words;

'Birth and death, creation and dissolution, are like the crest and trough of eternally moving waves of consciousness in the cosmos.'

Kevin nodded at Chris, aware he had changed a little forever. He placed the paper carefully in his pocket next to his notebook.

He had one more thing to do – he sought out Nurse Kathy, who excitedly met him in the cafeteria, but she was soon to be brought down to earth with a bump. Seated discretely at a corner table furnished with steaming drinks, Kathy's big blue eyes shone with anticipation.

Her wide mouth was flapping faster than usual as she greeted him with a torrent of mindless chatter. Kevin put his hand up to her big pouting lips in a gesture that he hoped would stem the tide of babble. Kathy's false eye-lashes fluttered in surprise but she fell silent.

'Listen Kathy, I can't see you again,' muttered Kevin, ashamed.

Kathy's babyish eyes filled with tears and her whole face fell. Grasping the proverbial bull by the horns, Kevin wrestled out his words.

'This whole thing with Chris has been wrong – I've written bad things about him and, until today, I couldn't see that there was a better way to act. Chris deserves better than gossip. He's an amazing kid; if it wasn't for him, I would never have found my mum...' he broke off, his shoulders heaving with pent-up emotion, '...to say goodbye. She's, she's just passed away...' he stuttered, as the floodgates opened and the tears cascaded down his face.

Kathy averted her gaze in embarrassment, realizing that she had instigated the gossip; a twinge of conscience made her shuffle awkwardly in her seat. She reached for a serviette and wiped away her tears.

'Listen, I'm really sorry about your mum,' she said uncomfortably. 'I understand what you're saying, so I'm not going to hassle you.' Kathy grabbed Kevin's chunky hand in one last ditch attempt to hang on to him; 'But if you ever need me, you know where I am...'

Kevin's half-closed eyes didn't meet her imploring blue gaze, so she knew it was over. She nodded, squeezing his hand one last time then let it fall as she fled from the room, tears tumbling down her cheeks again.

Kevin stayed in his hunched pose for what seemed like forever – statuesque and dejected, hands clasped in his tightly curled locks – trying to gather his scattered thoughts. Eventually he became aware of the continuing hustle and bustle around him – such disrespect for his departed mother, he thought. Why does the world carry on, when it should just stop turning at a time like this, he questioned.

A song floated to his ears from the hospital radio...the

lyrics made him sit up and listen;

> *'Light is good,*
> *but blinding light is not good.*
> *Love is good,*
> *but binding love is not good.*
> *The inner spirit represents light, whereas*
> *the body represents the opposite.*
> *When we find a source to reflect our being,*
> *the answer emerges like a lotus flower*
> *in the lake of the heart...'*

The lyrics floated around in his head and realization dawned. He realized he didn't want to be alone. Thoughts of Merry filled his mind, beautiful sweet Merry; he finally knew that he really loved her. Taking his phone from his pocket, he called her and in a flash she promised she would be right over.

As he awaited her arrival, he pondered his future involvement with Chris' story and vowed that he would only release positive articles from now on, with Chris and his family's full approval. He also decided to put his research skills to better use, helping the family to find answers concerning Chris' unusual symptoms. He picked out his notebook from his jacket pocket and started to jot down some ideas.

76

CHRIS RETURNS TO SCHOOL

The summer vacation was over and Chris needed to go back to school. The experts had poked and prodded, observed and tested, postulated and pondered and having gathered all their data over the course of three Full Moons, they had observed enough patterns to conclude that Chris' extra-sensory powers were at their height at the Full Moon, and waxed and waned in sync with the moon's appearance in the skies of San Francisco.

Agreeing with his parents that he needed to try to integrate back into normal life, the experts requested for Chris to return to the hospital for more observations only during each Full Moon, assuming that he would continue to have the same experiences.

Joe and Donna were pleased to have Chris back home. They shared time together doing fun family activities with him and his grandma to help Chris catch up with some of the things he had missed out on. They had grown much closer as a family and Chris' relationship with his mother had reached a new level of understanding as her eyes had been opened to Chris' capabilities and insights. Much as she still wished more than anything for his return to normality, she found herself relating to him differently, with a deeper respect for him, which he reciprocated by opening up to her more.

Equally, Joe and Donna's relationship had gone from strength to strength having spent lots of time together as a couple during the summer, attending the hospital to support Chris through his ordeal. Their interaction was almost like the old days as if they were back in their honeymoon period, but with an expanded mutual admiration and acceptance.

Chris was over the moon to be back home with both his parents, watching them behaving like a normal couple in love. The strong family unit that had reformed around him was more therapeutic than anything else. Although to his knowledge that he was very different from everyone else he was also keen to get back to some normality – and even to go back to school.

He dived into his school work. The teachers were amazed at how well he was able to focus, and his depth of knowledge was astounding for his age. He had matured a lot over the last few weeks.

Some of the children at school had heard about his experiences through Kevin's news reports, realizing that there was more to Chris than met the eye.

Boys and girls would gather around him in the playground at recess – even those that had previously bullied him – and fire question after question at him about what he was able to see and hear and what he saw in the Moon. Many of those that had previously taunted him were suddenly almost worshipping him as a hero; Chris found this particularly confusing as he knew he was still the same boy he always had been inside.

Hannah stood by him protectively; her Doc Martin's a formidable reminder that she would kick anyone who messed with him. She drew together a group of like-minded children from the Science Club to work together with Chris on some of his key points.

He would teach them about the things he had intuited and the group would go off and gather information from the Internet to support his theories and to explore how these new ideas could be applied in the world. This new network of young brains proved prolific in its production of innovative ideas.

The teachers asked them to present the ideas in assembly and many were astounded by their innovations. They entered the children and their ideas into science competitions, which were easily won by this intrepid group of young pioneers, so the unusual fact that Chris was able to see beyond the ordinary was soon seen as a gift to be prized.

Soon, children dropped their obsessions with playing electronic games and watching T.V. The desire to read was rekindled and children spent hours gazing up at the stars and Moon, watching and observing, hoping to be given the same extra-ordinary ability as Chris of encountering micro-universes and gaining seemingly super-human powers. Soon a craze for 'Moon-gazing' had infiltrated the school – even amongst those children that had mocked Chris in the past.

Some students seemed to want to follow Chris purely because of his fame, but he soon set them straight about the fractured nature of a celebrity life. He explained that celebrities miss out on simple life at the heart of society, complaining that ordinary people want to be like them, but can barely appreciate their own freedom, space and simplicity. Both the extremes of fame and anonymity are missing something, thus continuing the mystery of the human mind. He added that *the more you think egotistically that you are unique and irreplaceable, the easier it becomes to replace you. The simpler and humbler you are, with a subdued ego, the harder it becomes for Nature to replace you.*

Chris was not just sought out by his peers; he was even invited by the Principal to teach the meditation technique he had learnt with the yogi, starting first with the children in Science Club, then in whole-school assembly, and finally as a night class for the parents and teachers.

When Chris was once questioned by a sceptical parent on his rights to teach within the school, he pointed out that *'Learning is self-cultivation. All who make it possible are teachers.'* He also urged his meditation students to realize that *'Mere knowledge will not bring total realization of the self. Deeper insightful experiences should accompany it'*. He believed that meditation was a tool for learning about yourself – no-one else would teach you that.

Many people reported back various positive benefits from the meditation practice – such as a heightened sense of clarity and awareness, a greater sense of self and calm, more energy and focus and a better understanding of topics taught at school.

Teachers reported better behaviour in class and a general sense of peace, connection and respect between the students. The school adopted the meditation as a regular morning practice and co-operation between the students was palpably increased.

Chris' popularity soared and he became increasingly confident in his social skills. The school seemed to be pulling together as a cohesive network, which was drawing in the teachers and parents into a greater understanding of the connection between people and indeed other elements in the Universe.

77

News of Chris' healing abilities spreads

However, back at home, Donna continued to wrestle with her perceptions of Chris' abilities. She couldn't shake the anxiety that Chris was sick and needed to be cured of his illness.

She wanted Chris to keep seeing healers, but Joe was keen to let Chris flow with what was happening, as his perception was that this was all for a good reason; his faith in this idea kept him going throughout all the upset and uncertainty.

Donna was wary about Chris revealing his thoughts and revelations, yet Joe pointed out that knowledge held in conceit is like a plant in the dark – it will not grow vigorously. He persuaded her that it was in Chris' best interests for him to share his wisdom, as this would be how Chris' wisdom would continue to flourish.

Friends popped in to show their support, many of whom had read Kevin's news stories about Chris that were making headlines in the papers.

He was being hailed as a 'Wonder Boy' by some, a new 'Superman' with Extra-Sensory Perception – more like 'Extra Sensationalized Perception'! However there was no denying that Chris was showing some remarkable abilities that seemed to be bringing new helpful knowledge to people.

As the sensational news spread, the fame the boy experienced inevitably became somewhat invasive. Sick people began turning up at the family's door as news of their home address leaked out. The invalids would stand outside, or sit in a wheelchair at the door pleading for Chris to come out and heal them.

Joe and Donna tried to protect him the best they could, telling people that he was unavailable, but Chris wanted to help, so often he would come to the door and see the sick people. If he was able to, he would try to tune in to any information he could get about micro-organisms on the sick people, offering any advice that he picked up. Often he would just play the meditation song on repeat, until the neighbours complained of a disturbance.

Local police got involved to protect them from endless visitors, Joe and Donna received endless bags of letters and e-mails, requesting help with this problem and that health issue. They decided the best way to help the masses was to send them information about the meditation, to see if they could get their own answers through their own self-enquiry.

With Kevin's help, Chris made a film on YouTube showing himself practising the meditation; within days, the number of hits it had received rocketed exponentially. With Joe's help, they also created a website to explain what had happened to Chris, with a blog to keep people informed of his latest visions.

October

Full Moon: 12.50 pm on October 29th

78

Chris deepens his meditations

In between all this hectic activity, Chris was keen to continue his own meditation, to deepen his connection with the micro-organisms so as to understand their messages. As the Bright Moons came and went, he would tap into their consciousness, downloading more and more insights, which he shared with the medics and other interested researchers.

He found that as his knowledge developed, he desired to be more and more in a darkened room during the Bright Moon phase, realizing that the darkness minimized his view of the micro-organisms and their frenzied activity.

With this reduced sensory input, he seemed better able to connect with the micro-organisms to communicate with them. It felt like more of a heart-based communication as he shut out the extra 'noise' that the visuals created in his mind.

He found himself understanding more and more about the nature of life – not just that of micro-organisms, but of all life. Understanding that all is connected, whether through the presence of the micro-organisms in most entities, or through the deep consciousness emanating from all living entities, he found himself seeing the way the Earth and the Universe function as a whole. He spent as many hours as he could manage away from the public disruption, to feel out the revelations from the micro-organisms.

He found himself keen to impart this information to others; he wanted to express himself in the language of poetry, reflecting the beauty and the love in this new understanding.

He dictated poetical extracts to his dad, who then compiled them into a regular blog on his website, which soon received cult status throughout the world as people downloaded the quotes and marvelled at their deep wisdom.

79

CHRIS IS AN INSPIRATION TO PEOPLE WORLDWIDE

Children on the other side of the world became inspired by his story and took up Moon and star observation, passionate to experience the same level of super-human understanding. Astrology and astronomy Clubs boomed in many parts of the world. At the top of the presents hit-list were telescopes, microscopes and books about microbiology and the Moon.

The website became a phenomenon in its own right, as Joe indulged his passion for alternative therapies and philosophies by adding links through to like-minded people, who created an online forum. They discussed Chris' experiences and the implications they had for the world of alternative therapies, the potential for a new world-paradigm, a new belief system, based on the new philosophies that Chris was imparting.

This underground network spread the new ideas like wildfire, creating a sub-section of the population who believed that evolutionary change was imminent. They felt that when enough people believed in the new ideas, the whole world's belief system would be able to change, adapting to a new more harmonized way of life. Some people that read the website felt that it was all just one big hoax; they set up counter-websites that dismissed everything that Chris was imparting as a load of garbage. Sensationalized news articles continued to spread around the world – some positive, others trashing Chris' viewpoints and experiences – and those that knew about him seemed to stand in one of the two categories.

Some religious individuals were rocked by what Chris was saying and achieving; again these communities were split between those that believed him and those that thought what he was doing and saying were sacrilegious. Huge conferences were initiated, where speakers from many different religions came to discuss the healings and the revelations.

Although feelings were mixed, paradoxically there was a sense of unity amongst the religions created by the need to discuss Chris and his experiences – such is the nature of life; we rarely see the bigger picture created by contentious events.

Meanwhile Donna continued to seek answers, determined that he would be better off without his 'abnormalities'. Many came forward, offering therapies varying from cranio-sacral therapy to colour therapy. She invited many to the house and Chris politely indulged his mum by partaking in each session.

He had to admit that each session helped him in different ways – perhaps helping him to sleep and relax, or to feel less achy and connected to his heart, or to receive the messages from the micro-organisms more clearly, but health-wise he actually already felt better than he had ever felt. He was at the pinnacle of his well-being and the doctors continued to verify this fact each Bright Moon.

November

Full Moon: 6.47 am on November 28th

80

CHRIS PROPHESISES A TERRIBLE TRAGEDY

Donna was very happy that he seemed fit and healthy in most ways, but her concern that this almost God complex he was experiencing could lead to a nervous breakdown, was increasing. One day she thought her fears had been realized.

Chris had been deep in contemplation one evening staring blissfully up at the Moon, when his mother had overheard a cry from his room. She ran upstairs to see what the matter was. His troubled stuttering revealed that all was not well. His consciousness was associated so deeply with the Moon now that his intuitive sense had become non-localized, hence he could sense some indications in the reflection of light falling on his upturned face that the Earth would quiver strongly in the Far Eastern region.

'I believe that something terrible may take place in the world!' cried Chris.

'What do you mean?' enquired his anxious mother.

'I'm not sure what it all means, but I can just sense that something tragic will happen; maybe somewhere in the Far East, but I believe it's going to take place on Boxing Day after dinner!' Chris' eyes were wide and staring in angst.

'Chris darling, how can you possibly think such a thing?'

asked his mother incredulously.

'I just know, Mum! The micro-organisms, they're making unusual sounds too. I sense that they've picked up some unusual geo-magnetic behaviour on our planet; I think they are readying themselves for something cataclysmic!'

'Chris, how can they possibly know such a thing?' asked Donna in frustration.

'Mum, they know so much! You just don't understand! They can sense everything! Atmospheric changes, magnetism, temperature, any form of environmental change that might threaten them - they also have the abilities to affect those factors, to a certain extent. They know what to do to protect themselves from all those dangers too! They have a central point within their bodies into which they simply withdraw their consciousness until they become impenetrable by any means!'

'Sweetheart, I really don't understand. How can they withdraw like that? That's not possible, surely?'

'Well it is, and they do it, whether we understand it or not,' countered Chris. 'I think we should listen to them, Mum, they are the first to know of any environmental changes and, if they are reacting, then we should be worried.'

Donna, unsure what to do with this new information eagerly awaited Joe's return to discuss the matter. He was working late at the store, as his business had boomed as a result of the family's media exposure.

When Joe came home from the store clad in his white loose yoga clothes, Chris explained his latest revelation about some forthcoming tragedy and how micro-beings were withdrawing themselves in some kind of protective reaction.

Joe was silent for a while then shared his thoughts;

'Well, that sounds possible – even people have been known to withdraw themselves enough to be able to withstand extreme temperatures and pain,' he said thoughtfully.

'Remember there are yogis who can lie on beds of nails and walk through fire? And karate experts who can chop through wood just by using their mind in a special way? Maybe this is the same kind of idea?' he pondered.

'But honey, how can Chris possibly know all this?' exclaimed Donna, bemused. 'How awful it is to know that something terrible is going to happen! I'm not sure I like knowing about such scary things.' Donna seemed close to tears. Then, pulling herself together, she said;

'The question is, what are we supposed to do about it? It's not like we've got any information or proof about what this tragic event will be, so we can't warn anyone...'

They nodded. Chris agreed to continue with his meditations to see if he could find out more about this potentially terrible event. He slipped to his room for peace and quiet.

81

How can they warn the world?

With more contemplation, Chris foresaw that the 'catastrophe' may be some kind of meteorological event, perhaps on a par with hurricanes of recent history, or the terrible floods of New Orleans.

If this wasn't enough to make someone buckle at the knees, there was more revelation to come. He understood that microbes may be playing a key role meteorologically in changing the world's weather patterns. Due to excessive deforestation and extinction of flora and fauna world-wide at the hands of mankind and its materialistic behaviour, there had been a massive effect on the water cycle. All the water that was contained within these entities when they were alive had to go somewhere.

Chris knew that in the world's water cycle, all water was accounted for and endlessly recycled. With the help of microbes, whose job it was to break down organic materials, the water had been released from the decayed matter and taken back up into the atmosphere, ready to fall again from the clouds – not just as light rain, but as a massive storm or hurricane.

The news hit Chris like a clenched fist to the stomach; tears welled in his eyes as he realized the immensity of the revelation. All that responsibility was falling back on the heads of Man. In a flash he was able to see how much of the recent flooding that had plagued the world could be traced back to Mankind; so much needless suffering and loss.

As the tears rolled down his cheeks, he felt great sorrow for the harm that humans had done – not just to the planet, but also to innocent people and animals on the Earth. In his heart he realized with great certainty that Mankind must cease its heartless treatment of the Earth's resources, or suffer more of these ecological consequences. It was as though he was literally able to sense these events of the future today, through picking up and reading the signs he received from the microbial world.

Chris relayed his fears to his parents, whose concern for the consequences of NOT sharing his predictions outweighed their doubts about his story, so after much discussion, Donna and Joe decided to share these predictions with a couple of congressmen, but they were divided in their reactions. Many would not take his predictions seriously; only a small minority empathized and promised to try to help, but their intervention was sadly lacking in weight.

Minimal discussions were held with meteorological specialists, but as their machines and computer programs saw insufficient evidence of any foreboding event looming, Chris' predictions seemed to fall on deaf ears – who was going to trust the words of a young boy over readings from intricate, expensive equipment designed to pick up every nuance of meteorological activity?

December

Full Moon: 2.22 am on December 28th

82

Tragedy strikes – the world's scientists sit up and take notice

December passed by in a flurry of activity. Consultancy work for Chris came in thick and fast, which he tried to fit in around going to school, but as the Christmas break approached, Chris was desperate to spend some quiet time at home with his family.

He was hoping that nothing would get in the way of him having a normal Christmas – no hospital visits, no demands from sickly patients, no tragedies to deal with…yet his recent predictions of an environmental tragedy on Christmas Day left him with a terribly sick sensation in his stomach every time his thoughts dwelled on what might be around the corner.

Concerned about Grandma Larkin's safety, Chris had begged his mother to let his grandmother come to stay with the family for Christmas, just in case his predictions came true in their area. Donna reluctantly agreed; on Christmas Eve, Joe fetched Christina to their home.

Chris awoke on Christmas Day with mixed feelings. First, he was ecstatic that his vision was pretty much devoid of micro-organisms, which was a blessing. He could see details on things well enough without his glasses again. He could make out the intricate weaved patterns of the stocking material under his gaze. Eyeing the bulging stocking suspended from the end of his bed, he was suddenly filled with a boyish excitement!

However, his hearing was also pretty acute and, distracted by the howling wind sounds coming from outside, he peeped through the window and saw the rolling dark clouds sweeping across the skies. He felt a sudden angst. Turmoil was in the pit of his stomach, as he remembered his tragic prediction.

Troubled, he called for his parents, who ran to his bed and cuddled him. They gazed out at the Golden Gate Bridge which was swathed in foreboding heavy clouds. Holding hands they gazed silently and anxiously at the gathering storms.

The twinkling festive lights that adorned the many surrounding houses were like beacons of hope in the midst of the threatening darkness. Donna broke the silence, determined that they would not let it spoil their Christmas.

'Come on Chris, let's open your presents, eh? Don't you want to see what you've got?'

Chris' eyes were round like saucers – his gaze filled with uneasiness as he fretted over his predictions.

'Why don't you wake up your Grandma so she can watch you open them?' suggested Joe trying to distract him from his worries. Chris nodded, his eyes lighting up. He jumped up to fetch her, and he dragged the still-yawning Christina back to his room, chattering excitedly.

With Christina, Joe and Donna all huddled in Chris' bedroom, it was quite a squeeze, but he was keen to get started.

'Chris, catch this son!' Joe dropped a mystifyingly heavy festive parcel into his son's hands. Chris grinned as he caught the mysterious present, feeling a giggle rise up out of his throat. He could feel a ripping frenzy overtaking him! With reckless abandon he tore the wrapping paper away, sprinkling shreds of paper like confetti over his bed. Catching sight of the exciting contents he let out a thrilled gasp.

'Mum, Dad – wow, I love it!' He pulled out a magnificent new book about Space and the Wonders of Life, which Chris proceeded to leaf through, suddenly absorbed in the spectacular array of breath-taking photos of constellations, nebulae and planets.

Joe and Donna grinned at each other and Christina stepped forward and placed a shiny flat parcel into Chris' hands. 'Happy Christmas, sweetie; I hope you like it,' she grinned affectionately.

Chris tore open the star-drenched sparkling paper to reveal another book – a novel about cosmic travel. He grinned from ear to ear and ran to hug his grandma. 'Thank you, I love it,' he whispered into her ear.

'You're most welcome, little man!' she tousled his golden locks, teary eyed.

'Hmmm let's see, whose might this be?' asked Joe curiously, holding up a card and wafting it around. Chris tried to grab it out of his hand, jumping around the room like a demented meerkat, as Joe teased him with it.

'Please, Dad, it's for me, isn't it?' pleaded Chris. Donna was giggling, as Chris finally succeeded in catching his prize. He ripped open the envelope in a feverish hurry. He knew what he wanted, but he didn't dare to dream that it might be coming true. As he hurriedly pulled the card out, a piece of paper fell out too onto the floor. He grabbed it and read the words on it, bursting out;

'Oh yes, yes, yes! Tickets to the NASA Space Centre in Florida! Mum, Dad that is just AWESOME – thank you so much!' He ran to their arms and they hugged excitedly.

As Chris enjoyed his cuddle, he could see out over the bay; the brooding clouds were starting to dispense their drops in a flurry of wind. He snuggled in closer to his parents. Joe and Donna stared anxiously out of the window too; exchanging a nervous glance they squeezed their boy tighter.

'It's alright, Chris, we warned them about the storms; it's over to the authorities now to do the right thing,' said Joe supportively.

'That's right Chris, there's nothing more you can do. Just try to enjoy the day,' added his grandma soothingly.

The family had a wonderful day together sharing presents, games, anecdotes and jokes. The excitement culminated in a delicious dinner, shared with Grandma Larkin, which was filled with festive fare. As the day drew to a close and the family sat together contentedly curled up, they roasted chestnuts over the fire and sang Christmas Carols together.

However all the while they were enjoying their festivities, a storm was blowing outside, battering against the windows and the doors as if trying to enter the house. Each time a loud noise crashed into their consciousness they jumped in their seats.

That evening, when Joe turned on the television to catch the news, they were faced with a terrible newsflash.

'An almighty storm is devastating parts of the Far East. Flood waters are rising dangerously. People in affected areas are being warned to abandon their houses and evacuate in what is proving to be one of the worst meteorological tragedies to have ever hit this part of the world. Reports are coming in of houses and people being swept away. The army has been drafted in to help people to escape from their homes. The area is in uproar as many members of the public are demanding answers as to why there were no warnings from the Met office of this terrible storm...'

Chris cried out in shock.

'I TOLD them this would happen. Why wouldn't they listen? Why didn't they get the people out?' he cried incredulously. He started to cry as scene after scene of devastation and horror came on the screen. Animals were shown washed away in a turbulent muddy river of flood water. Parents and children were crying as they were separated by the rising flood waters. Cars were swept along as if they were toy boats in a bath.

The terrible scenes were etched in his mind as he anxiously lay in his bed that night, unable to sleep. He thought sometimes that Nature's cruelty provided more of a message and a deeper meaning for humans than compassion. He tossed and turned, as questions rose in his mind about his abilities. What was the point of being able to predict things if no-one would listen? He fretted angrily and wished he was older – they would never listen to a boy! He stared out of the window, which showed a surprisingly calm scene following the heavy storms of the day.

He was relieved that nowhere else had been badly affected by the storms, but he couldn't get the devastation of the news pictures out of his head. He caught sight of the Moon floating in the sky. Its almost-spherical face seemed to smile down reassuringly. He hung onto its essence and floated away with its whispers, soothed by the thoughts that came to him.

As Chris floated into dreamland, people on the other side of the world were battling with the terrible floods. The devastation in the Far East on Christmas Day took many by surprise. Little had been put in place to protect the population. Inevitably, it soon came to light that a boy in California had tried to warn them of the impending disaster; the resulting furore was to spark a great debate.

Predictably – as so often happens after a tragedy – the proverbial stable door was closed after the horse had bolted. Soon Chris was tracked down. He was inundated with questions from the media, from environmentalists and from meteorological experts. His wise words triggered more people to follow Chris' predictions about meteorological events. More research was carried out into ecological disasters and their causes and prevention. Many societies pledged their intention to heed Chris' advice in the future.

As more of his intuitive guidance came to light, Joe worked on disseminating it to the public. The world's scientists were able to access his reports on-line and his scientific fame spread; growing numbers of scientists sought out his collaboration with their research projects. The Centres for Disease Control were keen to initiate new research into disease prevention and ways to combat some of the big killers of the microbe world. Partners in the mix included various faculties of Immunology and Microbiology at a number of Universities, with Cousins as a focal linchpin communicating with Chris so as to minimize his exposure to strangers.

Extensive research was carried out to do with his audio-visual experiences and perceptions. Baines continued to lead visual research and a new sound expert was called in to investigate Chris' auditory functioning.

Chris' results continued to impress the science specialists

– his data and advice sometimes concurred with their current understandings, sometimes built upon them, yet sometimes blew original theories out of the water completely, but progressively he was able to explain to them how they could understand such leaps using sophisticated technical language that demonstrated his scientific intellect.

Increasingly, Chris was called upon as a living source of information in order for scientists to gain insights – not only into how to cure illnesses, but also how to avoid natural disasters and how to understand the nature of space and the Universe, but he needed silence and solitude to gain these insights, which was difficult amidst the intrusive interference of the monitoring medics.

So when Chris was back in hospital for his monthly investigations when the Bright Moon shone on December 28th, Chris begged to be left in deep contemplation under its cool rays, in a darkened room in the hospital, to help him shut out the creepy crawly wriggle-some visions and gain access to intuitive consciousness.

The hospital staff complied with his wishes, but placed a multitude of electrodes on his head in an effort to monitor his brain wave activities during this most active time of his gifts.

January

Full Moon: 8.40 pm on January 26th

83

CHRIS BALANCES WORKLOAD AND SELF-DISCOVERY

Chris found it increasingly difficult to juggle his school work with all this extra research, consultancy work, meditation, healing, problem solving and blogging that he was trying to do. His parents called a meeting with the school, negotiating special dispensary for Chris to work from home, with Hannah bringing him work assignments for him to fit in as and when he could manage.

During Chris' journey of self-discovery, he honed in on the duality of the behaviour of the micro-organisms. He sensed that some of them could be described as 'good', showing behaviour, sounds and sharing communications that could be described as 'beneficial' to mankind. However other micro-organisms seemed to be an antithesis, demonstrating a 'desire' to cause harm to mankind.

Chris discovered that he was not affected by these unfriendly micro-beings during a specific time-frame each month, i.e. from 12 midnight of Bright Moon nights for a subsequent 24-hour period. This time proved to be particularly fruitful for him to interpret antidotes for pain and disease from the sounds and faint whispers of the friendly micro-beings.

Health officials keenly absorbed his intuitive health advice, acknowledging his successful track record. They asked him to assist them in dealing with the most deadly ailments such as A.I.D.S., cancer and other terminal diseases.

Through discussions with Cousins, Chris was able to impart new ideas about the behaviour of unfriendly microbeings. He described them not as individual beings, but collective beings, that communicated with other beings of the same kind, or at the same level of physical structure and consciousness or intelligence. They communicated in many ways, including through sound signals which registered as very low infra-frequency.

Cousins decided to speak with the sound specialist about this, who explained that Ultra Low Frequency sounds had a frequency of less than 20 cycles per second. Although certain machines were able to detect these low rumbles, such as those that were designed to predict earthquakes, these sounds were usually undetectable by the human ear; however the vibrations might be felt in different parts of the body. Cousins puzzled over whether somehow this was true for Chris, wondering if somehow Chris 'felt' these low frequency sounds in some part of his body. He found out that ULF sounds were used to help study the heart's mechanics and he wondered if Chris might be somehow 'tuned in' to his heart.

The sound specialist explained that these low frequency sound waves could travel long distances and were able to get around obstacles with little loss. This was how some animals were able to use this sound frequency for communication, allowing them to pick up changes in the Earth's infrasonic waves to predict natural disasters. Cousins wondered if this was part of how Chris was getting his predictions about the environment.

Yet human detection of these low frequencies had also been linked by some researchers with feelings of awe, or suspicion of supernatural occurrences. These frequencies also appeared to match the natural resonant frequency of the human eye; some people thought that that explained why some individuals experience supernatural sightings – or bizarre visions. Could this somehow be at the root of Chris' visions? Yet Cousins had been convinced time and again that Chris really was able to see microbes as his descriptions of them were so factually correct.

Then one day Chris had a revelation about microbes that was to rock Cousins' world. Chris explained that he thought microbe communities, despite being spread out around the globe and the atmosphere, could use their signals to communicate globally – in an instant. This behaviour was a feature that implied there was a more subtle and highly complex microbiological world in existence than anyone had hitherto believed.

Chris thought that the capacity of microbes for detection and measurement was on such a fine scale that it made our scientific measurement devices a vague, approximate and laughably pale imitation in comparison; where our known mathematics ended was where the micro-biological zone began.

Cousins was astounded. What was he going to do with this remarkable idea? He couldn't help but think of the incredible recognition he would get from publishing research that provided evidence of all these breath-taking theories. It was any researcher's dream to be able to get themselves published in a peer-reviewed scientific journal; Cousins was closer than ever to this incredible dream. He was on the verge of scientific breakthroughs, and his bosses at the University were lapping it all up! The funding continued to roll in, yet he knew that he may never have got so close without Chris' revelations. How was he ever going to repay Chris for all his help?

84

Chris' knowledge is exploited

The research conducted using Chris' abilities was developing into new medical practices which were enabling many sick people to start recovering from their illnesses, as well as help to prevent sickness.

However, predictably, certain large pharmaceutical corporations started to become greedy. They exploited the boy's knowledge by charging ever increasing prices of production for the medical accessories necessary to fulfil his medical advice. Over the course of the next few months, health authorities worldwide would be reaping the benefits of the research initiated by utilizing the boy's extraordinary knowledge and sighting ability of the micro-beings.

Donna was increasingly in awe of Chris' knowledge and the benefits to humanity that he was able to initiate.

Yet she was no fool. She could see how people were benefiting from her son – both financially and in their career progression. She decided to talk it through with Joe.

'How much longer should we stand for it? All these people are making a fast buck out of Chris and some of them are doing really well because of him. It just doesn't seem fair somehow, Joe.'

'Hmmm, I see what you're saying Donna, but what can we do? He just wants to help people. It seems to make him happy to know that he's making a difference in the world. I'm really proud of him. I think he's an amazing role model for kids today. It makes a real change to see someone giving without expecting anything in return. I think it sends a positive message out to young people.'

'You would say that though wouldn't you Joe? I mean, you can't see the point of money, can you? You'd live on love if you could, you old hippy!' she laughed, but Joe didn't reciprocate, as old wounds began to open. Donna could see she had upset him, but she pressed home her point;

'Well why shouldn't he try to make some money out of all this, Joe? Lots of other people are making money out of him, why shouldn't he be getting some financial reward for all his efforts? I'm sure people would pay handsomely to get their hands on some of these ideas he has? Take Cousins, for instance, where would he be without Chris? I bet he'd still be stuck in his lab staring down his microscope if it wasn't for Chris? He would never have sealed those great funding deals, or met all those fabulous scientists, or been invited to all those gala dinners and research conferences if he hadn't met Chris!'

Joe was very quiet. He could see that Donna wasn't going to let this one go, yet he didn't want things to turn nasty. He valued Cousins greatly and had nothing but respect for all the hard work he had put in to help Chris understand what was happening to him.

'Why don't we see if we can get Chris some sort of deal out of Cousins?' pressed Donna. 'He should give something back for what he's getting from Chris in my opinion!' Donna's arms were crossed in annoyance.

'Well I don't know, Donna, he's been such a help for us all. I don't think he has taken advantage of Chris, he's only helped him. Why can't you get some kind of legal thing going to protect his intellectual property? I think it's the big companies that should pay if anyone's going to!'

'Hmm I wish I could, but you can only do that if the ideas are written down. You know; trademarks, design rights, patents and copyright – that sort of thing. No we don't have anything like that, because Chris only talks to people and they just lap it up and make their profits from his ideas. Nope, I'm going to pin down Cousins and get him to pay up – he can't keep taking all these ideas and getting all this kudos for nothing!'

Donna was on a mission. The next time Cousins came over she was ready to pounce. She sat in on their discussions.

'Hiya Chris, great to see you again little fellah!' greeted Cousins affectionately – he had grown to really love this quirky young boy with his incredibly grown-up traits.

'Hi Dr. Cousins, how's the research going?' interjected Donna, eyeing his ginger-framed face.

'Well, really great, actually. I just secured more funding to look at the physical communication systems of micro-organisms and my boss has given me a pay rise, and a new job!' gushed Cousins innocently. Donna grabbed her chance;

'Well that's just great that you're doing so well Dr. Cousins. I wanted to talk to you about that...'

Donna proceeded to wheedle her way round the scientist in such a way as to tie him up in knots. By the time she'd finished with him, she'd skilfully manipulated him into offering them a deal whereby he would give the family a monthly payment for consultations with Chris. He would loath to lose his connection with the insightful boy, so Cousins weighed up his options and opted for the one that allowed him to still get essential information from Chris. After all, what good was his research without the boy's help? No, he wanted that prized published article; his sights were firmly set on being the first past the post.

Donna was buoyed up by her successful negotiations with Cousins and went on to negotiate sponsorship deals with mega-corporations vying for Chris' data and advice. She felt Chris had every right to claim some income from all this corporate exploitation. The money came in extremely handy for the family to put right all sorts of financial issues, including paying back the loan from Christina, who was delighted that her family was thriving. Their comfort level had risen agreeably.

Hard as it was for them to see their child seemingly transformed into some kind of prodigy – some soothsaying prophet of scientific understanding – Joe and Donna needed to oversee the situation to ensure Chris' emotional and physical welfare. Donna negotiated reduced working hours with her firm in order to spend more time helping Chris.

Joe equally needed to pass the running of the store over to a trusted colleague as he no longer had time to help out Chris and deal with all the internet questions as well as work at the shop. Something had to give. Then he had a brainwave which he thought might just right a few wrongs; he made a call.

'Hi Joe, how's it going?' answered Holly in surprise. 'Is Chris alright?' she asked – suddenly concerned.

'Oh he's just fine thank you Holly. I just wanted to call you and see how you're doing, oh – and make you an offer you can't refuse!' laughed Joe.

'Oh?' Holly's curiosity was roused.

'Listen, you know how much you love the store?' teased Joe.

'Uh-huh...what is it Joe?' she couldn't stand the wait.

'We-ell, I just wondered if you loved it enough to want to manage it.' Joe's words hung, scintillating in the air like they were part of a magnificent firework display. Holly's reaction was joyful.

'Manage it? Run it all by myself you mean?' she asked excitedly.

'Yup – with no-one interfering and no-one to stop you from stocking it with whatever wonderful items you like!'

'Wow, Joe, I don't know what to say!' she stammered. 'I mean, how? I mean, why?'

'Look, I just want to give something back to you, Hol. You've been such a good friend despite me breaking your heart; I just want to show you how much you mean to me. We can negotiate terms to suit you. Besides, I can't think of anyone else who would do a better job, so whaddya say?'

'Well, I guess...yes, alright I'll do it!' she was smiling from ear to ear. Joe was delighted to have made her happy again and relieved that his beloved business would be in safe hands.

With Donna and Joe's regular work managed, and money coming in from sponsorship by various pharmaceutical, geological and astrological sources, they were freed up to support Chris. So many companies were keen to pull Chris to their side. Chris was increasingly pulled from one meeting to another; Cousins struggled to keep up with mediating all the communications with the global scientists via video conferencing.

Krefeld – a constant supporter of Chris and his emotional welfare – was concerned about the ethics of the whole idea. He kept reminding the representatives from the corporate giants that the boy was only 12, so the situation needed to be handled properly, yet increasingly there was in-fighting between the representatives as they vied for Chris' attention for help with their latest commercial endeavours.

Underhanded practices were uncovered by the authorities as they found certain corporate giants guilty of paying extortionate amounts to spies asked to steal information in a form of industrial espionage. Yet people were also prepared to pay the extortionate amounts that the pharmaceutical companies were charging for their new innovative medical solutions, as many were desperate to replace the life-saving medications and interventions.

Visitors to the Larkin-McKenzie household were too much to count. The streets were lined daily with sick people on stretchers and in wheelchairs, all desperate to see Chris.

Many were convinced that he held divine healing powers, whilst others were just curious. The police authorities set up blockades around their street to prevent the unmanageable waves of clamouring people from overrunning the household.

Now unable to reach him, the sick set up camps around the blockades, chanting Chris' name to get his attention.

Sometimes he would go down to the crowds, to try to help them. The only way he knew how to help them en-mass was to try to get them to meditate together. Right there in the street or, if there wasn't enough space, down at the park, the crowds took part in the sound and touch meditation. The effect of the mass meditation and the union of the voices sent chills down the participants' backs. The sounds rose up to the heavens in a beautiful symphony of sounds, a heartfelt mass prayer for healing. Chris always held the intention of healing, peace and love with his mind and heart throughout the sessions; the healing effects bounced out on his voice-generated sound-waves and washed over the gathered crowds.

In the weeks that followed such sessions, many sick people began to recover – they were astonished at first, but ever stronger in their faith in his healing abilities as their bodies recovered. The people who were healed created a new underground wave of support for Chris, which extended into every community, every religion and every political persuasion, in a way that blurred the boundaries between otherwise distinct groups of people.

Yet as the good created by Chris' luminous services to humanity ever waxed, the dark forces attracted by his brilliant light were ever growing in parallel and reacting to the massive changes that were initiated by his kind, compassionate acts.

Several pharmaceutical companies were experiencing reduced profits from the ever reducing number of sick people – a hitherto unknown phenomenon. Greed ruled the hearts of some; the bottom-line profits proved more important to these damaged individuals than the actual health of the nations. Sabotage plots were initiated to undermine the advice coming from Chris. Some individuals created media campaigns to destroy his reputation and to try to expose him as a fraud.

Throughout this dark time, there was one man who, contrary to his past record, proved to be a reliable and loyal support to the family – Kevin. He counteracted the negative stories with his more positive stories of hope and healing that Chris was involved with. He investigated the instigators of negative propaganda, trying to expose their hate campaigns as lies and slander.

85

Dark thoughts of exploitation unleash sinister revenge

Chris slept; his fevered brow was covered in perspiration.

As he lay tossing and turning in his bed, duvet binding his limbs and trapping him tightly, he was suffering. His nightmare tossed him from scenes of destruction to images of apocalypse. Fires and damnation, demons and monsters filled his head. His nostrils seemed clogged with acrid smoke and his throat felt choked and constricted. Piercing chilling screams filled his ears. Humanity was on the brink.

Nature appeared to him in all her burning glory, carrying enormous golden scales. Her scales were tipping precariously between construction and destruction, good and evil, light and dark, humility and ego, coherence and chaos, evolution and devolution. Mankind's choices were the weights that would tip the scales of their future either way.

She revealed to him that if her balance were upset, she would revolt. She pointed at Chris – he gazed down and saw in his hand a gift, a gift from Nature that should have brought benefit to the world, but it had created imbalance and disharmony and she rose up in his vision like a great burning effigy, furiously reclaiming the gift she bestowed upon him.

Bright Moon

As mankind's sinister thoughts of greed, exploitation, lies and slander prowled over parts of the Earth like a looming black cloud threatening to cover and quench Chris' luminous good deeds, he saw a stirring amongst the unfriendly micro-organisms, as if they were feeding off the black thoughts.

He saw a huge black and white chess board, filled with wooden chess pieces. He watched as Nature moved her chess pieces into check-mate. Then Chris felt his body vibrating with a deep low booming pulse. In an instantaneous sharing of ultra-low frequency sound waves amongst the insidious micro-beings, their community formed an understanding that a human had received illicit intelligence and knowledge in a communication from advanced extra-terrestrial beings that had been traversing the galaxy to colonize elsewhere. Chris absorbed the meaning of this communication and realized they meant him.

The pulses continued and in his mind, Chris translated; unsure how an inferior-intelligence being had been gifted such advanced knowledge, the dark micro-beings concluded that it must have slipped out of the extra-terrestrials' consciousness through some sort of mind meld with the human under the powerful electro-magnification force of a Bright Moon. Then Chris saw the Full Moon shining fiercely overhead in his horrific dream and he saw himself attached to it, as if it were an extension of his energy systems, like another chakra that extended outside of his physical body. He felt dizzy and ungrounded.

Then, out of the blackness he saw a ball of light appear, which diversified into pinpoints of light like stars, which shone around his head. Each star was a friendly microbe uttering words of encouragement, wisdom and love. The dark micro-beings pressed in picking up the signal pulses from the human-friendly micro-organisms, discovering that they were assisting the human by relaying messages of significance concerning human and environmental health. Chris watched in horror and confusion as he saw scenes of destruction, dying screaming microbes and planetary harm. He heard another booming pulse of sound which vibrated through his energy field, as the dark micro-beings shared information amongst their colonies about the resulting detrimental effects to their populations.

Paralyzed, unable to intervene, Chris felt the words form in his head; many humans are still incapable of dealing with cosmic knowledge and intelligence in a responsible and consciously aware way. The dark micro-beings exchanged units of information in pulses of light and sound that pierced right through Chris' soul, until they had formulated a plan that would retrieve the information from the human, to bring back balance to Nature.

In horror, he watched as the glorious glowing effigy of Nature handed a lethal gift to the sinister microbes. Then the dark micro-beings unleashed an unforgiving relentless microbial war aimed at bringing disruption to the human and friendly micro-being populations, as well as silencing the human responsible for the devastation to their colonies.

86

Chris succumbs to dark micro-beings

In Chris' nightmare he was being smothered and attacked by billions of micro-beings; he was gasping for breath. Burning up, he dreamt he was sitting by an inferno. He kicked off his bedclothes and writhed in his fever. He tried to cry out, but no sound would come.

Abruptly he awoke and his vision was filled with a cloud of dark micro-beings suspended above his bed in a fog of his own breath. Their cacophonous sounds grated in his sensitive ears like fingernails scraping down a blackboard. He tried to move his hands to his ears to block out the awful noise, but he couldn't! His hands were stuck by his sides, as if he was paralyzed.

He tried to scream out, but no sound would come from his searing throat – the pain was like knives slashing his vocal chords and his tonsils.

Trembling, he turned to view his clock and noticed that it was late. Where were his parents? They would usually be up by now. He strained his ears to hear any sound coming from the house, but he could hear nothing.

Terrified, and unable to scream or move his hands, he felt an urge to look out of the window. There was an eerie quietness about the place, with nobody walking the streets, or driving vehicles, or cycling. It seemed like a ghost town! Focusing, he was able to see clouds of dark micro-beings around the houses.

He rocked himself from prostrate into a sitting position; his head spun dizzily. With his head pounding and his hands useless at his sides, he shakily pushed himself to his feet. Wobbling weakly, he shuffled to his parent's room and found them both lying in their beds, groaning. They too were sick; he could see the same dark micro-beings swarming in the atmosphere of their bedroom.

Alarmed, he tried again to speak, but no sound would come. He flopped down next to his parents and they suffered together.

After dropping in and out of fitful sleep, the family woke again towards the evening. Joe and Donna thought it was just some kind of flu virus that had hit them all, but when the parents rallied that evening from the worst of the fever, they anxiously realized that Chris was unable to speak or move his hands. Chris nodded his head towards the window, to indicate that they should look out. Puzzled, they stared into the streets and realized that everywhere was deathly quiet.

87

CHRIS REALIZES THE VIRUS HAS GONE PANDEMIC

Turning on the T.V., there was an emergency news report from a very sick-looking reporter that explained that people all over the world were suffering from an unknown virus – no matter where they lived, or what geological temperature there was in their location and no matter what food habits the people kept.

Many businesses, factories, stores and public services had ground to a halt. The hospitals were overrun with sick patients, but there were no staff well enough to help them. They had succumbed to the disease just like everyone else and lay around the hospital in whatever space they could find with any spare blankets and sheets they could muster up.

The World Health Organization reported substandard care in hospitals due to staff shortages. The government was preparing to announce quarantines and schools were shut.

A sick-sounding U.S. government representative declared a state of emergency and a sickly representative from the Centres for Disease Control promised that they would work over-time with the W.H.O to try to establish what the unknown virus was and what would cure it – just as soon as they had any staff fit enough to come back to work.

The family jumped as the phone rang. Joe answered. It was someone from the C.D.C. asking for Chris.

'I'm sorry,' said Joe weakly, 'he's really sick; he can't come to the phone.'

'Well sir, it's imperative that we speak with him. I'm very sorry that he's not well, but it's a matter of National Security that we try to establish contact with him. The bottom line, sir, is that we don't know what this virus is. It has affected what seems to be the entire population of the world, which categorizes it as a pandemic. W.H.O. has issued a global health alert about a new infectious disease of unknown origin; we need your son's help to get some insight into its nature.'

The C.D.C. representative was breathing heavily down the phone, clearly exhausted by his efforts to speak.

'Well I understand your predicament; we are of course as keen as you to get to the bottom of why we are feeling so utterly awful, but as I said, Chris is unable to come to the phone to speak. He actually can't speak at all. His throat seems to have been badly affected by this virus. He hasn't been able to utter a single word to anyone all day. Not only that though, he's unable to move his hands either, as if he has become paralyzed. I'm sure he's been working too hard. I think he's got so run down trying to help everyone else that he's been hit really hard by this virus.'

Joe was in tears. He scraped back his damp floppy brown hair from his feverish face.

'So unless you've got any ideas how to help my boy, I suggest that if you have any compassion, you just leave us alone, alright?'

Joe slammed the phone down, and fell back onto the bed

utterly spent.

88

CHRIS GETS MEDICAL HELP

Fifteen minutes later, an armed guard arrived at the door of their house. Donna weakly wobbled her way to the door and opened it to see a bunch of white-coated scientists accompanied by the guard. All of them appeared utterly exhausted, clearly sickening from the virus, but they had been sent by the authorities to try to help Chris and his family.

With great effort, they carried out all sorts of tests on Chris, checking his throat, his temperature, his pulse and his blood pressure, taking samples of his blood and swabs from various mucous membranes, trying to establish why he was suffering so badly. The scientists kept sitting down, exhausted by their efforts.

They tried to give him antibiotics as a precautionary measure, but Chris refused to take them, shaking his head wildly and refusing to open his mouth. He clearly was still able to have an opinion about how to deal with the infectious micro-beings, but apart from his head movements they were barely able to discern it, as his ability to communicate his knowledge was completely impaired.

The scientists were astonished how rapidly and profusely the disease had spread. The world had never experienced such an outbreak before. They could only compare it to previous flu and S.A.R.S. outbreaks, but such illnesses were caused by viruses that had taken time to spread and had caused significant respiratory symptoms, unlike this new mystery virus. They had no medicines that were yet working to deal with the virus and the symptom profile was unlike any that they had seen before, apparently peculiar to this new viral strain.

They postulated that it was a mutation of another virus – perhaps it could be related somehow to S.A.R.S. or a particularly nasty case of influenza – but until the scientists were well enough to work properly, everyone was working in the dark and without help from Chris' insights, they were thoroughly stumped.

They administered the drug acetaminophen for Chris' fever and packed up to leave, promising to send more help as soon as they could. The sick scientists struggled back out to their military truck and collapsed in their seats, completely exhausted.The instantaneous spread of the disease went against all known understanding of viral behaviour and created chaos amongst the network of people expected to roll out the procedures that would usually be followed in this situation.

The staff of 'San Francisco's Communicable Disease Control Unit' were themselves decimated by the virus, so the usual response to widespread that was supposed to help with infection control, medical back-up, investigation of the virus and possible treatment protocols was disrupted.

For several days sick people arrived in their droves at the family's door, hoping to get help with their sickness, but Chris continued to suffer and was unable to communicate or assist anyone else. The armed guards and blockades were reformed to keep people away. Joe posted news of Chris' predicament on their website and contacted Kevin to report on his condition, hoping that if the news spread of his sickness, that they would leave him alone.

Kevin had also been unwell, but came as soon as he could to interview the parents about Chris' symptoms and his inability to communicate. He promised to spread the news and see if he could campaign for help.

89

CHRIS DETERIORATES

Then, as mysteriously as it had started, the sickness seemed to lose its grip on people. Joe and Donna recovered, as did the others who had been affected throughout the world, but Chris did not. The internet communities that usually kept up to date with Chris' activities via his website were shocked to hear that the boy who had helped the world so much was now struck down by a terrible sickness that wasn't alleviating.

With hospitals back up and running, Chris was taken in for more medical tests, but the medics were unable to understand why he continued to succumb to the virus when everyone else was getting well. Even with the intervention of experts from the Department of Public Health they found nothing that would help – no medication, no therapy and no treatments.

They even took serum from the blood samples of individuals that had recovered from the illness, giving it to Chris to artificially create the anti-bodies in his blood to fight the illness, but to no avail. He seemed to be responding differently from everyone else to this unidentified illness. They considered moving him into isolation until they knew more about his condition, but as everyone else already seemed to have had the virus and recovered, there didn't seem much point.

Experts in virology, lab techniques, epidemiological investigation and the control of unusual infectious diseases were sent to Chris' house in case it was the source of the outbreak. The teams were multi-national, drawn from the institutes participating in the W.H.O. Global Outbreak Alert and Response Network.

One of the most positive things that came out of the crisis was that it forced international cooperation and openness, bringing everyone together, as each person realized that they were all equally susceptible to being infected by new unknown virus strains – whatever their nationality.

The most effective way to deal with viruses was believed to be specially developed vaccines, but they took time to research, develop, test and produce. Once developed, the vaccines had to be produced on a massive scale to meet the protection requirements for future potential pandemics. The influenza pandemic led to the production of 350 million doses of vaccine in 2006, 900 million in 2009 and 1.4 billion million doses in 2011 as manufacturing efficiency improved, but international co-operation was key to this success. W.H.O. was now seeking to place agreements to encourage the sharing of information about new virus strains between different countries, vaccine manufacturers and biotech companies, in the hope that this would speed up the process of creating global protection against such viruses.

The researchers investigated the unknown virus' genome, its behaviour, its weak points, but even with all the international co-operation they were not getting far without Chris' help, even those that had been successful in mapping out the S.A.R.S. genome. Samples of the S.A.R.S. virus were held safely in San Francisco, so the virologists were able to compare it with the new virus, but they did not seem to be of the same family.

They compared the genetic sequence of the new virus with that held on the website of the Genome Sciences Centre in Vancouver, but could only confirm that this virus was something new. Any suitable vaccine against this unusual virus would still be months, if not years away.

90

People of the world send their support to Chris

Visitors now came to the hospital in droves to offer their good wishes to Chris.

There were friends from school, including Hannah and the other Science Club members, Cousins (who was trying to find a microbiological answer to Chris' predicament), Grandma Larkin, Joe and Donna's friends, members of the internet community, alternative therapists (including Chinese Medicine specialists such as those that had tried to treat the S.A.R.S. outbreak of 2003), various scientists and priests. The people kept on coming.

Joe and Donna held vigil at Chris' bedside in Intensive Care throughout, as he got sicker and sicker. Out of the hospital window they saw crowds gathering in the streets, holding lanterns, cigarette lighters, torches, tea-lights – indeed any kind of light they could find. They remained in prayerful vigil on the hospital grounds.

Religions worldwide claimed that Chris was the boy predicted in their sacred texts that would be born on the Earth in order to bring peace to the world, to promote faith and religion. Each religion held regular prayer sessions in their sacred places asking for Chris' healing.

Ironically, certain less spiritual members of the different religious sects were soon at loggerheads with each other over this point, each claiming that Chris was the Chosen One of their own religion only. The resultant conflicts led to violence in the sacred places, as each side refused to back down on their viewpoint.

Donna and Joe were at their wit's end worrying about Chris, but they allowed Kevin to interview them once more at the hospital. In the interview they appealed for people to come forward if they thought they could help Chris to get better. They also begged the different religious sects of the world to overcome their differences for the sake of their son, to unite in their prayers for Chris, for a more powerful cohesive prayer.

The yogi came to the hospital to visit Chris. He sat with eyes closed in deep contemplation with him. After some considerable time, the yogi's eyes flickered open, and he began to speak;

'Truth does not lie on the horizon or beyond the stars; it is in the palm of your hand and in your heart. In silence you may realize it and if your son survives this illness, he may emerge from his silence having found a deeper truth, even enlightenment. Donna, Joe, I feel that the only way that your son can survive, is with some unusual interference of Nature which the world may not welcome. The question is, how can this be done?"

The yogi turned his liquid brown compassionate eyes to the couple, sensing their deep sorrow and hopelessness.

'If there is truth in the Universal systems, I think that it will happen soon.'

Donna nodded her thanks and she turned to Joe, crying.

'Some gift! I knew this so-called gift was hurting him somehow. I've always known it, and I just want him rid of it and well and normal again! What are we going to do?' she wailed anxiously.

Joe hugged her tightly, as much at a loss as she was. They stared wide-eyed at their ailing son, pale, weak and unmoving from his continued illness.

*

The leaders of many religious groups of the world came together at a meeting and agreed to hold a united prayer day for Chris.

From Christian to Buddhist to Hindu, Sufi to Hopi, Jewish to Jain, a representative from each and every religion made their pledge to bring many of their followers together on one named day, to pray for Chris' healing.

On the day, vigils were kept in all sacred places and prayers chanted by huge crowds, unanimously pleading for Chris to be made well again.

91

CHRIS STARES AT THE MOON AND SEEMS TO IMPROVE

It was a freezing cold night late in January. Chris stirred in his hospital bed. He felt a little stronger. Sensing the silvery rays of light falling on his eyelids, he felt an enormous temptation to go and watch the Bright Moon that was shining in through the hospital window, as if he was pulled by its very gravity.

With difficulty, he heaved himself onto his side and pushed himself up on his elbow. His mother was sleeping in the chair by his bed. Trying not to wake her, he quietly rolled himself off the edge of the bed, swinging his weak legs over the edge. His feet found the floor; he very slowly tried his weight on them, pushing gingerly against the rubber tiles.

Carefully, he stood, wobbling with the effort. He took a teetering step towards the window. Then another, and then another. Finally within reach of the window he steadied himself with his forehead up against the freezing cold pane. Down below he could make out lots of flickering lights in the hospital grounds, gathered around his window. He could hear songs of praise, hope and divine worship emanating from the crowds below. He smiled, feeling the love from them all. His gaze tracked up to the Moon's bright silvery face and he mentally acknowledged his old friend.

Exhausted by his efforts he rested there a while, stuck up against the window, staring intently at the Bright Moon. His consciousness ebbed and flowed, but as he focused in on the Moon, he felt a strange quickening within, a sensation of attraction and magnification of his consciousness.

The Moon appeared to be growing bigger and bigger, then – like entering some kind of vortex – he felt as if he were spinning closer and closer towards the Moon and he was flying unaided, defying gravity. The spinning winds buffeted him and he felt something pulling at his throat, like a strong vacuum was pointed around his larynx. Then as suddenly as it had started, the sensations stopped; he realized he was still at the window, his face pressed up against the pane.

Regaining normal consciousness, he could sense feeling in his hands! He cried out in surprise, surprising himself doubly by the ability to vocalize his feelings once more. His throat was sore, but he had a raging thirst, so he rubbed around his throat, and pushed himself away from the window back to the bed. Reaching for his water glass, he took his first unaided sip of water in days, barely noticing that he could see no micro-organisms to put him off from quenching his thirst.

Krefeld was on-duty; he spotted Chris tottering back to the bed.

'Hey! Good to see you up on your feet, kid! How are you doing?' Krefeld was not expecting a reply, but to his intense pleasure, Chris laughed out loud – a hoarse whispery laugh, but a vocal sound all the same.

'I'm feeling much better thank you!' he whispered, grinning; although weak from his illness, Chris' elation brought him some stamina.

Donna stirred, disturbed by the noise. She was in happiness as she realized Chris was up and speaking again.

'What's happening?' she said, confused but excited.

'Mum, my voice is coming back!' he quietly stuttered, 'and look, my hands – I can feel them again!' he reached out to hug her warmly with his painfully thin arms. They hugged intensely for a while.

'Let me call your father!' she said excitedly. Chris lay back on the bed, exhausted but happy.

Joe arrived shortly from his trip home, carrying a bag of clothes for everyone and an Tablet-Gadget full of meditation songs, he had procured in the hope of them initiating some healing in Chris.

'Hey buddy! You're awake! Your mum says you're feeling a bit better!' said Joe, elated.

'Hi Dad!' grinned Chris. Joe leaned over his son and pushed back his damp curly locks to kiss him warmly on the forehead.

'Good to have you back!' Joe laughed. 'Can you see the micro-organisms, son?'

'No Dad, but I can hear them today.'

Joe excitedly tripped over to the window, throwing it open to the night-time air, and leaned out, yelling;

'Chris is talking again! He can feel his hands! Thank you all so much for your prayers. Bless you all, my friends!'

Cheers broke out below and the songs changed from imploring to celebration. Joe could see people dancing and offering thanks up to the heavens.

Joe and Donna offered their own thanks in their own quiet way – Donna acknowledging her God, Joe thanking his 'Divine Source of the Universe'.

92

CHRIS IS INTERVIEWED ON HIS OBSERVATIONS ABOUT THE VIRUS AND BACTERIA

The medics crowded round to see Chris and to take further observations. The news of his improvement spread quickly; scientists were keen to hear as soon as possible what he had to say about the virus that had afflicted the world.

Joe and Donna begged them to leave Chris alone to get stronger, but Chris insisted he was well enough to speak. He wanted his words to broadcast globally, as he had some important messages for the people of the world.

A press conference was called, but the medics insisted that only one reporter was allowed to speak to him as Chris was still very weak. Joe and Donna nominated Kevin as their preferred intermediary.

Kevin excitedly came with a cameraman and, very thoughtfully and empathetically, posed his list of questions whilst broadcasting live to the T.V. and internet. Pushing his thin-rimmed glasses up his fox-like nose, he began;

'The world is very pleased to see you getting better, Chris; may I ask you how you are feeling?'

'Pretty exhausted actually' smiled Chris weakly. 'But

I have had a long time lying silently in bed to think about all this and I have a lot to say. I am almost afraid to speak now though because I have found that when you speak it is usually imperfect; yet in silence you are strangely perfect.'

'Well let's get this over as quickly as we can shall we?' grinned Kevin. 'Nations and religions have come together, united as one, to pray for you whilst you were ill Chris. How do you feel about that?'

'I think it made all the difference! I could feel the waves of love coming from them and it made me stronger. Love is like a thread that weaves the body, mind and spirit into oneness. Everything we can imagine stands upon love. It's the basis of our lives and the foundation of all our achievements.'

'True love radiates without our knowledge. It's a profound positive energy that no passer-by can miss. It is a connective force, an attractive, mystical force; the only force that can unite the world.'

'Unconditional love has the power to heal, unite and inspire both the giver and the receiver. The unity of the different religions sprang from their inner spirituality – which alone can weave different cultures and religions into a garland of oneness. Our lives involve so many people and our circumstances are always changing. We can't make the novel of our lives meaningfully complete without the inspiration and good wishes of others.'

Kevin nodded with the look of someone absorbed in reflection, then commented;

'Well you certainly have my good wishes, Chris. What do you think happened over the last few weeks? How is it that the world's population all came down with the same virus?'

'Whenever you visit a new place – whether it is just a

new building or an entirely different country – bacteria and other micro-organisms, they're all around you, wherever you look. They are on guard just like invisible immigration and customs officers, or police officers, watch dogs, or security cameras; always watching, always checking us out. They are more powerful than any armed guards and they don't arrive as just one, or in their tens, or their hundreds, but in their millions – and even more than that.'

'As soon as we arrive somewhere new, bacteria sniff us out, surrounding us like a pack of hounds. They can even instantly get right into our bodies and examine us with more precision than an X-ray. You can't hide anything from them – sometimes you doubt whether even your mind belongs to you...'

'They have bodies like transparent gel and minds sharp like razor blades. They are so resourceful; they have more features and facilities than us, because they can change their shape or their size, or curl up on themselves and resist anything you may threaten them with; chemicals, temperature extremes, you name it, whatever you want to throw at them to destroy them, they can find a way to adapt themselves and stay alive. It's as if they withdraw themselves from their bodies, into another dimension that's completely off the spectrum of what we understand!'

'We don't even know their names – we have to make up our own names for them, and that's without really understanding what they are and what they are capable of. It's almost like they're civilized – maybe even more than we are! They create communities, customs, habits, personalities and even their own language – sometimes this involves sending out viruses, which I think is what happened in this case. Everyone succumbed to the same horrible virus.'

'But how could it happen throughout the world at the

same time?'

'They communicated instantly and each individual micro-being knew what the rest of the community was doing and why. We may think they are nothing because our ego gets in the way of us realizing, but they have more and better control over their lives and of others' than we do.'

'We are at their mercy; they are always many steps ahead of us. As soon as we think we've learnt all there is to know about them, they change and adapt; they always know more about us than we know about them. They are so much faster than us. We can't even begin to appreciate how much more advanced they are than us. They are always evolving, always learning, always improving and refining themselves and keeping us at bay.'

'So do you think this was some kind of a super-bug?' asked Kevin.

'Well, yes. As they are so adaptable, we can never disable, arrest or kill them.'

'Is that why none of the treatments seemed to work?'

'Yes. Through their adaptability they can keep emerging like weeds – yet their needs are minimal. They hardly need anything to survive and flourish. We are so different! Our needs are endless – we are never satisfied. We want to take control of Nature and the world, but you know, with a little awareness and effort on our part, we could control our senses and our mind to be more like them...'

'More like them? Why would we want that?' asked Kevin.

He scratched his dark curly locks in confusion.

'We need to be able to live alongside them, rather than just believe that we will succumb to the illnesses they are associated with. We can never eliminate them all – they are too pervasive. Why would we want to anyway? Some are beneficial to us – some people believe that all micro-organisms can be beneficial to us if we learn to work consciously with them rather than against them. Not a single entity, whether living or not, exists without its opposite. There is a perfect balance and each micro-organism thus has its own distinct and essential role.'

'We can never beat them with our ego or our so-called intellect. We need to understand them better – and not just with our minds, but also with our hearts and our feelings. They are the ultimate expression of living beings on our planet; yet they are the tiniest. We only live on land, but they can also live in the air, in other atmospheres, in the water, under the Earth, or even on other planets. They can live anywhere.'

'That sure would be useful for us humans too!' laughed Kevin. 'So why can't we live alongside them without illness breaking out?'

'When they check us out, if they can't see any signs of our understanding of them in us, then we are like foreigners traveling in an exotic primitive land, teeming with tribes jabbering in a nonsense language. We don't understand what they are saying and we can't speak to them; we don't understand their civilization.'

'Everyone has their own language at the end of the day – their own body language anyway; their own way of thinking, their own vibrations and emotional currents, their own distinctive body odour and perspiration.'

'Micro-organisms are ultimately the ones that decide what to do with us – whether they let us entertain them, or they decide to treat us like a prisoner, or humiliate or make fun of us. These clever bacteria, they figure out whether they could accept us; each of us measure up differently. That's why different people are affected in different ways by the same bugs.'

'Most people feel the pinch when they are in a totally new place; some people might feel a little under the weather perhaps, but generally they have 'adapted' enough or been accepted by the new bugs sufficiently for them to be left alone, mostly unaffected. Other people don't do so well, some fall sick and recover fairly easily, others fall seriously ill and take longer to get over the illness, whilst some unfortunate people fair really badly and might even become paralyzed. Of course the worst case scenario is if someone succumbs completely to the attack of the bugs; the person loses their battle against them and dies. Usually we say that person didn't have enough 'resistance' to the bugs.'

'Well, we're sure glad that you managed to resist this bug, kid!'

'It's funny – we talk about having 'resistance' to bugs, but I actually wonder if that's completely the wrong attitude? If we were to adapt to them, to go along with them and their ways, I think we would all get on much better. I think it's the lack of resistance that leads them to accept a person and not make them sick.'

'So were you resisting these bugs then?'

'Well yes, I guess I was. They seemed different to all the others. They were like dark forces of evil. I was so overcome by fear that I just couldn't get on their wavelength.'

'And I guess when the doctors didn't have a clue what to do to get you well, that didn't help your state of mind?'

'You could say! Doctors are always throwing antibiotics

at bugs, thinking they are the answer to everything. Yet antibiotics are a joke to most of them! In fact, in many cases, instead of the bugs becoming sedated or wiped out, they are only provoked. Then they are able to rise above the drugs and come back with even more power, causing multiple problems in the body.'

'This is so confusing for the medical experts; the bugs just don't fit into their neat little theories requiring them to wage war on bugs with drugs; in the end the infected person just loses out, no-one can help them.'

'We seem to have no respect for the abilities of bugs to live harmoniously together. They are able to set up their own ecological systems in which there is a natural order of different micro-organisms living side-by-side, engaged in some sort of mutual understanding about their combined – perhaps symbiotic – presence. Most people remember Alexander Fleming for inventing antibiotics. This name was coined by a pupil of Louis Pasteur's from the term 'antibiosis'. Yet Pasteur was known to have said 'Le terrain est tous', which means he understood that the health of the micro-organisms' ecological network is the basis for ecological balance in a living system. I think we could all learn from the symbiotic behaviour of micro-organisms, some healthy give and take, some harmonious and network-centred living traits would benefit our society enormously.'

'Do you mean you are proposing a new community-centred way of living for the people of the world?' asked Kevin, mouth agape.

'Essentially, yes! Going back to the old way, where each of us looks out for each other, co-operating for mutual benefits and survival and having more awareness of each person's role in the success of their future. Your body is a vehicle. You are the driver. Your genetic map is a fixed destiny, but you have some choice about steering in the direction you want to go. Our future depends mainly on the way we think at present. To change our lives, we must change the way we think. If we don't make positive wishes firmly, if we don't give a certain shape to our destiny with our positive wishes, then destiny becomes a dustbin of our negative thoughts. This influences our life towards downfall.'

'Everyone has the power to shift their consciousness towards either destruction or construction. The former breeds guilt, the latter brings happiness. In destruction you provoke; when you act constructively, you inspire. The past is solid and carved; we cannot change it. The present is liquid; it is flowing and we can steer it – especially if we raise our conscious awareness of this fact. The future is vaporous, unknown. The clue to the future is in the present moment, in the choices we make from moment to moment, in the intentions we set.'

'So what advice would you have for us were this superbug ever to attack us again? I take it from your words that we must change the way we think about bugs?'

'Absolutely, I believe there is another way apart from antibiotics that we can all try to deal with the bugs; not always, but sometimes it works, so it's worth a try. It's nothing to do with chemical protection, which is what everyone seems to try at the moment, with the masses of drugs we all take. No, this other way – it's not even taught at Universities, or Medical Schools, or even by any scientific discipline, or religion. You have to learn this way by trial and error, by regular practice, as if you are carrying out your own little experiments on yourself.' Chris tapped his head knowingly.

'That sounds incredibly strange!' declared Kevin, aghast.

'I know that sounds a bit weird, but you can do that with

your own body, it is yours after all; you know it better than anyone else. It's like a house that you live in, but you are the only one who can live there. You know exactly how you feel so you can always keep track of that.'

'You have to remember, we are not completely different to bugs. They have a mind and soul of their own and a life-force, just as we do. These are common elements that prevail throughout all living entities. This fact is true wherever we may travel one day in the Universe – throughout all the galaxies and even beyond – wherever else there may be living entities.'

'Careful, we're getting into "Star Wars" territory now!' uttered Kevin in disbelief.

'In a way I guess I am!' laughed Chris. 'I'm actually talking about consciousness here, the main commonality between all living entities. So when everything else fails, we can use our soul power – not aggressively – but gently, by generating meaningful and peaceful vibrations from our being and body, coupled with a sense of appeal to the bugs, a sense of respect, combined with an approach of humility and harmony. It is essentially just another form of communication. Words are just containers outside ourselves, whereas meanings are inside us. Just like with humans, on the surface we all think and speak differently, but deep down we are the same. Despite that, finding harmony amongst us remains a challenge – perhaps because we don't recognize that we are the same. So, freakish as this may sound to you, this approach may work – even if it only works to lessen the aggressiveness of the bugs.'

'I'm not quite sure I understand?' asked Kevin, confused.

He pushed his sliding glasses back up his sharp nose, as if that would help him comprehend.

'Imagine a burglar has broken into your house carrying a weapon, which he intends to use on you to attack you first. Of course normally you would react with fear and perhaps resist aggression in order to defend yourself physically; but let me try to explain how else the scene could play out. Imagine then that you are playing a musical instrument as the burglar arrives, but you don't even notice him because you are completely absorbed in a state of meditative bliss from playing.'

'The sounds that you are making with the instrument are actually generating a vibrational frequency of harmonious sounds, which create a certain electromagnetic field around you that actually enhances the magnetic field of the room you are in, so as the burglar enters the room, despite his original intentions to harm you, he is stopped in his tracks by the sensation he picks up from the surrounding magnetic field. The vibrations he senses are soothing and calming, causing a feeling of unity within, which somewhat counteracts the original negative and harmful intentions and feelings he had arrived with. It truly is an amazing thing, isn't it?'

Kevin nodded – slightly bemused by all this science. Boy this kid is bright, he thought to himself. So small and frail, but he's such a powerhouse of wisdom.

'That's why nearly everyone loves to hear music – so many people play it and appreciate it in the world, no-one will ever get upset or annoyed by that fact because it is just a mystical truth.'

'But here's the thing, it's not just music that can have that effect. A similar effect can be brought about by generating certain harmonious thought waves; guess what these thoughts are?' Chris' eyebrows were raised high above his shining silvery eyes in a question.

'Beer?' asked Kevin humorously.

'No!!' laughed Chris. 'It's not beer, even though I know it's your favourite. It's LOVE! Yes, love has been recognized for centuries, ever since the dawn of human awareness, as an essential transformational thought and feeling. Think about it! Who hates love? Who rejects love?'

'Well now you come to mention it, I guess love is kinda neat!' said Kevin, grinning and thinking of his girlfriend Merry.

'All beings need love, whether they are a scientist, a religious person, an illiterate, rich or poor, an animal, or another creature, or a plant or creeper, or even a reporter!' Chris broke off as Kevin was laughing now. Chris grinned amicably and continued; 'Everything and everyone needs and deserves love. Even in our broken society, it has been proven 100% accurate that speaking with even just a fragment of love communication, your communication becomes warm, effective and productive. What might these fragments be? Well – humanity, courtesy, politeness and modesty to name but a few!'

'That reminds me of a Sunday school song – what was it? Fruits of the spirit, I think! My mum used to love that one,' Kevin said wistfully, a tear welling in his eye as he recalled a fond memory of his departed mother. 'How did it go? The fruits are love, joy, peace, patience, kindness, goodness, faithfulness, gentleness and self-control...' Kevin was humming the song to himself. Chris smiled.

'You've got it! Christ's teachings were very astute!'

'So let's say I'm armed with my fruits of the spirit; what would I do in the case of bugs?' asked Kevin curiously.

'Well, when you go to a new place and you are surrounded

and invaded by all the bacteria there, you won't feel anything until they enter your personal space, but if you are sensitive and intuitive, you can sense them there even with your first breath in that location. This is the awesome thing, guys;' he gazed straight into the camera. 'You can actually communicate with them through meditative consciousness, so by creating waves of harmonious emotional currents (that's love of course!), they somehow sense this mystical language and it helps them to relax and back off a little.'

Kevin whistled through his teeth.

'Ultimately, what do the bugs actually want from us?' asked the reporter.

'Well, I can tell you; it's not just food. It's more than that. If food was all that was needed, then no-one should have to fight, because although food is not available to everyone and there is much hunger experienced around the world, the actual supplies of food that should be available to all are abundant and perfectly sufficient on this planet for all of its inhabitants' needs – a kind of ecological balance – but we would only see that if the people of the world were to share the food fairly.'

'No, we also need a type of food for all our cosmic components – our body needs nutritional food, our mind needs its own kind of food; that's peace. Our heart needs yet another kind of food – love. Our spirit needs the food of truth. All beings survive according to this formula – bugs included!'

'Well there we go; the recipe for life!' laughed Kevin.

'We forget that life evolved from micro-organisms. They created the first communities here on Earth. When they extended themselves to include many different bacterial types living in harmony, they protected themselves within a skin – a bio-film – a bacterial community.'

'These bio-films then evolved into a new organism known as an amoeba, which then evolved to work with other amoebas to create new organisms known as plants and animals. These also lived in harmony with each other in a symbiotic dance known as the rhythm of life, whereby each species had its own niche and its own role to play in the bigger picture of Nature.'

'Then, as Nature went out of balance again, humans evolved. Our role was to be the ultimate expression of potential adaptive power for bringing balance back to Nature, by stewarding this planet and its environment. We – like all other creatures – evolved as a community of amoebic cells, which in our case became a new organism called a human.'

'Well, some friends of mine have never evolved past the amoebic stage!' Kevin guffawed at his own joke.

Chris giggled, but ploughed on with his important message.

'Now the evolutionary nature of life is being called in to play, and – as the highest level of organized cells – we should be participating harmoniously in the balancing of Nature and the environment. We need to learn to live together as one functioning unit, one organism with one head or consciousness shared amongst all for the well-being of all.'

'Oh boy, that's a far-cry from where our heads are at the moment!' declared Kevin, wringing his hand.

'That's right Kevin! What are we doing? We are each competing as individuals, as if we are single-celled organisms lost in a sea of other single-celled organisms, each with no rudder to steer our ships. You know, I think life is like a sail; if we don't steer it, then the wind will sail us. It's better if we steer ourselves to an intended destination using the power of our intent.'

'Right, so if we continue to live the way we do, competing as individuals, what is the result going to be?' asked Kevin seriously.

'It is nothing short of evolutionary chaos.' Chris was staring straight down the camera again. 'Our own self-destructive behaviours are destroying the world and Nature. In the process we are destroying humans too. What we see as evolution – in the form of new technologies for mass convenience and ever-developed materialistic acquisitions – is leading us down the path to mass extinction.'

'Mass extinction – now you're getting really heavy.' Kevin's eyes had widened in horror behind his thin-rimmed glasses.

'Well it's our own fault. We evolved from simple micro-organisms. They are the stuff we are made of, so what we are doing is trying to bring them down too. Well, they've been around way longer than we have, they have far more wisdom than we do and they are not prepared to go down with us.'

'I think they are fighting back and killing off those of us that are not prepared to adapt to the ways of Nature, to the symbiotic harmonious circle of life that is the key to evolutionary progress on this planet. This latest virus was another wake-up call. I think we've been lucky to escape with our lives this time, but we may not be so lucky next time.'

Kevin appeared shaken.

'Until we realize the role we have to play in all this and the responsibility each and every one of us has in this experience we call life, I don't think the bacteria are going to give us an easy time. No, we've had our chance; until we pull our socks up and evolve as connected humans into a functioning society and integrated civilization, I fear we are at risk of losing everything we think we stand for. What price must we pay to continue this so-called civilized life?'

'Well when you put it like that, Chris, I hope the viewers are sitting up and taking notice!' Kevin stared meaningfully down the camera.

'I think it's time for a fundamental change in our belief systems. It's time that we realized our connectedness and behaved accordingly. Damaging ourselves and each other is no longer acceptable. It is damaging to the whole of our humanity; if we want humanity to survive and thrive, we have to embrace all that we are and all that we can be, through love.'

'Do you think that's what helped you to pull through this time?' probed Kevin.

'Cohesive prayers from a mass of people are incredibly powerful. I felt the waves of love coming from people around the world. We are a bizarre duality of good and bad, love and hate, yet we could be so perfect were we to embrace the whole and feel the oneness between us. The unity displayed by the religions is a huge step forward. After all, if only they would realize that the fundamental tenets of each of their religions are similar, that they are trying to teach different facets of the same spirituality. You know, spirituality without humanity, without awareness, is dogma. Yet their cohesive prayers came from the flower of their hearts – a fragrance of purest inspiration which has only one expectation – the well-being of others. This is a basis for understanding the true lessons of religion. We should all believe in and faithfully practise humanity, through which the truths of all religions can be comprehended.'

'Let's hope this message of hope reaches all the religious

leaders of the world,' said Kevin into the camera.

'Micro-beings are here to stay and they will outstay us if we don't evolve to catch up with them,' said Chris clearly.

'So how do we do that Chris? What do you suggest that we all do?' asked Kevin desperately.

'Work on your communication skills, but don't just expect others to understand you. Develop the ability to understand others. Practise symbiosis – working for the common good, in service to each other, fuelled by a consistent connection to source, to love – this is the only way for humanity to continue life here on Earth.'

'Tell me, Chris, how is it that you know all this stuff?' asked Kevin curiously, tapping his sharp nose.

'We have an inner, mystical eye. This is the mother of all our senses because it is more powerful than the physical senses. While the physical eye can only receive light, the inner eye can also hear, smell, sense and feel. We only realize this when we experience it for ourselves. Some people call this inner mystical eye intuition, or precognition, or a sense of deep, though logic-denying feeling. We may not yet know what it is, yet we all know that it is somewhere within us.'

'The heart may be the mother of all senses. With it, we move into different dimensions in consciousness, just as our galaxy is moving in space all the time. We also journey into the cosmos, but in mystical ways and, although these experiences are stored within our hearts, we can't always remember them. Sometimes the only way we can express these vague impressions is through inspirational poetry.'

Kevin remembered the beautiful poem Chris had written on the back of the note his mother was holding on her death bed. He smiled luminously, as if he was starting to understand.

'What do you think it is about you that has singled you out for this amazing gift of wisdom?'

'Through the heart we receive many gifts. Remember that we are all the direct embodiment of Nature, Kevin. Perhaps the Universe wants to give us all more, but how much more do we deserve? There is a veil between the past and the future, between birth and death, the mind and the heart, body and spirit.'

'This is what makes life interesting and exhilarating. There is anticipation, incentive and motivation to live life, to know, explore and experience the truth behind and beyond the veil. I think this is what drove me to keep searching until the veil drew back for me, revealing these gifts and these truths.'

'Why do you think you have become such a phenomenon – even an icon, a hero – to so many people at such a young age?'

'Success and failure are relative; there is no absolute standard to measure them. No-one has ever been absolutely successful or has utterly failed. Successful people are those who do not run after success, but pursue their cause and vision. I was never after success - I only ever wanted to pursue the truth of my identity. I asked so many questions – all day, all night, to anyone who would listen. Yet – as a great teacher once explained to me – often when we become occupied asking questions, we may miss the whispers of answers emerging from within.'

'Many complex questions have simple answers. Some simple answers spark remarkable discoveries, inventions and revelations, but it is what you do with these revelations, how you share them, that helps you grow as a person. Only those who can think ahead can go so far as to change the world.'

'Chris, as ever you blow my mind! Please tell me, what is the main thing that you have learned from your experiences of the last few months?'

'Hmm, that's a hard question. I found out that I didn't always have to ask other people in order to find out things. Truth is self-powered just as the stars are self-luminous. When you feel like you aren't getting your answers, it is only that the Truth may have been eclipsed today, but it will emerge again like the morning sun. I had so many questions, but now I know that questions can't arise in us without us being in possession of at least a seed of the answer.'

'One day we suddenly find ourselves answering our own questions. Maybe we find ourselves intuitively explaining an answer to someone else who has asked the same question, or we find the answer in a book and realize that we knew the answer all along. When questions are reflected back and resound within us, this is spiritual enquiry; it can even lead us to experience new and different dimensions of our being.

'Life is a journey to reach higher and higher levels of consciousness. We should embrace both truth and love in our spiritual quest, to make our inner journey whole and cosmic with fulfilment and enlightenment. Love is experienced in the heart and can unite everything into oneness; truth cannot. If there is no harmony within, love can't be felt and the currents of love can't flow. Empathy, harmony, compassion, kindness and forgiveness are all petals of the same flower of love.'

'Once we have reached higher levels of consciousness, our new understanding naturally leads us to serve others without inhibition or selfishness, even if it's only through our encouraging presence. When we observe the Universe with conscious awareness, we find so much meaning in every moment.'

'I also learned that a moment of deeper experience is more powerful than a lifetime of words, but I guess the main thing I realized is that we are never really alone.'

'Do you mean we are always surrounded by bugs?' laughed Kevin.

'Yes, but not only bugs, Kevin. Wherever you walk the whole Universe walks with you! Not only that, it has our best interests at heart and it will work with you even better when you become consciously aware of it.'

'Wow Chris, that was amazing. We're out of time but thank you so much for your brave messages of peace and hope for humanity. We will continue to pray for your complete recovery.' Kevin wrapped up the interview and thanked the family.

'Thank you'. Chris fell back onto his bed in utter exhaustion.

Joe and Donna hurried Kevin away to allow Chris to get some well-earned rest. Both parents were tearful from the wise words they had heard their son say.

Kevin went to join the press conference, also somewhat exhausted by the deep conversation. He wondered what the fall-out from this show-stopping interview would be.

When Chris' broadcast went out around the world, the world sat up and took notice. It sparked many lively philosophical, environmental, political, spiritual and religious discussions and brought many government representatives of the world together to hammer out ideas for new legislations and international co-operation. Representatives from different religions gathered to discuss how they could move towards a new more cohesive interfaith understanding based on mutual respect and recognition of equalities over differences.

Change was in the air, but was it evolution?

93

CHRIS STARTS TO LOSE HIS EYESIGHT

After a restful night's sleep, Chris awoke in the hospital, well refreshed. He extended his arms and legs into a delicious stretch.

What a blessed relief it was to be able to move his hands again! As he laid there listening, eyes still closed, to the early morning sounds of the patients and staff, (where were the microbe sounds?) he pondered on the interview he had given. He wondered if he had done enough to spread the message he had felt so urged to give. He wondered what the future held for the world and what part he might play in it all.

Hearing something clatter to the floor near his bed, he opened his eyes. He tried to focus to see what had made the noise, yet all he could see were blurred images, fuzzy and vague movements. He cried out for his mother, who rushed to his side.

'What is it Chris?' she exclaimed– she was still wound up like a coiled spring after all the stress of the last few weeks.

'Mum, I can't see properly!'

Donna, distraught that the boy may be going through yet another crisis, leaned over his face, but Chris could only see a disjointed vision where her face should be.

'My eyes, they're not working! Please help me Mum!' he cried.

'I'll get help, try to stay calm son.'

Donna rushed to the desk and explained his symptoms to the Staff Nurse. Kathy glided to his aid, launching into various checks and noting his oxygen saturation. She called for help and Dr. Krefeld ran over, pocket watch swaying wildly.

'What's the problem, Chris?'

'It's my eyes, I can't see – everything is blurred and disjointed.'

'Try to stay calm, Chris – we'll page Dr. Baines.'

The staff flurried into activity, and Chris was bustled off to have his eyes checked, his parents anxiously in tow.

94

Baines examines Chris' failing eyes

Dr. Baines glanced up through his enormous glasses as Chris arrived in his examination room, assisted by his parents. They all had anxious expressions on their gaunt faces.

'Hello Chris, we meet again! How are you?' questioned Baines, his large head cocked on one side.

'Well, not so great really.' Chris was struggling to peek at him through screwed up eyes.

'Here, take a seat son, Donna please help him sit down.' Donna seemed close to tears as she guided her son into the plastic seat next to the optical equipment.

'May I examine your eyes today Chris,' asked Dr. Baines with a mischievous grin, remembering the struggle that Chris had put up on previous occasions.

'Sure, go ahead,' agreed Chris, evidently not planning to put up a fight this time.

'I'm just going to shine a light into your eyes – ready?'

Edward peered into Chris' eyes with his small torch, making Chris feel a little like a deer caught in headlights.

'Hmm, there's minimal dilation today – a bit sluggish even. Chris, just take a look at my letter chart for me?' Chris looked towards the Snellen chart, but he was unable to focus on any of the letters, apart from guessing the very top three lines.

'I'm going to pop these anaesthetic drops into your eyes and when they've taken effect we'll have a little look.'

Chris nodded. Edward carried out several specialized tests to check the health of Chris' eyes.

'That's rather strange,' Edward muttered to no-one in particular. Grabbing his retinoscope, he checked how Chris' eyes were focusing its beam of light.

Confused by the acute deterioration in Chris' eyesight, Edward examined Chris further with his Volk lens at the Slit lamp, to observe his retina at the back of his eyes.

'Hmm, the blood vessels appear a little thinner. The head of the optic nerve – that's the 'electrical cable' that connects your eyeball to your brain – seems inflamed'.

Edward wondered if Chris' ability to transmit visual information to his brain was impaired by this inflammation.

He knew that some viruses could cause this nerve inflammation and lead to sight loss.

'It seems a bit like optical neuritis, which can affect your vision.'

'Is that permanent?' asked Donna anxiously.

'Well it depends what's caused it. If it's a virus, then the inflammation may go down when the virus goes.'

'But if it's not a virus, what happens then?' Donna eyed

Joe worriedly.

'Well let's not jump to any conclusions until we know more,' side-tracked Baines. He continued his examination.

'I'm looking at your retina now for any damage. The retina is made up of light-sensitive nerve tissue that contains photosensitive cells called rods and cones, which convert light into electrical signals that are carried to the brain by the optic nerve. If it's damaged you may have some issues picking up light signals.'

Chris shuffled uncomfortably.

'The macula in the middle of the retina seems a bit strange; maybe it's affecting your ability to see fine detail in the central part of your vision. This is the part that was working extra-ordinarily well before – presumably enabling you to see the micro-organisms. I wonder if it has somehow burnt out with all the extra work it's been performing.'

'Is that serious?' asked Joe, concerned.

'Well it's not great. It's kind of like early macular degeneration, which I'm afraid usually progresses over time, causing loss of central and detailed vision.'

'That sounds horrible!' Chris was understandably alarmed.

'What do you mean?' demanded Donna.

'Well let's not jump to any conclusions shall we; let's try some more tests – it's certainly not clear-cut. Please look at this grid pattern.' Baines showed Chris a regular criss-cross grid of lines. 'How does that seem? Is it straight or distorted?'

'Pretty distorted actually,'

'A bit like a black hole in the space-time continuum?'

joked Baines.

'I guess,' Chris wasn't laughing. He was breathing heavily, clearly upset.

'I need to get a second opinion on this first Chris. Try not to worry – it might not be anything serious. We'll take a retinal photograph and I'll confer with my colleagues.

'Right, I'm nearly done now. I just want to check something else. Pop your head on this chin rest.'

Edward observed Chris' eyes with a slit lamp illuminated microscope.

'Hmm, I can still see a silvery film on your eye; I don't think it is conjunctivitis, as it covers your cornea too. Let's see the depth of your visual field; I'm checking to see if you have any blind spots, which would affect your vision.'

'Are you nearly done?' asked Chris, feeling uncomfortable.

'Sure son. I'm all done.'

'So what's the matter with him, Doctor?' demanded Donna. Baines hesitated, unsure how to answer;

'To be honest, it's a bit of a mystery to me – the tests have not actually proved anything. I'm sorry but I can't diagnose any specific reason for the sight loss, although there are signs of inflammation which could be linked to other issues. My colleagues and I will discuss the results and let you know as soon as we have any answers.'

Edward escorted the family back to the ward, and Chris and Donna held each other's hands tightly. This really was the last straw.

95

BAINES DISCUSSES CHRIS' DIAGNOSIS WITH KREFELD

Baines was in discussion with Krefeld over Chris' eye examination.

'I just don't get it. The last time I checked his macula, it appeared to be in pristine condition. There's no family history of macular degeneration and usually when it appears it takes much longer to deteriorate to visual impairment.'

'Is there any chance you made a mistake last time?' asked Krefeld, slicking back his silvery hair distractedly.

'I don't think so. I would have had to miss it every time I examined Chris, which is pretty unlikely. However if he had been suffering from macular degeneration all this time, that might have explained his visions.'

'What do you mean?' asked Krefeld. Baines adjusted his humongous glasses on his nose.

'Well, long-term eyesight impairment has been known to lead to the brain creating strange conclusions about the disturbed visual signals coming in. What's the condition called now? Charles Bonnet Syndrome. The patient ends up seeing hallucinations, visual disturbances created by the brain. Yet that doesn't make sense either. He was able to see perfectly well before; the brain only creates these hallucinations to fill in missing information from visual impairment.'

'I see, and what about the auditory component of his experiences?'

'Some sufferers have those too, but usually these sufferers are aware that what they see is not real. Quite often they won't tell anyone about them in case someone diagnoses them as mentally sick.'

'Well Chris certainly believes these visions have been real, so perhaps that would imply some kind of psychiatric illness, I don't know, even dementia, but I have seen no other evidence of dementia in him and at his age – well... nor did I spot any brain lesions. Also, how can you explain how advanced and medically correct his visions and auditory messages have been? No, we've been over this time and time again. Most people – including me – think it must all have been real.'

'Well whatever causes the visions and auditory phenomena, there is still this possibility that he may have something akin to macular degeneration,' admitted Baines, 'but I don't know if there is a fault lying in the top pigmented layer of the retina, or in the photo-receptors. I need to do more tests to check that.'

'Could it be another symptom of his virus?' wondered Krefeld.

'The vision loss could be – there are viruses that have been known to cause optical deterioration because of inflammation to the optical nerve; the nerve does appear inflamed,' said Baines, 'but we've never seen this particular strain of virus before, so I can't confirm anything. Plus we'll need to do more tests to rule out multiple sclerosis or toxicity issues or any of the other things that cause optical neuritis. Did anyone else get this type of visual symptom when they were infected?'

'We've seen nothing like that in our other patients. Maybe we should check the symptoms with the I.C.D. database again.'

'Good idea. It would be a tragedy if Chris were to lose his sight; after all he's done for the medical world that would be just too ironic.'

'It sure would. I've heard there is remarkable stem cell research to replace cells that have been damaged in macular degeneration,' said Krefeld hopefully.

'Hmm, I've heard about that too, but I doubt they're advanced enough to help Chris right now. We don't know how fast his eyesight might deteriorate either. At its current rate, he could be blind in a few weeks...'

'You must consult with your ophthalmic colleagues to see what they think. I won't inform the family about this unless we're certain of the diagnosis. Not after all they've been through already.'

Baines agreed, promising that he would do his utmost to help Chris.

96

N.I.H. RESEARCHER SEEKS HELP FROM CHRIS

Joe and Donna were sat with Chris, who remained under observation as his eyesight was deteriorating. A man approached the family, with a clipboard and a recording device.

'Hello – may I introduce myself? My name is Dr. Bentley; I'm a research scientist from the National Institutes of Health in Bethesda. I have been informed about your son's remarkable abilities to detect micro-organisms and understand their behaviour. On behalf of the N.I.H., I've come to ask your son some questions in the hope that he can help us with our research into micro-organisms and pathogens.'

'Our vision is to develop treatments and protections against microbes that allow us to perfect our health and extend human longevity beyond a century.'

Bentley smiled broadly – evidently very proud of his work and certain that he would be met with co-operation and enthusiasm. He was most certainly unprepared for what ensued.

'You've got to be kidding me!' yelled Donna, protectively.

'Visions - what kind of sick joke is this? If you think I'm going to let you waltz in here and bombard my boy with more questions, you've got another thing coming!'

'But, I don't understand, ma'am,' stuttered Bentley, 'Chris has been co-operating on a wide-scale with all sorts of scientists, so what is the issue with him speaking to us about such a noble cause?'

'Noble – you scientists are all the same. You're all stuck up and full of your own self-importance. Selfish, thoughtless, I could go on!' Donna was close to tears. Joe was holding her shoulders trying to restrain her.

'Well, I've never been so insulted in all my life!' Bentley was in shock of Donna's Rottweiler-like behaviour, at which point Joe stepped in.

'Dr. Bentley, is it? I'm very sorry about that – Donna is very upset, well – we all are actually. Poor Chris has had a set back – I don't know if you heard that he has been badly affected in the recent virus pandemic?'

'Well, yes I did know that, but weren't we all! I saw his very eloquent broadcast that went out recently and I assumed that he was well on the road to recovery?' Bentley blustered.

'Yes, so did we, but I'm afraid that his eyesight is currently affected, so if it is micro-organisms that you're asking him to look at, I'm afraid you will be sadly disappointed.' Joe gave his son a hug.

'Oh I see, well that's certainly a terrible shock for you all. I do of course wish him a very speedy recovery.' Bentley was preparing to leave, sensing that he was not welcome.

Chris interjected – 'I'll speak to him. I can still talk, can't I?'

'You need your rest son,' Donna affectionately responded. Joe whispered in Chris' ear;

'Yes Chris, you've been pushing yourself too hard, too fast against the clock for all these months. Time will always walk parallel to us; your mind has been running faster towards the future, trying to solve the world's problems, but your poor body can only run as fast as the pulses of time in the present. If you push and push yourself, your body will not get a chance to catch up and recover.'

'I know you're trying to protect me, but I'll be fine. Please let me try to help him Dad, please Mum.' His pleading expression was too much for Donna. She reluctantly gave in, replying to Bentley;

'Well – alright then, but make it snappy! He needs to recuperate and you're not helping him with all your badgering.'

Bentley and Chris huddled together for half an hour, exchanging information. It was all revolutionary ideas that were being discussed and Chris was excited to help create some innovative ways to reduce suffering.

However his stamina was low; very soon he was too tired and unable to answer any more of Bentley's questions.

'I'm sorry, I need to rest – can we stop there?' asked Chris weakly.

'Sure, Chris; you've been most helpful; I'm very appreciative of your assistance at such a difficult time. Rest assured that the information you have passed on will be put to good use!' Bentley smiled broadly and waved goodbye to the family.

Donna scowled after him. 'Come on Chris, let's get you

back into bed,' she fussed, tucking the sheets around her fragile boy.

February

Full Moon: 12.28 pm on February 25th

97

Visitors; well-wishers or manipulators?

Chris' eyesight continued to deteriorate throughout his birthday month. He had only been able to detect the sounds of the micro-organisms in the day following the last Bright Moon.

He stayed in the hospital as the medical teams wanted to observe his progress, to determine whether his symptoms were to do with the recent virus.

Meanwhile he continued to receive a constant stream of visitors – Hannah and her Science Club buddies brought homework assignments, which he dictated back to her, to help him stay up to date with his school work. Her dad, Dr. Cousins, regularly dropped by to discuss his research projects and their progression. Kevin dropped in daily to monitor his welfare, recording Chris' predicament on behalf of the world's curious media. His Grandma Larkin came often, with sweets, home-baked cookies and plenty of lunar stories to keep him occupied – especially as his eyesight wasn't up to reading.

Many unknown visitors also came, who had heard about him from his broadcast. Many more scientists came and went, hoping for insights into their latest research. Representatives from major corporate companies came by to try to discuss products and marketing strategies, which would allow them to delude their rich clients about eliminating diseases and pains. Joe and Donna politely but firmly steered such visitors away as efficiently as they could.

Valentine's Day brought a special card to Chris' bedside – a thoughtfully produced bumpy card that he could feel even if he couldn't see it! Hannah blushed until her freckles seemed to vanish as he ran his fingers over the embossed heart on the front of the card. She was relieved he couldn't see her embarrassment as his mother read out the message Hannah had written in the card. At least it brought a warm smile to Chris' wan face.

Poor Chris also spent a somewhat quiet 13th birthday in the hospital. His entry into the world of teenagers was heralded by a rocket-shaped cake baked by his grandmother. The sparkler on the top fizzled and popped as the ward staff sang a rousing rendition of ' Happy Birthday,' however it wasn't the same as a proper teenage party; neither could he see his presents.

Donna lamented his difficult life. When would he ever be normal again?

98

The Bright Moon glows again

Throughout the waves of visitors, the Moon quietly and relentlessly waned and waxed through yet another monthly cycle of changing faces.

Donna watched the Moon phases too and noticed their passing as a mark of how relentlessly she had to deal with Chris' illness and this uncomfortable lifestyle. She worried most about how – after months and months of this terrible ordeal – she would be able to continue dealing with it all. How would she cope if he stayed like this for the rest of his life?

As the Bright Moon rose in the night sky once more, Chris was tempted to go to the window again to try to observe its attractive face – yet bizarrely, from what blurred images he was able to perceive, this time its dimensions appeared smaller than normal, as though the Moon was more like a star. He stared at it, bemused, observing clouds dashing past the Moon's tiny face.

With the window open, he was able to feel the buffeting of a strong breeze against his pale face; his eyes began to sparkle, as if he had just woken up.

He tore himself away from the beguiling charmer and –

sighing – he eased himself back between the starchy sheets of the hospital bed, falling rapidly into a deep sleep.

99

Chris' eyes deteriorate

The Bright Moon had dipped below the horizon, making way for Father Sun to spread his golden rays across the azure skies. Such beauty, pouring forth such great illumination for all to see – except Chris couldn't see it. At least, as he awoke he could barely make out the difference between light and darkness, let alone any fine detail of objects around him.

Horrified by this worsening state, he clamped his eyelids shut again in an attempt to block out the latest disappointing evidence of his rapidly failing eyesight. Crying for his mother, Chris made a courageous attempt to open his eyes and search for her, but his eyes were cloudy – as if he was trying to see through a screen. He couldn't even make out the shape of objects right in front of him.

Terrified, he cried out again for his mother, who came running from the coffee machine down the corridor.

'What's happened, Chris?' Donna's breathing was laboured from her run.

'I think I'm nearly blind!' said Chris, hysterically. 'I can't see you anymore, Mum! What am I going to do?' he wailed, heartbroken.

'Oh darling, I'm so sorry' said Donna, tears streaming down her cheeks.

The medics crowded round his bed, fussing and messing with him, but there was very little they could do. Baines had ruled out macular degeneration as the vision loss had spread wider than the central part of the retina. He found that the optical components of Chris' eyes seemed to be losing their transparency in a strange and foreboding turn for the worse.

Mother and son lay in each other's arms. Donna rocked her boy back and forth, distraught by the latest turn of events. Her mother's instincts kicked in; she offered care for him as best she could – she suggested that she could draw Chris a bath to help him relax and unwind.

Chris nodded his consent and Donna grabbed a wheelchair for him – there was no way he would be able to see well enough to navigate his way to the washroom.

As Chris backed himself into the chair he turned his head towards the next-door beds, suddenly aware of a grating grinding sound which he recognized as a harmful micro-organism. As Donna wheeled him away he shouted back towards the sound and the fuzzy outline of two people;

'Please don't stand over there, you will be in danger! There is a weird sound coming from near you. Move yourself away back towards my bed, or you will get infected!'

The surprised patients stared in surprise at the mad blind boy, then back at each other, eyebrows raised. Shrugging, they continued their mundane conversation.

100

A NEW PATHOGEN IS DETECTED

Chris received extensive support from Baines and Krefeld as well as numerous other medical specialists during his confinement with deteriorating eyesight, yet they were distracted by another serious illness that struck down the two patients in the beds next to Chris, plus a nurse who had been treating them.

Having come in with relatively simple health problems, the medics were surprised that the patients became so rapidly and seriously ill, with seemingly unrelated and unexpected symptoms and that the nurse had followed suit with the same symptoms.

The research teams were tearing their hair out trying to understand what had gone wrong – everyone was still on high alert after the recent virus incident. As they fussed around trying to diagnose the illness, Chris weakly whispered to his mother;

'I heard them – I heard the sounds of the pathogens. I told them to move away, but they wouldn't listen!' He turned his head on his pillow, exhausted.

'I know, son. Don't worry yourself over it,' Donna soothed. She'd had enough of her boy being questioned and consulted;

she wanted him to be left alone to get well while the others sorted out their own problems.

101

A plea for help

Baines came to carry out some more tests, but Chris' eyesight was deteriorating further.

He went to discuss the results with Krefeld, who showed him the latest brain scans. They agreed that they could draw no diagnosis conclusions from the collective results, so they were back to watchful waiting.

With Chris' worsening eyesight, it was increasingly difficult for him to interact with others, so Joe and Donna tried to field as many visitors away from him as possible, unless they were offering some kind of hope for getting him well again.

Joe tried to keep up with the endless internet enquiries and phone calls asking for help from Chris for various problems, but finding this difficult he enlisted Kevin's help to create another broadcast dedicated to spreading the word about Chris' deteriorating eyesight and his indisposition to working.

He requested people to come forward if they had any similar experience with failing eyesight that had been cured – be it from the alternative therapy world, or otherwise.

Donna added a plea for help from the religious communities to come together in their prayers for Chris once more, which instigated religious leaders to perform mass prayers on his behalf.

Donna was increasingly turning to her faith to get her through the ordeal; she spent time in the hospital prayer room offering supplications up to God for her son's healing. In her desperation she even tried meditating with Joe and Chris; she found respite to her usual anxious thoughts as she turned her thoughts inwards.

Many healers came – nutritionists, hypnotherapists, acupuncturists, cranial osteopaths, 'Neuro-Linguistic Programmers' and 'Emotional Freedom Technique' experts, naturopaths, sound therapists, counsellors and so on – each offered their own support and tried to help Chris and his family to be more comfortable.

March

Full Moon: 2.30 am on March 27th

A Shaman calls

The visitors continued to arrive throughout March.

One spring-time visitor caused a great stir within the hospital – he wandered in with a smoking pipe, which released acrid smells of burning herbs. The staff jumped on the unusual-looking character, asking him to put out his pipe and leave it at the door.

The man refused and was about to be thrown out, when Kevin showed up, on his way to visit Chris. He noticed the exotic-looking man's small cloth bundle and saw that the dark-skinned man was dressed in leathers and moccasins. He also had feathers and teeth on a string around his neck.

Having seen a regular stream of unusual visitors arrive for Chris recently, Kevin guessed the man was also coming to visit Chris, so he intervened in the fracas, grabbing the man by the arm and tugging him to the corner.

'Are you here to see Chris McKenzie, sir?' Kevin whispered urgently. Surprised, the man replied in a faltering accent;

'Yes, Chris McKenzie. Bear Mountain. You smoke with me?' The Native American Indian proffered his pipe at Kevin, who quickly tucked it into his jacket, saying;

'Listen we have to hide this for now, yes? Follow me, I'll show you where he is.' Turning back to the astonished staff, he shouted;

'He's with me! I'll make sure he puts out his pipe, alright?' The staff just stood there open-mouthed as Kevin whisked the tribal man to the elevator.

They found their way up to Chris amongst a cloud of excited whispers from onlookers, who rudely pointed and stared. Kevin pointed out Chris in the ward, who was talking with the microbiologist, Cousins.

The healer shaman approached Chris' bed, arm outstretched, with a small rolled up cloth in his hand. Donna jumped as she spotted the curious character right by her side. His silent footsteps in the soft moccasins had concealed his advance. She shifted awkwardly, but Joe put a comforting hand on her shoulder.

'Donna, don't worry! This is 'Bear Mountain'. I invited him to come. He promised he would bring something he thought would help Chris to get well.' Joe nodded to the Native American Indian to proceed, then spotting Kevin in the doorway, he gestured to Kevin to come over and join them.

Finding Chris' hand, the shaman dropped the bundle into it.

'I bring help,' he announced. 'You wear this round your neck. You get better.'

Unable to see the gift, Chris felt the soft folds of the small bundle and found the edges of the cloth. Pulling gently, they unwrapped to reveal a tiny cylinder. Chris' face gave away his confusion.

'You open it, you feel inside,' uttered the shaman.

The whispers from the staff in the room had now increased in volume to a low chatter of astonishment.

Chris found the end of the minute cylinder with his fingers and delicately prized open the lid. Upending the cylinder, a tiny rolled-up copper sheet slid out onto the bed. Joe gasped, reaching forward to touch it.

'Son, let me help you!' Joe fumbled with the copper sheet until, with difficulty, he unrolled it; the onlookers inhaled an astonished breath. Some type of fragrant herbs and a small leaf pouch fell out onto the bed, releasing heady scents of an exotic nature.

Crowding round to see the tiny copper sheet better, the onlookers saw a strange geometric diagram, somewhat reminiscent of a maze.

'What the...?' muttered Donna. An awed silence descended on the group.

'What is it? I can't see!' exclaimed Chris, impatiently.

Cousins leaned forward to stare at the tiny diagram. His thoughts whirred as he tried to make out the detail of the shape. In awe he recognized the shape was reminiscent of a specific friendly bacteria which he knew aided human health; a friendly micro-entity.

'Wow! That looks a bit like a bacteria!' exclaimed Cousins.

'You've got the microscopic world on your brain, Cousins!' laughed Joe. 'I think it's some kind of symbol, Chris,' explained his dad.

'Yes, Sacred Symbol of Healing,' nodded the shaman. 'It is a yantra. Come, I start now.' The shaman deftly rolled up the minute copper sheet again. 'I must do it to make healing,' uttered the man determinedly.

'Well at least do it discretely!' muttered Kevin, shielding the event behind his jacket to try to hide it from the eyes of the staff.

The shaman placed the herbs back inside the cylinder and closed the lid. He took a string and hung the cylinder around Chris' neck like a pendant. The cylinder began to release fragrant smoke, which wafted gently towards Chris' nostrils above.

'What are you doing?' hissed Donna. Joe put a comforting hand on her shoulder.

'Let him do his work, Donna, he might be able to help Chris,' he reassured.

They jumped as the shaman suddenly broke into strange sounds; the sounds growled in his throat and erupted into piercing noises, which seared through the air and hit their very consciousness. The combination of the heady herbal scents with the ethereal sounds created a mysterious atmosphere, which made the group feel like they had been sent into another world.

'Why is he making that awful noise?' asked Donna, disturbed. Cousins clapped his hands over his ears, almost knocking his glasses off.

'Shush! He's reciting a mantra,' whispered Joe.

'What's that when it's at home?' whispered Donna – a little too loudly.

'It can be a sound, a syllable, a word or a group of words. Silverman told me about them. You know who I mean, the sound healer guy? He thinks that mantras are capable of creating transformation. The sounds have inherent meaning, whether we understand them or not. They are supposed to be manifestations of ultimate reality,' explained Joe.

'I didn't get a word of that...' hissed Donna.

'It's like a thought-form symbol representation of a divine or cosmic power. Their influence is exerted by the shaman's sound vibrations.' Joe put his finger to his lips to request silence so the shaman could complete his work, but of course Chris couldn't see him.

'The yogi I visited mentioned something about mantras; he explained that the sound 'AUM' and its Sanskrit syllable represent a mantra meaning "The sound of the Universe,"' gabbled Chris, excitedly.

'That's right, son! Now let's stay quiet and let the man finish his work.' They stayed transfixed as the shaman continued to create incredible sounds.

The staff intervened soon enough when the smoke alarm sounded.

103

Bayside mantras

Chased by security, Cousins and Kevin whisked the shaman away out of the hospital. Kevin was keen to get an angle on this man's story.

'You come with me,' stated the shaman to the men, as they rounded the corner of the hospital.

'Sure, where are we going?' asked Kevin, laughing.

'I take you to beach tonight and show you how to get boy better.' The shaman walked quickly to a near-by bus stop. Kevin and Cousins hurried along after him, excited by this new turn of events. They'd never met anyone as strange as this man, but somehow they felt they could trust him.

On the bus, the men stared awkwardly out of the window at the passing people and vehicles. Sat next to the shaman, they felt all eyes were fixed on the odd man. Soon enough, the bus terminated by the Bay. Everyone got off and the shaman hurried down to the beach. Kevin and Cousins rushed along trying to keep up with the tall long-legged tribesman.

'Wait here,' instructed the shaman. Kevin watched as he ran down towards the shore line of the nearby beach, where the waves had rolled a flat clean surface on the sand. Unaware that his mouth was gaping, Kevin watched the shaman fly into action, first locating a large piece of wooden driftwood, which he proceeded to use like a pen in the sand.

'What's he doing?' whispered Cousins.

'Shush, just watch' said Kevin.

Kevin stared transfixed as he watched something take shape on the sand. Unable to make out what the shaman was drawing, Kevin ran back up the beach shouting Cousins to join him. They scrambled up higher to get a vantage point over the beach. From above, in the gloomy light of the descending night, they were able to make out an unusual shape in the sand by the light of the Bright Moon rising overhead.

'What is it?' asked Kevin.

'I'm not sure, but it reminds me of something,' said Cousins. He thought the large ovoid shape looked like some kind of diagram, yes! Like the one he had seen on the copper sheet. He tried to take a picture, but it was only faintly visible under the lunar illumination. Never the less he filed the picture to research it later on.

'It is done!' shouted the shaman, as he threw his arms up in the air. The men jumped as the shaman commenced chanting. They listened, as the sounds welled up in the shaman's throat and burst out into the night air like a piercing wail. Cousins found the recording device on his mobile to capture the incredible sounds he heard.

As Kevin stared out from his high look-out over the glistening waters of the Bay, he felt transported to another dimension – or was it just his vertigo? He spotted the reflection of the Moon sparkling in the water; he stared, transfixed whilst the shaman completed his mantras. He felt like he was flying.

104

Hannah comes bearing healing gifts

Chris was lying exhausted on his hospital bed. The herbal scents had left him completely zonked out; he was barely able to respond when Hannah dropped in with her dad to see him.

'Hi Chris,' she smiled shyly. 'I brought you these flowers and some fruit. I thought they might help,' she added hopefully. She had been a faithful companion throughout his hospital incarcerations. Chris smiled weakly at her friendly voice.

'Thank you, will you bring the flowers over here?' he asked. 'I'd like to smell them.'

Chris heard the clumping sound of her boots on the floor, then suddenly he smelt the scent of the flowers as Hannah brought them under his nostrils; he inhaled deeply. They somehow roused his energy enough to banter with her;

'Yup – they're definitely flowers!' he joshed.

Hannah laughed, but she was worried about Chris, who seemed so weak and pale.

'Here, take a bite of this fruit too?' she offered the rosy apple up to his lips and helped him to take a small bite. The fruit tasted sweet and delicious on his tongue; he licked his lips in appreciation.

'Do you wanna hear some music?' she asked. 'I downloaded something new on your Tablet-Gadget.'

Chris nodded feebly. Hannah slipped the earpieces into his ears and pressed play. Chris soon heard the wafting lilting sounds of strings and an angelic voice singing a melodious song. He grinned and relaxed into the comforting music. Hannah hoped that it was healing him.

Soon Chris fell into a deep slumber. Donna nodded her grateful thanks to Hannah, who sat down next to her while Cousins spoke to Joe.

105

COUSINS SHARES HIS DISCOVERIES ABOUT THE SHAMAN

Kevin and Cousins were reporting back to Joe after their antics with the shaman on the beach.

'You know, that shaman guy was amazing!' exclaimed Cousins. 'You'll never guess what he did!'

'Nope, you're right. I won't!' laughed Joe.

'He was only drawing shapes in the sand!'

'What – like his name or something?' asked Joe, bemused.

'No! Like a bacteria! It looked just like a bacteria! I had a nagging thought when I saw the copper-sheet drawing that it was like a bacteria, but it just didn't make any sense! Then there he was drawing the same thing on the beach under the moonlight, chanting his mantras like there was no tomorrow! I'm telling you, the diagram looked just like Lactobacillus!'

'Wow...' that left Joe lost for words. The world was indeed a strange place; Joe felt like he for one was never going to understand all its strange facets.

'Hey, Krefeld, come over here!' Cousins gestured to the

neurosurgeon that had entered the ward. 'Get a load of this!'

Cousins drew out his iPhone to show Krefeld the gloomy picture of the beach diagram.

'What is it? I can't see anything,' complained Krefeld, rubbing his goatee beard.

'Look here! This faint outline was drawn out by the shaman.'

'The who-man? You mean that crazy kook that set the alarms off! What's he done now?' scoffed Krefeld.

'This shape, what does it remind you of?' persisted Cousins, hopping in excitement.

Krefeld peered over the faint picture and the shape started to jump out at him, like a 3D image. 'Oh boy, is that what I think it is? That's just weird! What would he be drawing bacteria for?' Krefeld was rubbing his beard, deep in thought.

'Listen, that's not all!' Cousins seemed like his ginger hairs were about to explode right out of his head, he was so agitated. 'Listen to this recording of the shaman!' Cousins played back the sounds that the shaman had sung. The wails floated back to their ears and transported them once more to strange far off lands.

'Now listen to this!' exclaimed Cousins, barely keeping the lid on his already explosive contents. He played another recording back to the listening men; bizarrely, there was a certain similarity between the two recordings.

'So what was the second recording?' asked Joe, perplexed.

'That's the really weird thing! It was Ultra Low Frequency sounds that I've recorded myself, coming from real live bacteria! I had to process the sounds to make them audible to us, but surely you agree that they sound alike?'

April

Full Moon: 12.59 pm on April 25th

106

Physicist Gets on the Case

With Joe's encouragement, Kevin wanted to record and understand everything that was happening to Chris, so with the help of Dr Cousins he had invited an expert to join a discussion about the shaman's diagrams and chants. He'd invited Krefeld to join him, Joe, Cousins and a physicist who had a special interest in wave theory.

'May I introduce you to Dr. Sandy Cromwell-Parks – he's a Scottish physicist who went to my University.'

Cousins gestured towards a tall moustachioed bear of a man who gazed back at Joe, Krefeld and Kevin with twinkling, humorous eyes.

'Well hello lads!' Cromwell-Parks bared his great white teeth in a charming grin. 'I hear you have a bit of a physics mystery on your hands! Don't worry, I'm here now, the brains are on the case.' He pointed to his temple and tapped, adding 'Up here for dancing, down there for thinking' as he pointed at his feet.

The others looked on, somewhat bemused by the self-effacing British humour.

'Well don't just stand there gawping!' he chivvied, 'show

me the pictures!' His great belly laugh was infectious; his good-natured banter eased everyone into an excited discussion about the photos from the beach and the copper sheet diagram that the shaman had produced.

Cousins explained about his revelation that the shaman's sounds had very distinct similarities to those he had recorded of real live bacteria.

'You know, I have a theory on all this...' reflected Cromwell-Parks in his delicious accent. 'I suspect that the diagrams are really meant to represent an object and its energy. I think that the shaman constructed a symbol that represented bacteria and that he used his energy and intention through the mantra's sound waves to create an equal but opposite pattern to that which has been set up in Chris.'

Cromwell-Parks was twiddling his moustache as he talked. Joe, Krefeld, Cousins and Kevin were staring incomprehensibly.

'Look, it all goes back to the wave-particle theory,' explained Cromwell-Parks. 'Each object can be either in a wave form or in a particle form, but not both at the same time. In wave form it is in its form of optimum potential. When observed, the wave form collapses under the interaction and becomes a solid object made up of particles. I think each particle in the Universe has the potential to become an instrument or medium to disseminate or echo the vibrations or waves of meanings given out by our brain and our consciousness.

'It's like a chain effect; the vibration goes on retaining its original wave structure, and energy bounces from particle to particle in a chain that can affect an infinite number of particles, like radio waves can, until they are picked up by another's brain or consciousness. I think that's what happened to Chris; I think he picked up some kind of signal from another object, perhaps sound waves or electromagnetic waves from bacteria. Once it got into his electromagnetic field, it was automatically sucked in and digested by his subconscious.

'Then the shaman was trying to recreate the same but opposite signal message in an attempt to cancel out what was lying in Chris' electromagnetic field. Perhaps his yantra message is also intended to help enhance Chris' cellular capacity and his immunity, to help him to fight back.'

Cousins interjected;

'This does explain what Chris said about how he received his information. In Chris' mind, all humans are like antennas, or radios. We can turn our 'tuning dial' to a specific 'station', then information starts downloading in the form of signals. Chris told me that we have this innate faculty in our mind and body to tune into a specific subject that deep down we desire to know. This is our innate intense curiosity, which is one of the essential components required for all this to happen. The second component required, he said, is to pursue it single-mindedly.'

'Well Chris certainly displays those two attributes – he's like a dog with a bone when he wants to know something,' chortled Joe, affectionately.

'When the system senses a perfect match or synchronicity, the special information starts 'downloading', in computer terms.'

Cousins eyed the group willing them to understand this rather complicated theory.

Krefeld seemed to get it; he rephrased it in his psychological language; 'Or in epistemological terms, I would describe it as knowledge descending into the conscience of the pursuer.'

'That reminds me of 'The Matrix', where the character searches intensely for truth and ends up being able to download information straight into his brain through a special cable from a computer into the back of his neck,' laughed Kevin.

'There you go! It's an idea that has already been conceived; I think it's actually been known about for much longer than we can possibly imagine – obviously not in computer terms, but certainly in consciousness terms. If the shaman knew about it, then I suspect the knowledge has been retained since ancient times, passed on through the generations. I think these ancient cultures, like Native Americans, Mexicans, Egyptians, Indians and Tibetans probably know more about the power of these symbols than we give them credit for.'

'Symbols, visuals and diagrams are rapidly assimilated by the brain, and could stimulate the pea-body – the pineal gland – in the brain. When they are written or drawn on a copper plate, which is a good electrical conductor, perhaps they are better able to transmit some kind of electrical signal.' Krefeld's hands were waving in an excited gesture.

'The shaman said something to us about healing, didn't he Cousins? What was it?' Kevin was scratching his thick head of curly black hair trying to remember.

'Um, I think he was trying to explain that healing is not in the belief, but in the words and acts of the person's intention projected towards the disease, the illness or the problem.'

Cousins nestled his glasses back into his ginger hair.

'Well I remember the yogi saying that Chris would be healed but with some unusual interference of Nature, maybe he meant he would have to compromise with the Gift, so I agree, that sounds like what the shaman was trying to do, create some sort of counteracting wave of energy made up of the energy of the symbols, the sound of the mantras and the energy of his healing intentions,' said Joe, who had sat back listening up until this point.

'Well I still wonder where Chris actually got the information or signal from,' pondered Cromwell-Parks, cracking his great knuckles. 'You say he spent a lot of time staring at the Moon? Was he somehow gathering photons and there were some encoded energies and consciousness within the photons that he downloaded?'

Joe shrugged. 'How much do we really know? I think most of what we've suggested has just been speculation. Maybe we should just admit that we know nothing!'

'You speak for yourself' scoffed Cromwell-Parks, his great teeth bared in a guffaw. 'I didn't spend six years at University to be told that I know nothing!'

'Well it wasn't meant to be a personal comment! You can see that admitting that we know nothing hurts our ego! But do you know what; truth need not have to satisfy our ego. I've spent all year trying to puzzle out what's been happening to my boy and I still don't feel like I'm anywhere nearer to getting any answers.' Joe shrugged at the group again. 'It's a bit like your wave-particle theory,' he said, turning back to Cromwell-Parks. 'All this sounds like 'seeking Love and searching for Truth' seems to take you down one of two routes, but you can never be on both paths at the same time.'

'Aha now you're talking my language! Sounds like the Heisenberg Uncertainty Principle!' said the physicist, tapping his temple knowingly.

'You've got it! I think we can either get lost in understanding the labyrinths of the process involved in trying to get answers, OR we can be immersed in the joy of searching for our intended objectives!' Joe's silvery eyes sparkled humorously.

'Oh – you mean the fun is in the chase!' laughed Kevin.

'That's it! Either you are in the mind or in the heart. You cannot be in both at the same time. You cannot be consciously aware at the same time as being logical and emotional,' explained Joe.

'Right, in that case, I'm off to enjoy chasing a whiskey!' said Cromwell-Parks with a big belly laugh. 'Who's joining me?'

'Well I'm not sure it's appropriate for us to go off and enjoy ourselves when poor Chris is still so sick,' said Krefeld, empathetically.

'Listen, I meant what I said about needing to find joy in life. Take your moments for celebration whenever you can. Go and have a break and I'll see you when you get back,' said Joe, shaking their hands.

The others left to continue their discussion in more sociable surroundings, whilst Joe went to join Donna at Chris' bedside, to continue their long vigil, wondering when it would all resolve.

107

WHAT IS TO BECOME OF CHRIS' SIGHT?

Several weeks later, still with no answers forthcoming from the puzzled medics, Chris continued to vegetate in a sickly state in hospital. He was effectively blind, but the medics were at a loss as to how to help him.

All the crises and restless nights were taking their toll on poor Donna, who was increasingly drained and gaunt-looking. Joe tried to encourage her to go home to get some rest, but she refused to leave Chris' bedside. Instead she told Joe to go home, whilst she settled uncomfortably in a chair by Chris' bedside to catch a few hours of shut-eye.

Her eyes wandered from Chris' even gaunter-looking face, lying silent and drawn on the pillow, to that of the Bright Moon at the window. She gazed up into its knowing face in wonder; perhaps she might find the answers to her questions too if she concentrated for long enough on the Moon. After all, it seemed to have worked for Chris. She kept her eyes trained on the Moon's bright presence, trying to fight the weight of her sleepy eyelids.

Willing herself to stay awake seemed to have the opposite effect; soon she fell into a restless slumber, cascading into a vivid dream scape that seemed so real, she was certain it was really happening.

She saw Chris rise from his sick bed and lurch towards the window through which poured the ethereal light of the Bright Moon. She watched as he gazed at the Moon, then she gasped as she saw something pulled out of his eyes, his mind, his body and his spirit. She could see the beads of perspiration sparkling on his forehead.

As if in slow motion, she tried to rise from her bedside seat to catch him as she saw his legs crumble under him. Her own legs were like lead and immoveable; she just watched, helplessly, as he collapsed to the floor in a heap.

Then her perspective seemed to change in her dream; she was suddenly observing as if she was hovering, gazing down over the scene. Chris was conscious and from the floor she heard him cry out to her in a joyous voice;

'Mum, I can see! I can see everything clearly! It's like a new world!'

Donna glanced across and saw herself diving to the floor, throwing her arms around Chris' huddled figure, ecstatically proclaiming; 'My son has returned to Earth!' Yet the noise really was emanating from her throat; she woke herself up with her own screams. Energy coursed through her like great rolling waves gushing towards a shore.

Shaking herself, she realized that she had been asleep but dreaming a most vivid scene. As she unpeeled her sleep-ridden eyes, she slowly focused on a moving figure in front of her. As her eyes gently came into focus, she was able to discern the movement was that of her son.

She saw Chris rise from his sick bed and lurch towards the window through which poured the ethereal light of the Bright Moon. As if in slow motion, she tried to rise from her bedside seat to catch him as she saw his legs crumble under him. Her own legs suddenly really were like lead and immoveable; she just watched, helplessly, as he collapsed to the floor in a heap.

She shuddered, all her hair standing on end, as the prophetic dream unravelled for real in front of her, just moments behind her dream reality. Tossed between the two realities – the physical and the dream consciousness – she had discerned them running parallel to each other, but with a fraction of time shift.

Following the long months of her intense attachment and anguished care for her son, her soul's enduring and unbearable pain had sent a dream message to the pinnacle of her body and mind, then something deep within herself, something nameless, brought her slipping down from the heights of the dream to the steep valleys of the physical world. It woke her from her dream consciousness in time to see the shocking spine-tingling reality of the repeated scene – a déjà vu.

If she did but know, dreams are the windows to a world that we cannot comprehend with our conscious minds. If we could interpret dreams with our intuitive language, who knows what major problems could be solved?

Chris was conscious; from the floor she heard him cry out to her in a joyous voice;

'Mum, I can see! I can see everything clearly! It's like a new world!'

Donna glanced across and dove to the floor, throwing her arms around Chris' huddled figure, crying ecstatically; 'My son has returned to Earth!'

108

CHRIS IS GIVEN THE ALL CLEAR TO LEAVE HOSPITAL

Medics rushed to the hugging pair and swarmed around them like bees round a honey-pot, fussing and clucking their approvals and slapping each other on the back, pleased as punch with the outcome 'they' had achieved.

Donna ran to the window and shouted down to the gathered onlookers keeping their vigil for Chris.

'Thank you all so much! My boy is alright! My heartfelt gratitude goes out to all of you!'

The onlookers cheered and those wearing hats threw them up into the air.

Joe rushed back to hospital and flew to Chris' bedside, hugging him as if he would never let him go.

Chris' medical team was assembled to check him over; Baines examined Chris' eyes and pronounced them 'normal'. Krefeld carried out a scan and pronounced the results as 'normal'. Barnes questioned Chris on his mental state and pronounced him 'normal' if suffering from a little amnesia, as he seemed for the moment to have forgotten his ordeal, even that he had ever been able to see or hear micro-organisms.

Chris was finally released from hospital amongst much

celebration, merriment and extensive public and media attention, during which Donna and Joe pronounced their immense gratitude to those that had helped their son in any way in his healing, expressing their appreciation for all the prayers and support. Donna and Joe drove their boy away from the hospital that had been the family's surrogate home for so much of the last year, turning to wave at the gathered crowds of well-wishers.

As Donna gazed out at the sea of kind faces, her thoughts turned reflective. She was finally able to perceive the precious value of his previous abilities from the secure perspective of knowing that her son was now well. Yet why had her son's gifts been taken away from him in the end? She was startled by her sudden realization that power conferred by nature was a cosmic gift, but from the perspective of the world it had turned out to be unsustainable. Why?

She realised that Chris had never solicited his remarkable powers. He loved the full moon innocently, with a pure heart. These powers though, as intriguing as they were, were taken away from the boy for two reasons: firstly the persecution he experienced from various competitive mega-corporations who were fighting about who should own the rights over his knowledge; and secondly, her soulful maternal interest in her son's well-being. Much to her own surprise though, Donna had opened her eyes to the publicity around her son's situation and how rich she or he could be in the future and, even more unexpectedly, she had even opened up her heart towards spiritual dimensions of human existence.

Donna's intentions had always been pure; aimed always at helping him to get well again. She had amazed herself by finally condoning the meditative path; she had taken the attitude that she should at least try the meditation methods he had been taught – as an ultimate last resort of course

– even though her mind had pondered such thoughts as 'this is the last option I have, what am I going to do with my stubbornness, my resistance to being open to it? Let me just open myself up and see if something could be possible beyond the laws of physics, beyond the laws of materialism.'

This very leap of faith had led her to something most profound; some experience which was expressed in her silent thoughts as prayers to the infinite Universe, seeking only for her son to be relieved of this great gift, 'All I want is to have my son back with normal health and for him to be accepted by other people so that we can be peaceful.'

Donna, as a lawyer, was seen as a respectable person in society and she had an in-built innate characteristic of seeing things through. This is why she had been so immensely happy when her son was finally relieved of the power. She identified her own achievements with his well-being and progress. Yet now that he was without his gifts, she could see clearly that this had never been about her, and felt a twinge of shame that she had acted so selfishly.

She sighed, shaking the confusing thoughts from her mind. She had what she wanted after all; her son's health was surely the most important thing. She grinned, a heavy weight lifted from her shoulders.

Turning with a radiant face to see her miraculous boy fit and well next to her on the back seat of the car, Donna remembered a time when she had lost sight of the miracle of family, of the wonder of unconditional love attached to bringing up a child. Her heart swelled as Chris hugged her tightly. There was nothing that could top this feeling! She squeezed him, as if she never wanted to let him go. She grinned infectiously at Joe, happy at last.

Her heart's desire had been granted – yet, a little tiny voice in her head whispered over and over... 'What is normal?'

109

THE MEDICS DISCUSS CHRIS' RETURN TO 'NORMALITY'

The medics sat around an oval table in the sun-drenched meeting room, each face lost in thought as they sought personal answers to the confusing scenarios they had faced with Chris' medical case. Krefeld rose to fill water glasses for each, watching the crystal clear water sparkle as it tumbled from the orbed jug.

Returning to his seat, Krefeld took his drink in his hand and raised it, toasting his companions in a tender moment of recognition of the invaluable part each had played in Chris' medical care. Cousins, Baines, Barnes, Holmes, and Callows raised their glasses in response.

'You know,' said Baines, scooping his enormous glasses back up his nose, 'I would love to know the truth about what happened to that boy. How on Earth was it that he was able to see on such a microscopic scale? If only we could have found the answers to harnessing that ability, we could have had an incredible gift for the world.'

'Oh Baines, are you still going on about everyone getting Superman-sight?' sniggered Barnes. 'You live in cloud cuckoo land, man! Who'd want to live like that anyway?'

'You may mock!' said the bespectacled genius, 'but can't you imagine the wonders that we could see with such ability?'

Cousins nodded, 'I agree. Of course I'm pleased for the family that Chris' eyesight has been restored and he can probably go back to some sort of normality now – if the media and the public will let him! – But hey, that microscopic sight thing he could do was providing answers to so many of our unanswered questions. All that research which we were able to understand, all those revelations about the microbial world, all the environmental clues he was able to give us. My God! All those layers upon layers of understanding he was able to describe to us – it made me feel the Divine in everything! What are we going to do without it?'

Krefeld nodded sagely, but underneath all the layers of emotions this case had stirred up, he felt the most important thing was that Chris should be allowed to get his normal life back. Chris had done more than enough for humanity. He had served the world well and he had earned himself a break.

Yet Krefeld too was confused by the appearance of such unusual symptoms, the evolutionary neural connections he had witnessed, the amazing brain wave patterns that the boy had been producing. It had all felt so ground-breaking and yet somehow so right. Could his colleagues have been right about this being a first appearance of a new ability? Could this have been a new evolutionary step that they had witnessed? Was that possible? If so, how would this affect the world if such abilities were to spread amongst the global population? How different would the world appear were that to happen? How differently would people behave were they to have access to such intuitive wisdom? Would people steward the Earth differently knowing now how profoundly man's actions affect Nature?

All he knew now was that millions of suffering patients

had been brought to a better state of health as a direct consequence of Chris' gifts; now that the boy was back to 'normal', what would happen to future patients? Without Chris' insights, would they still be able to help patients as astutely? No, there was a definite bitter-sweet feel to the way Chris' recovery had panned out.

His thoughts were interrupted by Callows and Barnes, who were crowing about their advice having been the key to the boy's recovery.

Krefeld shook his head, laughing; he caught Cousins' eye. Cousins raised his eyes to the ceiling at the brazen egotistical displays. Neither of them wished to take any credit for Chris' recovery, they simply took pleasure in the fact that he was better. Krefeld gestured in salute to his like-minded colleague.

110

Anonymous healing; Kevin's concluding story

Kevin was in a philosophical mood, fuelled by a visit to his mother's grave. His readers and his Editor had demanded a final story, a concluding summary, which depicted his views on what had happened to Chris, so he poured out champagne, drew up a chair in his apartment and opened his laptop, ready to type...

Anonymous Healing
By Kevin Masters

"Chris McKenzie – was he an extra-ordinary healer, a visionary, a mystic, bringing an incredible gift to the world as some like to think? Or was he in fact just a very sick young boy, whose strange symptoms were just the cruel and unusual effects of an unknown virus?

Whatever in the end caused the boy to see his incredible visions and experience strange sounds that he deciphered as voices of micro-beings, these so-called 'gifts' were apparently stripped from him by a mystery virus, which left him blind and paralyzed. Then as suddenly as the illness descended on him, he recovered his sight and the use of his hands, returning him to a state of normality which would lead people to distrust that he had ever been anything other than 'normal'.

Everybody believed that they had helped the boy to recover in some way; the musicians thought that their harmonious music had entrained his vibrations and his cells into health. The shaman thought that his herbs, yantra and mantras were the cause for his shift to health. The medics congratulated themselves on their extensive involvement with medications, research and nursing care. His best friend Hannah from school hoped that her flowers and fruit had contained a curative strain of bacteria. The therapists assumed that their interventions had facilitated his improvement and the religious groups each claimed that their particular prayers had brought Chris his healing. (Call me a disbeliever, but I doubt there will be a day when individual religions accept that other religions could have made a difference; many, in my opinion, will never get past the belief that theirs is the 'one true religion' judging by the current trajectory of their thoughts.)

No-one was prepared to believe that it had been a joint effort, that it had been a cumulative effect of a collective healing intention, which potentially had pulsed in from all over the world, given Chris' extensive fame and support. Each individual's ego was unprepared to share the limelight and each claimed their stake in his improvement like they were claiming their territory to affirm their ego presence.

In the end, perhaps the truth lay somewhere else – perhaps in Mother Nature. No-one could know though whether Nature may have worked through all these people, or whether Chris' shift back to health could have been purely down to Mother Nature herself. Perhaps Mother Nature is the only one with all the answers, but there was no one solution, not a single therapy or religious rite, no specific medication which could be named as being the true healer in the situation; all remained faceless and unsung.

I for one cannot answer the question of what happened to Chris McKenzie – despite my extensive research into his case, I am unable to conclude what caused his experiences and what took them away. I have no proof one way or the other that any of the theories postulated were correct. My attitude is one of 'seeing is believing,' and as there was no-one else to corroborate his experiences, my rational nature nudges me to believe that there was nothing mystical in Chris' abilities.

However after extensive exposure to the incredible results of his advice, I have to admit that my subjective approach feels inadequate, that my curiosity is piqued in the idea of there being more to life than meets the eye. In my subsequent confusion, I can only conclude therefore that I have no conclusion, that I cannot tell you what lies in the mind of Chris McKenzie. That – my dear readers – I leave to your own conclusions.

This search for understanding has been a long journey for me. A dear friend once explained to me that we can either get lost in understanding the labyrinths of the process involved in trying to get answers, OR we can be immersed in the joy of searching for our intended objectives. Perhaps, more simply put, we could say that – 'the fun is in the chase'!"

III

Chris discovers his true name

Chris was safely ensconced at home, writing messages of thanks and appreciation to all those that had prayed and sent their benevolent wishes for his good health. He relived his experience through the messages and questions posted in his e-mail inbox. He noticed one from the yogi, which addressed him as 'Shashanka'.

Unsure of its meaning, he surfed the web in search of an answer, discovering that it was one of many different Sanskrit words for 'Bright Moon'. He stopped in his tracks and gazed at the word, in awe that there were so many different names for one entity in this ancient Indian language. He wondered why in English there was usually only one word for an object.

He remembered that there were many Inuit words for 'snow'; he decided that such profuse descriptions must be down to the importance a culture granted an object, or the frequency with which they considered it.

Struck with the name 'Shashanka', he copied and pasted the word, so he knew how to spell it even if he couldn't pronounce it properly. He typed it again in capitals and printed it out. He folded up the paper and slipped it into his back pocket.

'Chris, are you coming?' called his mother up the stairs. Rushing down the steps two at a time, he leapt the last four like an eager tiger jumping out of a tree. Grabbing his hat and coat, he and his family took off for the bay.

Sat nestling together on a picnic blanket, Chris, Donna and Joe faced the rainbow hues of the sun-kissed water, watching the sun set peacefully on the horizon. Chris embraced his mother and father, feeling a great sense of peace as he appreciated his life, Nature and the Universe. Remembering his paper in his back pocket, he slipped his hand in and retrieved it. Unfolding it, he passed it to his mother, saying;

'Mum, I think this name fits me...'

'What's that Chris? What does it say? Let me see...SHA – what? SHASHANKA. What does it mean, son?'

'Bright Moon, Mum, it's a Sanskrit word for Bright Moon.'

Donna gazed at her son in awe – behind him the Bright Moon had appeared in the trees in the darkening sky and from where they were standing, the shape of his head seemed to fit right inside it, leaving a mystical glow of light emanating around his head.

'It fits you alright!' she said, smiling proudly. 'Shashanka' – she rolled the name over her lips a few times; then she truly saw him, as if for the very first time. 'My beautiful boy,' she whispered. 'You're perfect...and you always have been.'

Epilogue

Blog entry by Joe Larkin:

'My son is returned to Earth', as my wife says. Indeed Chris has been returned to us from the grip of his debilitating viral symptoms and from whatever strange phenomenon allowed him to observe and detect the communications of microorganisms.

Yet Mother Nature will not let only one person or entity take the credit for something good happening. Nature is the ultimate giver and solvent of all, whether we understand it and recognize it or not.

I am very proud of my son and his achievements. I believe that he evolved himself and his consciousness through deep and sincere contemplation, through an 'adventure in self-discovery' as a friend once put it. Ultimately he developed his unique abilities as a manifestation of his pre-destined gifts, through compassionate concern for his fellow man.

Unaware where his gifts would lead him, he has been very brave throughout his experience, however I would like you all to know what I believe; that every human is given some unique gift, which will come to light if they choose to patiently and positively explore and observe themselves with deep conviction, when placed in different situations and circumstances.

After the realization of such gifts, I believe that one will maintain them through expressing oneself with a heart for fulfilment and service to family, community and society. However the gift or position will be taken back if it is abused, misused or greedily exploited by anyone, even if it is by someone else. I am sad to say that we were witness to many misguided exploitations during this experience, despite Chris' best intentions to serve selflessly. Who knows what evolutionary heights mankind may have reached through my son's intuitive advice had he been able to maintain his gifts? What now of my son's consciousness? Yes, he is now diagnosed as 'normal', but what of his development? Has his progress been hindered?

We found ourselves at the hands of mega corporations and their twisted efforts to exploit Chris' knowledge. Saddened as I am by this, I am somewhat assuaged by their subsequent downfall. I would like to let anyone who thinks that this behaviour is acceptable know that if any corporate giant tries to gain ultimate control over the world and its people, the corporation will start to collapse by stages, especially when they start to misuse their power. This is not idle revenge talk, simply an observation of what happened to those mega-corporations that ignorantly, selfishly and greedily exploited Chris' advice.

Mother Nature creates a natural upper limit to success or benefits. Think of it as like a statistical levelling out, or like a mound of sand. How high can you build a mound of sand before it starts to collapse? Do such greedy organisations think that they can defy Mother Nature and her Laws?

There are situations in everyone's life when – regardless of their scepticism and pessimism – they are bound to become transformed to a higher level of consciousness and life. I would like to invite all of you, dear readers, to acknowledge this fact. Chris was not as alone in his experience as one might think – it's just that the way that his raised consciousness manifested appeared in a unique fashion.

One dear lesson that arose time and again for me is that unity is important; without it, life is not moistened with tender and emotionally reflective experiences, whether it be unity of a couple or a family through a difficult situation, or unity of a community through a testing time, or unity of religions despite apparently differing beliefs. We can only be truly happy when others around us are happy.

The realization and experience of one's spirituality becomes possible when the Universe and all beings in it are comprehended as a single, whole entity. Such an understanding and experience of wholeness raises one's consciousness towards enlightenment. Yet enlightenment can also be seen as the sum of two concepts; love is an experience, truth is a realization.

The Universe will not allow any one person, community or religion to take overall credit. It is always redistributed again and balanced out. Every faith and religion is important in its own way, each reflecting a different facet of the diamond of spirituality, a different flavour of truth in the garden of humanity.

I thank you all for your prayers, your good wishes, your healing intentions and your support. I truly believe that without it things may not have worked out so well. Yet my heart tells me that, in Nature, everything is counterbalanced. In our limited perception, we see only shortcomings and imprint our own interpretations, but at the end of the day, it is all well balanced.

Farewell, readers. I now close this blog and website, so we may return to our lives – back to normality, but in truth we *are forever changed and forever bonded with each and every one of you.*

THE END

Everything eventually returned to normal - the Larkins were able to absorb the events of the past year, and had finally settled their minds.

Although the full moon had reached his peak that night, Donna was relaxed, fully convinced that nothing otherworldly or cosmic would ever affect or communicate with Chris again.

After a lengthy goodnight ceremony and a kiss on his forehead, Donna gently shut Chris' door and made her way to her bedroom, with a habitual sigh of great relief - today marked the anniversary of her little boy's relief from the gift bestowed upon him by higher nature.

Chris' window was partially open - his translucent curtain gently swayed as the cool breeze tenderly touched his face. It felt so pleasant and soothing, and he could not resist peeking through his window before finally committing to his bed.

He walked in the soft moonlight spilling into his room through the partially exposed window, which reflected on and blended with his bedsheets. He stood watching the moon; half awake, with half a smile. After breathing in deeply the beauty and serenity of the moment, he turned to go to bed. Suddenly, there was a call of his name.

SHASHANKA echoed in the depth of his heart and in the heights of the sky, and his eyes widened - he became fully awake.....